A journalist by profession, **Douglas Jackson** transformed a lifelong fascination for Rome and the Romans into his first two highly praised novels, *Caligula* and *Claudius*. His third novel, *Hero of Rome*, introduced readers to his new series hero, the one-armed ex-gladiator Gaius Valerius Verrens. Five more novels followed, including *Scourge of Rome*, helping to establish Doug as one of the UK's foremost historical novelists. *Saviour of Rome* will be the seventh Gaius Valerius Verrens adventure. He is also the author – as James Douglas – of four successful adventure thrillers featuring art-recovery expert Jamie Saintclair: *The Doomsday Testament*, *The Isis Covenant*, *The Excalibur Codex* and *The Samurai Inheritance*. An active member of the Historical Writers' Association and the Historical Novel Society, Douglas Jackson lives near Stirling in Scotland.

To find out more, visit www.douglas-jackson.net

www.penguin.co.uk

SCOURGE OF ROME

Douglas Jackson

CORGI BOOKS

TRANSWORLD PUBLISHERS
61–63 Uxbridge Road, London W5 5SA
www.penguin.co.uk

Transworld is part of the Penguin Random House group of companies
whose addresses can be found at global.penguinrandomhouse.com

Penguin
Random House
UK

First published in Great Britain in 2015 by Bantam Press
an imprint of Transworld Publishers
Corgi edition published 2016

A CIP catalogue record for this book
is available from the British Library.

ISBN 9780552167956

Typeset in 11/13pt Sabon by Thomson Digital Pvt Ltd, Noida, Delhi
Printed and bound by Clays Ltd, Bungay, Suffolk.

Penguin Random House is committed to a sustainable
future for our business, our readers and our planet. This book
is made from Forest Stewardship Council® certified paper.

MIX
Paper from
responsible sources
FSC® C018179

1 3 5 7 9 10 8 6 4 2

For my wonderful, long-suffering wife, Alison

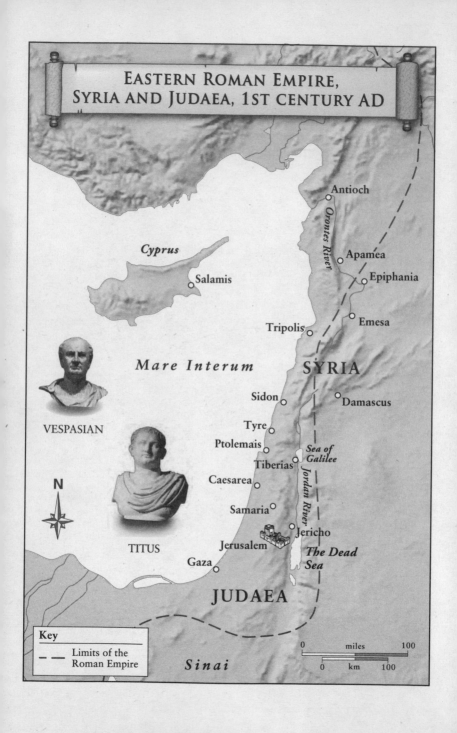

EASTERN ROMAN EMPIRE, SYRIA AND JUDAEA, 1ST CENTURY AD

Antioch

Orontes River

Apamea

Epiphania

Cyprus

Salamis

Emesa

Tripolis

Mare Interum

SYRIA

Sidon

Damascus

Tyre

Ptolemais

Sea of Galilee

Tiberias

VESPASIAN

Caesarea

Jordan River

N

Samaria

Jericho

TITUS

Jerusalem

The Dead Sea

Gaza

JUDAEA

Key

— — — Limits of the Roman Empire

0   miles   100

0   km   100

Sinai

THE SIEGE OF JERUSALEM, AD 70

Camp of Fifth Macedonica
and Fifteenth Apollinaris

Third Wall

N

Tower of
Psephinus

Mount of
Olives,
Camp of
Tenth
Fretensis

Bezetha
(the New City)

Antonia
Fortress

Second Wall

The Temple

King Herod's
Palace

First Wall

Xystus Square

Camp of
Twelfth
Fulminata

Hasmonean Palace

Hezekiah's
Conduit

Cedron Valley

| 0 | yards | 300 |
| 0 | metres | 300 |

Herod's Theatre

What I now recount is an act unparalleled in the history of the Greeks or the barbarians, and as horrible to relate as it is incredible to hear.

Flavius Josephus, *The Siege of Jerusalem*

Prologue

Rome, January, AD 70

'I fear I must report a failure in Athens.' The only reaction from the man on the throne was a slight lift of the head, but the messenger flinched at the menace his words kindled in the dark, unforgiving eyes. 'Our operative vanished,' he stumbled on. 'And the traitor was able to take ship for the East.'

'Could he have been warned?'

The messenger took time to consider his reply. This was even more dangerous territory. His dealings with Titus Flavius Domitian, younger son of the Emperor Vespasian, had made him aware that the new prefect of Rome nurtured an irrational hatred for the man they were discussing. The reasons were lost amid the murk of intrigue and conspiracy of the eighteen-month civil war that had come so close to bringing Rome to her knees. Not five hundred paces from where Domitian sat they were still sifting charred bones from the burned-out ruins of the Temple of Jupiter on the Capitoline Hill. The seeds of the bitter conflict had been planted by Nero's enforced suicide, after the erratic young

11

Emperor's downward spiral had cost him the support of the legions and the Senate. His successor, Sulpicius Galba, governor of Hispania, had made the mistake of cheating the Praetorian Guard out of the payment he'd promised them, and been murdered by Marcus Salvius Otho, the man he'd spurned as an heir. By the time the new Emperor took the throne, the German legions of Aulus Vitellius were already marching on Rome, and a disastrous defeat at Bedriacum had cost Otho his life. In a final twist, Domitian's father Vespasian, general of the eastern legions, had been hailed Emperor by his officers. After a campaign which had left the soil of Italia bloodied and littered with sun-bleached bones, Vespasian's supporters finally wrested the purple from Vitellius's hands and butchered him on the Gemonian Stairs.

Now Vespasian was making his triumphal progress to Rome from Egypt while Domitian protected his interests in the capital, and his elder son Titus commanded the legions putting down the Judaean revolt. For the moment, Domitian was the city's ruler in all but name, and he held the power of life and death over every inhabitant. The messenger knew his next words could bring that power into play. In the political crocodile pit that was Rome in the aftermath of Vitellius's ignoble death, was it in his interest to offer a sacrifice? A slight chill tickled the back of his neck. A draught from the open window looking out on to the Forum? Or a warning that the palace walls had ears and another might be close whom he could not afford to offend.

'I . . . I do not believe so,' he admitted eventually. 'The timings make it unlikely.'

Domitian rose from his cushioned seat and the messenger was struck by how slight he appeared in his purple-striped toga. Just a boy really, but one must never forget that the boy was his father's son. Domitian had been trapped in the Temple of Jupiter with his Uncle Sabinus, but while Sabinus's body parts still lay on the Gemonian Stairs, Domitian had reappeared to assume power in his father's name. To the messenger's surprise, the young man smiled.

'He would not be worthy of my enmity if he were not worthy of my respect.' Domitian shrugged. 'What have we lost? One man who promised more than he could deliver and no doubt paid the price.' The smile disappeared as quickly as it had come. 'The game goes on.'

'Of course, lord.' The man bowed and backed out of the room.

Domitian waited until he was alone. 'You heard?'

A figure in military uniform emerged from the balcony. 'These people are fools if they think their barrack room backstabbers and slow poisoners can kill Verrens. A man who stood alone against the rebel queen Boudicca and survived the intrigues of the past two years will not go so willingly to his grave.'

'You sound as if you admire him.'

'He's proved he can soldier,' the officer shrugged. 'And he has a gladiator's instinct for survival. If he lives your father may give him a legion.'

The suggestion brought a grunt of bitter laughter from the young man on the throne. He had destroyed Gaius Valerius Verrens' reputation by portraying his peace mission to Vitellius as treason; he would not let him recover it. 'Yet you want him dead?'

'I have my reasons. If he has a fault it is his honesty. One day it may be the death of him.'

A cold smile wreathed Domitian's narrow features. 'Then it suits both our purposes for you to join my

13

brother in Judaea. You and Verrens are very much alike. He will instinctively trust you. You can get close enough to . . .'

The soldier's stare silenced the younger man and Domitian bridled at the . . . contempt, yes, that was what he saw in the eyes, contempt. He was reminded that his physical weakness in the presence of men like these didn't match the power of his position. When this was over . . .

'Call off your dogs. They will only get in my way.'

'No.' Domitian recovered himself. 'It may be that your mission has been completed for you before you arrive in Judaea. In that case you will get close to my brother. I want to know everything. Who he sleeps with. Who he plots with. His attitude to my father and his attitude to me. Who are his allies and what are his plans. You will place my brother's fate in the palm of my hand, is that understood?'

'Perfectly.'

I

Roman Syria, one month later

A man would die in Antioch tonight. The assassin had stalked his victim for a week and knew his routine intimately enough to be certain of his destination. His target had taken lodgings in the cloth-making district where tight-packed, ramshackle houses lined the rat-infested Parmenian stream. It was a decision that spoke of an exceptionally tolerant sense of smell and a wish for privacy. The stench of fuller's piss permeating the streets meant the *vigiles* kept their distance unless provoked. A perfect sanctuary for a fugitive, and his man certainly acted like a fugitive.

Normally, the assassin would have finished the job in a single night, leaving his victim just another corpse floating face down in the festering creek among the turds and the dead dogs. A long-nurtured instinct for survival told him that this one was different: a man with an equally well-honed sense of self-preservation. Instead, the murderer had watched and waited, his eyes never leaving the lodging house in the narrow alley the locals called, with supreme irony, the Street of Perfumed Gardens.

His target left the house twice each day, at noon and in the early evening, and though his route varied the destination was always the same, a tavern-brothel named the Vengeful Tenth after the legionaries who frequented it while on leave. There, he nursed a single drink and ignored the half-hearted ministrations of the whores until one of the merchants who organized the eastern caravans made his daily call. A short conversation ended with a shake of the head and a shrug that meant another day's wait. Showing neither disappointment nor frustration, the target would hand the trader a coin and re-arrange the rendezvous before making his way to the stables where the two horses he'd bought were being cared for. He would check their condition and question the groom before handing over another coin and returning to his accommodation.

The assassin had assessed the route and calculated the possibilities before making his decision where to strike. His favoured spot was reached not long after the man left the tavern, when he passed through a shadowed alley a few dozen paces long on the way to the stable. If someone happened to be around, another convenient place presented itself between the stable and his lodgings. The assassin was adept with either knife or strangling rope, but he'd chosen the former because the victim was a well-built man of above average height who had once been a soldier; a holder of the Corona Aurea, if his sources were to be believed. Despite his ragged clothing and broken-down appearance, the high military honour identified him as a formidable opponent. The assassin was a man who took no chances. Death must be instantaneous.

One other factor required consideration. His victim had a feature that made him instantly recognizable but also created, if not a problem, then at least an interesting dilemma. One hand, the right, was missing – an old battle injury, he'd been told – and had been replaced by a carved wooden fist. The question was: did that make the victim more vulnerable or less so? A less experienced killer would immediately have opted for the first, but the assassin was a thorough man. After some thought he'd decided that the fact that this man had survived with the mutilation for so long probably made him more dangerous. A left-handed victim was unusual and his reaction to an attack less predictable. Better to give him no time to react at all.

Tonight he didn't follow the victim into the smoky, noisome interior of the Vengeful Tenth with its tawdry painted harridans and sour wine. Instead he wrapped his cloak tighter against the night cold and took up a position where he could watch the door. Patience was an exceptional virtue in his profession, and he was an exceptionally patient man.

As he waited, he watched the sky turn from dark blue to inky black. The hills looming over the ancient city transformed from grey to silver and finally a ghostly, insubstantial haze that was eventually consumed by the night. He saw the merchant arrive and leave in the time it took to sup a single drink. Any moment now. He took a deep breath. There. A tall man silhouetted in the light from the curtained doorway, the bleak grey eyes mere pits of darkness in a hard-edged face with a distinctive white scar that ran from eye to lip on the left side. The man hesitated a moment before trudging off in the direction of the stables, slightly favouring his right side as if to compensate for the missing extremity. The assassin gave his victim twenty paces of a start before following, not so much moving over the ground as flowing from one shadow to the next, deathly silent and oblivious of the nameless filth beneath his feet.

This close to the kill his senses, always well developed, heightened so that every sight, sound and scent was recognizable even in the murky depths of the alley. Wary and wound tight as a ballista rope, he nevertheless felt an almost brotherly affinity with the victim. For instance, this past two days the man had taken on a heavy-footed gait as if someone had placed a great weight on his shoulders. Was it caused by the knowledge that the assassin's patron nursed a vengeful hatred that knew no bounds and each day was likely to be his last? Well, the weariness and the worry were about to end. When the job was done the killer would take ship at Seleucia Pieria and return to the reward that was his due and the wife and daughters on whom he doted.

He didn't think of himself as an evil man, not even a bad one. He was just a professional doing a job. Every man had to die some day, and few had the choice of the where, the how or the why.

At least for the former soldier it would be quick. He could visualize the gap between two ribs where the needle point of the long blue-tinged blade would enter the body. A moment of exquisite agony as it penetrated the frantically pumping heart. The muscle spasming to grip the bright iron until the knife twisted to break the hold, triggering a terrible long shudder that transmitted its way through the blade from victim to killer. A final breath and the familiar look of disbelief in the dying eyes.

Now! He increased his pace. His cloth-bound feet covered the ground in long soundless strides that brought him so close to the inviting, unsuspecting back that his nostrils twitched with the scent of the victim's last cup of wine. The final rush was accompanied by a thrill of fear that the man would sense something and react, instantly replaced by the exhilaration of the faultlessly placed strike, the right arm punching forward, the aim and the angle exact. Perfection.

But why did the impact jar his arm? Why, instead of welcoming flesh, did the point meet something rigid and unforgiving? Even as the assassin's mind made the link with the sensation of a blade being turned by metal, it was already too late. A warning scorched his brain like a bolt of forked lightning. That heartbeat's hesitation gave Gaius Valerius Verrens his opportunity. He whirled in a single movement and his left hand came up to seize the attacker's wrist. The would-be killer felt the bones grind together and the knife dropped from his nerveless fingers. He looked up into eyes that surprised him because they were filled with regret rather than hatred or vengeance. As he struggled to break free the oaken fist he'd forgotten existed came up and smashed into his jaw with a force that sucked the strength from his legs. But the assassin had not survived for so long without an inner strength that would have surprised anyone who looked upon his doleful, priestly face. As he fell to the cobbled street his mind still whirled with possibilities. Surely he would be questioned? The man would want to know who had sent him and why. The assassin decided he would lead him back to his lodging house. Offer him money. Perhaps even give up the next link in the chain that led back to Rome. So many opportunities for a man of enterprise to escape or turn the tables.

Even as he considered his next move his disbelieving brain registered the sting as the edge of his own blade sliced across his throat. So this was how it—

*

19

Valerius stood over the dying man until the soft gurgling faded, careful to stay clear of the spreading pool of darkness that threatened his feet. When all movement ceased he threw the knife into a nearby cesspit and searched the corpse. As he'd expected, the findings were of little interest: a purse containing a surprising number of gold coins, the usual phallic charm for luck – he looked into the dead eyes and shook his head at the irony of it – a second knife in a pouch strapped to the arm, and a braided rope that needed no explanation. He'd supposed the man might carry some token identifying his origin, but it didn't really matter. Whether he was employed by one of the shadowy state-sponsored agencies in the Palatium or just another blade for hire, Valerius had no doubt who sent him.

He straightened with the weary grunt of a much older man and considered his options. The dead assassin was the latest of at least four killers who'd dogged his footsteps over the last two months. One of them had simply disappeared. He'd persuaded the second, a Moesian courtesan, that whatever she'd been offered wasn't worth dying for. But in Athens there'd been a much too friendly merchant who'd surreptitiously poured powder into his wine cup, then taken so much interest in the establishment's nubile entertainment that Valerius had managed to switch drinks with him. Such was his agony that the convulsions snapped his spine like an overstrained bow.

This one had been the best. It had taken Valerius two days to mark him and the assassin's only mistake was not to strike earlier. The one-handed Roman thanked the gods for the whim that had led him to buy the rusting auxiliary chain armour he'd seen hanging at the back of an ironworker's market stall. Without it, he would certainly be dead. Mars' sacred arse, the bastard had been quick. One moment he'd been a dozen paces back and the next Valerius had the breath knocked out of him. It had been pure luck the point hadn't punched through one of the armour's many weak spots. As it was, he was certain the knife had still bitten deep into the heavy leather vest he wore under the chain. He stretched his lower back. He was getting too old for this. The thought made him laugh. He was thirty-four years old. At thirty-four, Augustus had conquered Egypt and ten years later he'd still had the strength of will to invade Parthia and recover the standards lost by Crassus at Carrhae.

With a last regretful glance at the dead assassin he set off again in the direction of the stables. More imperative than ever to ensure the horses were being well cared for and the stable hands were following his instructions. He was fairly certain the killer worked alone, but that didn't mean there weren't others nearby ready to take on the job if he failed. Valerius's enemy was a man who could not be underestimated. Valerius had done that once and almost paid the price. To do so a second time would be suicidal.

He pondered whether to search the assassin's rooms, but decided he might alert an accomplice he'd missed. The killer must have some means of reporting his success and the man who had sent him was not known for his patience. Did that mean he'd already been told of Valerius's plan to join one of the caravans heading east for the next leg of his journey?

'Spare a few *as* for an old soldier down on his luck?'

The slurred words came from a doorway to his right. Valerius automatically checked his left side in case the approach had been designed to distract him. When he was certain there was no danger he turned back to the man who'd spoken. A single red-rimmed eye shone from a face destroyed by a sword blade. It had caught him high on the right cheek and removed the other eye, half his nose and several teeth. He might have been anywhere between thirty and fifty and sat on a bundle of straw with one leg tucked under him. The stump of the other, removed at the thigh, jutted out in front.

'What legion?'

'Tenth Fretensis, your honour, Corbulo's finest. Honourable wounds taken against the Parthian King of Kings.'

A shiver ran through Valerius at the reminder of Gnaeus Domitius Corbulo, the most successful general ever to wield a sword for Rome and the man who'd been like a father to him. Corbulo had become so powerful that Nero had grown to fear him and, despite his professions of loyalty, ordered him to commit suicide. The Tenth Fretensis had held the Parthian charge at the Cepha Gap as arrows turned the sky black and King Vologases' Invincibles crashed to their doom, but they'd suffered terrible casualties. Most of the badly wounded died in the unsprung carts carrying them back to the Euphrates crossing at Zeugma. This man must be tough to survive the ordeal – or he'd been graced with Fortuna's favour. He weighed the assassin's purse in his hands and threw it to the cripple.

'Spend it wisely,' he said.

Before he reached the stables he heard the cackle of laughter as the mutilated soldier discovered the value of the purse's contents. A roar of 'The drinks are on old Atticus tonight' echoed down the street and told him his advice was unlikely to be taken.

The pure joy in the shout made him grin. In truth he could have used the money himself, but he had a feeling the gold was tainted and, in the long run, would bring him bad fortune. Another old memory stirred and he touched his throat where a silver wheel of Fortuna hung on a leather thong. It was his only physical link to Domitia Longina Corbulo, the general's daughter, the woman he loved and the one who'd saved his life. She'd placed it round his neck on that last day in Rome. 'You must forget me,' she'd said. But her advice was easier to acknowledge than to put into practice.

In pursuing Domitia, Valerius had made a mortal enemy of Titus Flavius Domitian. That enmity had grown along with Domitian's power until it became a homicidal obsession to rid himself of his love rival. When Valerius had knelt in the Forum, falsely accused of treason and with an executioner's sword at his neck, Domitia had promised herself to his enemy to save him. Instead of death, Valerius had suffered permanent exile from the shores of Italia and been branded an enemy of the state.

Of course it wouldn't end there. There'd never been any doubt that Domitian would send his assassins in Valerius's wake. Even with Domitia's support he wouldn't have escaped Rome alive without the help of his former colleague Gaius Plinius Secundus. Pliny had loaned him money and supplied him with a list of contacts that allowed him to reach Antioch. Now he was on his own, and Valerius knew his only chance of long-term survival was to reach his friend Titus, Domitian's brother, and somehow redeem his honour. It meant finding a way to Judaea, where Titus commanded his father Vespasian's forces.

But Judaea was a province in revolt and a lone traveller's chances of crossing its war-ravaged deserts and mountains alive were slim. Valerius had sought a place in a well-guarded mercantile caravan that would take him some of the way in relative safety. Thanks to the assassin he must now consider that route closed. He could return to the coast and take ship from Seleucia to Tyrus or Appolonia, but Domitian would undoubtedly have the ports watched.

Which left him with only one option.

II

'I do not wish to appear ungrateful, lord, but the pittance I accepted to be your guide and protector on the road to Emesa did not extend to travelling through the hours of darkness.'

Valerius gritted his teeth and resisted the urge to snarl at his companion. He wondered how much longer he could stand the sing-song whine. For two hours now, or was it three, he'd been listening to a litany of complaint. The horse was too high-spirited. He'd have been much better with camels. The night was cold. The saddle was hard. The date was not auspicious. The route . . .

'Did I mention that the coast road would be quicker, more comfortable and, now I remember, safer?'

'I've seen enough of the sea.' Valerius's patience snapped. 'I told you I wanted to experience the interior. You assured me this was the scenic route, fit for conquerors, kings and emperors. We will walk in the footsteps of Alexander, you said.'

'Indeed, lord,' the other man said patiently, 'but it is so much more scenic, not to say less dangerous, if one travels it by the light of the sun. Who knows what djinns and sprites haunt the darkness? Foul shape-changers who lure

25

you in woman's lovely form before turning into monsters with hooked claws and fangs to rend your flesh asunder.'

'Then you should feel quite at home here,' Valerius responded through clenched teeth, 'given the quality of the women in the tavern where I found you.'

Ariston, for that was the name he went by, registered the dangerous quality in the Roman's voice and fell quiet. Dark-skinned and coarse-featured, he claimed to be of Greek origin, and had astonished Valerius with a laughable boast that he was descended from the Seleucid ruling house. If that were the case his bloodline had been much diluted. He'd been described by the barkeep who pointed him out as 'part Bedou wanderer, part Palmyran bandit, with a touch of Gandhara Zoroastrian fire-worshipper thrown in to make him interesting'. The result was a hooked nose any eagle would have been proud of and a pair of luminous green eyes that darted restlessly from beneath a bush of curly hair. His almost feminine, thin-lipped mouth never seemed to shut. For conversation he favoured Greek, which suited Valerius well enough, but like many of the nomadic people of the province he could make himself understood in a dozen languages. Wrapped in a shapeless, hooded cloak of patched cloth that might once have been white, he appeared the least trustworthy-looking human being Valerius had ever laid eyes on. Yet when the Roman remarked that he'd doubtless have his throat cut on the first night, the innkeeper insisted that Ariston had a reputation for delivering those with whom he set out.

'Then why,' Valerius had asked, 'if he is such a paragon, isn't he a guide for the merchant caravans out of Palmyra where the real money is made?'

The man had shaken his head in mock sorrow. 'That would be because the traders wouldn't let him within a hundred paces of their daughters.' He grinned. 'He may not look it, but our Ariston is a terrible one for the ladies.'

The Syrian had accepted the commission readily enough, but his protests started when Valerius insisted on setting out before daylight. Ariston boasted of being from a long line of fearless warriors whom no bandit would dare attack, but it seemed his fearlessness didn't extend to the dark. 'Only a fool or a fugitive creeps about after the sun has gone down,' he muttered peevishly. 'We should wait.'

But the dawn risked exposing Valerius to the eyes of his enemies and after further negotiation he persuaded Ariston into motion. They left the city by the Beroea Gate – two men and three horses, the pack horse heavily laden, helped on their way by a modest bribe to the gate guard. Ariston led Valerius along the eastern road, with the Orontes always to their left. It was his plan to follow the river to the next major stopping place, which meant a day's march east before turning south. With the gods' will it would take them another eight days to reach Emesa.

Flat slabs of local stone provided the road with a good surface and even in the dark they made good time. Dawn saw them skirting the foothills of the mountain range that hung like a wall over Antioch. The morning mist cleared quickly and they broke their fast in the shelter of an olive grove beneath a sky of pristine, eggshell blue while their horses drank from the foaming waters of the river. On the opposite bank, the valley was carpeted with fields already worked by slaves ploughing and planting the fertile dark earth. It was a tranquil pastoral scene, evidence of a land settled and at peace, and Valerius said so as they prepared to mount up.

His words drew a high-pitched laugh from his companion. 'Ayah, peace provided at a price by your legions for the Greeks who own this land and these slaves and those vineyards on the hills yonder. All paid for by the taxes of people who have never seen a legionary, nor asked for or needed his protection.'

Valerius favoured him with an indulgent smile. It was the argument of the barbarian from one end of the Empire to the other. They were simple people who couldn't understand that, just because the benefits provided by their taxes weren't visible, it didn't mean they didn't exist. 'But you have fine roads that can be travelled in all weathers,' he pointed out as he pulled himself into the saddle. 'Bridges that never wash away and wells that never dry up.'

Ariston shrugged dismissively. 'Does it matter if a man reaches his destination in a day, or a week? The destination will still be there when he arrives. Or he gets his feet wet crossing a stream that will, in any case, cleanse them or cool them on a hot day? A well is very fine, but only a fool does not know how to find water.' He looked towards the distant mountains. 'This river was once named for Typhon, the dragon who was its creator. It is said the gods sought him out with their lightning bolts and in his agony he tore up the earth and created this valley, before fleeing underground where he unleashed the waters. Now it is the Orontes. Who knows what it will be next?'

'Whether I reach my destination in a week or a month your mindless chatter isn't taking us any closer.' Valerius kicked his horse into motion, but Ariston's words still rang in his head. What the Syrian said was true. Nothing was permanent but the earth and the mountains and the sea. Everything else had its time, even empires.

Ariston turned moody and sullen after the rebuke and they barely exchanged another two words before they halted in the late afternoon. The Syrian wanted to use the daylight to continue a few miles to a *mansio*, one of the government lodging houses that dotted the highway. Instead, Valerius insisted they sleep under the stars away from the road. Muttering complaints beneath his breath, the guide tethered the horses and prepared the campsite.

For the hundredth time since leaving Rome, Valerius found himself wishing that Serpentius, the freed gladiator who had become his friend and bodyguard, had been able to travel with him. The Spaniard had suffered a dangerous head wound trying to save the life of Vitellius's son Lucius during the Flavian sack of Rome. If he still lived he would be halfway to his home province by now. Serpentius had acted as Valerius's shield when none was available, covering his right side in many a fight, and the Roman felt naked and vulnerable without his friend. A familiar itch reminded him that by now anyone who wanted to know would have discovered he'd left Antioch and might well be on the road behind them.

'We'll do without a fire this first night.' The order drew a stare from his companion, but for once Ariston didn't complain. He set out a cloth and laid it with rolled vine leaves stuffed with a moist, tasty combination of cereal and spiced ground lamb. Valerius pulled a flask from his pack and poured wine into two leather travel cups. The Syrian nodded his thanks and supped appreciatively as they ate.

'You are a well-travelled man, Ariston,' Valerius said. 'Tell me what you know of the situation in Judaea.'

Ariston didn't raise his eyes from his food. 'The Jews are fools to fight you Romans, but they are like a lion trapped in a cave with the hunter's spear at his throat. Ask them why and they will tell you that when a free man is forced to mortgage his lands and call another man master while he watches the flesh fall from his starving sons' bones, there comes a time when he has no other choice but to fight.'

'A fine speech,' Valerius commented. 'But I do not recognize this Rome you paint. Yes, Rome taxes, but it also builds, and it encourages those living under its rule to create further wealth that can be taxed in its turn. Surely to create wealth there must be peace, which benefits all?'

'Just so.' Restless green eyes stared out from beneath the heavy brow. 'But what happens when the wealth is created by the sweat and blood of the poorest and none is returned? For sixty years they watched their gold being shipped to Rome or used by their priests – priests appointed by Roman masters, mark you – to decorate the Great Temple of Jerusalem and glorify the Judaean god at enormous cost to his long-suffering people. Then your procurator marched his men to the temple and demanded seventeen talents of gold – the weight of ten men – in compensation for some imagined slight. In such circumstances all that is required is a spark.' The Syrian shrugged. 'They are a superstitious people and when a light in the sky appeared in the shape of a sword, the spark was provided. When they saw the anger of the common folk, the priests suspended sacrifices in honour of the Emperor.'

Listening to the other man's words, Valerius realized he hadn't been entirely accurate when he'd said he didn't recognize Ariston's Rome. A face swam into view, narrow and sharp-edged, with a long nose and a drooping petulant lip. Catus Decianus, procurator of Britannia, had also impoverished his subjects on behalf of Nero and provided the spark for a bloody insurrection when he'd scourged Boudicca, queen of the Iceni.

'What happened next?' he asked, though he could imagine it easily enough.

'Leaders appeared, and the country people rose up and invested the towns where they believed the riches of the land were stored. Roman garrisons were slaughtered along with any Judaean who supported them. So Rome had to act. A competent general would have smashed them in weeks, crucified a few of their commanders and sent the rest back to their fields.'

Valerius felt a flush of anger at the memory of his army's shameful record in Judaea. The Roman generals Nero sent had been far from competent. Cestius Gallus rushed his legions from Syria to suppress the rebellion, but after initial successes he'd been forced to retreat. Worse, the Twelfth Fulminata had lost its eagle. Rome had not only been defeated, it had been humiliated. Brute force had failed, but Rome did not negotiate with rebels in a backwater like Judaea. The answer was to find a more competent brute.

Nero had been a wastrel and a fool who alienated his generals, but he'd kept one old soldier close. While Domitian was detained in Rome under the watchful eyes of the Emperor, Flavius Vespasianus could be relied upon to put down the rebellion with all the power at his command. Valerius had met Vespasian three years earlier, at Alexandria, while the general was planning the subjugation of Judaea, and later at Ptolemais on the eve of the campaign. He'd been impressed by a logistical brain that rivalled Corbulo's and a decisiveness that didn't bode well for the Jewish rebels.

'When Vespasian took the field,' Ariston continued, 'the Judaeans had control of every town and city of any

31

strategic value, but within the year they had lost all. Gabara fell swiftly, but forty thousand died in the fight for Jotapata, betrayed at the last by their commander. At Gamala the streets ran with blood and the place was only taken when the general's son Titus personally led the assault. They are fanatics, the Jews, who would rather die than submit to authoritarian rule. Jericho followed, but when Vespasian heard of the trouble in Rome he was unwilling to commit his soldiers to a new assault when they might be required elsewhere. Of course, all that has changed. Vespasian is Emperor and Titus commands in Judaea.'

'Do you know where Titus is based?' Valerius asked. 'I would think that by now his troops will be coming out of their winter quarters and preparing for a new campaign.'

Something in the Roman's tone made Ariston frown. 'I do not know where he is, but I know where he will go.'

'Where?'

'Jerusalem.'

III

Valerius lay beneath his blanket with the ground chill gnawing at his insides like a hungry rat and listened to the other man's soft breathing. Despite his initial doubts he'd been impressed by the depth of Ariston's knowledge and the way he'd explained the political and military situation in a few simple sentences. Jerusalem was the key. That was where the real Jewish fanatics – Ariston called them Zealots – had retreated and regrouped during the breathing space provided by Vespasian. According to the Syrian, Jerusalem's walls had never been breached. The Great Temple was the centre of the Jewish religion and the Zealots would defend it to the last drop of their blood. To destroy the rebellion for his father, Titus must first take Jerusalem.

Titus the general. Titus the man Vespasian was likely to appoint as his heir to the throne of the world's greatest empire, though he would not only have to survive his father, but also prove his right to it, before he succeeded. When Valerius had first met Titus the young man had been a mere junior tribune newly appointed to command his father's auxiliary cavalry. They discovered they were of an age, they'd both served in Britannia at the time of

33

the great rebellion, and both took an unlikely joy in the art of soldiering. A shared background and shared interests led to friendship. Friendship brought Vespasian's patronage at a time when Valerius desperately needed it, which had undoubtedly saved his life.

But the cheerful, enthusiastic young soldier of that first meeting had vanished entirely by the time their paths had crossed again the previous year. The Titus who urged Valerius to help his father by reining in the reckless instincts of Marcus Antonius Primus, commander of the Danuvius legions, was much harder-edged; a man for whom command was natural and authority came easily. What kind of man would he be now?

Valerius tensed. Something almost imperceptible had changed in his surroundings. Beneath the blanket his left hand crept to the hilt of his sword. His companion's breathing, that was it. It had been regular and relaxed, but now the rhythm had an artificial quality, as if the other man were waiting for something. He pictured the campsite in his head. Perhaps four paces of open ground separated them, with the animals corralled to the right and the packs close by beneath the trees. He'd considered placing the packs between them, but that would have alerted the guide to his suspicions. Now he wished he hadn't ignored his instincts. The Syrian hadn't shown any weapon, but the voluminous robe he wore provided ample concealment for a sword or a knife. Valerius's ears strained for the sound of movement and he tensed to meet an attack.

'You will get very little sleep on this journey if you spend every night with a sword in your hand.' Despite the gentle admonition Valerius's fingers tightened on the weapon's grip. Ariston sounded reasonable enough, but a seasoned killer would use soothing tones to get close enough to put a knife in his victim's throat. 'If you do not trust me I will turn back tomorrow,' the Syrian continued. 'You will be safe enough as far as Apamea, which is as welcoming to a Roman as Antioch. The road is good and I've had no word of bandits in the Orontes valley this season. You will be able to hire a guide there who is more to your taste.'

Valerius hesitated. 'What makes you think I don't trust you?'

'You haven't even told me your name.' The other man's bitter laugh made the horses twitch against their hobbles. 'You think I don't notice how you always keep your right hand hidden beneath your cloak with your fingers on your sword? Why, tonight you even ate with your left.'

'My name is Gaius Valerius Verrens and perhaps you have not noticed that I do not have a right hand.' A shiver ran down Ariston's spine at the sound of the voice close to his right ear. He'd had no warning of Valerius's approach: the man must move like a ghost. 'Take your hand away from your knife.'

Ariston did as he was ordered. 'Please . . .'

'My right hand was once part of an oak tree.' The Syrian winced as Valerius tapped him on the forehead with something that certainly wasn't flesh and bone. 'It identifies me as clearly as a senator's purple stripe. As it happens I have reasons for not wishing to be identified.'

'So that is why you avoided the *mansio* and insisted on having no fire.' Understanding dawned on Ariston. 'You fear someone might be following us?'

'Perhaps.'

The Syrian waited for some further revelation, but the only sound was Valerius returning to his bedroll. 'Then

35

perhaps I can help,' he suggested. 'There are other ways than the road.'

'We will discuss it again in the morning.' Valerius lay back and pulled the blanket around him. His fingers automatically sought out his sword, but this time it was to return the blade to its scabbard.

'Your arm? They caught you stealing?'

Valerius laughed and shook his head.

Ariston looked put out at his mistake. 'It is the way of the desert tribes,' he said defensively.

'What happens if you're caught with another man's wife?' He saw the Syrian wince and smiled. 'I lost it in battle.' The explanation was simpler than the reality, but it would do. The elevation of the rough track Ariston had chosen to the east of the river allowed occasional glimpses to the road below. It slowed their progress, but Valerius was satisfied. He'd seen two groups of horsemen and a few individuals travelling south at speed and had no wish to make their acquaintance. 'It happened in a fight against an army led by a woman. A rebel queen.'

'A woman defeated Rome?' Ariston couldn't hide his interest.

'A queen,' Valerius corrected. 'She led an army of sixty thousand, while we were fewer than four thousand. At the forefront were her champions, giants who fought naked to prove their courage.'

'Still,' the Syrian sounded thoughtful, 'a woman.'

'We kept them from the temple for two days and watched as they burned the city around us.' Valerius shrugged. 'Sometimes there is only so much a man can do.'

'But you lived.'

'I lived.'

'Rome defeated by a woman,' Ariston repeated as if he didn't quite believe the words he was saying.

'She won every battle but the last.' Valerius's voice sounded so bleak that Ariston reined in his horse to study him.

'What happened then?'

Valerius met his gaze. 'Let us hope Titus is more merciful to the Judaeans than Rome was to Boudicca and her Britons.'

As they rode, Ariston explained that the old caravan road would eventually lead them to Darkush, famous for its healing waters, where they could replenish their supplies. After that they would cross the spine of the mountains into the next valley, far from any pursuit. 'The valleys eventually meet again about twenty miles south, but it's well-populated country and we have a choice of roads to take. I doubt anyone will pay attention to us.'

Over the next three days Valerius gained a better appreciation of his Syrian companion. For a start, Ariston possessed an instinct for danger rivalling his own. In Darkush he bought Valerius a hooded cloak as voluminous as the one he wore himself. It provided the twin attributes of perfect anonymity and, despite being light and airy, giving as much protection from the cold as a much heavier garment.

When Valerius quizzed him about his own history he looked troubled. 'A man like me has many lives. One for every town he visits and woman he lies with. My father owned a tract of good land north of Palmyra, but a neighbour coveted the sweet water that had been ours by right for five generations. When my father was found dead in his fields I sought out the neighbour and demanded compensation. He pulled out a knife . . .' Ariston shrugged; it could have happened to anyone.

'He had powerful friends, so I had to run or die. The Bedou took me in and I stayed with them for a while, but the desert is not for me. I found a position as a caravan guard and travelled deep into Persia and as far as the Indus. In Gandhara I took a wife, but she died along with our child.'

'Did you ever go back?'

'Only once. My mother was dead and my brothers worked the farm. I think they would have driven me off, but I only stayed an hour. After a few years in the saddle farming was not for me. A long road and a different bed every night are my life, and I am satisfied.'

'A different woman, too, I would wager?' Valerius attempted to lighten the mood. The Syrian's words stirred an unfamiliar emotion. For the first time since he'd left Rome he felt free of responsibility. Thanks to Domitia Longina Corbulo's intervention, his sister Olivia had been allowed to keep the family estate at Fidenae. Olivia had brought her newborn son to visit him on the day he'd left the city. She knew she could never formally marry Lupergos, the child's sire and her estate manager, and the boy had been named for Valerius's father, Lucius. He felt a rush of contentment at the memory. Perhaps it was the vibrant colour of the mountains that changed with every bend in the road and arc of the sun, or the sweet water and even sweeter air, but it felt as though he were on the cusp of a new existence. He knew it was dangerous to tempt the gods, but maybe, just maybe, he'd outridden the clutching fingers of the past.

That night they bedded down in a gully away from the road. Ariston estimated that they'd reach Apamea at noon the next day and boasted of the luxuries that would be available to them in the city's markets.

An hour later they heard the screams.

IV

Valerius reacted instantly. Even as he leapt from the blankets with *gladius* in hand, his mind was calculating the direction of the agonized cry. One thing was certain, it had come from a woman, and one in terrible pain.

He dashed up the gully wall with the branches of scrub oak and cypress tearing at him, praying she'd cry out again so he could fix her position. Sharp stones cut into his bare feet, but that didn't concern him so much as the noise he was making and the fact that he had no idea what was beyond the brow of the hill.

His brain only gradually came to terms with the fact that he was acting alone, with no Serpentius at his side. Reluctantly, he forced himself to slow. He would do the woman no good by getting himself killed. The best he could hope for from Ariston was that the Syrian looked after the horses and didn't simply disappear into the night with them.

Another scream. Much closer now, long and drawn out, and he angled to his left towards the source. The word childbirth entered his mind – he'd look a fool if he burst in with a sword as the baby emerged – but he quickly dismissed it. He'd heard enough women give birth in the baggage camps that followed a legion to know this was a different kind of pain. A pain accentuated by terror.

He reached the lip of the rise and crouched among the bushes, staring into the darkness across the broken ground ahead. Perhaps a hundred paces away he detected a faint glow just visible through the stunted trees among the dips and the hollows. On the point of rising he froze, paralysed not by any hint of danger but by a sudden, unexpected and uncalled-for sense of self-preservation. His brain told him he didn't have to do this. He had no obligation to whoever was out there being hurt. How many times had honour and duty driven him to risk his life, and for what? In Rome he'd been moments from a slow and agonizing death. In Armenia, Gnaeus Domitius Corbulo had sentenced him to be beaten with pickaxe handles. He'd lost his right hand in Britannia. He could turn back now and no one would ever know. No one but Gaius Valerius Verrens.

But Valerius had been fed a diet of honour and duty since he'd first suckled his mother's teat. His father had beaten it into him with a vine stick and with every blow had suffered more anguish than his victim. Corbulo, whom he'd loved as a father, had gone to his death because he believed that an honourable man did not have the luxury of choice, only duty. How could he be any less of a man? Gritting his teeth, he forced himself to his feet and slithered down the far side of the slope, leaving an almost invisible trace of dust in the darkness.

As he moved swiftly across the broken ground the soldier's questions ran through his mind. How many? More important, how many of them would be willing to die? It was a fact of war that for every ten men you faced with a sword six would rather be somewhere else entirely, and two would run at the first sign of danger.

And their dispositions? Would they have posted a guard? That depended on whether they were soldiers or brigands. He could hear the sound of mocking laughter now, and in the background a woman pleading for an unlikely mercy. He touched the little wheel of Fortuna and prayed that any guard would be distracted by the sport. These were clearly men intent on their work. Men who enjoyed inflicting pain.

By now he could see the bright flicker of a fire through the trees and he padded softly towards the source. Despite the urgency, he took his time, allowing his eyes to adjust to the changing light and testing the air for danger with every step. Gradually moving shadows appeared, crouched low over something that glowed pale gold in the light of the flames, their hands busy and their minds intent on their victim. Four at least, perhaps five. He calculated the odds and was undismayed. Civilians, or at least dressed in civilian clothing. In an ordered world that should mean the sight of a naked blade would give them pause. If Valerius had his way that pause would kill them.

Three of the men held down their near-naked captive while a fourth gripped her wrist and intermittently forced her hand into the flames, accounting for the screams he'd heard. The final torturer was a huge man with features hidden behind a striped scarf wound around his head in such a way as to leave only the eyes showing. His role seemed to be limited to questioning the tormented woman.

Valerius waited for the next scream before he moved forward another step.

41

The hidden guard's mistake was to charge from the bushes before calling out. Valerius caught the movement in the corner of his eye, and turned to meet the danger knowing he was already too late. The mouth of the swarthy, bearded face gaped wide as the man prepared to shout a warning to his friends. Before Valerius could even raise his sword, something like a silver bird flashed across his vision and the guard's head snapped back, the mouth gaping still further. The only sound that emerged was a soft croak caused by the little throwing axe that had cut his vocal cords and severed his windpipe.

Valerius stepped forward and caught the swaying body, taking the weight and easing the dying guard to the ground. A tall, emaciated figure with a shaven head and burning eyes stepped from the darkness. Valerius pulled the axe free and held it as if ready to throw. Instead, he wiped it on the dead man's ragged tunic before handing it silently back and nodding his thanks. He could still barely understand what had happened or why, but for the moment the newcomer's eyes held a question. Valerius answered it with a raised hand showing five fingers. His companion registered no emotion at the number.

Valerius pointed east, his mouth silently mouthing the word 'horses'.

The newcomer raised a rebellious eyebrow and held up a hand showing an identical five fingers, a gesture that suggested the odds would require more than one man. Valerius knew he was probably right, but something told him it was important that none of these men escape. That meant someone had to find their mounts and kill whoever was looking after them. He shook his head and repeated, 'Horses.'

The thin man acknowledged this with a soft grunt and set off silently over the rough ground on an arc that would take him to the far side of the camp without being seen. When he was gone, Valerius advanced directly towards the firelight.

The questioning must have been completed to the leader's satisfaction because he laughed and the four men began to tear at the screaming woman's remaining clothing. Two of them forced her legs apart while the others held her arms and pawed at her naked breasts. Valerius's instinct was to rush straight to her aid, but he knew this was not the moment for impetuousness. For the time being she must endure. He forced himself to wait.

His opportunity came when the tall man advanced towards his helpless victim. Dark eyes gleamed in the cloth-covered face as he hitched up his tunic in a movement that left no doubt what was to come. The woman squirmed beneath her captors' hands, but they only mocked her all the more, spitting in her face and making gestures that indicated they would be next.

Wait.

The big man forced his way between the pair holding the captive's legs and knelt over his victim. Valerius could hear him talking to her in a soft voice, but without warning the tone turned savage and guttural. The man's head rose and his hips prepared to thrust forward.

None of the torturers noticed the shadowy figure who emerged from the darkness and ran silently towards them. The triangular point of the *gladius* is its true strength in battle, but Valerius had always made sure the edge was keen enough to shave the hair on his arms. By the time the men detected his presence the sword was already coming down in a scything arc aimed at the point where the big man's skull joined his neck. The razor-edged iron would have taken his head off at the shoulders had it not been partially blunted by the cloth of the headscarf. As it was, the blow was powerful enough to slice through the spine; his skull flopped forward and the rapist's enormous body collapsed on top of his victim. The two men holding her legs were momentarily trapped beneath the still-shuddering corpse and Valerius used the split second to transform his sword swing into a neat back cut that slashed across a second man's throat.

Ignoring the torturer struggling to free himself, Valerius confronted the pair who'd been holding the woman's arms. They'd reacted to the sudden outburst of lethal violence by scuttling away from the danger on their backsides. Now they simultaneously clawed for their daggers as they struggled to regain their feet.

Valerius knew he had moments to win back the initiative. In desperation he leapt on the partially decapitated man's back and launched himself in a flying kick. It took the closer of the two full in the face and the blow sent the man backwards spraying blood and teeth. A spear of pain shot up Valerius's leg, reminding him he'd left his hobnailed sandals back at the camp. But the bloodied knifeman was far from finished. He sprang up and parried a thrust aimed at his abdomen. Somehow Valerius managed to turn his attack into a clumsy hack that chopped off his opponent's left ear and four inches of scalp. As the shrieking man collapsed the Roman just had time to whirl with a panicked slash that blocked the wickedly curved blade aimed at his midriff.

Valerius had practised with the sword almost every day for a dozen years. On many of those days he'd found himself up against former gladiators like Serpentius, fighters whose speed so mesmerized their opponents that they were knocking at the gates of Elysium before they realized they were dead. A civilian with a knife, however deadly in appearance, should have been no match for him.

But nobody had told this civilian. He had the balance of a gymnast and Valerius felt as if he'd been pegged to the ground as the man danced around him seeking an advantage. If ever there was a moment to regret sending his unexpected saviour to deal with the horse holders this was it. The knife darted and weaved in little half-moon arcs that threatened first one flank then the other. Valerius knew that somewhere behind him the man he'd left untouched would have freed himself, but he didn't dare take his eyes off that glinting blade. A howl of terror from the direction of the fire drew his attention for a fatal heartbeat. He realized his mistake just in time to suck in his stomach so the dagger point barely scored his flesh in a white hot bolt of fire. Another desperate hack at his opponent won him the room to hobble out of range, but it was only a matter of time. Where in the name of Hades was his ally?

The sound of galloping horses from the darkness behind the knifeman answered his question and the resolve faded from the snarling features. With a frustrated glance towards the fire the killer darted off, pausing to casually run his blade across his wounded comrade's throat as he went.

If Valerius was honest he'd expected the woman to be dead by now, but she had other ideas. She'd taken advantage of the surviving attacker's momentary incapacity to snatch up a flaming brand and defend herself. From the look of his face, now a blackened, unrecognizable mess, it appeared she'd been all too successful. As Valerius watched, she continued to hammer the branch home with short, vicious, left-handed blows that landed with a wet slapping sound.

'I'd have liked to be able to talk to at least one of them.' The words were in Greek and his weariness tempered any tendency towards sympathy.

The woman looked up and he felt as if someone had run a *gladius* point down his spine. The deepest blue eyes he'd ever seen glared at him from beneath slanted lids. 'Get this pig off me. Why did you let the other one get away?'

Her reply was also in Greek, which surprised him, because in Syria, as in Rome, it was the language of the educated and more affluent. He'd created an image of her as a village woman snatched by bandits to be used at their leisure and then discarded with her throat slit. But she was young, probably not yet twenty, and her tone was anything but that of a serving girl. If she'd been the daughter of a farmer or a merchant her skin would have been reddened by years of outdoor toil; instead it had the startling luminosity of a new-harvested pearl. A bruise to her right cheek was the only visible sign of her ordeal. She pushed vainly at the big man whose blood had drenched her torso and Valerius looked around for something to cover her.

A discarded cloak lay nearby. He handed it to her and hauled the near-decapitated giant aside, the dead man's head flopping like a strangled chicken's. The girl accepted the garment without a word of thanks, and struggled clear as the weight shifted. She wrapped the cloak around the tattered remnants of her clothing, spat on the man she'd killed and pushed him into the fire with her foot for good measure. His blood sizzled noisily in the glowing embers.

It was only when she tried to stand that it finally hit her. Valerius rushed to stop her toppling to join the man gently roasting on the fire. She was shorter than he'd realized, but the body beneath the cloak was full and well fleshed. Taking her by the shoulders he cursed himself as she flinched away from any contact on a right hand covered in blisters the size of ripening grapes.

'Thank you,' she said with enormous dignity before her eyes turned up in their sockets and she slumped into his arms.

At that moment, Valerius's deliverer emerged from the darkness, leading a saddled mare. Lean as a stockman's oxhide whip, his brutish features were a patchwork of shadowy planes that made an already frightening face all the more fearsome. Valerius felt a rush of pleasure at the appearance of this savage creature.

'Seldom has a Spanish horse thief been a more welcome sight,' he said with mock formality. 'Serpentius of Avala, I thought you'd be halfway back to that nest of barbarians you call home by now.'

Serpentius spat towards the fire. 'Do not think you can escape me so easily, Gaius Valerius Verrens. You're not a hard man to track. I followed a trail of bodies from Achaia to Antioch before I lost you in the hills. I must have been up and down the Orontes road three times before I discovered where you'd crossed. A prudent man does not invade another's camp by night, but when I heard the scream I knew you'd be around here some-where.' He nodded to the woman in Valerius's arms. 'You've been getting acquainted.'

'She's in shock,' Valerius laid the woman gently on the ground, 'and her fingers are badly burned. They were torturing her.'

Serpentius studied the woman's injuries. 'We should immerse the hand in cold water. Then a loose bandage soaked in olive oil.' It was more an order than a sugges-tion, but Valerius remembered how Serpentius had

47

treated his burns after an Egyptian shipwreck and knew better than to argue.

'I—'

Without warning Serpentius spun round and one of the little Scythian throwing axes he favoured appeared magically in his hand.

'No!' Valerius's shout made the Spaniard freeze a moment before he released the weapon. Ariston stood at the edge of the trees paralysed by fear, staring at the silver glint of death aimed at his heart.

'I think our journey might take a little longer if you killed our guide,' Valerius said with heavy irony. 'Ariston, this is Serpentius, a friend who will be travelling with us.'

Ariston glared at the Spaniard, but his attention was quickly drawn to the near-headless body by the fire. He stalked over to kneel beside the corpse, hesitating before he peeled back the scarf and let out a low whistle. Taking it delicately by the hair he tilted the head so Valerius and the Spaniard could see the unwholesome grey flesh and twisted features, so contorted and swollen by disease as to be rendered almost inhuman.

'No wonder he hid his face,' Valerius said.

'He didn't hide it because he was ashamed of it,' Ariston corrected him. 'He hid it because he didn't want to be recognized.' He dropped the head and picked up one of the distinctive knives the men had carried. 'His name is Shimon Ben Judah, and he is . . . was . . . high in the ranks of the Sicarii.' He saw Valerius's puzzlement and showed him the knife. 'A society of assassins,' he explained. 'This is their mark. I don't understand it.'

'What's to understand?' Valerius grunted as he picked up the unconscious girl. 'A murderer and rapist gets the justice he deserves.'

The Syrian shook his head. 'The Sicarii seldom venture far from Jerusalem and I have never known them to appear this far north.' He stared significantly at the bundle in Valerius's arms. 'They rarely kill for gain or satisfaction.'

As Valerius carried the girl back towards the camp he noticed that Serpentius hadn't moved. The Spaniard stood among the bodies as if unsure what to do next. The inertia was so unusual that Valerius stopped and called to him.

'Serpentius?'

The former gladiator shook his head with a look of bewilderment. 'Was I . . . gone?'

'You seemed a little strange, that's all.'

'It has happened to me a few times since this.' Serpentius turned so Valerius could see the back of his shaven head. Among the old scars was a clearly visible depression the circumference of a wine cup. Valerius tried not to show his shock at the sight of the terrible injury. Domitia had hinted that the Spaniard had been badly hurt defending Vitellius's son, but this blow must have come close to killing him. The bone of the skull had been smashed in by a sword or a club. If such a wound happened on the battlefield, the more experienced *medici* would use some kind of cutting tool to remove the shattered bone, then pick fragments of it from inside the head. Only one man out of a hundred lived to fight again. 'They said the dent was too big.' Serpentius read his eyes. 'If they opened it up more than likely they'd kill me. The lady Domitia stayed with me until I recovered, but sometimes,' he frowned as if the thought had just occurred to him, 'it's as if I'm just a memory. A ghost trapped between worlds.'

'How often does it happen?'

'I don't know.' Valerius saw a tear roll through the dirty grey stubble of his friend's cheek and it disturbed him more than anything that had gone before. He'd never seen Serpentius show self-pity, never mind weep, not even when he talked of the wife and son murdered by Rome. The Spaniard was the hardest man he'd ever known, and the quickest with a sword; indomitable and without fear. 'I let them down, Valerius.' Serpentius shook his head. 'I couldn't save the boy. There were so many of them and then everything went dark.'

'Nothing could have saved the boy.' Valerius's reply was harsher than he intended, but he knew Serpentius needed support, not sympathy. 'He was dead from the day Vitellius announced him as his heir and I would rather he died than you. Now come. We have the girl to treat and a war to fight.'

V

Her name was Tabitha.

When she woke the next day she possessed only a vague recollection of the previous night. Valerius offered to delay the journey until she'd fully recovered, but she insisted they keep to their normal schedule. Still, he watched her carefully for some reaction to her ordeal and saw her face grow pale as the memories returned. It surprised and pleased her that her injured hand had been bandaged so efficiently, and the oil Valerius applied reduced the pain to a dull throb. One thing puzzled her. A vague recollection of lying beneath a giant pig of a man who had bled copiously . . . Someone had roughly stitched together the remains of her dress. Her mouth dropped open and she stared at Valerius, her expression changing swiftly from dismay, to outrage, to devastation. When she finally realized what must have happened she burst into tears. Ariston and Serpentius exchanged a look and found something essential to do with the horses, leaving Valerius to explain the unexplainable.

'We couldn't leave you as you were.' He chose his words with exaggerated care. 'We didn't know if the blood came only from him or if you had been injured also. I . . .' She stopped weeping long enough to spear him with a look of open-mouthed incredulity and he hurried on. 'I treated you as I would the body of a dead comrade fresh from the battlefield,' he assured her. 'With reverence and respect. To me you were just an empty vessel, as if I were washing a bowl or a cup.' He stumbled, aware of his voice taking on a pompous solemnity as he fought the memory of skin with the texture of silk and intriguing curves and hollows and shadows. 'I did not look upon you as a person.'

'Truly?' she said.

'Truly,' he lied, hoping the word didn't sound as hollow in her ears as it did in his.

She frowned, unsure whether to be pleased his medical ministrations had been carried out with such professional detachment or dismayed that her charms had so little effect. 'I do not know your name, though I would guess by your accent you are a Roman.'

'Gaius Valerius Verrens, at your service, lady . . . ?'

'I am called Tabitha.' She bowed her head with grave dignity. 'It was fortunate you strayed so far from the road.' The statement contained a question he found intriguing.

'We are on the way to Emesa.' He shrugged as if the journey were of little consequence. 'Then perhaps I will continue on to Judaea. My guide,' Valerius sensed Ariston's ears twitch, 'pledged to show me the wonders of the Orient, but he turns out to have poor eyesight and not much sense of direction.'

Tabitha explained that she was the servant of a lady travelling from Chalcis to Hamah with a caravan of five hundred camels laden with precious frankincense. 'An escort of fifty mounted archers provided by the king rode with us and we were judged safe from any interference.' She lowered her eyes. 'I wandered away from our encampment . . . I did not like to . . . under the gaze of the soldiers and rough camel drivers.' She sighed. 'I was a fool. They must have been waiting.'

'They must also have been eager to know the dispositions of the guards.' Valerius nodded towards her injured hand.

'Yes,' Tabitha said too quickly. 'They put me to the question before . . .' A tear ran down her cheek and he placed a fatherly hand on her shoulder. The touch clearly surprised her and she raised her eyes to meet his. For some reason Valerius found breathing difficult. 'If we make reasonable time we could reach Hamah before the caravan, or perhaps meet them on the road,' she continued eagerly. Valerius must have looked doubtful because her expression turned downcast. 'I promise I will not be a burden to you. I can ride as well as any man, and despite my foolishness my mistress will reimburse you for any inconvenience I have caused. Please.'

Valerius hesitated. He'd discussed the conundrum with Serpentius and Ariston during the night. In their opinion she would hold them back and his first instinct had been to leave her at the next village with enough money to see her home. Ariston had suggested returning to the river and hailing one of the boats carrying olive oil from the Syrian heartland to Antioch. But if she could ride . . .

'I have seen a mouse put up more of a struggle against a cat.' Ariston's complaint to his mount travelled back to where Valerius rode beside the pack horse. Tabitha had forged a few yards ahead with Serpentius, the shapely form from the previous night engulfed in Valerius's hooded cloak. 'With one flutter of her eyelashes she has

53

him doing tricks like a trained monkey. I once owned a camel with such eyes and she was the most wilful, vain, pernickety creature ever spawned. I sold her to a Bedou who was not so impressed by her looks and less inclined to spare the whip.'

'If you've finished reciting the merits of your menagerie,' Valerius gave him a sour look, 'perhaps you could keep your eyes open for signs of the lady's caravan and we'll be able to dispense with our unwanted distraction.'

'Unwanted? Hah.' The Syrian dropped back to take station beside him. 'A caravan of five hundred camels would leave a trail a hundred paces wide,' he said soberly, 'which would be visible even to a guide with poor eyesight. In addition, it would create a dust cloud that could be seen for ten miles. I see no dust cloud.'

'What are you saying?'

'Six men, or even ten, why would they risk raiding a caravan guarded by fifty bowmen?'

'They might have been only the advance guard,' Valerius suggested.

'They were Sicarii, I am certain of it. The Sicarii are killers, not thieves. They usually work alone. Six men would denote a particular mission.'

Valerius caught the hint. 'You think our new travelling companion is not being open with us?'

Ariston shrugged; what did he know? 'She has made a remarkable recovery.'

'There was nothing false about what those men did to her,' Valerius pointed out. 'Maybe she is just a remarkable woman?'

The Syrian turned in the saddle. 'Her beauty blinds you. I hope it is not the death of us.' His eyes drifted to the man riding at Tabitha's side. 'Speaking of death, your friend with the wolf's eyes makes me nervous.'

'And so he should,' Valerius said. 'Serpentius survived a hundred combats in the Taurus amphitheatre. He has hands as swift as a cobra's strike and has saved my life more times than I remember. It is your good fortune, Ariston, that he only kills who I tell him to.'

He kicked his horse ahead to where Tabitha had reined in to water her mount in a stream that joined the Orontes. 'You ride well,' he complimented her. 'Is that a common skill among servants in Chalcis?'

'Common enough in servants of the royal court.' She gave him a searching look that made his cheeks burn. 'My lady often hunts in the desert with King Aristobulus, either with hawk or hound. She expects her servant to be at her side in case of need. We are different from Roman women, who I understand avoid such strenuous pursuits.'

'I know one Roman woman who could match you in the saddle.' Valerius smiled, remembering Domitia Longina Corbulo's fierce pride as they outrode their Batavian pursuers at Placentia. 'But you're right, it is not a skill of which many Roman ladies can boast. Your place at court would also account for your remarkable command of Greek.'

'Latin too,' she replied in that language. 'And Hebrew, though Aramaic is the language of my birth. Is this an interrogation, Gaius Valerius Verrens?'

'Let us call it a conversation,' he smiled. 'Ariston, our guide, is by nature a suspicious man. He thinks it is possible that the men who attacked you were members of a group of assassins who go by the name of Sicarii. Perhaps there is a reason other than the value of your frankincense why they were interested in you or your lady?'

'What other reason would there be?' Tabitha shook her head. 'They were bandits. They wanted to know the layout of our camp and the position of the guards. Nothing more.'

As the sun reached its height they entered Apamea by the Antioch Gate beneath impressive city walls, and Ariston grinned at Valerius's undisguised astonishment. The Roman had expected just another dusty provincial city. A working community with a meeting place for a market, perhaps a forum and a basilica, a few temples and a baths. Instead the city rivalled anything he'd seen outside Rome, in some places possibly even surpassing the capital.

'This is the longest street in Syria, perhaps the world,' Ariston informed him proudly. 'I promised you wonders, is this not one?'

The main street, the *cardo maximus*, ran for at least a mile; a broad avenue lined with fluted columns of creamy white. 'There are twelve hundred,' Ariston continued, determined everything must impress. 'I have counted them. Six hundred to each side and every one the height of five men.'

Serpentius rode a little way apart, ignoring the architecture. Instead, his restless eyes searched the street for any undue interest in their little party. The others forced their horses past carts shod with iron wheels that rattled over the rutted cobbles. Driven by labourers in dusty robes, they carried wood and stone and fought for space with dark-skinned traders leading heavily laden camels, which were in turn followed by slave boys vying to pick up their droppings for manure. Valerius noted men wearing the garb of a dozen cultures. Apamea, like Antioch, was clearly a crossroads between east and west. A bustling place that trade, natural resources – they had passed through ripening fields and lush pastures filled with sheep – and its location beside the river had made wealthy. Behind the columns lay myriad shops and basilicas, selling goods from all over the world. Some of the luxuries had been imported from Rome, but others were more exotic. Ariston insisted the intricately worked golden objects studded with jewels and pearls on one stall could only have originated in the Indus Valley and the Orient. Tabitha altered course to study the shops more closely and reined in her mare at the front of one festooned with multicoloured lengths of cloth. When Valerius joined her she was clearly wrestling with some decision.

'Here.' He held out his purse, solving her dilemma. The shop was a dressmaker's and beneath the borrowed robe she wore only the hastily stitched, bloodstained remnants of her clothing. Of course she would want to replace it. 'Take what you need and call it a gift.'

After a moment's hesitation she accepted the purse, her face breaking into a pleased smile that made the bottom fall out of his stomach. Whatever he'd been going to say next vanished from his head. Fortunately, she saved him. 'It will take me an hour,' her head tilted and she studied the shop front with more care, 'perhaps two. You could pass the time in the baths and we could meet later in the market place by the elephant fountain?'

Valerius looked to Ariston for confirmation and the Syrian shrugged. 'There is merit in what she says. I prefer not to use the baths, but I would be happy to show you their location. I have business to conduct here, but the market is not far. I will take you there first and show you the meeting place.'

Tabitha dismounted and passed Valerius her reins. 'The elephant fountain in two hours,' she repeated. He watched the diminutive figure almost skip up the steps as Serpentius rode up to join him.

'I will stay with her,' the Spaniard said.

'You think she'll be in danger in a dress shop?' Valerius smiled.

'Why take a chance?' Serpentius growled. 'Who's to say those men last night are all there was? Besides,' his savage features broke into a grin, 'I might see something I like.'

'We should leave her here,' Ariston interrupted the Spaniard. 'There is something not right about this.'

Valerius laughed. 'Am I travelling with an old woman who feels threatened by a pretty girl?'

'A pretty girl who is much too familiar with this place for a servant who has spent the bulk of her days in Chalcis,' Ariston scowled. 'You will see.'

Valerius ignored the dire prediction and spent a pleasant hour in the baths. He hadn't removed the leather socket covering his stump for days and it was a guilty pleasure to have the mutilated limb massaged and oiled by a slave girl. He tried to recall if Tabitha had noticed the wooden fist. If she had, she hadn't reacted and she was clearly too diplomatic to mention it. Later, when he lay face down to have the oil removed from his back by a metal strigil, an image of Domitia Longina Corbulo swam into his mind. Should he feel guilty that he hadn't thought of her for days now? She had sacrificed her future to save him, but the moment she'd made her decision she had reconciled herself to a life without him. His recollection of that last day was of a woman utterly remote, as if his existence were no longer of any consequence to her. He still felt the pain of the realization. Yes, it might have been partly to dull the terrible emptiness of their parting, but he sensed there'd been something else. As if she could only endure her new life if she expunged the memories of the old.

Whether Domitian's assassins succeeded or not, he was already dead to her. They would never meet again.

When he'd dressed, he walked south towards the market, stopping occasionally to look at a shop or a stall, but with one eye on the people around him. It seemed unlikely he'd been followed, but the cruel reality was that he wouldn't see the dagger that killed him. Even with Serpentius by his side, one day there'd be someone who was faster or more cunning than those who'd tried before. A troop of exotically uniformed cavalry rode past, hooves clattering on the stone slabs. Valerius kept his head down and his wooden hand covered.

Ariston waited by the fountain, which, as its name implied, was dominated by a statue of an elephant standing in a pool with water streaming from a lead pipe in its trunk. The fountain was at the centre of a paved square surrounded by columns. Beyond the columns houses and villas clung to a hillside where another pillared roadway snaked its way to a magnificent temple that reminded Valerius of one he'd seen in Athens.

Ariston stared at him. 'You have lost your charm?' He pointed to the Roman's neck where the wheel of Fortuna had hung.

Valerius's hand instinctively went to his throat, but he smiled. The slave girl had been delighted with her unexpected gift. 'I decided I didn't need it any more. Sometimes a man must make his own luck.'

Ariston's expression said he must be mad, but the Syrian shrugged. 'You like Apamea?'

'It's very civilized.' Valerius smiled. 'But perhaps a little brash for my taste.'

'You can blame my forefather, Seleucas Nicador.' Ariston ignored Valerius's look of disbelief at his unlikely claim to royal blood. 'He was Alexander's most successful general and named the city for his fourth wife, a Bactrian with the nature of a bad-tempered crocodile. He loved her despite this, and to prove it Apamea must be bigger and more impressive than Antioch and Palmyra. He ordered a channel constructed that brings sweet water all the way from Salimiye.' He rose and reached out to slap the elephant's enormous behind. 'This was where he kept his five hundred fighting elephants, and those fields we passed with the sheep would once have trembled beneath the hooves of forty thousand horses.'

Valerius looked up at the sun. 'She is late.'

'What do you expect?' Ariston's laughter echoed round the market place. 'A girl in a dress shop, of course she's late.'

A few men and women appeared and began setting up stalls for the next day's market. They worked quietly and efficiently, laughing and joking amongst themselves. Valerius noticed the moment several heads looked up in alarm, like deer sensing the approach of a wolf. A heartbeat later he heard the sound of approaching hooves and as he leapt to his feet cavalry troopers funnelled into the square from every side. Squat, narrow-eyed men with fish scale armour, pot helmets and strung bows tensed and ready to loose. Every viciously barbed arrow was aimed at the two men by the fountain.

'It would be unwise to allow your hand to get any closer to your sword.' Ariston glanced nervously as the circle of arrows edged ever closer. All it would take was one careless movement and . . .

'Unstring your bows, unless you want to provide another reason for the king to take your stupid heads.'

The order caused consternation among the mounted ranks as a familiar figure in a voluminous cloak forced its way through the ring of horses. Tabitha threw back her hood and glared until the bow strings loosened. Serpentius stood at her side, surveying the scene with a look of sardonic amusement on his haggard features.

A cavalryman in a prefect's sash dropped to the ground and ran to kneel at Tabitha's feet.

'My lady.'

VI

'Lady?' As they rode at the centre of an escort to the Chalcidean camp outside Apamea, Valerius couldn't hide his curiosity about Tabitha's reception from the leader of the mounted archers.

'A figure of speech,' she assured him. 'Gaulan thinks he can win my heart by flattery. He will sometimes be overly deferential no matter how much I chide him for it.'

Her manner was so offhand and imperious that Valerius decided he pitied poor Gaulan. He'd find it easier to command his desert tribesmen than the woman he'd been entrusted with. 'You must have many potential suitors,' he teased her.

Tabitha looked at him from below curved lashes. 'Or perhaps it is my lovely new clothes that deceived him?' She pulled back her cloak so Valerius could admire the crimson *stola*.

'It was fortunate the seamstress completed her work when she did.'

'Gaulan's men would have done you no harm, I'm sure. They are very disciplined.'

'Nevertheless,' the Roman smiled, 'having been the focus of so many arrows I must give you thanks on behalf of myself and Ariston. What I don't fully understand is how they managed to find us in the market place.'

Tabitha considered for a moment. 'My lady was so incensed the caravan guards failed to protect me that she insisted Gaulan and his men stay behind until they found me. She can be very forceful and she left them in no doubt of the penalty if they failed in their task.'

'She must value her servants very highly.'

Tabitha's eyes searched for any sign that she was being mocked, but Valerius kept his face expressionless and she continued her explanation. 'One of his riders came upon the bandits' camp and found their remains, along with some scraps of my clothing. When they could discover no trace of me, they decided I must have been killed and my body thrown to the wild beasts. They deduced from the tracks that the bandits had some sort of dispute and the survivors had set off in the direction of Apamea. Since the only way they could save their own heads was to provide proof that all the bandits had been killed, they followed. Travellers on the road gave them descriptions of our mounts. When they reached Apamea it was a simple enough task to check every stable until they tracked down the horses and obtained a detailed description of the men who had brought them. Gaulan sent soldiers to scour the town and they found you quite quickly.'

'What happens now?' Valerius asked, as they approached the colourful cloth tents the cavalrymen had set up on one of the lush meadows outside the city.

'We will continue our journey at first light.' She paused, the white pearls of her perfect teeth nibbling at her lower lip. 'It is my hope you will accompany us as far as Emesa. It will be safer and you will travel more quickly with the help of their remounts. Is that acceptable to you?'

Valerius bowed in the saddle. 'I would be honoured to share the journey.'

'Good.' She kicked her horse ahead, smiling at him across her shoulder. 'Serpentius assures me that despite your great age you are a warrior of repute among Romans. I have told Gaulan you will protect my honour should he prove incapable.'

Valerius was still trying to work out whether to feel flattered or insulted when Ariston appeared at his side. 'I told you she would be trouble.' The Syrian shook his head gloomily.

'She may have saved our lives,' Valerius reminded him. He explained Tabitha's invitation to travel on to Emesa with the column and Ariston's expression became even more lugubrious.

'I suppose this means you will no longer need my services?'

Valerius had already given the matter some thought. He shook his head. 'This land and these people are entirely unfamiliar to me,' he said. 'If I am to be of any use to Titus I need to understand how they think. How far from Emesa to Jerusalem?'

'Twelve days, if the weather holds. Fourteen or fifteen if not.'

'If you are willing to accompany us I will pay you for your knowledge of Judaea and for teaching me the rudiments of the language. You speak it?'

'Of course,' the Syrian bristled. 'Hebrew is my second tongue.'

'Then join us, and when we reach Titus you will have your reward.'

The Syrian considered for a moment and then nodded his acknowledgement. 'I will be happy to ride with you, even among these Chalcidean hellhounds and their vixen.' He frowned and his voice took on a tutor's solemnity. 'First, you must understand that Judaea is not one country, but an amalgamation of several. Galilee is in the north . . .'

By the time they reached Emesa two days later, Valerius had learned that the Judaeans were naturally rebellious, having previously fought both the Syrians and the Greeks. That despite their singular religion they were eternally divided, much as the tribes of Britannia had been and for all he knew still were. That the country wasn't really a province at all, not being worth the attention of a governor of senatorial rank, but ruled by a mere procurator. 'My knowledge of high politics is slight,' Ariston had admitted. 'But it seems to me that Rome's only interest in the place is ensuring the Parthians have no influence there.'

Emesa lay forty miles downstream from Apamea, on the east bank of the Orontes at the edge of a flat plain enclosed by hills on three sides, with blank, sterile desert on the fourth. During the journey, Gaulan had described it as a great metropolis, but Valerius considered it vastly inferior to the sprawling glory of Apamea. A massive mound topped by a palace complex dominated the city. Tight-packed houses surrounded the hill, hemmed in by the city wall and a scatter of suburb slums that lined the roads converging on it. The hilltop complex and a large temple apart, it looked a poor little place, and he said as much to Ariston.

'Do not be deceived,' the Syrian assured him. 'Emesa may not be as lovely as Apamea, but it is more important by far. The palace you see is the seat of Sohaemus, the powerful king who rules here, and the temple to the south is the home of Elah Gebal, the sun god. Thousands come to worship during the great festivals and tributes, even from as far as Palmyra, which Sohaemus covets but cannot move against without Rome's sanction.'

Valerius was disappointed he'd had no opportunity during the journey for further contact with the mysterious Tabitha. He'd planned to impress her with the few Hebrew phrases he'd learned, but she'd ridden with the baggage train and he wondered if she was deliberately avoiding him. The feeling was strengthened as the soldiers set up camp and he watched her ride out towards the city with Gaulan and an escort, heavily cloaked and with a hood covering her dark hair.

Serpentius appeared beside him. The Spaniard watched the riders. 'I wouldn't trust the Syrian camel thief to water my horse, but maybe he's right and we'd be better off on our own,' he scowled.

'You seemed happy enough to talk to her a few days ago,' Valerius pointed out. 'You're not usually so communicative with strangers.'

The former gladiator gave a grunt of a laugh. 'So she told you.' He spat in the dust. 'She asked and I answered, but only enough to make you sound interesting.'

'Well, from now on keep your gossip to yourself. What do you think of our travelling companions?'

'The cavalry? They're well mounted and they can use those bows of theirs. I saw one of them put an arrow through a hare's eye at a hundred paces. In fact the third squadron are getting ready to go hunting in the scrub along the river. A couple of them speak reasonable Latin. Maybe I should go along and see if I can find out a bit more. Not that it'll make much difference. We won't know if they have any fight in them until someone tries to kill us.'

'Then let's hope we don't need to find out too soon,' Valerius called after him. 'And Serpentius?' The Spaniard looked over his shoulder. 'Stop giving Ariston your murderer's stare. He knows his way around this country and I have a feeling we'll need that knowledge. I don't want him sneaking out on us one night because he thinks you want to kill him. In any case, I like him.'

'Then he'd better look out for himself,' Serpentius growled. 'Because I've noticed that the people you like have a tendency to end up dead.'

An hour later one of the escort returned across the plain to announce that King Sohaemus demanded Valerius's presence at his palace in the city. The summons came as a surprise and Ariston shot him a glance of warning that Valerius acknowledged with a barely discernible nod. 'Very well,' he told the man. 'I will accompany you once my interpreter and I are ready.'

The cavalryman gave him a troubled look. 'I was told to bring you immediately you were suitably dressed, lord, and to assure you that no interpreter will be required.'

Ariston shrugged and wandered off to ready Valerius's horse. Valerius went to his tent and returned a few minutes later dressed in his best tunic. The Syrian came back with a green cloak of fine wool provided by Gaulan's servant and pinned it at Valerius's neck in the Roman style. 'Be wary,' he whispered.

'Why?' Valerius demanded.

'Is it not said that the patronage of kings is like the desert storm? It passes swiftly and leaves victims in its wake. In truth, I do not know: I am not in the habit of meeting kings. But this is a strange honour for a simple traveller. I had hoped to acquaint you a little more with this king's character on the way to the city, but now you must discover it for yourself.'

Valerius frowned. He'd suffered the accusing stares of emperors, but he'd never stood before a king. 'Should I bow or kneel?'

'You are a Roman.' The Syrian's eyes twinkled as Valerius pulled himself one-handed into the saddle. 'He will be happy as long as you don't take away his throne.'

The closer they approached the city walls the more Valerius understood just how the great palace compound on the mound dominated Emesa. Massive fortifications and multi-columned buildings towered over the city like a giant sentinel. His mind automatically approached it as a military problem. First, any attacker would have to take Emesa's walls, which were sturdily built and high. Even so, they'd pose no problem to any competent legionary commander equipped with catapults and siege towers. His problems would begin when they were breached. From the little he could see, beyond them lay a rat-trap maze of interlinking streets and alleys, many of them barely wide enough to allow passage to more than two or three men at a time. By the time the walls fell the defenders would have created two or three further lines of defence and those watching from the citadel would see the direction of attack. Their commander would use his interior lines to focus his men and resources on the most vulnerable areas. As long as the defenders could wield a sword or loose an arrow they'd be able to hold the attack at bay. Casualties would be high. And that was before the attackers reached the citadel itself. From his vantage point the entrance wasn't visible, but the sides of the mound were near vertical and formed of smooth stonework. Anyone attempting to climb them equipped for battle would be swept away by a hail of spears and the slingshots he knew the Syrians delivered so lethally.

His suspicions were confirmed when they passed through the city's north gate. The gates themselves stood twenty feet high, were faced with copper and iron-bound, and wide enough to admit two carts at a time. A squad of guards clad in helmets and armour in the Greek fashion watched the riders pass, but had obviously been warned not to hinder them. Beyond the gate they entered a warren of narrow streets that wandered and twisted between two-and three-storey mud-brick buildings. Valerius would have lost his bearings within moments if it hadn't been for his escort, who forced his horse through the crowds, ignoring the protests of beggar and merchant alike. The heat between the flat-topped houses was stifling and the usual street smells seemed multiplied in the confined space, cesspit and unwashed body vying for supremacy with bittersweet horse and musky camel, heavily spiced stews and the odd welcome waft from a stall selling jasmine and lavender. It was a relief when they began to climb the winding road to the citadel, always under the watchful eyes of the guards on the walls above.

Away from the streets the air was clearer, though the heat from the mid-afternoon sun had a fiercer quality than that among the houses. As the road climbed, Valerius looked out across a panorama of flat roofs to an enormous building that stood out like a jewel in a handful of pebbles. Despite its scale it had been hidden by the shoulder of the mound. Now he could see it had the pitched, tiled roof and marble columns of a Roman temple and the sun glittered on the golden statuary that surmounted it. To the north, the silver ribbon of the Orontes snaked through the plain, flanked by the dusty emerald of fertile fields and meadows. To the east, across his left shoulder, the air shimmered like a living thing over the golden carpet of the desert. The hill reminded him of the Palatine in Rome and he stifled a shiver at the memory. How many nervous journeys had he made up the Clivus Palatinus to appear before Nero, any one of which could have ended up with him dead? Which brought him back to the question that had been plaguing him since they'd left the Chalcidean camp: why was he here? As far as this Sohaemus was concerned he was just another traveller on the dusty road from Antioch.

Unless this was another of Domitian's tricks.

Ariston had hinted that Sohaemus sought Roman support for his ambitions to take control of Palmyra and its revenues from the eastern caravans. Could word have reached Emesa that a certain one-handed Roman might be travelling this way and should be stopped at any cost? Even as the thought occurred he decided he was starting at shadows. If that was the case, the deed would have been done somewhere down in the shadowed streets below: a rush of bodies and no escape; a struggling figure dragged into a workshop and his throat cut, ready for disposal. Discreet and tidy. Why take him to the palace where the arrival of a Roman would be noted, and no doubt reported? Domitian wanted him dead, but as far as Valerius knew he still had the confidence of Titus and Vespasian. No, Domitian wanted him to disappear with as little fuss as possible. He was safe enough for now.

They reached another massive gate and rode into an inner courtyard where the leader of the escort took Valerius's reins and nodded for him to dismount.

'You are to wait here to be called, lord,' the commander informed him.

Valerius nodded distractedly and studied his surroundings. To one side stood a guardhouse where a few Emesan soldiers studied him with unguarded curiosity. They were plainly relaxed in the presence of Gaulan's cavalry troopers, who joined their comrades in the shadow of a stables at the opposite end of the cobbled square.

A tall figure appeared in the doorway of a substantial honey-stone building that ran the length of the fourth side of the courtyard. The man affected a braided beard that reached to his chest, but the intricate golden diadem encircled a scalp entirely devoid of hair. Beady, deep-set eyes stared at Valerius from above a long nose. He wore a flowing robe of shimmering azure dotted with golden sun symbols. At first Valerius thought he might be in the presence of Sohaemus himself, then he noticed the familiar courtier's expression that sent the unmistakable message: 'you are beneath my contempt until you prove to me otherwise'. The man introduced himself in fluent Greek as Helios, the king's chamberlain.

Inside the door two young slave boys held silver bowls and towels. Valerius looked on perplexed as one bent to wash his feet. The other offered a bowl for his hands, struggling to keep his face impassive as the Roman dipped his single hand into the water and held it out to be dried.

Helios sniffed and led the way along a marble-lined corridor with a short, almost feminine stride. As he walked, he talked in staccato bursts. 'You will prostrate yourself in the king's presence. You will only speak when you are spoken to.' He twisted his head and grimaced at Valerius's rustic military cloak. 'If we had time my slaves would find you something more suitable.'

'Perhaps you could explain why I am here.' Valerius reflected that the loss of his rank was a drawback when dealing with royalty. How much more at ease would he have felt in helmet and armour, draped in the pristine white cloak of a *tribunus laticlavius*. A soldier of

71

the Empire, instead of an outcast in a borrowed cloak, living on borrowed time.

'That is for the king to decide,' Helios snapped. 'Just remember you are on his ground and subject to his justice.'

'Yet he bends the knee to Rome.' Valerius came to a halt, forcing the other man to stop and glare at him. 'And I am a Roman citizen. So do not dare to threaten me, chamberlain, lest you bring down Rome's wrath upon you and your master.' He saw something in Helios's eyes and his lips formed a cold smile. 'I wonder if King Sohaemus knows how his doorkeep treats his honoured guests?'

The look changed to one of pure hatred and the chamberlain swept on. A few minutes later they reached a doorway guarded by two armoured men. Helios glided through and stood to one side, beckoning Valerius forward. 'Prostrate yourself before his majesty, mighty Sohaemus, High King of Emesa, protector of far Commagene and Sophene, commander of the Blue Guard, slayer of thousands, Foremost Priest of Elah Gebal and Guardian of the Black Stone, may the sun for ever shine on his countenance.'

Valerius almost had to shield his eyes as he strode into the room to meet the Sun King. Frescoes covered in gold leaf lined the walls and every ornament shone with the same buttery glow. A cunningly sited opening in the high domed ceiling allowed the sun's rays to illuminate a golden throne and its occupant. A bull of a man in the prime of life, King Sohaemus was dressed more simply than his chamberlain in a robe of golden silk, but looking into his dark eyes was like staring into an empty tomb. They glared from coarse, pitted features, deep-set beneath a heavy brow. He had a beard of oiled black ringlets in the Parthian style, and a beaked nose hung threateningly over a mouth like a bear trap.

'Advance five paces and throw yourself upon the Sun King's mercy,' Helios commanded.

Valerius marched forward the required distance, a soldier in bearing if not in uniform. He met the obsidian eyes and kept his face emotionless as he bowed his head in a nod of respect. Helios emitted a hiss of outrage, but Sohaemus's features broke into a broad smile that seemed out of place on the fearsome mask.

'So this is your protector,' the king said to the room's only other occupant, who sat in a chair behind a screen to one side of the throne, at the outer limit of Valerius's vision.

'I owe him my life and my honour, majesty,' a familiar voice replied quietly.

Tabitha.

VII

The crimson dress had been replaced by virgin white, but of a much finer material and cut in a style that left one silken shoulder bare. A golden brooch in the shape of a sunburst held the cloth at her other shoulder and a belt of gold links circled her narrow waist. Only the bandaged hand looked out of place. Her sapphire-blue eyes studied him with the cool appraisal of one entirely at ease in her surroundings and he felt fire in his cheeks at being so easily deceived. No lady's maid this, but a princess or a priestess.

'My lady,' he bowed, placing an emphasis on the second word that brought the shadow of a smile to her lips. He wondered why she'd maintained her guise for so long when it would have made more sense to announce herself for what she was. Nothing about her was what it seemed, a fact confirmed by the king's next words.

'My sister's daughter,' the sombre voice announced. 'A wayward child who charmed her way into my affections and whom I have never been able to marry off. But she has her uses and it seems I am in your debt. Name your reward and if it is within my power I will grant it, Gaius Valerius Verrens.' The king stood up and studied Valerius for a moment, nodding to himself. 'Your bearing and the marks you wear tell me you are a military man. Your confidence in my presence that you have held a position high enough not to be overpowered or awed by kings. Yet you travel alone, more or less, and in little state, which I find intriguing. I would offer you a position at the head of one of my regiments, but I fear it would be an insult to a man who has commanded Roman soldiers. Come, gold I have in plenty, or land; an estate on the Orontes and the revenues that go with it?'

It was a generous offer and one that would go a long way to restoring his fortunes, but Valerius felt Tabitha's eyes on him and it made him uneasy. No matter how perceptive the Emesan ruler was, Sohaemus knew far too much about him to be justified by such short acquaintance. The question was where he had got his information. Valerius had talked to Tabitha on the ride to Apamea, but only in the most general terms. He'd never discussed his past or his current situation. Yet here was the king of Emesa offering him gifts that could be as valuable as life itself to a fugitive. He tried to think back. How much time had she spent with Ariston? Only Serpentius and the Syrian knew he was on the run, but even Ariston didn't know why.

'All I ask, majesty, is that I be allowed to continue my journey.' Valerius bowed again. 'My thanks for the offer of a place in your service. If the fates had dictated otherwise I would have been proud to accept, but I have made a pledge to join the Imperial forces fighting in Judaea.'

The king returned to his throne and exchanged a glance with Tabitha. Valerius was certain some unspoken message passed between them, but he had no idea what it was. Eventually, Sohaemus nodded. 'Very well,' he said. 'But I insist that you do so in a state that befits your rank and your deeds. You travel to join the Romans in Judaea? In four days I will have gathered a force of five hundred archers and cavalry to send to General Titus as a signal of my fealty to Rome. I had hoped it would be more,' he looked to Tabitha again with a frown, 'but King Aristobulus insists that Chalcis has none to spare. His spies report Parthian cavalry massing on his border, and it is true that King Vologases has had little to occupy him since your General Corbulo taught him such a harsh lesson in tactics at Cepha.'

'Aristobulus is afraid of his own shadow.' Tabitha's interruption took Valerius by surprise. 'He is like a child hiding behind his mother's skirts in a storm. If we had supported Gaulan against him as I suggested, I would have returned with ten times the number of cavalry.'

'But Rome supports Aristobulus,' Sohaemus said reasonably. 'And it would have meant risking the wrath of your mistress, who would hardly thank me for aiding a man who removed her uncle from the throne. Gaulan is young and ambitious. It will do him good to take out his frustrations on the Zealots. If he impresses General Titus he might end up with a kingdom of his own. The father is no longer young; who knows—'

'And that is why it is important to provide the general with as much aid as possible.' The king acknowledged Tabitha's new intervention with a curt nod. It had been designed to prevent further indiscretion. Any discussion of the Emperor's age or health was dangerous ground even for a client king like Sohaemus. She went on smoothly: 'Of course it would help if we had a champion at the heart of his court. Do not be too angry with Ariston,' she added, confirming Valerius's suspicions. 'He is garrulous and susceptible to flattery, especially from a woman, but so are many men. I feigned an interest in you, and how much more impressive to have a master who is an intimate of the Emperor's son than a mere desert wanderer.'

'He is a gossip and a fool,' Valerius growled. 'I should have him whipped.'

'Perhaps it is I who should be whipped?' She rose smoothly to her feet and approached so close that he scented a wisp of perfumed oils. 'For the fault is mine. No?' She smiled at the startled expression on Valerius's face. 'Then I plead for mercy on his behalf. Should I kneel?'

'That won't be necessary.' The turmoil in his breast made the words gruffer than he intended. 'But I will ensure he knows whom to thank for his escape, and of course,' he turned to bow to the king, thankful to escape relatively unscathed, 'I will be happy to carry any message you wish and to ensure it reaches General Titus's hands.'

'Good.' Sohaemus clapped his hands and the chamberlain reappeared. 'Arrange for food to be brought: our guest will eat with us. And send for my armourer.' He smiled at Valerius. 'If you will not accept a reward at least you will travel as a prince of the East in the finest armour and on the finest horse my stables can provide.' He waved away the Roman's protests. 'If you are to escort my sister's daughter to Jerusalem, you must be suitably armed.'

Valerius frowned as Tabitha walked towards her uncle. 'But I thought—'

'Where would I be if not at my mistress's side? And where General Titus is my mistress will not be far away,' she said, mystifying him even more.

'Then it is settled.' The king rose from his throne. 'You will move into the palace until my soldiers are

77

ready to leave. Now we will feast.' As they were leaving the throne room, Valerius's eyes slid to a stack of scrolls on a table positioned to get the most light. Sohaemus noticed his interest and beamed proudly. 'Of course, you are an educated man. After we have eaten I will show you my library.'

To Valerius's disappointment Tabitha didn't join them for the sumptuous banquet Sohaemus provided. There were questions he wanted to ask her and it would have made it easier to disguise how little of the king's food and wine he actually consumed. After months on the road eating the most simple of foods, he found that his stomach rebelled at the sight of the thick sauces and heavily spiced meats served from golden platters. Even the wine, a sweet, heady vintage from one of the king's vineyards on the coast, couldn't tempt a palate more accustomed these days to the thin vinegar served to servants and slaves.

But if the meal wasn't to his taste, the aftermath was a feast for the mind.

For a man who loved books the library at Emesa was like stumbling on an oasis after a ten-day ride through the desert. King Sohaemus led him into an enormous room illuminated by tall windows. Row after row of stone niches rose the height of the walls. Each opening held at least a single leather-cased scroll, but most contained several. Many of them could only be reached by the polished wooden ladders which stood ready for the purpose. The musty scent of ageing leather and decaying papyrus tickled the nostrils and a dozen clerks toiled at wooden desks drawn up in lines. Valerius's father had kept a small collection at the family estate at Fidenae, but the villa had been destroyed during the civil war. In Britannia, he'd never been without his copy of Thucydides' *History of the Peloponnesian War*. It too had burned, in the sack of Colonia Claudia Victricensis, and he'd never been able to replace it. Fortunately, before he left Rome, Valerius's friend Pliny – Gaius Plinius Secundus – had managed to smuggle him the early chapters of Xenophon's *Anabasis*. The old soldier's adventures on campaign with mighty Cyrus of Persia had relieved the boredom of the long trip east. Before he died, Corbulo had created a fine library in his palace at Antioch, but it was dwarfed by the collection Sohaemus had amassed here at Emesa. Not a single room, but three or four echoing halls, linked by doorways guarded by soldiers in light armour.

Sohaemus smiled at Valerius's puzzlement. 'They are not here for my protection, or even the books',' he explained, 'but to save them in event of a disaster. Some of these scrolls survived Caesar's destruction of the library at Alexandria – see, this copy of Plato's *Apology* still bears the scars. There are books here in Latin, Greek and Hebrew, Aramaic and Phoenician, Egyptian and a dozen other languages we have yet to decipher. Each man is tasked with the preservation of certain treasured works in the event of fire or earthquake.'

'It is wonderful,' Valerius said sincerely. 'A marvel surely to rival Alexandria itself.'

'Ah,' Sohaemus smiled modestly at the compliment, 'but did Seneca not say: "What is the point of countless books whose titles the owners cannot possibly read through in a lifetime"?'

'The learner is not instructed, but burdened by the mass of them.' Valerius quoted his old mentor.

'You are familiar with him?' A row of white teeth shone through the ringlets of the king's beard. 'Then you will also know he was not in the least impressed

79

with Alexandria. Livius may have praised it as the most distinguished achievement of the good taste and solicitude of kings, but Seneca bemoaned the collection of books not for learning but to make a show – decorations for the dining room, as he put it.'

'But he too had a great collection.' Valerius smiled at the memory. 'And I doubt he ever read more than half of them.'

Sohaemus's dark eyes twinkled. 'Would he have been embarrassed, do you think, by his hypocrisy?'

'No.' Valerius thought back to the Seneca he had known. Bombastic and secure in the knowledge of his own greatness, but never arrogant. A man who, for all his faults, had always been able to laugh at himself. 'I think he would have pointed out that his own situation was the irrefutable proof of his genius. He never paraded himself as an example of perfection, either as a Stoic or in the way he lived his life. His duty, as he saw it, was to point out the contradictions and imperfections others did not, or would not, see.'

'You are something of a philosopher yourself, I find.'

Valerius shook his head. 'My father had ambitions for me in that direction and I was guided by a master. But I found that though I could memorize and repeat the views and conclusions of others, I never once found a way to contribute something of my own to a debate. Spending your days mouthing another man's words soon becomes like digging the soil from one hole only to fill another. Seneca recognized it and pointed me towards the law.'

'Yet you became a soldier?'

Valerius smiled. 'Sometimes a man's fate is not his to decide.'

'Seneca?'

'Gaius Valerius Verrens.'

When Sohaemus had finished laughing he showed Valerius some of the treasures of his collection. Calling on a servant to climb a ladder to this alcove or that, he directed them to retrieve the scrolls with an obvious knowledge of their whereabouts and contents.

'I try to heed Seneca's exhortations that books are tools of learning and not mere decoration,' he assured Valerius. 'Clearly, I cannot read them all, but much of the knowledge contained here is duplicated and some of it discredited. My clerks seek out the gems among them and bring anything of interest to my attention: new information or innovative approaches to a philosophical problem.' He pointed to a table where a clerk was working with a papyrus scroll, copying the contents to a long strip of soft leather using a sharpened reed and a bowl of black ink. 'Goatskin,' Sohaemus said proudly. 'Expensive, but parchment is so much less fragile than papyrus. The third book of Herodotus, I believe, Philippus? One of nine. He has been working on it since the festival of Elah Gebal. Where have you reached, Philippus?'

'I am transcribing the passage where Cambyses goes mad, majesty,' said the clerk, clearly at ease with his master despite the ferocious scowl Sohaemus affected.

'A timely reminder of the consequences of the cares of state,' the Emesan ruler nodded ruefully. 'Is it true that Nero went mad?'

Valerius hesitated, remembering a warm night and the garden of a villa outside Rome; blood spurting black in the moonlight and the final sigh of an actor leaving the stage. Despite the time that had passed since Nero's death, this was treacherous ground. The young Emperor had been more popular in the East, where his excesses were less visible, than among his own people. Vitellius, whom Vespasian had just displaced, had been in the process of declaring his predecessor but two divine, and it was just possible his successor might fulfil his wishes.

'I think he was ill-advised,' he said carefully. 'And lost sight of his duty to his people. Without Seneca there was no guiding hand, and more important, no restraining one. His mistakes were more a young man's folly than madness.'

Sohaemus studied him shrewdly. 'A good answer.' He paused and became thoughtful. 'As a young man I too could have been accused of youthful folly in my relentless pursuit of additions to this collection. I would dispatch agents far and wide seeking out new treasures, with orders to take any steps necessary to acquire them. I convinced myself that in attempting to bring together all the world's knowledge in a single place I was furthering the advancement of humanity. Of course, now I know that I was only feeding my own vanity. That is why I have decided to have all the most important scrolls copied so that they can be distributed and more widely read. Most new additions these days are sent to me, though few books drive me to the kind of passion Homer or Herodotus once did. Only one acquisition would truly excite me now. A book I have sought for many years . . .'

'I'm sure Valerius has heard enough about your dusty old books, Uncle.' Tabitha made her entry without warning and Valerius turned just in time to see her expression change from one that didn't quite match her tone to a smile as bright as the Sun King's throne. 'In any case the armourer wishes to take measurements and discover our guest's requirements.'

Valerius bowed deeply to Sohaemus. 'Thank you for sharing your wonderful collection with me, if only for a short time. I would have been happy to learn about the book that so excited your passion, but it would be impolite to keep your armourer waiting.'

The king beamed at the praise for his collection. 'You are an honoured guest of the house of Sampsiceramus and free to come and go as you will, Gaius Valerius Verrens,' he said. 'I will leave word that you may visit the library at any time for the duration of your stay.'

VIII

'I haven't had the opportunity to thank you for your kindness in naming me to King Sohaemus,' Valerius said as they walked side by side through a long corridor to the guest apartments. 'It was a small enough thing I did, but a king's gratitude is not to be scorned and now I am in your debt.'

Her reaction surprised him. 'A small thing?' She stopped without warning and studied him with narrowed eyes, her mouth pursed dangerously. 'You call saving my life a small thing? If I were not familiar with your rough Roman ways, Gaius Valerius Verrens, I would believe I had suffered a mortal insult.'

'I only—'

Tabitha stood with her hands on her hips, her breasts rising and falling beneath the thin material of her dress. 'Is it a small thing for a one-armed man to risk his life against many – Ariston told me you left your camp alone – to save the life and honour of a lowly serving girl? If it was such a *small thing*, perhaps you dallied on the way, uncertain whether a mere woman's life was worth the effort? Perhaps you thought about turning back and leaving her to her fate? If . . .'

He stepped forward and placed a finger on her lips. She blinked at the intimacy and scowled at him, but the tirade faded. Something in his eyes sent a shiver through her body.

'Once more, I must apologize, my lady. It seems that whenever we talk my words turn into great clumsy boulders in my mouth. If, knowing what I know now, I had even considered such a thing, I would gladly fall on my sword. If you had not fought with such courage I would not have arrived in time. In truth, you were your own saviour, but you are right, it was no small thing to go to the aid of someone so worthy of saving.'

Their eyes locked and he knew he only had to lower his head and their lips would meet in a kiss that would change everything. But the moment passed. Instead she reached out and soft fingers touched his cheek. 'It seems I misjudged you, Valerius, for the boulders are transformed into pearls. It is I who must apologize for behaving like a petulant child. The stink of those men is still thick in my nostrils. I can smell the blood and the roasting flesh. And,' her face dissolved into a quizzical smile, 'I am confused. Perhaps the event is still too fresh, for my head spins. I should have known you would never say anything to hurt me. The debt is mine and I vow to repay it one day.'

In the focus of her blue eyes Valerius suddenly understood why Ariston had been so willing to part with his secrets. They had a mesmerizing quality and he was drawn into their depths by the flecks of gold in their shadows. He had to make a physical effort to break the spell.

'One thing still puzzles me. I can understand why you did not tell us who you were at first, but surely it would have been safe after Apamea?'

She considered for a moment. 'Yes,' she nodded, 'it might well have been, but what was there to be gained from it? If it became known that I'd survived there was always a chance that the associates of those men would have tried again, even with Gaulan on the alert.'

'So they knew who you were?'

'And why I had travelled to Chalcis.' She saw the question in his eyes. 'Persuading that fool Aristobulus to part with his precious troops was only part of my mission.'

'If we had known, we could have done more to protect you. Found a different route . . .'

'Do not look so annoyed, Valerius.' Tabitha's laugh was like the tinkling of a silver bell. 'Even now you do not trust me with your entire story, so why should I trust you with mine? Still, perhaps that will change. Here are your quarters.'

He watched her until she disappeared before entering the curtained doorway. Ariston and another man were waiting for him inside. The Syrian looked uncomfortable amid the sumptuous surroundings. Brightly coloured tapestries depicting hunting scenes and ancient battles lined the walls and the couches and low bed were scattered with soft cushions. A window opened on to a courtyard with a fountain at its centre surrounded by trees bearing exotic fruits. The two men eyed each other suspiciously, like dogs ready to fight over a bone.

'He says he's the royal armourer,' Ariston announced sceptically. 'But he looks more like the king's catamite to me.'

The second man gave Valerius a courteous bow. He wore a long, flowing robe and appeared very young for his position, with jet black hair that hung in ringlets to his shoulders. His skin was pale, smooth and unlined.

Unlike most Emesans Valerius had encountered he had handsome, fine-boned features and a beardless chin. The Roman noticed a strong smell of perfumed oils. He sighed. 'You're right,' he said, 'he doesn't look as if he's been near a forge in his life.'

'He can wield a hammer as well as any man in the armoury,' the young man said easily. 'And he speaks Greek more fluently than this fleabag of a servant of yours. I'm surprised they allowed him through the doors without throwing him in the horse trough first.' He repeated the bow. 'Dimitrios Dan at your service, lord.'

Ariston spluttered through his beard at the insult, but Valerius grinned and raised a hand. 'Well, Dimitrios Dan, your king said you could turn me into a prince. I doubt you have ever had a more difficult commission, but perhaps we can cooperate. While we discuss our business this fleabag will find us some wine.' Ariston stalked out of the room muttering to himself. 'Where did you learn your trade?'

'Under a Roman, lord. The armourer of the Sixth legion found me in Jerusalem. I was working in a metal shop doing fine work on copper salvers and he liked what he saw. He used me to create the decoration for officers' breastplates and the like and taught me how to mend a sword and rivet a piece of plate. When the Sixth left for Antioch I found employment here.'

'I'm intrigued,' Valerius said. 'How did someone so young find favour with the king?'

'I am known,' Dimitrios couldn't keep the mischief from his voice, 'but not always loved, for my innovation, lord.'

'Well, you can keep your innovations to yourself.' Valerius returned his grin, immediately liking the young man. 'I'm all for progress in tactics, but all I ask of a piece of armour is that it protects the places it is supposed to protect.'

The armourer couldn't hide his disappointment. 'Do you have any other requirements, lord?'

'I've seen your eastern princes and they wear more ornament than a Thracian auxiliary. So no peacock-plumed helmets or anything outlandish in the armour line. Do you have anything in the Roman style?'

'I believe we can accommodate your wishes,' Dimitrios said gravely. 'A few adjustments with the straps and buckles and I think we have the very thing. If you please, lord?' He pulled out a length of twine marked at regular intervals of a kind Valerius had known legionary armourers to use. With a few deft movements he measured Valerius's chest and shoulders, the length of his arms, the girth of his waist and the circumference of his neck.

Valerius put up with the fuss without complaint, but eventually he lost patience. 'Are you finished yet?'

'Almost, lord. Ah . . .'

'What is it?'

'Your right hand?'

'Is old bones buried beneath a burned-out villa in Britannia.'

'May I?' Dimitrios lifted the wooden fist on its cowhide stock with a look of distaste. 'But the replacement is so crude.'

'A friend carved it.' Valerius remembered the endless hours Serpentius had spent whittling the block of oak and the terrors of the day he'd worn it for the first time. 'I like it as it is.'

'Of course, lord, but a few adjustments, a polish . . .' He studied it more closely. 'The grip is designed to fit a standard legionary *scutum*, I believe?'

Valerius nodded.

'But you find it a little loose, the angle not quite perfect?'

Valerius pinned him with a glare, but he realized the armourer was right. 'Yes,' he said grudgingly.

'Then it will take only a few hours.' Dimitrios's handsome features broke into a grin. 'It will be the same hand, but more fitting for a man of such rank, and,' he forestalled Valerius's opposition, 'more efficient in a fight.'

Valerius looked down at the primitive wooden fist, scarred and dented and not quite firmly fixed to the stock. It had been the best Serpentius could do with a fruit knife in the camp at Cremona where they'd waited to die in the sands of the amphitheatre for Vitellius's pleasure. He doubted the Spaniard would mind. A little care and attention would do it no harm and he could spare it for a few hours. He worked at the bindings with his left hand and pulled the socket free with a soft groan of relief. It was time he oiled the stump in any case.

'I want it back tomorrow.'

'Of course, lord. May I check one final measurement?' He stretched the cord across the Roman's chest, bending to study the marks and muttering numbers to himself. The position brought his mouth close to Valerius's ear, but even so the Roman barely heard the whispered words. 'Be very wary. All is not as it seems in the palace of Sohaemus. Trust no one.'

'Then why should I trust you?' Valerius's lips barely moved as he answered.

'You will see, lord. Undoubtedly, you will see.'

Dimitrios stepped back and bowed, reversing out of the room past a hovering Ariston. The Syrian placed a jug of wine and two cups on a table. 'What was all that about?'

'I'm not sure.' Valerius poured wine from the jug into the cups and passed one to the Syrian.

'Your hand.' Ariston's eyes widened as he noticed the missing wooden fist.

'I'm told it will be returned in even better condition,' Valerius smiled.

'But it leaves you . . .'

Valerius saw the words 'half a man' freeze on the Syrian's tongue. 'Vulnerable,' he agreed. 'So you will have to be my trusty right hand until Serpentius returns from the Chalcidean camp. Can you do that, Ariston?'

'I am your man to the death, lord.'

'Then tell me everything you know about this city and its king. I've never seen so much gold in a single place, nor so many gems. Yet there are people starving in the streets.'

Ariston nodded slowly. Where to begin?

Emesa and Palmyra, it transpired, were tied by trade and blood, and had once been part of a larger federation that included Apamea, Laodicaea and Heliopolis. The rulers of the two cities were, in times long forgotten, members of the same family. 'A mongrel breed of Assyrian, Armenian, Greek and Medean,' Ariston spat, conveniently forgetting he was of similar lineage. For generations the two cities had coveted each other's wealth, only constrained from violent action by the fact that each depended on the other for the artery that provided that wealth: Emesa's to the east on the desert road controlled by her rival; Palmyra's to the west, on the coast road controlled by Emesa. 'They were like the right hand and the left hand of the same body struggling to cut the throat for control of the whole.' Fortunately for the Emesans and the Palmyrans, Rome imposed its rule before either could prevail or it could have been the ruin of both.

Ariston paused in his narrative, but Valerius stayed silent, sensing there was something more to come. Something important.

'Yet even the power of Rome is not strong enough to stem the level of ambition or jealousy inspired by vast wealth,' Ariston continued in his sing-song Greek. 'And vast wealth had come to Emesa as a gift of Elah Gebal, the Sun God and the God of the Mountain. Some say it was the king's namesake, Sohaemus of Chalcis, who discovered the black stone on a hunting trip, led by the gods to where it had fallen after being plucked from the sun. Others say that it was Iamblichus, who then ruled this city. It is certain that the king's father built the Temple of the Sun God with tributes from every ruler in the East, freely given because all wished to share in the glory of this offspring of mighty Sol.' Valerius remembered the vast temple that had caught his eye as he'd climbed the hill, with the sun glittering on its golden statues. 'Every year the tributes have continued, allowing Sohaemus to build his great palace and swelling his coffers to bursting. He uses the power it gives him to undermine Palmyra and the other city states; meanwhile they covet his wealth with hungry eyes and work to bring him down.'

'Why not use the gold to increase the size of his army?' Valerius asked. 'Even half of what I have seen would pay for another five thousand spears.' But he realized the answer even as he posed the question.

'Rome,' Ariston nodded. 'It is not in Rome's interest to foster strength or ambition, only stability. And stability is best maintained by keeping men like

Sohaemus in their place, even if it means he can only send five hundred archers to Titus. When Vespasian's legions proclaimed him Emperor, Sohaemus travelled to Berytus to pledge his loyalty, along with the kings of Commagene, Palmyra and Chalcis. He was well treated for his consistent support for the Empire, but he knows he is just one among many.'

Valerius looked at the man sitting uneasily on the couch opposite. Ariston had his eyes to the floor and his face was creased by a frown of concentration as he searched for ever more detail. The amount of information he had gathered in the few short hours since they'd arrived outside the city was truly remarkable.

'You have been a spy, I think, Ariston?' The dark eyes came up and speared him, the frown replaced by a scowl.

'You must remember where you are, lord,' the Syrian warned. 'This is not Rome. From Antioch to Alexandria every man is a spy and today's friend is tomorrow's deadly enemy. Loyalties shift like the desert sands in the Khamseen and the right information is as valuable as the gold that decorates this palace. You have asked me for information, and I have given it. Now you mock me, perhaps because in the gathering of it I spoke too freely?' He raised an eyebrow and Valerius smiled.

'She is not our enemy, Ariston, of that I am certain.'

'Not today.'

Valerius shrugged, but it was acknowledgement of the possibility rather than a dismissal. 'Tell me what you have discovered of our mysterious companion.'

The scowl disappeared and Ariston laughed. 'From what the palace servants were whispering when I fetched your wine, you would know more than I.' He saw the dangerous glint in Valerius's eye and hurried on.

'Her bloodline has given her royal connections all over Syria and Judaea. Sometime handmaiden to a queen. Sometime courier and plenipotentiary for Sohaemus. Seductress or spy, no one is sure. Loved by most, but hated by an influential few. She grew up in the king's court in Emesa, from which stems her learning and her manners . . . and the waywardness that would have been beaten out of any other woman long ago. The only mystery is why, despite her evident beauty, she has never married.'

'Perhaps she is more use to Sohaemus unmarried?' Valerius suggested. 'While she flutters her eyelashes at you she is stealing your secrets.'

Ariston sniffed, not pleased to be reminded of his indiscretions. 'She was in Sohaemus's service when she was attacked, but was that why she was attacked?'

'You can ask her on the way to Jerusalem.'

The Syrian gave him a sour look. 'The gods keep me from wilful women, especially beautiful ones. There is one other thing you should know. Sohaemus fears none of his rivals, but he does fear Rome.'

'But Rome seeks stability, you said so yourself.'

'Only Rome has the power to remove him from the throne. Why should Rome do so? Because Palmyra is not the only power that covets the wealth of the Sun God. Sohaemus visited Rome a dozen years ago and befriended Nero. The years since the Emperor's death have left him confused and insecure. When Cestius Gallus passed this way with the Twelfth legion to put down the original Judaean revolt he insisted Sohaemus pay tribute of a year's pay for the legion. They say that when he entered the treasury his eyes shone like beacons at the sight. Only the fact that the Twelfth was smashed at Beit Horan by Eleazar ben Simon deterred him from

93

coming back for more. Now Vespasian is Emperor and Sohaemus hears that Rome's coffers are empty.'

'Vespasian would never be so foolish as to antagonize an ally.'

'Not when he's fighting a war,' Ariston agreed.

'But when the war is over . . .'

'So you would not be surprised if Sohaemus was arming the Judaeans as well as reinforcing Titus. It is only a rumour, and that from a single source, but . . .'

'But a long war would be in Emesa's favour if Sohaemus thinks his wealth or position is in danger.'

'Precisely,' Ariston nodded gravely. 'Is it any wonder the king wishes to keep close this mysterious Roman who has just wandered into his territory? A man of obvious rank, and a soldier, well equipped to assess his true strength. He can't afford to have you killed because he believes you have been sent on Titus's orders, so he must court you – and spy on you. And who better than . . .'

'Our encounter with Tabitha could never have been staged,' Valerius insisted. 'Those men were definitely going to kill her.'

'No,' Ariston agreed, 'but it presents the king with an opportunity. And now she travels with us to Jerusalem where Titus gathers his forces. No doubt on the way she will flutter her eyelashes at you and steal more of our secrets. I am reminded of a spider of the Tigris valley where the female of the species devours her mate after she has done with him.'

Valerius laughed. 'I fear there are more dangerous enemies.'

'You are right,' the Syrian said earnestly. 'The place is filled with them. You are a Roman and there are Emesans who resent the king for doing Rome's bidding.

There are Judaean slaves who are undoubtedly spies for whom any Roman is an enemy.' He drew himself up to his full height. 'I will sleep by the doorway tonight to ensure none passes but those who have the right.'

He waited for some recognition of this sacrifice, but Valerius only looked thoughtful. After a time, the Roman said: 'Ariston?'

'Yes, lord.'

'It comes to me that your most diligent efforts to gather information on my behalf will have confirmed the king's suspicions about my presence here.'

'Yes, lord,' more warily.

'And while I have the king's protection . . .'

'Perhaps, on further consideration, I will sleep by the window.'

Valerius smiled. 'I appreciate your offer, but no doubt Serpentius will be back soon and I'm sure someone will be able to provide you with more suitable accommodation.'

IX

Northern Judaea

The man was dressed in rags and lay in the dust on his right side with his legs splayed at an awkward angle. A dark stain surrounded his head and closer inspection revealed the cause. A terrible wound split his features from brow to chin in a way that almost gave him two separate identities. The eye that was visible looked oddly serene in the ruin of his features and ivory fragments of teeth surrounded his head like a diadem of stars. Back cut, Titus decided, admiring the deadly efficiency of the strike. His killer would have been level with him, the heavy cavalry *spatha* already falling as his mount swept past, the force of the blow knocking the man backwards in a spray of red mist.

'Another we don't have to worry about.' The words were innocuous enough, but Tiberius Alexander's tone questioned why the commander of Rome's Army of the East was wasting time over one dead rebel among the hundreds scattered along the road from Gadara.

'Placidus knows his business.' Titus ignored one minor provocation among many.

'So he should,' the chief of staff said. 'He and his Phrygian barbarians have been slaughtering these vermin for close on five years.'

'Who commands the infantry?'

'Longinus. He has a cohort of Spaniards and another of Gauls with orders to press hard and keep them moving. I've ordered the flanking cohorts to force march until they reach the river. Our scouts report that the waters are high and continue to rise.' The olive features split into a savage grin. 'Don't worry, lord, they won't escape. It's like herding sheep.'

Titus turned in the saddle to face the older man. It was difficult to conceal his resentment at his father's imposition of the Alexandrian – could one be a former Jew? – with twice his own military experience, who understood Judaea and the Judaeans better than any Roman. He felt his anger growing. Mentor or wet nurse, it didn't matter. He was old enough to make his own decisions. He had commanded legions and he could command an army. 'I don't want any mistakes, Tiberius.' He saw the other man flinch at the hardening of his tone. 'This is one of the last rebel forces of any strength outside Jerusalem. I can't afford to have them causing trouble at my rear while we're taking the city. I want them destroyed.'

The sound of a trumpet alerted him and he urged his horse to the top of a mound beside the road. Alexander and the rest of his staff rode in his wake to share the vantage point.

As always, auxiliary light infantry made up the van of the marching column – a cohort each of Thracian spearmen and archers, ready to deploy into a skirmish line at the first enemy contact. In the far distance, Titus could see the dust of the legion's cavalry contingent, scouting the vulnerable flanks and the route ahead. In the wake of the auxiliaries came the camp prefect, responsible for march discipline and accompanied by junior tribunes who weren't much good for anything but carrying messages. Behind them followed the signallers with their curved trumpets.

Titus's heart beat a little faster as the eagle came into sight – the eagle of the Fifteenth Apollinaris – the golden wings raised and beak open in a scream of defiance. The eagle was a legion's pride and a legion's soul, presented personally by the Emperor and every man was oath-sworn to protect it. It was borne by the *aquilifer*, a veteran of twenty years' service, sweating in the heat beneath his leopard skin, the face a snarling mask over his helmet. Eight men accompanied him, the eagle's personal guard, the *phalerae* that proclaimed their valour on their breasts. A legion could experience no greater shame than to lose its eagle. Titus reflected that in a way it was the loss of an eagle that had brought him to this place and to this command.

The revolt, now in its fifth year, had been sparked by Flacus's foolish decision to loot the temple at Jerusalem in revenge for attacks on Roman citizens. Judaeans led by the fanatical Zealots responded by butchering the small Roman garrison in the city before the insurrection spread across the country. The growing threat forced Cestius Gallus, Syria's legate, to march on Judaea with the Twelfth Fulminata, a highly experienced unit which had fought with success against the Parthians under Corbulo. The campaign had begun well, but Gallus became convinced that the enemy forces were too strong to be defeated by a single legion and retreated towards the coast and reinforcements. Instead, the idiot had walked into a trap. The Twelfth was ambushed on the march, outnumbered and outfought by a rabble of Jews. The victors carried off the Twelfth's eagle and brought eternal shame to the legion and its commander. There could only be one reaction. Nero looked to his commanders for one experienced enough not to repeat Gallus's mistakes, ruthless enough to pursue the rebels to destruction however long it took, and astute enough to win over those other fractious states in the region who might become a threat. Only two men fitted that description. One was Gnaeus Domitius Corbulo, who had thwarted the ambitions of the Parthian king, Vologases, in Armenia, but was suspected of ambitions of his own closer to home. The other was Titus Flavius Vespasian. Vespasian had commanded legions in Germania and Britannia, but was a man of humble birth who did not pose any sort of threat.

Titus had sailed with his father from Athens, taken command of the Fifteenth Apollinaris in Alexandria and marched north. Meanwhile, Vespasian continued to Syria where the Fifth and Tenth had been tasked with the subjugation of the Jews. What followed was a campaign of destruction and terror, carried out with merciless efficiency by the cheering men who now marched before him. The elite First cohort led, their uniforms and armour coated with gritty Judaean dust. Eight hundred legionaries followed the standard-bearer, five double-strength centuries of a hundred and sixty men each. These were the legion's bravest and best troops, soldiers who could be relied on to break the enemy line, or hold their own under any pressure. Every man wore a polished iron helmet with a neck protector, cheek guards and a reinforced brow. *Lorica segmentata* armour protected his torso, a complex arrangement of case-hardened iron bands that covered the chest, shoulders and back. He carried a pair of *pila*, weighted spears designed to punch through shields and light armour, and on his hip he wore a twenty-two inch *gladius*, the short sword that had almost literally carved out the Roman empire. On his back, he bore the brightly painted *scutum*, the big shield that was cursed on the march for its weight, but would save his life in the battle line. It was prone to chafe the shoulders, back and legs, but it was the work of a moment to unsling it and face the enemy ready for battle. They were short, wiry men, with uncouth habits and a soldier's tendency to complain, but – the Twelfth, those dozy bastards, notwithstanding – they knew that if they kept their discipline they were invincible. Titus had learned to love them like recalcitrant children who required regular beatings to keep them honest.

Nine normal-sized cohorts followed the First, each with six centuries of eighty men and each century in turn identified by its standard. Of course, these were the nominal complements. The last roster Titus had seen showed that sickness, battle injury and troops needed for security details had left the Fifteenth with a strength of four thousand two hundred men. Still, it should be more than enough.

Vespasian initially targeted the rebel stronghold of Galilee, where the enemy had turned the region's towns and cities into what they believed were impregnable strongholds. Instead of attacking the Judaeans' strengths the Roman commander ravaged the Galilean countryside, bringing fire and death to villages and farms. The carnage forced the survivors to flee to the towns where they became a drain on the enemy resources and spread tales of terror and unspeakable savagery. Titus had linked up with his father just as Judaean morale weakened enough for him to invest their cities. At Japha, the Tenth and Fifteenth combined to take the walls, driving the defenders back into the narrow streets where women had pelted the legionaries with whatever household missiles came to hand. Every male – fifteen thousand of them – had been slaughtered in revenge for the insult done to the Twelfth, and every woman and child sold into slavery. At Jotapata, the Judaean butcher's bill numbered forty thousand after a siege of forty-seven days, and most of the women killed their children and themselves rather than be taken away in chains. Then Joppa, where the population tried to flee in ships but were dashed upon the shore by a great storm and massacred by the auxiliaries who met them there.

Ambush, betrayal, confusion and slaughter.

Tarichaeac. The name brought a cynical smile to Titus's features as he reviewed his troops. 'Your opportunity for glory,' his father predicted. Opportunity for an early grave, more like.

Strong walls on three sides and the fourth facing the shore of the Sea of Galilee. The Judaeans kept a strong force outside the walls to maintain contact with a fleet waiting offshore, covered by archers and slingers from the ships. Vespasian had ordered him to sweep them away with a reinforced cohort. When Titus's men refused to charge against such odds he'd been forced to take the lead. So many arrows smacked into his shield that it looked like a porcupine, while slingshots spanged off armour and helmet, leaving his head ringing and his body bruised. Six hundred Romans against four times their number. He remembered the stink of sweat and fear and torn entrails thick in his nostrils and the leaden taste of blood in his mouth. Wielding his blade until the muscles of his arm screamed and the shield felt as heavy as a cart wheel, cursing bearded faces shrieking defiance and invoking their god even as the *gladii* took their lives.

Surrounded and knowing the awful shame of failure he'd felt the bowel-liquefying fear of approaching death. He was too young. He had so much to do.

'Are you well, general?' The concerned voice of Genialis, the camp prefect of the Fifteenth. The man who had saved his life by sending archers to overwhelm the storm of arrows from the ships and cavalry to drive the Zealots back.

Titus felt the sweat streaming down his cheeks, but managed a smile. 'Chasing rebels is hot work. Your men are up for a fight?' he said to change the subject.

'They'd rather fight than march,' Genialis snorted. 'If there's a foot of this godsforsaken dustbowl they haven't covered, I'd like to know where it is.'

Tarichaeae. Flames and screams in the night after Vespasian commanded that the ships be destroyed along with the thousands who had fled to take refuge on them. A soft, breathless morning when the charred corpses of men, women and children bobbed and dipped in the waves along the shore. Another morning watching a long column of non-combatants stream from the city after being urged to throw themselves on the mercy of Rome and guaranteed free passage as far as Tiberias. Rome – in the shape of his father – showing the true meaning of Roman mercy. Twelve hundred of the old and sick slaughtered in the stadium at Tiberias, the rest, almost forty thousand, sold into slavery to be worked to death at their masters' pleasure. Vespasian justified the decision by the fact that as the story spread all but three of Galilee's fortresses surrendered. Meanwhile, Tarichaeae's gates hung open, the only occupants the dead or the soon to be dead beneath a giant pall of smoke that stank of roasting flesh.

And after Tarichaeae, more of the same at Gamala and Gischala, Jamnia and Azotus, Gersa and Jericho.

The long pause to draw breath after Nero's death, waiting to see what would unfold. The day in Caesarea when the impossible happened and three legions declared a 'new man' Emperor of Rome. Hail, Caesar! His father's dry, self-deprecating humour as he offered his son either a death sentence or an opportunity for his name to live on through history.

'Whatever my legions say, I am not the Emperor until I am made so by the Senate and people of Rome. The day that happens I will appoint you my heir. For the moment I must ask you to command my armies in Judaea, though you may feel a cup of hemlock laced with honey would be a more attractive proposition.'

For weeks afterwards Titus had no time to dwell on his new status because of the huge amount of preparation needed for the next phase of the campaign. Three legions must be manoeuvred into position to destroy the last surviving pockets of rebel resistance. Yet they'd still have to rely on supplies of fodder in country stripped bare by the rebels and along roads always vulnerable to ambush by the insurgents. The critical shortage of cavalry and archers concerned him and he had to endure interminable negotiations with the jumped-up rulers of the city states of Syria, Armenia and Cappadocia. He commanded three legionary legates, each of whom demanded their unit should have the place of honour and the final glory. Well, he was resolved there would be glory enough for all when the time came. In the meantime they could obey orders with good grace. And always at his shoulder, Tiberius Alexander; mentor, wet nurse or spy?

Yet at least once a day came a moment of startling clarity as he realized who and *what* he was. One step away, at the age of thirty, from being the ruler of the greatest empire the world had ever known. Yes, a war must be fought and won before that was certain, though let no man believe it was a war either he or his father had wanted. But it had to be fought, and now it *was* won. Vitellius was dead. In a few months Titus Flavius Caesar Vespasianus Augustus would be hailed Emperor of Rome and on the same day he would declare Titus his heir. Did he deserve this honour? Of course not. He was but a simple soldier, who, he prayed, had risen to his present position by his abilities and not by hanging on to the laurels won by his father. Yet what else could he do but stand by Vespasian and accept the responsibilities placed upon him? What son would do otherwise? Of course, he had doubts. He'd felt the entire weight of the Empire looming over him like a collapsing *insula* the moment his father announced his intentions; all the breath knocked from his lungs as if he'd been punched by a boxer. Yet there'd been excitement, too, and a growing inside, an expanding of the mind as he understood that he, Titus Flavius Vespasian the younger, was capable of greatness. He had already shown courage and leadership; he must learn wisdom and statesmanship and how to wield authority.

If he'd been in command at Tarichaeae, Titus would have stuck to the principle of the bargain and freed the non-combatants. By killing a thousand sick and elderly and sending the rest into slavery, his father showed a superior understanding of the situation. The dead were useless mouths who would have died in time anyway. Many were troublemakers who had flocked to Judaea to join the rebellion against Rome. Sacrificing a few thousand saved tens of thousands of lives by sending a clear message to the other fortified cities of Galilee that if they didn't surrender without a fight they were doomed. Titus had absorbed the lesson. Sometimes a man must harden his heart in the present to save the lives of his soldiers in the future.

A rider approached and he heard the man pass his message to Tiberius Alexander. 'We have them trapped against a bend of the Jordan, tribune. The river is in flood and they have no escape.'

Titus made his decision before the Alexandrian turned to ask for orders. The slave pens were full and he had no provisions to feed prisoners. Other battles must still be fought and he couldn't afford to have insurgents operating at his rear.

'Kill them. Kill them all.'

X

Serpentius sent word that he'd spend the evening at the Chalcidean camp and he still hadn't returned when Dimitrios, the armourer, reappeared as promised the next day. He carried a leather bag and was accompanied by three slaves bearing bulky, cloth-covered packages. From the bag he produced the Roman's wooden fist on its cowhide stock, buffed, polished and almost unrecognizable from its earlier incarnation.

'I have made certain modifications of which I hope you approve, lord.' He slipped the stock over the freshly oiled stump of Valerius's right arm and tightened the leather thongs to hold it in place.

'It's more comfortable,' Valerius admitted. 'And a better fit.'

Dimitrios's eyes twinkled at the praise. 'I added a lining of soft calfskin, which should stop any chafing. A simple addition that will make wearing it for lengthy periods less demanding.' He snapped out an order in Aramaic. One of the slaves uncovered his burden to reveal a large shield – a full-size legionary *scutum*, the face painted in the colours of the Tenth legion. 'Please . . .'

Two leather straps had been fitted to the right of the grip for better stability. Valerius pushed the wooden fist through them and pulled back to engage the hooked fingers of the carved hand with the shield's grip. The balance and feel was much better and he said so.

'I am glad you are pleased.' The armourer waved to the other two slaves to unwrap their packages. 'And I think you will be even more so. Of course, this is only a fitting. I will make adjustments later and by the time I am finished you will believe it was made for you.'

Valerius studied the gleaming pile of metal with disbelief. 'I . . .'

'It was a gift to King Sohaemus from the Emperor himself,' Dimitrios said proudly.

It was a Roman general's breastplate worked in silver and gold. A set of protective armour fit for a prince and, judging by the decoration, originally made for an emperor. A golden chariot pulled by a team of silver horses raced across the well-muscled chest, while below Mars, Jupiter, Juno and Minerva looked on approvingly. The breastplate lay on a scarlet tunic and a legate's scarlet cloak, beside a helmet of equal quality. The brim of the helm was inlaid with four roaring lions' heads and it had a crest of stiffened scarlet horsehair. As Valerius watched, the slaves each produced a pair of similarly worked greaves and arm protectors.

'I can't wear this,' he protested.

'But the king insisted.' Dimitrios looked terrified. 'It would be a mortal insult to refuse his gift. Please, at least try it on.'

Valerius knew he had no choice. He stripped off his tunic and replaced it with the scarlet version, which turned out to be made of the finest cotton he had ever worn. Dimitrios fitted the gilded breastand backplate over his head and strapped them in place, then attached the greaves to his shins and the arm protectors about his wrists. Finally, the armourer produced an elaborately decorated scabbard on a leather baldric. He placed the strap diagonally across Valerius's chest, so the sword rested on Valerius's right hip, ready to be cross drawn by the left hand. Satisfied, he stepped back and studied Valerius with a look of almost religious awe. Valerius's fingers automatically sought out the sword hilt and drew the *gladius* from its sheath with a spine-chilling hiss.

As he took the sword in his hand, Valerius felt a surge of immense strength run through him and he saw the awe in Dimitrios's eyes momentarily turn to fear. Valerius studied the weapon in his hand. But for the decoration it might have been a standard military *gladius*, yet it was probably the finest sword he had ever held. It had been manufactured from the best carbon-rich iron to give it strength, yet the balance was perfect. Even with the ornamental eagle on the pommel it felt almost weightless. The ghost of the five or six carefully selected bars of metal that forged it were visible as silvery traces in the blade. Like the pommel, the hilt was heavily ornamented. Valerius knew that in a fight even a hand as calloused as his would soon be blistered and bleeding. Still, a strip of leather wound around the grip would make it more of a killing weapon. The feel of it reminded him of the sword of Julius Caesar that Vitellius had taken from the Temple of Mars Ultor. His friend had carried it with him to the great Golden House in Rome where he'd ruled the Empire for eight short months. He only hoped fate would be kinder to this sword's new owner.

The armour, like the *gladius*, was made of the finest materials. It was a little too full at the chest and shoulders, but an adjustment of the straps and some padding would fix that. He knew it was an illusion, but the combination made him feel taller and stronger, and he grinned; a shark's grin that sent a shiver through the other man. These glittering baubles had one purpose, and one purpose only: to project power. He replaced the sword to a sigh of relief from Dimitrios, picked up the helmet and placed it on his head.

'No wonder the Romans conquered the world.'

Valerius looked round to find Tabitha staring at him from the doorway. 'I must look like a golden peacock,' he grinned.

'No,' she said seriously. 'You look like a warrior of old.' She walked round him and he felt his face redden as she studied the effect from every angle. 'You could be Titus, or his older, much more dangerous brother.' She ended up facing him and it was as if she were seeing him for the first time. 'What could a man like you not achieve,' she frowned, 'if he had an army at his back?'

Valerius glanced warily at Dimitrios and the slaves. 'My loyalty is to Rome, lady, and let none think otherwise.'

'Yet Rome has abandoned Gaius Valerius Verrens. Why else would he be wandering in the Syrian mountains with a single servant and the clothes on his back, relying on the goodwill of an old friend?'

'We will speak no more of this,' he insisted, working at the straps of the breastplate.

She smiled and gave a little shrug. 'Just a girl's silly reflections, Valerius. Not to be taken seriously.'

'Perhaps I'll keep it for Saturnalia.' He handed the armour to an appalled Dimitrios, but Tabitha laid a hand on his arm.

'Do not discard King Sohaemus's gift so lightly, or underestimate the importance of appearances in this land. There will come a time when you need to impress, and no matter what you think of these glittering baubles, you look mightily impressive in that uniform. Think on it, Valerius. Will you arrive at Titus's camp like a beggar seeking alms, or at the head of five hundred of Sohaemus's desperately needed archers, looking what you are? A warrior. A leader. A Hero of Rome.' The pause that followed reinforced her point, but it was her next words that caught his attention. 'And there will be others watching, people who may have a profound influence on your future in the East.'

'You make it sound like a threat.'

'Not a threat, Valerius. An opportunity. Sohaemus is not the only person with reason to be grateful you saved my life. Titus will also hear of your valour.'

'You are very well acquainted with kings and princes for a lady's maid.'

'That is because my *lady* is Queen Berenice of Cilicia, for which you also may have reason to be grateful.' She laughed as she swept out of the room, leaving him with the slaves and Dimitrios, whose face was a picture of consternation.

'Lord?' the armourer pleaded, holding the breastplate like a sacrifice across his hands.

Valerius sighed. 'Very well, but I will need a padded scarf for my neck and shoulders . . .'

Dimitrios nodded and began to withdraw, ushering the slaves with him.

'. . . and I want a shirt of chain of a similar quality to here.' He put his hands to the bottom of his ribs. 'And make sure to pay particular attention to the sleeves. Those open armpits are an invitation for any spearman who wants to leave a battlefield a rich man.'

'Of course, lord.' Dimitrios hesitated. 'And, lord, I hope you will not feel it an imposition if I add my own gift?'

Valerius smiled and shook his head, but eventually he bowed. 'I would be honoured, Dimitrios, but only as long as it has a use and a dearth of golden decoration.'

When he was alone, Valerius poured himself a cup of water from a jug and marvelled at Tabitha's ability to keep him off balance. Had she been hinting something when she talked about an army? Or had she just been blinded by the sight of the armour and, he allowed himself a smile, the man in it? Was it coincidence he'd been presented with a general's uniform, or was this some subtle piece of trickery by Sohaemus? Certainly, from what Ariston had discovered, the Emesan ruler was devious enough. He'd already more or less offered Valerius a command in his army, what there was of it. Perhaps the armour was a clue to the rewards that went with the offer. He noticed a small cloth-wrapped bundle on the table beside the jug. Dimitrios or one of the slaves must have left it by mistake. Reluctant to see yet another golden trinket though he was, his curiosity soon had him tugging at the white material. It came away to reveal a highly decorated *pugio*, a legionary dagger and an unusual addition to a general's regalia. He turned it over in his hands. Highly decorated, but killing sharp, with a needle point and curved edges. He returned it to its sheath and placed it back on the table.

By now it was late afternoon. Valerius had sent Ariston to the market to learn what he could about the kinds of threats they might encounter between Emesa and Jerusalem. Sohaemus had promised one of his cavalry commanders would brief Valerius before they left, but the Roman preferred to have his own sources of information. Until the guide returned there was nothing he could do to prepare for the journey. He decided to take up the king's offer by visiting the palace libraries while there was still enough light to read by.

He guessed it would be cool by the time he returned and threw on the cloak Gaulan had given him the previous day. Standing by the curtained doorway he hesitated for a moment. Only the guards were allowed to carry weapons in the palace, but he remembered Dimitrios's warning. Had he left the dagger for a purpose? On impulse, Valerius picked up the knife and strapped the belt beneath his cloak where it couldn't be seen.

To reach the library he had to pass through a series of corridors in the sprawling guest quarters and cross a large, paved courtyard. The guards at the library door were big, bearded men in fish scale armour with spears in their hands and curved swords at their sides. He realized Sohaemus might not have passed word that he was free to enter and resolved not to make an issue of it. There would be other times and there was no point of making a nuisance of himself. In the event, he had nothing to fear. When he presented himself at the door the two soldiers nodded him through into the great echoing space of the first room. The clerks were at their desks, hunched over rolls of parchment, their narrowed eyes darting between the original manuscript and the copy they were making. Valerius wandered among them, trying to view the books they were working on without getting in their light.

'Is there a particular work you are interested in, lord?' The speaker was Philippus, the young man Sohaemus had spoken to the day before. His cheeks were smudged with dark streaks where he'd rubbed ink across his face.

'The king asked me to ensure you were given every facility as well as access to any book, however obscure, and we have many of those.'

Valerius complimented him on the fluency of his Greek and the clerk blushed beneath the ink.

'So it should be, since I was born in Athens. My father made sure I was taught to read and write from a young age and my tutor soon discovered I was an acceptable copyist. A few years later King Sohaemus heard of my ability and persuaded my master to allow me to come here. He treats me well and I am rewarded for good work. I have no complaints.'

'How long have you been with him?'

'Ten years now.' The young man frowned. 'But a copyist is only as good as his eyes and I do not know how much longer I will be able to continue.'

'I am sorry to hear that.'

'It is the fate of many in my profession.' Philippus's tone was philosophical. 'Fine work seems to drain the ability to see clearly the way a tiny pinhole will eventually empty a wineskin. No one will employ a copyist who writes large, because of the high cost of a roll of parchment. I am one of the fortunate ones. I have some money put away and King Sohaemus says he will find me a position teaching the children of his lords their letters. Still, I hope to complete the Herodotus. For the moment that is all I could ask. Would you like to see it?'

'I would be pleased to.'

He followed Philippus to his desk, where the original of the book was still pinned. Perhaps forty lines of writing were visible on the crumbling papyrus. On the copy to the right stark lines of Greek symbols leapt from the creamy white of the softened goatskin. 'We combine soot, vinegar and wood gum to create the

113

ink,' Philippus explained. 'I am just waiting for this to dry before I roll it up for the night. King Sohaemus prohibits us from working by lamplight because of the risk of fire. He is very conscious of what happened in Alexandria. Some of our books were recovered from the library even as it burned. But I am boring you.' He shook his head. 'You did not come here to listen to me talk about my work. What would it please you to read?'

Valerius assured the Greek he was far from bored. 'There are so many books here it is impossible to choose. Perhaps I could ask you to do so for me. I am a military man, with an interest in philosophy and the law.'

Philippus nodded thoughtfully. 'Philosophers we have by the basketful, and legal cases so lengthy and dull your head would fall off before you were halfway to the conclusion. But writers on military matters . . .' His eyes scanned the niches and their contents. 'Yes, I have it. I can offer you Polybius' *Histories*, though it is not an original and I fear the copyist had literary ambitions of his own.' Philippus sniffed to show what he thought of the changes. 'We have Homer, of course, but you will be familiar with his works, and Aeneas on siege operations . . .'

Valerius dredged up a memory from the long days spent with Seneca during the philosopher's exile on Corsica. The old man had insisted Valerius read military texts as well as the dry, dusty tomes of the Stoics because: 'I am not sure you are cut out to be a philosopher, Valerius. Your father will thank me one day.'

'Aeneas of Stymphalos?'

'The same.'

'Then I would be happy to read him, and anything else you have on the subject.'

Philippus called for a slave. 'Room two, section four, niche five,' he ordered. The man dashed off, returning a few minutes later with a set of scroll cases. Philippus selected one and took out a roll of papyrus. 'This is the start.' He unrolled the scroll, revealing faded brown writing: σοις τῶν ἀνθρώπων ἐκ τῆς αὐτῶν ὁρμωμένοις χώρας ὑπερόριοί τε ἀγῶνες . . .

'When men leave their country and engage in warfare and encounter perils beyond their own frontiers . . .' Valerius read aloud.

Philippus went back to Herodotus, leaving the Roman alone with his book. Valerius's choice was not entirely random. Ariston had described Jerusalem as a massively fortified city occupied by fanatical defenders determined to hold their sacred places to the last man. A siege appeared inevitable. Valerius had experience of sieges from the point of view of both defender and attacker. Did Aeneas, who had himself been a general, have anything new to teach him? Disappointingly, it turned out that most of the Greek's analysis proved to be very basic. He began with organizing the defenders and placing sentries, keeping the population in order and pooling food and supplies, creating passwords and making sallies against the besiegers. Valerius carried on reading and discovered the author mirrored his observations on entering Emesa by suggesting a series of fallback positions in case the walls fell to the enemy. There were sections on mining and counter-mining and methods of repelling the besiegers by destroying their siege machines with rocks. This last brought an image of Juva, the Nubian he'd fought beside at Placentia, hurling a great grinding stone over the parapet to smash an enemy ram. At last he found a section that truly interested him. Aeneas suggested several devious ways of smuggling a

115

secret message through enemy lines. And, though he'd compiled his treatise almost four hundred years earlier, he proposed the use of coded letters. A simple enough system, using pinholes invisible to the naked eye to identify certain letters in a book when the parchment was held up to the light. He also advocated the use of ciphers. Seneca had always claimed that Julius Caesar had devised the first code, but for once it appeared the old philosopher was wrong.

By now the light had begun to fade and Valerius found himself squinting to make out the words. He blinked his eyes to clear them. No wonder Philippus and his fellow workers suffered eye problems if they had to concentrate like this every day. He rolled up the scroll and placed it back in the leather container, looking round for a slave to take the book back to its niche. Instead he found Philippus approaching.

'I came to warn you that King Sohaemus allows no one in the library after dusk. It is part of my duty to make a final check of the rooms. Perhaps you would like to accompany me?'

Valerius followed him through the echoing halls and the rows of empty desks.

'It seems you have every book in the world here, or at least every book worth reading,' the Roman commented.

'Not every book,' Philippus smiled. 'But certainly a vast fount of knowledge.'

'Yet the king mentioned a single book that would make his collection complete?'

'He told you about that?' The clerk laughed. 'The Book of Enoch. No one is even certain it exists, and if it does, whether it is a work of genius or madness.'

'Why is the king so interested in it?'

'There are many reasons. The first is that it is possibly unique; a single copy in the entire world. The second, that it is said to encompass the entire span of the Judaean race from the creation to the apocalypse and the king believes that he cannot know too much about his neighbours.'

'So this Enoch could see the future?' Valerius had come across several men who had claimed to be prophets, but most had been obvious frauds.

'So it appears.' Philippus's tone was scornful. 'The other reason the king seeks the book is because it is said to foretell the coming of the man Christ whose followers the Jews hate so much. A delegation of these Christians appeared at the gates of Emesa a few years ago demanding to search the library for the book, which they claimed as their own. They also pleaded with the king to give up the Black Stone of Elah Gebal and worship Jesus. He told them he would be happy to do so if they could prove the gift of eternal life they offered was a reality. He had them executed in a number of individual ways in an attempt to provide the proof. None came back to life, but one who was about to be burned to death offered to renounce Jesus and worship the Black Stone if he was allowed to live.'

They'd reached the doorway of the library and Valerius said farewell.

'Do you wish me to accompany you, lord? The palace is a maze of corridors.'

'I know my way, Philippus.' Valerius smiled his thanks. 'I'll be safe enough on my own.'

117

XI

Words are like arrows: once loosed they cannot be taken back. Before he'd gone a hundred paces Valerius wished those words unspoken. Instinct saved him. Instinct, speed and the little knife Dimitrios the armourer had thoughtfully provided. But instinct most of all.

He'd just passed a curtained doorway in a corridor illuminated by oil lamps when he felt the faintest whisper on the back of his neck. The flames of the lamps barely flickered in the still air so the draught could only herald some new factor.

Another man would have hesitated. The warmth of the king's friendship might have lulled Valerius's senses, but instant, violent reaction had kept him alive through battle, skirmish and ambush. Before the thought had even formed, his left hand swooped to the knife while the right arm flung his cloak wide as he turned, instantly creating a distraction and a threat.

Curved blades glinted evilly in the yellow light from the lamps. Three men running towards him, swift and silent across the marble tiles. The closest attacker had aimed his stroke at Valerius's unprotected back, but the unexpected movement caused it to slide a hair's breadth past his side and become engulfed in the folds of his cloak. Its owner, a big bearded man, barely had time to register disbelief at missing such a simple target before Valerius's *pugio* came up to slice across his throat. A beautiful stroke; simple and deadly and almost casual in its delivery. Valerius experienced a liquid surge of elation as he felt the flesh separate beneath the razor edge and the momentary resistance of the windpipe before the tendons parted. The would-be assassin fell away gurgling horribly, his eyes huge discs of ivory and his bulk momentarily obstructing a second killer who'd been at his shoulder.

Valerius ignored this second man. Instinct told him the greatest threat lay with the third, who'd loitered at the rear and now attacked from his left side with his curved dagger raised shoulder-high. By Fortuna's favour the billowing cloak masked the weakness of Valerius's open flank and caused a moment of confusion. The hesitation lasted for less than a heartbeat, but long enough for Valerius to rake the studded sole of his sandal down the front of the killer's shin. As wounds went it was trivial enough, but the assassin shrieked as the iron rivets peeled strips of flesh away from the bone. Before he could recover Valerius followed up with a crunching shoulder charge that sent the knife flying and hammered the man back against the door jamb. By now the rhythm of the fight was pulsing in his head like the slow beat of a drum. He could visualize his surroundings as clearly as if watching from above. The impact forced the breath from the assassin's lungs, paralysing the man long enough for Valerius to haul him round in time to take the knife aimed at the Roman's back. He screamed as the point entered where shoulder joined neck and blood fountained from the wound. Valerius stepped away and faced the surviving killer with the *pugio* in his left hand. The man gaped as he realized his error and with a cry of frustration he plucked the knife free from his comrade's body and dashed up the passageway. He'd covered a dozen paces when he stopped as if he'd run into a stone wall.

Valerius watched as he clawed at his breast before falling back so that his head bounced from the marble floor with an audible crack. Serpentius stepped from the shadows and bent over him to tug his knife free from the man's chest, absently cleaning the blade on a handy piece of tapestry.

'You took your time.' Valerius's chest heaved as he struggled for breath.

The Spaniard straightened, swaying slightly, and his words were slightly slurred. 'You wanted to know about the archers, so I took them drinking with your money.'

For as long as he'd known Serpentius, Valerius had never seen him even mildly affected by wine. He could drink an amphora of the sourest tavern piss and wake up with a head as clear as a child's. Still, he decided not to pursue it for now. 'Couldn't you have found a way of stopping him without killing him?'

'I thought it better to kill him before he did the same to me. In any case,' the Spaniard nodded towards the men whose blood was spreading over the marble at Valerius's feet, 'yours won't be telling us much any time soon either.'

Valerius bent to check the man who'd been stabbed in the neck, but the Spaniard knew a dead man when he saw one. 'A pity.' He shook his head. 'It would have been interesting to question at least one of them.'

'We should—' Serpentius's mouth shut like a trap as the rhythmic clatter of well-shod feet heralded the arrival of a troop of guards. Tabitha strode purposefully in their wake and Valerius experienced the odd mixture of thrill and wariness he always seemed to feel when she entered his orbit.

'What has happened here?' Her face turned pale as she saw the dead men. 'I was told there had been a disturbance, but this?'

Valerius explained the details of the ambush and she frowned. 'But there should have been guards on this corridor.' The words were aimed at the guard commander, who paled under her wrath.

'I was ordered to remove them by the chamberlain, lady,' the veteran soldier stuttered. 'He said it was a waste of manpower.'

Tabitha closed her eyes and took a deep breath. 'Leave us, and take this offal with you.'

'Wait,' Valerius commanded. 'Shouldn't we try to find out who they were?'

'Very well.' Tabitha glared at the guards. 'Search them for any clue to their identities.'

'Nothing here,' the commander said after his men had rummaged through the clothes of the three corpses. 'But they have the look of Judaeans and the knives are such as the Sicarii use.'

'This one has some kind of charm at his neck.' Serpentius crouched over the man he'd killed and cut the leather thong holding the talisman. He held out a crudely carved wooden cross. Valerius recognized the symbol as the mark of the Christ worshippers Philippus had talked of less than an hour earlier. Coincidence? Before he could mention it Tabitha snatched the cross from Serpentius's hand. The Spaniard gave her a look that would have stopped a charging elephant, but she ignored him and turned to the guard commander.

'Get rid of these animals, but quietly, and mention this to no one.'

'The king . . .'

'I will inform the king,' she said coldly. 'Mark me well, if this incident becomes market gossip you and your men will spend the next five years eating dust at a checkpoint on the Palmyra road. Do you understand?'

The captain lowered his eyes and Valerius reflected on this further evidence of the power Tabitha wielded. This was an Emesan nobleman, an experienced soldier trusted enough to be part of the king's personal body-guard, but he accepted her authority without question.

As the guards carried the dead men away, he moved closer to her and asked quietly: 'What about the chamberlain?'

When she turned to him, the dark eyes were full of deadly certainty. 'I will deal with the chamberlain.'

Tabitha insisted on accompanying them to Valerius's guest quarters and surprised him by leading the way inside. She noted his reaction with a sniff of disdain. 'My reputation is safe unless some garrulous fool,' her eyes went to Serpentius, 'announces my shame in the market place. Of course, we have ways of rewarding garrulous fools in Emesa.'

'She means she'll cut out my tongue,' Serpentius grinned. 'I'm beginning to like her. I'll be outside. Safer there, even with all the murderers who seem able to slip past Emesa's guards at will.' He ignored the poisonous glare she shot him and stalked out of the room.

Valerius went to the table and poured two cups of wine, hesitated long enough to give them a thoughtful inspection and left them where they were. Tabitha smiled. 'I will have a sealed amphora sent from the king's private supply. You take the attempt on your life very calmly.' She folded herself on to one of the couches. 'Almost as if you expected it.'

'I was wondering when you were going to tell me who tried to kill me, and why.'

Now it was her turn to be thoughtful. She rose in a single flowing movement and poured a little water into one of the cups before returning to sit at his side on the second couch. They faced each other and he experienced that sensation of drowning in the dark eyes.

'Why do you think I would know such a thing?'

'Because it appears the lady Tabitha knows everything that goes on in Emesa – and elsewhere.'

She drank some of her water and nodded, lowering her voice so he had to lean closer to hear the words. 'You have to understand that there are many factions in Emesa, Valerius, and factions within factions. Loyalties change with the ebb and flow of power between various highly influential families. The greatest division is over the king's policy towards Rome, which some see as wisdom and others as an invitation to complete and perpetual domination. Of course, any fool can see that it is both, but what is the alternative except to give up power altogether? It causes much enmity, sometimes deadly enmity.' She paused and took another sip from the cup. 'I do not *know* who is responsible. My *guess* is that someone opposed to Rome saw your arrival as a new threat to Emesa's independence and decided to have you murdered. We have many refugees in the city, from Judaea and elsewhere, some of dubious background. It would be the work of an hour and the price of a small camel to persuade one or two of them to kill you.'

Valerius wondered if he should feel insulted to discover his life had so little value. At least Domitian's assassins were proper professionals.

'This is the East, Valerius.' Tabitha smiled at his reaction. 'A small camel is a great prize to a man who cannot afford shoes.' The smile faded to be replaced by a frown of irritation as a thought struck her. 'I was not aware the chamberlain's sympathies lay in that direction. It was careless on my part, but it also leaves open the possibility that the pro-Roman faction was prepared to sacrifice you to implicate their enemies. The king has a gentle disposition, but in the past he has acted with great severity against rivals. That is why I insisted this be kept from him. It is not beyond Sohaemus to purge the entire anti-Roman faction and slaughter every Judaean in Emesa if he discovered what occurred tonight. That is not what Emesa needs at this moment.'

'What does Emesa need?'

'Stability,' she said firmly. 'The opportunity for King Sohaemus to earn not just the respect of the new Emperor, but also his gratitude.'

'Could the Judaeans be acting alone? And what about the Christ worshipper? I've crossed swords with his kind in Rome and they're fanatics. Perhaps they wanted revenge for the leaders executed by Nero?'

'It is possible they acted alone,' she admitted, 'but I think it unlikely. They would not be able to buy the chamberlain's assistance. As for the Christ worshipper, either he wore the cross for some other reason, or, more likely, he kept his allegiance from his companions.'

'Maybe we should get out of here tonight,' a voice rasped from the doorway.

'A loose tongue and long ears,' Tabitha sniffed at the interruption. 'That would be unwise, and an insult to the king.'

'Then what would you advise?' Valerius asked, so close to her now that he could feel the heat of her body.

'It is unlikely they will make another attempt before you leave. I could suggest staying in your rooms, but King Sohaemus wishes you to choose a horse from his stables tomorrow.' She laughed at his consternation. 'You need not be concerned that you choose too well. His grooms will have removed his favourites. Later, as High Priest of Elah Gebal, he will sacrifice to the Sun God in the Temple of the Black Stone to solicit the god's aid for the expedition to help Titus. He would be pleased to have you witness the ceremony as an honoured guest and sit by his side at the banquet that follows.' Tabitha had communicated the invitation in a voice loud enough for Serpentius to hear. Now she lowered it almost to a whisper. 'I have other information which can only be conveyed in the utmost privacy. Find a reason to have your pet wolf spend tomorrow night elsewhere and be here two hours after sunset.'

Valerius opened his mouth, but she put a finger to his lips.

'He will protest that he cannot leave you alone, naturally, after what has happened today. You may reassure him that all routes to this room will be guarded by men of the utmost loyalty and experience, which they will.' Her mouth came close to his ear. 'Everything will be in place, Valerius, all you have to do is find a pretext to keep Serpentius away.' As she shifted, her lips brushed his cheek and the touch, coupled with the promise of her words, sent a flush of heat through him. By the time he'd recovered she was gone.

The next day passed in a blur of anticipation and frustration. Valerius spent the morning with Serpentius and Ariston, choosing a horse from the king's stud. The enormous complex lay to the west of the town among the lush meadows by the Orontes. By noon they'd whittled the options down to six from the hundreds originally on offer. They were beautiful animals and he reflected that if Sohaemus had truly removed his favourites they must be fine horses indeed.

'And they're all cavalry trained?'

The king's horsemaster grinned, showing a row of yellowing, crooked teeth that could have graced the mouth of one of his charges. 'Of course, lord. They don't understand Latin, but they'll respond to heel and knee and they won't take fright if someone shouts at them. Why don't you try them and find out?'

Grooms took the animals away and the first returned with a grey mare. Valerius saw with relief that the horse had a four-pronged Roman saddle rather than the simple padded rug the Syrians favoured. Ariston helped boost him into position and the groom handed him a long spear, which he gripped loosely in his left hand, and a circular light shield, which he declined. The horsemaster led him to a narrow paddock about four hundred paces in length. It had a double target in the centre consisting of two of the round shields on a horizontal bar fixed to a central pole. Valerius knew from his experience in Armenia with Corbulo's auxiliary cavalry that the shields would rotate when struck by the lance. Sometimes the Thracians would replace the second shield with a heavy sandbag designed to knock the unwary trooper from the saddle if he hit the target at the wrong angle.

The familiar Roman saddle provided a steady seat and after one or two short canters up and down the paddock Valerius was ready. The grey was a pretty animal, long in the back and lithe of limb with long-lashed deep brown eyes. She was the type of animal you could fall in love with, but after two runs at the target – one near miss and one hit – he knew she was too highly strung for a cavalry mount.

On the fourth ride he found what he was looking for. The horse was a gelding, its coat the shimmering black-blue of a magpie's wing feathers. He had a noble head, but a short, broad back and stocky legs. More important he had no mind of his own. The animal reacted instantly to every change of pressure from Valerius's thighs and its low centre of gravity provided a perfect platform for a mounted warrior. His gait was a little awkward, with an odd little half twist at the trot, but a deep chest hinted at endurance and stamina. Valerius tried four runs to be certain, making the horse jink and dance and hitting the targets plumb every time.

'This one will do,' he informed the horsemaster as he trotted up to the start line. The man shrugged, but his expression said he didn't think much of Valerius's choice. 'What do you call him?'

'This one? This one we call the Screw.'

Valerius laughed. It was appropriate enough given that twisting ride, but no name for a war horse. 'Then he will have to get used to a new name. I will call him Lunaris. There was never a better name to accompany a man into battle.'

They arranged for Lunaris to be taken to the palace stables and Valerius and Ariston rode back to Emesa. 'Who was this Lunaris?' the Syrian asked. 'A hero of old?'

Valerius smiled, remembering the towering, indomitable figure who had stood beside him on the steps of the Temple of Claudius. 'A hero, yes, but not of old. A simple Roman soldier who did his duty.'

'He was your friend?'

Valerius stared at the distant hills to the north, remembering Serpentius's warning to keep the Syrian at a distance. 'Yes, he was my friend, but he died.'

When they returned to the guest quarters Valerius found that someone had laid out a milky white toga, the symbol of Roman citizenship, on the bed. Beside it was a note on a piece of reused papyrus. 'A servant will call for you at the seventh hour and take you to your position.'

'It wouldn't do to turn up for the sacrifice smelling of horse,' he said to Ariston. 'You'd better bring me a bowl of water and a cloth.'

Washed and shaved, he was ready when the servant – a young boy of fourteen – arrived. Serpentius wanted to accompany him, but Valerius insisted he would go alone. 'And Serpentius?'

'Yes.'

'Tonight I'd like you to take Ariston and test the mood of the city. Trawl the bars and inns for information.' He tossed the Spaniard a small purse. 'With what you already have that should last you a good few hours. Should you end up in a woman's bed so much the better, for we will be on the road in a few days.'

Serpentius gave his bark of a laugh and the light of understanding flickered in his eyes. 'If you want to be alone for a while, why don't you just say so? After what happened yesterday, though . . . maybe I should stay within shouting distance.'

'Don't worry about me. The guards in the corridors have been doubled and I'm assured that their loyalty to the king is total.'

'All right,' Serpentius agreed. 'But be careful. Sometimes the deadliest adversaries aren't the ones with beards and skinning knives.'

XII

Valerius found himself an object of curiosity in the parade of Emesan noblemen making their way to the Temple of the Sun God. He returned the frank stares and wondered idly if any of these men had ordered his death. The Emesans were tall, uniformly bearded, their hair falling in oiled ringlets to the shoulder, and scented with exotic oils. They wore long flowing robes of gaudy colours and patterns that would have attracted ridicule in a Roman market place. Gold chains hung at their necks and from their wrists, some of such weight it was a wonder they could stay upright. The most heavily laden drew gasps of wonder from the Emesan mob, who were kept at bay by armed soldiers not slow to wield their spear butts.

Despite the previous evening's attack Valerius felt no sense of threat. The aristocrats talked excitedly among themselves and a festival atmosphere prevailed. He noticed the highest ranking – those wearing the most gold – ensured that they only addressed their equals, looking down on those of humbler status in a manner that would have made a Roman consul proud.

Soon the column approached the temple, perched on a raised promontory to the south of Sohaemus's palace complex. In style and scale it was similar to the Temple of Apollo on the Palatine Hill, though Valerius noted that the precinct was much less elaborate. Where the Roman version had high walls and colonnaded walkways, a low parapet of cut stone enclosed the Temple of the Sun God. As the Emesan elite dispersed to positions allotted according to rank a servant, who went by the name of Julius, guided Valerius to a vantage point reserved for honoured guests.

In the hush that followed Valerius studied the scene before him. The first things that caught his eye were the great double doors sheathed in gold and decorated with an enormous sunburst. A substantial wooden ramp covered the marble steps that led to the ceremonial platform and a distinctive pattern of scratches and chips scarred the paving inside the wall.

A cacophony of horns made his ears ring and the temple doors slowly opened to allow an enormously tall figure swathed in purple and gold to back out. Valerius belatedly recognized Sohaemus, his height emphasized by the largest crown the Roman had ever seen, almost half as tall as the wearer and elaborately worked in gold and jewels. The king moved slowly, and it became apparent that he was leading something from the shadows. Valerius sensed the excitement in the crowd grow as the tossing heads of four white horses gradually appeared.

A loud shout went up – 'Elah Gebal!' – immediately repeated and magnified by a hundred voices and a hundred more, until every mouth chanted the name of the god. The tumult made the horses restless and the king hesitated, uttering calming words to the animals before resuming his progress, slowly inching his way backwards on to the ramp. Now the tempo of the chants grew as the crowd caught their initial glimpse of the chariot attached to the horses.

'Elah Gebal! Elah Gebal!'

'My lord king has vowed never to turn his back on the god,' Julius shouted to make himself heard above the increasing volume of the crowd. 'He wears the robes of the Foremost Priest of the Sun God and the great crown of Emesa, which has been passed down from his ancestors for time immemorial.' The sun's rays caught the golden chariot, but despite its brilliance the roars weren't for the chariot, but for the object it carried. Sohaemus led the horses carefully down the ramp with priests hauling on ropes to keep the vehicle from picking up speed.

Valerius strained his eyes for his first sight of this marvellous god, but he was destined to be disappointed. In a gilded cage stood a pyramid-shaped piece of rock about twice the height of a legionary *gladius*. It was a deep, almost subterranean black and gave the appearance of being enormously hard. Fissures and indents scarred the surface, but Valerius could identify no discernible pattern.

The chariot reached the bottom of the ramp and Sohaemus, still walking backwards, led the horses on a circuit of the temple precinct. The god cruised slowly past and the Emesan nobility dropped to their knees before rising again and tearing golden chains from their necks and arms to throw them over the wall. Priests followed the chariot picking up the treasure and one took a careful inventory of the donations and presumably their donors, for the throwers immediately looked to the king for acknowledgement of their gift.

Valerius estimated that, in the visible portion of the precinct alone, ten *talenta* of gold had been thrown in the wake of the sun god. He wondered just how often Sohaemus called these ceremonies. Not as often as he would like, or the Emesans would soon be impoverished. He said as much to Julius.

The boy smiled at his naivety. 'Those who pay tribute today know they will have their investment repaid tenfold in treasure and influence. Our great festivals occur only twice a year, during the summer and winter solstice,' he explained. 'Then, the rulers of Commagene, Palmyra, Chalcis and Laodicea send wagonloads of gold as tokens of their esteem for the god.'

Despite the great devotion shown by the Emesans, Valerius found it difficult to imagine worshipping a stone, unique or not. Yet clearly these awed people believed Elah Gebal was the true incarnation of the sun god. It was also true that Nero had encouraged the cult of Sol in the last years of his reign. Valerius supposed it was little different from pouring a nightly libation to the kitchen god, or leaving tribute to the god of the crossroads after a wedding. He was as sceptical about the power of the gods as anyone trained by Seneca could be, but he still made the ritual sacrifices. A man, especially a soldier, had to make his own luck. In Britannia they'd believed every lake and river held a god, and the druids had held their bloody rituals in oak groves.

The king reappeared at the head of the chariot and the roars subsided as he led the horses to the bottom of the ramp. Four priests used a special frame to lift the sun god from its chariot and place it between the temple columns. A fifth steered the golden chariot away from the crowds. His eyes never leaving the god, Sohaemus took his place at the top of the temple steps.

The sacrifice was as familiar to Valerius as his morning exercise with a sword. Priests led a white bull to the bottom of the steps where a *victimarius* used a hammer to stun it. A *haruspex* cut the collapsed animal's throat and examined the entrails. Sohaemus smiled as the man declared the omens for the coming expedition auspicious.

During the ceremony and the excess that followed only one thing dominated Valerius's mind. All he thought about during the feast was the fire in Tabitha's eyes and the promise in her voice. He picked at his food, the finest cuts from the white bull, and barely touched the wine. Fortunately they'd seated him well away from the king, between two foreign dignitaries who were more interested in the food than in his company.

When he finally returned to his rooms his heart fluttered like a lovestruck boy's and he cursed himself for his weakness. What if he'd entirely misread her intentions? It wouldn't be the first time. But then there was the touch of her lips on a cheek that still felt as if a glowing brand had seared the flesh. He lay on the bed for a time, then rose to pace the floor. What if she didn't turn up? He tried to conjure up a vision of Domitia, but the face that appeared was always Tabitha's. Where was she? Eventually he lay down again. His eyes closed of their own volition and the next thing he knew was the sound of whispered voices that made him sit bolt upright.

A single oil lamp illuminated the room. Valerius slipped silently from the bed and smothered it, breaking his stride only to pick up the dagger from the table. In a heartbeat he was by the doorway.

By now the whispers had faded, but he could hear a soft rustling and the sound of cushioned footsteps. The curtain rippled and he tensed, the knife ready in his left hand, held horizontal for the cutting stroke that would take out a man's throat before he even felt the kiss of the blade. Another twitch and the heavy wool drew back and a shaft of light illuminated a hooded figure in a long cloak who stepped stealthily into the room. Valerius delayed his strike until the inevitable second assassin followed, but none appeared.

The hood slipped back to reveal lustrous dark hair and a pale, slim neck. Tabitha turned with a look of mock irritation before her eyes caught the gleam of the knife and she smiled. 'Is this how you greet all your women, Gaius Valerius Verrens?' Valerius's heart thundered fit to burst. He stepped forward to take her into his arms, but she pirouetted away like a dancer. 'What better disguise for a spy?' she asked, clearly pleased with herself. 'Naturally, King Sohaemus would send a supple and experienced slave girl for the pleasure of his honoured Roman guest.'

'Spy?'

She laughed at the bewildered dismay in his tone. 'I said I would bring you information, Valerius,' she said, her voice suddenly turned low and husky, 'but in truth I bring you a gift.' Her hands went to her throat and the cloak fell away.

A night of wonder. A night of discovery. A night Gaius Valerius Verrens would remember in every detail until his last breath. For a moment he froze, bewitched by the naked form silhouetted against the lesser darkness of the window, and then he picked her up in his arms.

*

134

Much later she lay draped over him, one leg thrown across his thighs. A combination of softness and warmth, curves and hollows, the sweat still damp on her skin and the scent of their coupling a heady reminder.

'Why did you come?'

'You need to ask?' The words were almost a purr and he could hear the smile in her voice. In the silence that followed she sensed he required a genuine answer. 'I need a strong man, Valerius, a protector.' Her hand stroked the stump of his mutilated arm. 'I see in you a strength in mind and body I have seldom encountered before. And you . . . needed to forget.'

He nodded. She had looked into his soul and seen the emptiness there. The loss of everything he had ever loved. He searched with his mouth until it covered her nipple, nibbling the tiny bud gently between his teeth and sucking deep. Tabitha gave a soft groan and moved against him. With a single movement he rolled on top of her, arching his back so he was looking down at her. The harsh need in his voice surprised him, but seemed to please her. 'Make me forget again.'

Valerius thought himself experienced in love, but she taught him things about pleasing a woman he would never have discovered for himself. He used the strength that had impressed her to impose his will. She quivered beneath him, the royal lady gone, replaced by the captive he had first happened upon. It was a contest that neither wanted to end, but when it did there was no loser, only winners.

When the first pink of the coming dawn touched the sky, Tabitha stirred and slipped into her cloak, raising the hood to conceal her identity from the guards. Valerius rose and joined her at the doorway. She clutched at him and he willed her not to go, but eventually she raised her head to be kissed and slipped from his arms.

'I will come to you on the march,' he whispered, holding back the curtain.

'No.' The want in her eyes denied her words, but she would not be moved. 'It would not be seemly. We must be patient. When we join Titus it will be different. Please, Valerius, you must trust me.'

'With my life,' he insisted, but she was already gone.

XIII

Valerius was still basking in the soft glow left by Tabitha's presence when the Emesan guard commander appeared at the door with two of his soldiers. The Roman suspected trouble the moment he saw the man's face.

'What is it?' he asked.

'I must ask you to accompany me,' the officer said coldly. 'I'm sorry, I have my orders.'

A chill ran through Valerius at the tone of the response. Clearly the situation was worse than he'd imagined. 'Am I under arrest?'

A look of momentary confusion. 'No . . . not unless you refuse.'

'Then let me get my cloak and I will be happy to come.'

Despite the guard commander's words it felt like an arrest. Valerius expected to be taken to the king's quarters, but they passed the entrance to the palace and headed towards the citadel's gates. His mind fought for some explanation that would explain the sudden change in his treatment. Had someone informed Sohaemus about Tabitha's visit to his room? Or worse, had something happened to her? It could be as simple as a change in the king's policy towards Rome. Emesan loyalties seemed to fluctuate like the direction of the wind.

He felt the men beside him stiffen as they approached the guardhouse. The commander forged ahead and threw open the door, and Valerius saw an untidy heap of blanket lying on the cobbled floor. An icy dagger of dread pierced his heart. 'What . . . ?'

A guard drew back the coarse grey cloth and Valerius stifled a gasp. Ariston's dark eyes bulged from their sockets and a permanent grimace twisted his face as if the ragged wound below his chin had come as an irritating surprise. He held his clawed hands at chest height as if he'd been fending off his attacker, which was odd. Valerius had seen enough wounds on the battlefield to know that whoever killed the Syrian had cut his throat from behind. The question was: where had Serpentius been?

'Someone reported a brawl in one of the alleys in the tavern district,' the guard commander explained in a flat voice. 'When the watch arrived at the scene they found the dead man and his killer.'

Valerius felt a surge of anger. He'd resigned himself to hearing that Ariston's murderer had escaped, but now a desire to see justice done swelled his heart. 'What will happen to him?'

'The penalty for murder is crucifixion.'

Despite his grief for Ariston the dread word sent ice water running down Valerius's spine. Not six months ago Domitian had sentenced him to be crucified. Still, the man must be punished.

'Where is the killer now?'

The officer gave him an odd look. 'He is in the next room. We were holding him here until you could be informed.' He marched across the floor and pulled back a curtain.

Valerius's voice almost failed him as he studied the manacled figure seated on a bench with his head in his hands. 'Serpentius?'

'What do you mean you don't know if you killed Ariston?'

The Spaniard shook his head. He was grey-faced and exhausted, with a distant, bewildered look in his eyes. 'We'd left a tavern a few minutes earlier – Ariston said it was as welcoming as a Portus cesspit, the wine as sweet as the black heart of a Bactrian camel, and the women . . .' he shrugged. 'I think some men followed us.'

'Think? Mars' arse, you have to do better than that or they'll have you hanging from a cross before nightfall.'

'We were drunk,' Serpentius said, as if that explained everything. 'Ariston more than I. We talked; argued, maybe. Then something happened. I remember shouts, the flash of a blade and then it was like falling into a black pit, only the stars were whirling around like fireflies. When my eyes cleared Ariston was lying on the ground leaking blood and the watch had a spear at my throat.'

Valerius considered the story. He wanted to believe that Serpentius hadn't killed Ariston, but this wasn't the Serpentius he had known before the head wound. An argument. A fight. A man with a bloodied sword standing over one with his throat torn out. Everything pointed to only one outcome. The Spaniard must die. All except one thing.

'You saw Ariston's body?'

Serpentius nodded dumbly.

'Serpentius,' Valerius hissed. 'You have to concentrate. If you give up you're a dead man.'

The former gladiator looked up and Valerius shivered at the message in his eyes. 'We've been dead men for years, Valerius, only we won't acknowledge it.'

A bitter laugh escaped Valerius's lips. 'If only our friends could see you now. Old Marcus, the *lanista*, Juva of the *Waverider*, and all those other men we fought beside. The great Serpentius led unresisting to his slaughter like a sacrificial lamb. Going to a coward's death without putting up a fight.'

Light flared in the leopard's eyes at the word coward and Serpentius's chains rattled as his muscles tensed. His upper lip twisted into its customary sneer. 'Take these chains away and I'll show you how to die, Roman.'

'With a sword in your hand and a friend by your side?' The Spaniard stared at him for a long time before he nodded. 'Then help me.'

King Sohaemus sat on his golden throne staring balefully at the chained figure surrounded by his guards. 'The situation is clear. You killed a man – it matters not whether it was in a drunken brawl or that you have no memory of it – and under Emesan law you must be crucified.' He turned to Valerius. 'My respect for you forces me to allow you to speak for your friend, but,' he shook his great head, 'you must know it will count for nothing.'

'What if I can prove he didn't kill Ariston?'

'All the evidence says he did.'

'Even so . . .'

The king waved a dismissive hand. 'Speak, then. We are wasting time.'

Valerius marched across the floor so he was standing directly in front of Serpentius. 'You remember nothing?'

'I remember a fight, and confusion.'

'But you saw the wound in Ariston's throat?'

The Spaniard growled and would have spat, but he remembered where he was. 'Butcher's work, and from behind. I know I did not kill the Syrian because I have killed a hundred men and more, and every one of them looked into my eyes as they died.'

'Lord, this means nothing,' the guard commander interrupted. Valerius turned to stare at him and he lapsed into silence.

'The king needs proof that Ariston's death was not your work. Can you give him it?'

Serpentius turned to the king and bowed low. When his head rose there was a gleam in his eye that contained a warning to any man who knew him. 'Lord king, place a sword in my hand and six of your best men in front of me in full armour. Then you will see that the wound that killed the Syrian could not have been placed there by Serpentius of Avala.' He shrugged, and a mirthless smile appeared on the ravaged face. 'You see, I am an expert at my trade and this was the work of an amateur.'

Valerius shook his head. 'I don't think King Sohaemus can spare six men.' He nodded towards the doorway and Tabitha ushered in the display Valerius had requested. Slaves carried six spear shafts with the butts fixed into square wooden blocks for stability. Each shaft was topped with a water melon the size of a man's head. A murmur of bemusement ran through the courtiers seated below the golden throne as the slaves placed them carefully in a circle five sword lengths in diameter. 'Now, unshackle him.' The request prompted an audible gasp and the beginning of a protest from the guard commander, but Sohaemus raised a hand for silence.

'You will take responsibility for his actions?'

141

Valerius felt Tabitha's eyes on his back, but there was no way out now. 'If he spills one drop of Emesan blood I am prepared to die for it.'

'Very well,' the king said. 'Release him.'

Two guards strode forward and removed the Spaniard's chains. He rubbed his wrists where the iron rings had rubbed raw spots on his skin and flexed his shoulders. With a glare at the men guarding him he stepped forward into the circle of spears.

'Your sword,' Valerius ordered the nearest guard. The man looked towards his commander who gave the briefest nod of consent. He slipped the long blade from its scabbard and handed it hilt first to Valerius. 'Are you ready?' he asked Serpentius.

'This is nothing but a child's game!' The impatient cry came from one of the Emesan aristocrats.

'I'm ready,' the Spaniard said. 'Give me your knife.' Valerius handed him the ornate dagger and he took it in his left hand. 'Let's get this done.' He studied each of the melon-topped spears in turn as if he were trying to squeeze every detail from them, then closed his eyes. After a moment he repeated the operation.

The men around the king sneered, and Sohaemus said: 'In truth, Gaius Valerius Verrens, I do not see what cutting up a few melons is going to achieve.'

'If you will give me a moment, lord.' He turned to the nearest guard. 'Blindfold him. Make sure he cannot see anything.'

Now he had the attention of the entire room. Necks craned to gain a view as the guard removed his sash and tied it around Serpentius's eyes. Even the king leaned forward for a better view. Valerius obliged him by walking silently across the circle and moving the melon-topped spear in front of him a foot to the left.

'Are you certain he cannot see?'

'Certain, lord.'

'Good.' He moved out of the circle. 'Begin.'

Valerius had witnessed Serpentius in action a thousand times, yet each time he found himself awed by the incredible swiftness and precision of the former gladiator's sword work. The Spaniard had been born with a natural aptitude for killing, but his skills had been honed to a razor's edge in the arena, where only speed, accuracy and an appetite for extreme violence kept a man alive. Serpentius must have marked his surroundings with the accuracy of a hawk fixing its target below. His feet never faltered and he was so quick none of the watchers registered a single stroke. A blur of movement. The sightless progress round the inner circle a continuous twirling dance. The path of the sword blade marked by a single gleam as it carved unerringly through the melon targets in a series of curving arcs, turning the air red with the sweet juice of the opened fruit. In what seemed less than a heartbeat only one melon remained. A groan went up from the spectators as they realized Serpentius was on the opposite side of the circle from the melon in front of the king, but the Spaniard didn't hesitate. The eyes behind the blindfold homed in on their unseen target. His arm drew back and, with a flick of his left wrist, he sent Valerius's dagger spinning towards the target the Roman had moved.

'No!' Sohaemus cried out as he saw death fly towards him, only for the dagger to pierce the green and gold outer skin of the melon, an inch from the edge.

A collective sigh went up from the men in the room and Valerius went to his friend. As he took the sword from the former gladiator's hand, he noticed that Serpentius's ribs were heaving and sweat glistened on the hairs of

143

his chest. The Spaniard reached up to unwind the sash from his face and Valerius found himself the focus of the piercing gaze he knew so well. Gradually the fire faded from the dark eyes and Serpentius let out a long breath. Valerius turned to face the king. Sohaemus stared at the dagger that had been kept from his heart by an inch of over-ripe fruit.

'Does any man here still think that Serpentius of Avala killed my servant Ariston in such a crude fashion?' Valerius's eyes searched the room for any sign of dissent, but they were all looking to the king for their lead. Sohaemus pushed himself up from his throne and marched down the steps. He studied the melon that had been pierced by Valerius's knife before reaching to pull the blade free.

'I declare Serpentius of Avala innocent of this crime.' He swept from the room followed by a crowd of his courtiers. Tabitha left with them and when he met her eyes Valerius was sure he saw her lips twitch in a smile.

'Come,' he said to Serpentius. 'We have much to do.'

They left the throne room side by side and the Spaniard turned to Valerius. 'I thought you said you'd move the shaft a handspan to the left. That must have been a good foot. What would you have done if I'd missed?'

'You never miss.'

XIV

Valerius was studying a map of Judaea from Sohaemus's library when he heard the shuffle of footsteps outside the door and Dimitrios the armourer begged entry.

'Come in.' Valerius rolled the map and the Greek marched in followed by four servants, who unwrapped their burdens at his order. Slaves had polished the body armour and helmet so they shone like glass and had an almost blinding lustre. When Valerius pulled the *gladius* from its scabbard he saw that the armourer had followed his instructions to the last detail. It was still a beautiful example of the sword-maker's art, with the golden eagle glaring from the pommel, but Dimitrios had wrapped the hilt in a sleeve of wet leather which had dried tight to the polished bone beneath, resulting in a perfect grip.

'Lord?' Dimitrios held up the red tunic and scarlet cloak.

'Must I?' Valerius winced.

'Of course, lord. The king's gift must be perfect.'

Grudgingly, Valerius stepped out of his tunic and into the new one, which Dimitrios belted at the waist with a chain of fine gold loops. He then helped the Roman into the ornate breastplate, buckled on wrist and shin greaves, and slung the leather baldric so the scabbard fell on his right hip. He draped the scarlet legate's cloak across his shoulders and pinned it at the breast, stepping back to study the result with a look of pained reflection. Finally, he placed the plumed helmet on Valerius's head with a flourish worthy of a fanfare of horns.

Serpentius walked in as the armourer fussed with the folds of the cloak. 'Very pretty,' he whistled. 'When does the war start, general?'

'Don't call me general,' Valerius snapped, conscious he wasn't even a soldier until they reached Titus, and who knew then? He'd already decided to present the armour to the Emperor's son or some other deserving general at the first opportunity.

'There is one more thing, lord.' Dimitrios held out a final linen parcel. 'A gift. The personal gift I mentioned and,' he hesitated, 'to be received in private.'

Valerius nodded to Serpentius and the Spaniard shrugged and followed the servants from the room.

Dimitrios waited until they were alone before he began to unwrap the parcel with nervous fingers. 'It came to me, lord, that these are particularly dangerous times . . .' He peeled back the final fold of linen and lifted out a perfect replica of the wooden fist fitted to Valerius's right wrist on a toughened leather stock.

Valerius studied the wooden hand with bemusement. What did he need with two of them? 'I . . . I thank you, Dimitrios. I'm sure a spare will come in very useful. I can keep one for ceremonial occasions.'

'But you don't understand, lord.' A mysterious smile wreathed the Greek's features. 'This is different entirely.' He held out the wooden hand and Valerius vainly studied it for any anomalies. As he reached out he heard a sharp click and a glittering knife blade the length of his longest finger snapped from the centre knuckle of the wooden hand. Valerius automatically backed away from the bright iron and Dimitrios laughed at his discomfiture.

'It will still hold a standard shield perfectly,' the Greek cried enthusiastically. 'But sometimes a man in battle – or in dangerous times – can profit from the element of surprise. I noted by the marks on the original that it has often been used as a defensive weapon. This has the added benefit of being potentially offensive.'

'How does it work?' Valerius reached out to touch the point with the tip of his finger and winced as he drew blood. Dimitrios tutted and handed him a cloth.

'Why don't you try it?' the armourer suggested. 'You will note that the weight, dimensions and balance are the same,' he went on, as Valerius stripped off the cowhide stock of the original, slipped the new version over his stump and tightened the leather ties with his left hand. 'In fact, it is identical in every detail but one. Where the fist meets the cowhide you will now find an angular protrusion. Simply press it firmly . . .'

Valerius followed the instruction. The same sharp snick and he had a knife in his right hand. He twisted his wrist to study it from every angle and shook his head at the fiendish potential of having a concealed weapon like this at his disposal. 'Do I have to walk around with it for the rest of the day?'

Dimitrios took the hand and turned it. 'Inside the fist you will find another small protrusion. Simply press it, place the point against a solid surface and push until the top button engages. Like so?' He stepped away and looked to Valerius for the fitting expression of wonder his invention deserved.

'It is unprincipled,' Valerius began warily, 'underhand, sly,' the Greek nodded, his grin growing wider with each word, 'dishonourable and quite possibly criminal. It is a marvel. I love it.'

'It is based on the principles of Archimedes,' Dimitrios explained proudly. 'But I must give some credit to Philo of Byzantium for his treatise on experimental catapults. I combined Archimedes' lever theory and Philo's work with metal springs. That is what gives it the power. In a way it is the same as a bow, but the stresses and tensions are provided by the spring. The length of the blade is dependent on the dimensions of the hand, of course, plus a comparable length which extends back into the stock when the knife is retracted. It provides the necessary stability when the blade is in use, while the second protrusion holds it in place. The mechanism is quite robust. For care, a few drops of olive oil in the button holes. But I wouldn't advise getting it too wet.' Valerius waited for the inevitable explanation. 'Rust,' Dimitrios said. 'Once it rusts you would be as well throwing it away.'

'It is truly ingenious,' Valerius said. 'I look forward to showing it to King Sohaemus.'

'Please, no.' Dimitrios had a look of horror on his young face. 'The king has become uncomfortable with innovation of late. When I suggested using a similar mechanism to improve his catapults he threatened to have me impaled. If he knew I had forged this for you, he would carry out his threat, but he would castrate me first. In the name of the Black Stone, please tell no one. Promise me.'

'Of course,' Valerius readily agreed. 'It would be a pity to deprive the world of such a talent.'

XV

Serpentius walked in without warning as Valerius prepared for their departure the next day. 'It seems you're not the only Roman who will be riding with Sohaemus's archers,' he said. 'A broad stripe tribune rode in last night with an escort of cavalry from Tripolis. According to Gaulan he was on his way to join Titus, but Judaean fanatics cut the coast road and he came inland rather than wait for a ship to Caesarea.'

Valerius considered the news as he dried himself. A broad stripe tribune meant a senior officer, probably the second in command of a unit. 'He'll be joining his legion as aide to the legate, perhaps even an aide to Titus himself.' He felt Serpentius's eyes on him. 'It would be best if we didn't meet. Tell Gaulan to structure the column to ensure it doesn't happen.' The Spaniard nodded, but Valerius could see something was troubling him. 'You think I'm being over-cautious?'

'You can never be too cautious when people are trying to kill you.'

A grunt of acknowledgement. They'd discussed who might have murdered Ariston, raising a dozen possibilities but coming no nearer to an answer. The likelihood was that someone wanted to separate Valerius from Serpentius. Without the gladiator guarding his back he'd be a much easier target. But then why kill Ariston and not Serpentius, who'd been as vulnerable as he ever would be, drunk and alone in the Emesan alley? Then again, perhaps Ariston had been marked as a spy, or already had enemies in the city. Valerius would have liked to discuss the question with Tabitha, but he could hardly go pursuing her through the palace. It seemed likely they'd never know.

He finished dressing just as light began to filter through the courtyard window. Now, a dilemma few other men had ever faced. The thought brought a wry smile to his face. Which hand should he wear today? He oiled the stump of his arm and laid out the two artificial fists on the bed.

Serpentius studied the wooden twins. 'What . . . ?'

Belatedly Valerius remembered he hadn't mentioned the armourer's gift to Serpentius. He picked up the new hand and pressed the button. Serpentius's eyes lit up admiringly as the lethal little blade snapped out.

'I like it,' he grinned. 'A proper lifesaver.' He saw Valerius's look of puzzlement. 'That's what we called a hidden blade in the arena. Even if your opponent smashed your shield away and bludgeoned you into the dust you always had a chance with your lifesaver. A quick thrust into his balls or even his thigh and he was yours for the taking. It took timing and nerve, but it worked. You should wear it all the time. Just in case.'

'You don't mind?' Valerius indicated the other fist, which had taken Serpentius countless hours to carve.

'This?' The former gladiator laughed. 'It's just a rough old thing. It probably has woodworm. You should be ready for your audience with the king.'

Valerius reached for the armour and, with the help of Serpentius, transformed himself into a glittering example of a Roman officer, clad in armour forged for a god, with the scarlet cloak of a legionary legate over his shoulder. When they met, King Sohaemus apologized for Ariston's murder and made a pledge to hunt down his killers that Valerius doubted he intended to keep. There was no mention of the attack on Valerius himself, which presumably meant that Tabitha had managed to suppress all mention of it. Sohaemus was polite, but wary; perhaps a hint that the Roman had worn out his welcome. Nevertheless, he asked him to convey his regards to General Titus, greetings to the Emperor and assurances of Emesa's continued loyalty to Rome. He pledged to send more troops if they came available and he would attempt to persuade Chalcis to do the same.

'I have not had the opportunity to thank you for your magnificent gift, majesty,' Valerius said with overblown courtesy. 'It is far beyond my expectations and the value of any service I have provided. I will wear it with pride against your enemies and the glory of it will strike them blind.'

The king's lips twitched to show he understood the compliment's underlying message. 'I also have a more personal gift.' He waved forward a servant bearing a scroll case and Valerius opened it to find the papyrus copy of Aeneas on sieges he'd been reading in the library. 'No thanks are required,' Sohaemus assured him. 'I have other copies and I believe the contents may be of some use to you when you reach General Titus.'

An hour later, Valerius joined the column of archers formed up beneath the cheering crowds lining the walls of Emesa. There were five hundred of them, in addition to Gaulan's Chalcideans, a full cohort divided into ten squadrons each led by a standard-bearer carrying a flowing pennant. As a reinforcement for Titus's army of forty thousand, they'd barely be noticed, but Gaulan assured Valerius that Titus desperately needed archers and their value went far beyond their numbers. Few or not, they were well equipped. Every man wore a padded tunic beneath a chain vest polished by rolling in barrels of sand, and on his head a shining brass helmet with chain neck guard.

Valerius had spent time watching them exercise and he'd been impressed by their horsemanship and skill with the bow. They could half turn in the saddle, fire three arrows over the horse's tail and return to a normal riding position in the time it took to blink. Their bows were short, double curved weapons of wood and sinew that could launch an arrow twice as far as any hunting bow, and with the same accuracy. Though the archers carried the bows unstrung in pouches strapped to their backs it was the work of a moment to attach the cord and pluck an arrow from the leather quiver attached to their saddles at the knee. Fiercely independent men, they could have been brothers to the Parthians he had faced in Armenia.

To the rear, a baggage train of fractious, roaring camels and braying donkeys hauled supplies for the journey. A legionary cohort would have used bullock carts and been half the length, but the journey time would be double. Gaulan estimated it would already take two weeks or more if, as the king had hinted, Titus was already at, or close to, Jerusalem.

The column's departure was delayed by King Sohaemus's speech from a tower by the city gate. Valerius only heard a few unintelligible words on the breeze as he sat taking in the scent of nervous horse and fresh manure while the men shifted impatiently in their saddles and their officers fretted at the wait. Finally, the king waved a hand and they were on their way. Gaulan, who had overall command, rode at their head with Valerius at his side, but the Roman had seen no sign of Tabitha.

They'd been on the road for less than an hour when the sound of cantering hooves heralded the arrival of Serpentius at the front of the column. 'A certain person is comfortably housed in a sprung wagon at the front of the baggage train, as befits her status,' the Spaniard quietly informed Valerius. 'Sohaemus has allocated twenty horses to ensure the pace of the column is not impeded and to show his love for his niece. She is protected by twenty of our Chalcidean friends who change guard every two hours.'

They followed the Orontes through a patchwork of lush fields and meadows and that evening they camped on a height above the banks on grass spun with spring blossoms. A legion would have fortified the temporary camp with walls and ditches, but the Emesans simply built fires and unrolled their blankets before cooking the evening meal. Valerius mentioned this to Gaulan, but the Chalcidean only shrugged. 'They know their business. We are safe enough while we are in Emesan territory. It will be different after Heliopolis when we turn into the mountains. Ambush country,' he said significantly, 'and the Judaeans are masters of ambush, as your Twelfth legion discovered to their cost.'

Valerius woke to the usual military dawn chorus of coughs and farts, the familiar rattle of equipment, groans of complaining men and the rasped commands of their officers trying to get them moving with kicks and curses. The closest Emesans looked on with frank amusement as he oiled the mottled purple stump of his right arm. He

153

ignored them and slipped the cowhide socket in place, tying the leather thongs with practised movements of his left hand and teeth. When possible he liked to exercise with his sword every morning, something he'd learned from Serpentius. He searched for the former gladiator, but Serpentius's bedding still lay where he'd slept and there was no sign of the Spaniard. Valerius was unsure whether to be relieved or disappointed he wouldn't face that lightning sword and relentless savagery today.

He shrugged off his tunic and slipped the ceremonial sword from its sheath, shivering slightly in the still air. Men watched curiously as he walked through the camp and down the slope through the trees until he found a small clearing. He instinctively checked his surroundings for potential threats, but the only sound was the gentle twitter of birds somewhere close among the branches and the soft rush of the river from further down the slope. Satisfied he was alone, Valerius began a series of cuts and thrusts, parries and counter-thrusts, dancing first backward then forward, switching his weight from one foot to the other. Gradually he increased the pace until his mind began to soar to the rhythm of the movements and the sweat coursed down his back. Now the sword wove increasingly more intricate patterns and he darted from one side of the clearing to the other, performing pirouettes and changing direction without warning, ducking and weaving. Attack low, change in mid-thrust to a controlled throat-high slash, and use the movement to sweep aside the point that's about to skewer your liver. Dance left away from another attack. Regroup and counter. Hear a rustle in the bushes behind you, spin and . . . thrust.

The stranger didn't even blink as the *gladius* point came to a halt a belt notch from his eyeball.

'So it is you? An impressive display.' Valerius ignored the cosy familiarity in the words; the voice a little slurred, but with a cultured, educated Latin. The reason for the slur wasn't difficult to work out. One side of the man's lips – the left – hung lifelessly, as if they'd given up on the rest of his features. Like most of that portion of his face they were a wrinkled, mottled purple, the colour and texture of a turkey crop.

'You don't recognize me?' Valerius's sword point didn't stray the width of a hair. 'Perhaps . . .' the newcomer moved his head only to freeze again as the point touched the flesh at the base of his throat, 'perhaps if you allow me to show you my more attractive profile?'

Valerius's expression didn't change, but his eyes shifted from the disfigured features to the trees beyond the newcomer's shoulder. Tabitha stood silently twenty paces away, a ghostly, ethereal figure dressed all in vestal white. How long had she been there? Had she seen the man approach? Her face remained unreadable and when he looked again all that remained were leaves fluttering in the soft breeze.

He turned his attention back to the scarred interloper. The sword point moved an inch away from the man's throat, allowing him to turn his head to reveal the unin-jured side of his face. A handsome profile, fine-boned, with an aquiline nose and thin lips that curved slightly upwards in a smile that, for all its allusions to friendship, remained devoid of any humour or warmth. Dark hair flecked with grey flopped over his brow above an eye as cold as a misty Iceni morning. A man whose visible scars were not the only ones he bore, but Valerius knew all about that.

'No?' The other man broke the silence. 'I am disap-pointed. Britannia? The Twentieth? You were returning

155

to Rome while the rest of us cursed and sweated trying to prepare for Paulinus's march on Mona. Of course,' the eye drifted to Valerius's wooden fist, 'you didn't get there. I heard about your exploits at Colonia and winning the Corona Aurea. That came later, of course, after Paulinus had us patrolling in the woods and some Celts decided I should make closer acquaintance with the coals of their fire.'

Valerius studied him more closely. Still no hint of recognition, but that wasn't surprising. When he thought of Britannia it was the faces of the dead who came to him, as if those still living and breathing had never really existed.

'Claudius Florus Paternus,' the newcomer introduced himself. 'We served together for two weeks and I was the most junior tribune. I'm not surprised you don't remember me, but I remember you. There was a Celtic hill fort on the Silurian border. Legate Drusus reckoned he'd never seen an assault better planned or led.'

Valerius frowned. This he did remember. The stink of sweat and fear at the centre of a *testudo* formation as the spears and boulders battered down on the roof of shields. A grinning gap-toothed face that disappeared in a spray of scarlet. He still had the scar on his leg from the burning fat, and the memory of a soldier's worst nightmare: the enemy who decided that the pleasure of killing him was worth dying for. He allowed the sword to drop, but not so far that Paternus was out of range.

'Why are you here?'

'No joyous welcome for an old comrade?' Despite the admonition, Paternus visibly relaxed. 'Given your particular circumstances that's probably understandable. I am ordered to join the army of General Titus as aide to his chief of staff Tiberius Alexander. A storm forced us into Tripolis, but the rebels had cut the coast road. My guide advised that the Emesans might provide safe passage, and here I am.'

'No, I mean why did you follow me here?'

The disfigured face twisted into what passed for a grin. 'I caught glimpses of a legate's helmet and cloak during the march yesterday and it naturally made me curious. The Emesan cavalry troopers of my guard talked of a Roman officer with one hand who had won King Sohaemus's favour. The single hand stirred a memory. I was under the care of Paulinus's personal *medicus* when we camped somewhere close to Verulamium. He'd given me some herb concoction and I was only semi-conscious, but I remember him treating a man who'd lost his hand. He was quite proud of the leather cover he designed to protect the stump. When I saw you leaving the camp I decided to follow. It seemed the best chance to introduce myself.'

A plausible enough explanation for his sudden appearance, with the added advantage that Valerius remembered the man who'd treated him in the hospital tent. A Greek. What had his name been? Cornelius? No, Calpurnius, that was it. Tiberius Calpurnius. He'd wanted to remove more of Valerius's arm for the sake of neatness, and been quite put out when Valerius refused. Still, something didn't quite fit.

'You say it seemed the best chance to introduce yourself, but wouldn't it have been a little odd if I'd been at the latrine?'

The scarred face creased into a perplexed frown. 'What kind of man takes a sword to the latrine?'

Valerius raised his *gladius* so the point touched the other man's breastbone.

'A careful one.'

XVI

'The legate's uniform and armour were the only things that made me think I might be mistaken,' Paternus explained as they walked back through the trees to the camp. 'It would have been a sudden and unlikely elevation for a man in your position.'

Valerius turned to stare at him. 'You mentioned my *particular circumstances*. What did you mean by that?'

'I heard what happened to you in Rome.' For the first time the scarred tribune looked uncomfortable. 'I was on garrison duty in Achaea during the troubles, and glad of it. My commander declared first for Galba, then Otho. Dithered in terror for six months when Vitellius came to power, before declaring for Vespasian. By the time the Palatium recalled me to Rome it was all over, though the ruins of the Capitoline still smouldered and they were cleaning blood from the Forum. Mucianus, Domitian and Primus apart, Gaius Valerius Verrens was the talk of the city. To some . . .' He looked to Valerius, wondering if he should continue, but the one-handed Roman gave him no hint.

I heard what happened to you in Rome.

Just how much, Valerius wondered, had Paternus heard and from whom? Pliny would have told him that Valerius risked his life to reach Aulus Vitellius, persuade him to give up the purple and spare Rome from sack and massacre. He would have said the Vitellian attack on the Capitoline, in which Valerius had taken part, and the burning of the great Temple of Jupiter were the result of the cowardice, intransigence and downright foolishness of Vespasian's brother Sabinus. Domitian's allies, on the other hand, would have condemned Gaius Valerius Verrens as a traitor who betrayed his friends and his Empire and quite possibly threw the brand that razed the temple to the ground.

Paternus read the message in Valerius's eyes. 'I'm sorry if this causes you pain, but if we are to travel together I feel it is wisest to be frank. To some, you were the traitor who had destroyed and defiled Rome's most sacred site. Still, I wondered how such a man could escape execution. I spoke to a young tribune who'd been deputy commander of the Seventh Galbiana . . .'

'Claudius Ferox?'

'I believe that was the name,' Paternus nodded. 'He had a different story. Of a soldier who had lived up to his reputation as a Hero of Rome, saved Primus's command on the road to Cremona, and somehow become involved in negotiations too secret ever to be revealed. He didn't believe what he heard at your trial. His version went some way to explaining why Domitian chose to sentence you to exile instead of crucifixion, so I reserved judgement. I had no idea you were travelling east.'

Valerius knew Paternus expected some kind of reaction or explanation, but what was the point? Words would change nothing. The only way he would regain his reputation was on the battlefield and only Titus could give him the opportunity. Still, politeness required a response. 'I suppose you should . . .' The words froze in Valerius's mouth and his sword came up in a blur of light as a figure appeared on the slope above them.

Paternus placed a hand on his arm. 'My servant, Gavvo. He must be searching for me.'

Valerius studied the man, who stared back impassively. He reflected that the last time he'd looked into eyes with quite that hint of menace had been on the day he'd first met Serpentius. Nondescript and so ordinary as to be almost featureless, he none the less possessed a stillness that sent a message to anyone capable of understanding it. Valerius lowered the sword.

'You pick your servants well,' he said with heavy irony. Paternus laughed and they continued up the slope. Valerius avoided making eye contact with the lithe, shaven-headed figure who sat unnoticed among the trees on a stump, cleaning his fingernails with a fruit knife.

Later that day the column left the river for a broad valley and made good time on another of the well-found roads that spoke so eloquently of Rome's long-term presence. At first the surrounding country appeared barren – a few isolated farmsteads eking out a living on the thin, dry soil – but with every mile south the land became more fertile. Soon they rode through a landscape of well-cultivated wheat fields and vineyards. Valerius the farmer noted a familiar golden tinge to the wheat crop that warned a landsman to start preparing for harvest, and the individual ears had begun their characteristic bow in homage to the sun. It didn't look like a place ravaged by civil war for five years.

'The land all the way to Heliopolis and beyond belongs to the city of Berytus, which is loyal to Rome,' Gaulan, who accompanied them, responded to a question from Paternus. 'Most of the farms you see are owned by the families of retired legionaries settled here by Augustus. They are Roman citizens and Rome's rule here is absolute. You are as safe in the valley as you would be in Antioch or Apamea, even Rome itself. That is why the men are so relaxed. Any Judaean rebel who ventured this far north would find the entire countryside against him. We will not reach Judaea proper for another three or four days. Then it will be different.'

If Paternus realized that Valerius was doing his best to ignore him he took no obvious offence. The scarred tribune seemed to assume his fellow Roman would be desperate for news of Rome. Valerius faced the choice of listening politely or dropping back to ride beside Serpentius a few files back.

'You know about the Temple of Jupiter and the Castra Praetoria, of course? Domitian, who rules as city prefect, has pledged that his father will rebuild them in greater splendour than before. He sent two of the three legions that took the city south under Primus to mop up the last of the rebels. The third provides security until a new Praetorian Guard has been formed.' Valerius heard Gaulan curse as they came up behind a farmer driving his herd of skinny goats to another field or a nearby market. Despite the muttered grumbles from his rear, the ragged herder showed no inclination to allow the column to pass and they were forced to slow. Paternus frowned irritably at the delay, but he could see no solution and continued: 'Most of Vitellius's supporters died when the city fell or in the bloodletting that followed.' Valerius had to grit his teeth. Had the man no feeling? Valerius had *been* there; he'd seen the chopped-off limbs, gaping mouths and staring eyes. 'But Vespasian

161

has pledged that any man who takes the oath to him will be pardoned. For his own reasons Domitian claims not to have received the instruction. He continues to hunt down any former Vitellian he can find, especially those involved in the murder of his uncle, Sabinus. Despite his youth he commands respect as well as fear among the populace, but he will never be liked for himself. Any popularity stems from the efforts of the lady who is to be his wife, Corbulo's daughter Domitia, who it is said works tirelessly for reconciliation.'

Valerius flinched at the mention of the name. Had things been different Domitia Longina Corbulo would have married him. Instead, she'd sacrificed her future to save his life, pledging herself to Domitian. Valerius still didn't know whether to admire or hate her for it.

'It is Domitia,' Paternus continued, 'who controls the effort to feed the poor and hungry, who are legion in a city where most of the supplies burned during the fighting. She persuaded Domitian to send aid to the city of Cremona and to incorporate the survivors of the old Guard into the legions rather than executing them . . .'

I am my father's daughter. Valerius heard the words ringing in his head as the goatherd bustled his animals on to a track with whistles and the use of his staff. That was her fate and what defined her. Of course she would use Domitian's power to help the poor and the dispossessed. What power could Valerius have offered? Ruling over the little farming estate at Fidenae they'd have shared with his sister Olivia and her husband? It would have been like putting her in a cage. And what was the alternative? An army wife playing hostess at a crude fort on the Danuvius frontier or in the wilds of Britannia? How could he ever have dreamed she would be his?

He looked up to find Paternus staring at him. 'I asked what you expect from your meeting with Titus, but you seemed distracted for a moment. Perhaps my news of Rome troubled you. I apologize; I didn't mean to cause offence. I have always lacked subtlety, even before this.' He indicated the burns on his face with a tight smile.

'Titus knows what I did to advance his father's cause.' Valerius cursed the lack of confidence in his voice. He'd failed utterly to achieve what Titus had asked of him. 'Tame the tiger,' Titus had said of Marcus Antonius Primus, Vespasian's impulsive general of the Balkan legions. Instead all Valerius had achieved was to hang on to the tiger's tail as he launched his army impetuously into northern Italia. Primus's victory at Cremona changed the course of the war, but at what cost? Blood and fire. Raped women, merchants crucified on the shutters of their burning shops, and babies spitted on spear points. Primus lost control of his legions and Valerius could do nothing to stop it. Desperate not to repeat the disaster, Primus had sent Valerius to Rome to talk his old friend Aulus Vitellius into giving up the purple. But Vitellius's soldiers refused to let him abdicate, Rome burned and Domitian branded Valerius a traitor. Valerius counted Titus a friend, but why would he reward failure or risk being tainted by dishonour? 'All I can ask of him is an opportunity for redemption,' he said stiffly. 'A chance to prove myself in battle.'

'Perhaps I could be of some help,' the disfigured veteran offered. 'As aide to Tiberius Alexander I will have his ear.'

Valerius shook his head. 'I prefer to fight my own battles.' Paternus froze and Valerius realized he'd been more blunt than the generous offer deserved. 'Now it is for me to apologize.' He gave the other man a conciliatory smile. 'These past months have not been easy and I find it difficult to talk about. Titus will listen to me, I hope, and, if not, he is unlikely to be swayed by anyone else, however persuasive.'

Paternus nodded his understanding. Valerius knew what he was thinking – bad enough to lose your hand, but your reputation too? – and willed him not to say it. Perhaps Paternus had the same thought, because he wisely changed the subject. 'What do you know of these Judaeans?'

'Poorly armed fanatics.' Valerius repeated Ariston's estimate of their fighting qualities. 'But men who will fight to the death rather than surrender. They are split into several factions, and when they're not trying to kill us they're killing each other. They even kill their own women and children to stop them becoming Roman slaves.'

'Fools then,' Paternus sniffed. 'For even a child growing up a slave has opportunities for advancement in Rome.'

'Perhaps,' Valerius agreed, 'but brave fools. An enemy that can destroy a legion and take its eagle is worthy of our respect. Titus's strategy is to break the back of the rebellion in the countryside and force the survivors to flee to Jerusalem. But Gaulan tells me Jerusalem is like no other Judaean city. It won't be easy to take even with three or four legions.'

'It was simpler in Britannia where the Celts hid behind their pathetic wooden fences on top of a hill and thought themselves invincible.'

'If Boudicca had listened to her advisers,' Valerius pointed out, 'and drawn us to her, neither you nor I would be here to discuss it. In the end the Celts were defeated by their own courage. Even Paulinus admitted that if he'd been forced to attack that day he would have been beaten.'

'More brave fools,' Paternus conceded with a bitter laugh. 'And of all the brave fools in Britannia,' he added significantly, 'Paulinus awarded only one the Corona Aurea.'

Valerius might have dismissed what amounted to an impertinent question, but despite his earlier doubts he'd begun to warm to Claudius Paternus and he didn't object. The scarred tribune reminded him of someone, but he couldn't think who. Something in his mannerisms; the way he held himself? 'One man was awarded the Corona Aurea,' he agreed, remembering a similar conversation a decade earlier with Julius Agricola, Paulinus's aide. 'But only because the men who truly deserved it were already dead. We couldn't hold Colonia's walls, so we did what a legion does best and fought them on ground of our own choosing.'

'A legion,' Paternus frowned. 'I thought . . .'

'Two thousand militia,' Valerius corrected himself, 'and a few hundred stragglers rounded up from the Londinium garrison. The militia were veterans of the battles against Caratacus and legionaries to their core; men past their prime, but their swords were sharp and they could still hold a shield. The rebels covered the entire north slope across the river, but we had left them only one bridge. The Colonia militia defended it to the last man and gave me a breathing space to retreat to the temple perimeter.'

'Where you held them for three days.'

'Just two. Two days of stifling heat and all-pervading fear as the glow of the fire eating through the oak door grew ever brighter, but every man who fought for the Temple of Claudius was a hero who deserved the Corona

Aurea more than I, because it cost them far more than it cost Valerius Verrens. We beat off a dozen attacks before they swarmed across the walls, then the few of us who were left fought our way back to the temple. After that it was just a question of waiting.'

'Yet you survived.' Paternus glanced at the wooden hand.

'Let us just say that the gods were kind to me that day.'

Paternus knew he would get no more. 'I liked Britannia,' he said, 'apart from the weather. Good soil and lush pastures. I think I could have settled there.'

'Even after what happened?'

'This?' Paternus laughed. 'We were on patrol. Armed reconnaissance, Paulinus called it. Clever Ordovice swine managed to separate the head of the column and captured a few of us. Of course, we knew what was coming next. They strung a few poor bastards from the trees by their entrails, and got ready to burn the rest, but they wanted information from me. So they set this little fire, and forced my face closer and closer until my hair was burning and I thought my head was going to explode. When I wouldn't say anything they pushed my face into the embers. Venus' wilted tits, how I screamed. I would have told them anything, but I was fortunate. The cavalry arrived and a second later the fellow holding me down didn't have a head. The *medicus* did what he could and treated my face with a salve, but when it came off I looked like a piece of roast pork, and here we are, ten years later and nothing has changed.'

'Yet you're on your way to be aide to one of the most powerful men in the eastern Empire,' Valerius pointed out.

'Ah,' Paternus smiled knowingly, 'but previously I had been destined for greatness. I had been promised a quaestorship and that was only to be the start. My family had influence, through my father, and money through my mother. Who knew what honours were to be mine?'

'But?'

'But when I went for my interview on the Palatine, the Emperor happened to catch a glimpse of me through a window.' A shadow fell over the unravaged portion of his face. 'Nero, as you know, had an eye for beauty and I must have been the least beautiful thing his eyes witnessed that day. He banished me from the palace and my hopes of advancement were gone. Fortunately, I had been a decent officer and in the legions there were plenty of men with worse injuries. I have been content enough, but I haven't seen my family for five years.'

They rode in silence for a while before Valerius excused himself and dropped back to join Serpentius, who slipped away from the Chalcideans he'd been regaling with tales of his romantic triumphs.

Valerius drew the Spaniard to one side. 'What happened back at the camp this morning?'

Serpentius shrugged. 'When the first one came down the hill, I followed him, but I could tell he was unarmed. In any case I was sure you wouldn't find him any trouble. The other one, the one with the killer's eyes, was different. When I saw him slipping through the trees I decided he was the bigger threat and stayed with him.'

'You're sure he was following me?'

'I can't be certain,' the Spaniard admitted. 'He might have been going for a piss or down to the river to wash himself. But you've seen the way he moves, and all it would take was a half turn and he'd have been coming at you from behind with all your attention on the handsome one. It was only when the Emesan vixen . . .'

'Lady Tabitha,' Valerius corrected him.

'. . . appeared from nowhere that he took himself off in a different direction. Then she saw you were occupied with your new friend and disappeared back up the hill.'

Valerius tried to visualize the scenario as Serpentius described it. Had Paternus been distracting him to allow Gavvo to surprise him from behind? But if he were going to do that surely he would have been armed as well. 'Paternus didn't have a hidden blade?'

Serpentius nodded. 'He wore only a tunic. You know how a man carries himself a certain way if he's armed.'

'What about the servant?'

A shrug. 'He was wrapped in a blanket so it was hard to tell, but I know the type and their hand seldom strays far from the knife hilt. For a servant, he moves like a soldier, but he's too young to have been pensioned off.'

Valerius looked thoughtfully at the soaring hills to right and left and made his decision. 'All right. Gavvo will never be far from his master, so keep your eyes open and don't mention this to anybody.'

'Not even . . . ?' Serpentius grinned.

Valerius allowed himself a smile. 'I suspect she already knows more than we do.'

XVII

The road took them into the mountains and they spent two days on narrow, precipitous pathways before finally descending a long, gentle slope into a broad river valley where a paved road led south. Tabitha discussed the location with Gaulan and they agreed the column had at last reached Judaea. They identified the river as the Jordan, which dissected the country from north to south.

'We are ten miles from Caesarea Philippi, according to the marker.' Gaulan pointed to a crudely carved milestone half hidden by scrub and thorn. 'But I would have expected the road to be busier. We haven't seen a patrol or a wagon in the last hour.'

They turned south and soon the ground on both sides of the road became impassable. Dense reed beds alternated with dark pools surrounded by banks of black, glutinous mud, and occasional small islands colonized by scrubby, undersized trees clinging to survival. Every stretch of water teemed with ducks and wading birds. Gaulan had to issue orders to the Emesans not to waste arrows by trying their luck against the local wildlife. At intervals the birds would take to the air without warning in huge flocks, rising and falling in wide circles before settling on some favoured spot. Gradually, the road surface rose until it became a causeway dissecting broad wetlands to left and right.

Their tactical situation concerned Valerius more than the bird life. The causeway confined the entire column to this single road, with no space to deploy if the enemy attacked. Logic told him that any attacker would have to have webbed feet, but still . . . Gaulan wondered aloud if he should order his scouts into the swamp, but they knew the riders would have trouble keeping up with the main column. Besides, what would they find among the reeds and bulrushes apart from frogs?

During a rest halt the Chalcidean ordered a patrol to move ahead and check the length of the causeway and what lay ahead.

Shortly after they'd ridden off a skiff emerged from the wall of papyrus stems to the right of the road with a single man on board. The hunter, his nets crammed with dead birds, gaped at the soldiers long enough to be snatched by two cavalrymen who plunged their mounts into the waist-deep water.

'A good catch,' Valerius complimented him, hoping the man would provide more than just fowl to supplement the rations. At least now they might get some up-to-date information. 'Tell him we'll pay him well for his ducks and leave him enough to feed his family.'

The Chalcidean commander questioned the hunter in Hebrew, eliciting frowns, shrugs and a sideways glance at Valerius's wooden fist. 'He says the road has been quiet for three or four days,' Gaulan reported. 'But he doesn't know why. He minds his own business, netting ducks and trapping eels to sell at the market at a place he calls Egret Hill. We are the first soldiers he's seen for some time, but that means nothing. He was due to meet someone here and he's wondering why they haven't appeared. That's the only reason he was coming ashore on the causeway.'

'Which direction would they be arriving from?'

Gaulan repeated the question and the man pointed south. Valerius stared in the direction the scouts had disappeared. Some instinct reminded him of being young in Britannia, where a Celt could be hidden in every fold in the ground. He studied his surroundings and didn't like what he saw.

'Ask him how well he knows this swamp.'

'Every bank and every pool and every stand of reeds, he claims. But he only hunts the northern part, because the governor's licence gives him the right.' Gaulan grinned. 'I think he's lying. He probably knows when and where his neighbours hunt at any given time and poaches on their territory whenever he gets the chance. But there's something else. He's frightened, and not just of us.'

The sound of galloping hooves distracted Valerius as the patrol galloped up the causeway, their horses blowing hard.

'Rebels,' the leader called as he reined in before Gaulan. 'A mile ahead where the road crosses a piece of dry ground. They've barricaded the causeway and fortified a patch of land to the east within bowshot.'

'How many?' Gaulan demanded.

'We counted at least a thousand, possibly more. They must have known we were coming.'

'Two to one.' Gaulan directed the words at Valerius, but the Chalcidean's eyes were on the hooded figure beside the Roman. 'Not bad odds for cavalry against infantry, especially mounted archers against untrained rebels.'

Valerius felt Tabitha's eyes on him. Despite Gaulan's rank he knew the final decision was to be his. 'Not bad odds in the open,' he agreed. 'But these rebels are behind walls and you'll have no room for manoeuvre. If I read it right you'll charge the barrier and when you're trying to tear your way through they'll be slaughtering you from the flank with spears and slingshots. There's a possibility you'll succeed, but no guarantee. No matter what happens you'll lose soldiers, and Titus needs those men.'

'Then we stay out of range and kill them from a distance. My men can put an arrow through a sparrow's rearmost orifice at a hundred paces.'

'You can't kill what you can't see,' Valerius persevered. 'You'd just be wasting ammunition and you'd still have to take the barricade.'

'You think we should retreat?' Gaulan's outraged tone said more than his words.

A commotion on the road behind interrupted the discussion. Valerius glanced back to where a member of Gaulan's rearguard was forcing his way through the column towards them. 'I have a feeling that may not be an option.'

'What would you suggest?' Tabitha asked.

Valerius pointed to the duck hunter. 'Ask him if he can lead us through the swamp and past the rebel lines.'

'He will betray us.' Gaulan looked dubious. 'He must have known the Judaeans were close.'

'That's true,' Valerius conceded. 'But perhaps he is as afraid of them as he is of us. We can't go forward so we have to find another way. There must be deer tracks through the swamp we can follow. Ask him.' He stared hard at the man. 'But in such a way that he understands if he refuses we'll cut his throat and give the eels something to chew on.'

Gaulan spat the question at the Judaean hunter and the man swallowed and went pale. He shook his head, but when the Chalcidean commander snarled another barrage of Hebrew he started to babble in the same language, pointing to the reeds.

'He said it was too dangerous, but when I pointed out the alternative he changed his mind. There are paths through the shallows and some from island to island, but the way is often unclear. To miss a step could take a horse into quicksand or send it to the depths. He said he would lead us in the skiff, which means he'd give us the slip the first chance he had.' He smiled at the man, but it wasn't a pleasant smile. 'I told him we'll give him a horse and he'll have a sword at his back every step of the way. I don't want him leading us to some watery dead end and paddling off into the distance.'

A thought occurred to Valerius. 'What about the camels? Will they go through the water?'

'I think so, as long as they are led.' The Chalcidean frowned. 'We'll double up the drivers behind my archers. Any animals that refuse we'll slaughter and distribute the baggage between the rest.'

'We will need a rearguard.' Tabitha pointed out what neither man had considered. 'Enough men to make a demonstration to those in front and behind and convince them we are still trapped. Otherwise . . .'

'Otherwise they'll be waiting for us when we reach land.' Valerius completed her thought.

'I will command the rearguard,' Gaulan said in a tone that allowed no argument. 'You deal with this fellow.'

'Very well,' Valerius agreed. 'Give us to the count of a thousand after the last man is out of sight before you follow. We'll mark the trail where we can and leave men to provide a guide where it's not possible.'

Gaulan nodded and went off calling for his officers, leaving Valerius and Tabitha alone with the hunter. He turned to her. 'Even if Gaulan succeeds, it's possible they'll be waiting for us when we try to leave the swamp. If that happens, stay close to Serpentius. If there's a way out he'll find it.'

She shook her head. 'You do not know me very well, Valerius. I will stay with you, and if necessary I will fight and die alongside you.'

The decision to flee into the swamp didn't meet with universal approval. Most of the Emesan archers would have preferred to fight on dry land. But they were soldiers and soldiers obey orders. The cavalrymen urged their horses down the bank of the causeway and pushed their way into the reeds in twos, churning the water a muddy brown. Valerius rode at the front of the vanguard, his sword blade only a flick of the wrist from the hunter's throat. The man sat rigid in the unfamiliar saddle of a horse led by a Chalcidean trooper, his hands hooked like claws on the leather pommel. Tabitha took her position just behind Valerius, beside Serpentius and ahead of Paternus and his servant. It clearly irritated the tribune that he hadn't been consulted before the decision, but this was no time for argument. The first hundred Emesans rode with their bows strung and at the ready, but in the ranks behind each horse bore a camel driver as well as its rider. The drivers sat facing their charges and linked to them by a length of rope. It was an uncomfortable position, but better than wading through water of uncertain depth, and preferable by far to being left to the tender mercies of the Judaean rebels.

The horses whinnied and skittered nervously as they entered the water and their hooves fought for purchase in the clinging mud. A few of the more highly strung bucked and danced, threatening to spook their neighbours, until their riders managed to get them under control. Valerius would have said this patch of reeds and bulrushes was like any other, but gradually his eyes discerned a faint path through the shimmering green barrier. Even so, the bottom was uneven and more than once his heart leapt into his mouth at a sudden feeling of weightlessness as Lunaris stepped out of his depth. It was clammy and airless among the thick stems and the reeds restricted visibility to a few yards. Swarms of black flies plagued horse and rider alike and the monotonous buzz of insects filled the air. The men rode in silence, but there was no quieting the coughs and snickers of the horses or the braying of the camels. Valerius knew that for all their precautions their progress would be easily monitored by anyone within a hundred paces.

In the sullen depths of the dense stands of bulrushes it was easy to lose all sense of time and distance. It came as a surprise when they broke through to an expanse of clear water that twinkled into the distance where rafts of ducks and geese, patches of yellow water lilies or low, reed-fringed islands broke the shining mirror of the lake surface.

Valerius wondered how any man could tell the difference between the shallows and the hidden depths. But the hunter had spent more than half his life poling his skiff across these waters and with every push the pole touched bottom. The Judaean indicated a course running parallel to the reed bank and pair by pair the Emesan archers emerged into the sunshine. At regular intervals the guide would indicate a change of course to avoid an underwater obstacle or hidden pit. He seemed resigned to his fate now, and Valerius allowed himself to relax and sheathed his sword. Another mile, or perhaps a little more just to be safe, and they could begin to work their way back towards the causeway.

Serpentius called out a warning and Valerius followed his pointing finger. About two hundred paces back he saw a shimmer run through the reeds. The men closest to the phenomenon didn't appear to notice what was happening, or perhaps they thought it was caused by a gust of wind. They were wrong and it might have killed them. The reeds parted and a shower of spears arced out to slice into the flanks of the nearest horses, creating a screaming chaos of panicking men and injured animals. As quickly as it opened, the gap in the reeds vanished. Valerius witnessed the same shimmer in reverse as the attackers retreated. Men floundered in the water as others came to their aid and two of the horses were down, their legs thrashing as the water turned red around them.

A hundred paces further down the column cries of consternation rang out as a second ambush caused more casualties. Valerius grabbed the guide's reins and dragged the horse with him as he doubled back down the line of men, sending spray flying. As he rode, he ordered the bowmen they passed to stay alert and watch the reeds.

The quick-witted *decurio* closest to the point of the second attack led a ten-man section of archers into the bulrushes in pursuit of the attackers. Within moments a violent flurry of activity among the reeds ended with shouts of fear and cries of agony. When Valerius arrived a camel stood with its head down and a spear hanging from its belly. Nearby, a cavalryman was up to his waist in a cloud of red, cutting the throat of a dying horse. Valerius spun as the reeds parted behind him, but it was only the officer returning. One of his archers hauled a flat-bottomed skiff with four bearded men lying in the bottom riddled with arrows, their blood staining the wood crimson.

'Judaean rebels,' he announced unnecessarily.

The sound of churning water heralded the return of Gaulan and his rearguard, galloping up the side of the column in a flurry of spray. 'You too?' The Chalcidean shook his head. 'They've hit the rear five or six times. No casualties among the men, only horses and camels.'

'They only need to kill the horses.' Valerius's heart sank as he worked out the implications of what had just happened. 'A horse is an easy target and every man on foot in this swamp slows us down to a crawl. They know exactly where we are and all they have to do is shadow us, picking off a few horses at a time. We can't afford to keep taking losses, so we'll eventually be forced to return to the causeway.'

'Where they'll be waiting for us.'

Valerius knew what the cavalryman was thinking. It would have been better to risk charging the barricade and accepting the casualties needed to make a breakthrough. At least some of them would have survived. Maybe he was right, but they couldn't turn back time. 'Form the men into half-squadrons in tight formation. Those leading the camels will need to be on the outer flank away from the reeds. Ten paces between each squadron.'

Gaulan nodded approvingly. 'So each half-squadron is close enough to support the next. If one is attacked the units to the front and the rear hook round to snap up the attackers.'

'They can't have that many boats. Every one we capture weakens them.'

'We should kill him.' Gaulan glared at the hunter. 'He must have known they were collecting skiffs.'

'Not yet,' Valerius said. 'I may have a use for him.'

He returned to the front of the column with the guide. The attacks became less effective against the new formation, but they continued, with a steady loss of horses that he knew couldn't be sustained for much longer.

'Couldn't we fire the reeds and burn them out?' Tabitha suggested. It would have been a good idea at the height of summer and with the wind in the right direction. But this was spring and the reed beds glowed with the emerald shoots of moist new growth. There had to be another way.

But there was no other way. The only option was to continue plodding southwards with every step through the glutinous sucking mud and belly-deep water taking its toll on their mounts. An hour later even Valerius was beginning to despair. Gaulan reported that men and horses were close to exhaustion and called a halt to allow them to rest. The animals stood with their heads down to the water, flanks sweat-slick and breath coming in sharp snorts; even the camels, hardiest of beasts, appeared diminished by their ordeal.

'We must either find somewhere dry to rest and feed the horses or we have to fight,' the Chalcidean insisted. 'But the decision has to be made soon or the horses won't be fit to fight at all.'

Valerius nodded, hopelessly searching the watery landscape for somewhere that would provide sanctuary. He pointed to the guide. 'Tell him we have to find a way back to the causeway road. If possible we need somewhere we can form up to sweep aside any rebels who oppose us there.'

178

The guide looked aghast. 'He says there is no such place,' Gaulan translated. 'All he knows is paths where two men might ride side by side. It would be suicide. I believe he foresees his own fate if he is captured and known to have helped us.'

'Suicide or not, we don't have any choice.'

'We could form up into smaller groups and scatter,' Gaulan suggested gloomily. 'Some might get through.'

'But we would have failed Titus,' Valerius said. 'And I will not fail him.'

Suddenly the guide burst into animated voice. The Chalcidean commander ordered him to slow down, then turned to Valerius. 'Finally, he understands the true gravity of our situation. It appears there is an island large enough to accommodate us. It is the most distant of that group there.' He pointed to a barely visible clump of brush on the horizon. 'Reaching it will be difficult and dangerous. He says there are sinkholes and quicksand, and he's not completely certain of the shallows. Ordinarily he would not have suggested it because of the perils it involves, but in the circumstances it may offer us sanctuary, if not salvation.'

Tabitha came to Valerius's side and laid a hand on his arm, ignoring the looks of surprise on the faces of the men around her. 'If we take the path to the causeway you think we will all die?'

'Most, if not all.'

She looked across the wide expanse of water separating them from the islands and shivered. 'But if we survive the night we will give the gods another chance to look kindly upon us.'

'The horses are almost done,' Gaulan counselled. 'If he's wrong and we can't reach the island, we may never make it back.'

Valerius met Tabitha's eyes. 'We go,' he said loudly enough for the men around him to hear, and immediately shouted commands echoed down the line of cavalrymen, horses and camels. He lowered his voice. 'But no arguments this time. You stay close to Serpentius in the centre of the column.' The order clearly annoyed her, but she bit her lip and allowed the Spaniard to lead her away.

Despite the attacks, the beds of reeds and bulrushes had offered an illusion of safety. Out in the open water at the head of the long column of twos Valerius felt terribly exposed and even the most experienced cavalrymen looked nervously around them. With reason. Beyond the far end of the column a flat-bottomed skiff emerged from the reeds and floated just out of bow range. Valerius had a sense of the two occupants shouting to someone in the reeds. He had no doubt that in moments another skiff would be speeding back to the causeway to inform the leader of the Judaean rebels of their change of course.

The water grew appreciably deeper as they moved towards the centre of the lake and Valerius was relieved when it settled at chest height on his horse. It appeared obvious their guide was less sanguine about their prospects. The hunter stared at the water in front of him with an intensity that should have parted it, all the time muttering to himself and emitting occasional squeaks of alarm. Fortunately, he retained enough nerve to direct a string of panicked instructions at Gaulan and as a result the column snaked across the lake like a giant python. Whether by Fortuna's favour or good judgement they'd managed this far unscathed, but Valerius knew it couldn't last. Inevitably a rider would react too late and the turn would be a little further ahead than the original order.

If he'd had spears he would have marked the turns with their shafts. Without any points of reference he feared any error would be multiplied across a thousand animals and the deviation might be as much as fifty or sixty feet.

A loud bray of alarm alerted him. When he looked over his shoulder a camel near the rear had floundered out of its depth, weighed down by sacks of fodder. Two riders went to try to drag it back, but soon their horses were swimming and it was clear the beast was doomed. The handler had thrown himself from the lead horse to rescue his animal, but all he could do was cling to the mane of one of the rescuers. Meanwhile, the animal bellowed plaintively and struggled to keep its head above water, until, inevitably, it disappeared altogether.

'No!'

The shrill cry came from Tabitha a hundred paces away and at first Valerius was surprised that she should be so concerned about the loss of a single camel. It was only then he noticed the original craft monitoring their progress had been joined by six or seven more. While the rearguard stared at the drowning camel, two of the skiffs darted in and launched spears that brought down more precious horses. The first fled out of range before the Emesan archers could reply, but the man poling the second panicked and lost control. Valerius saw him pirouette like a dancer and plunge over the edge of the skiff. It wasn't difficult to imagine what was happening when the Emesans surrounded the vessel, their swords flailing at the unfortunate occupants.

'Let's hope they've learned their lesson.' Valerius couldn't hide his irritation. 'We can't afford to lose any more horses.'

But the fate of the horses lay with the gods and some-times the gods do not appreciate being lectured. The moment Gaulan urged the guide's mount into motion it reared up as if it had seen a snake, almost pitching the duck hunter from the saddle. One of the animal's rear hooves had become entangled by a root or trapped between boulders and it gave a panicked scream. With a convulsive heave the horse broke free before anyone could react and bolted in a shower of spray. It had barely gone a dozen strides before it found deeper water and stopped as if it had run into a wall. This time the guide pitched over its shoulder and disappeared instantly beneath the surface. An expectant hush followed as the men at the head of the column waited for him to reappear.

Like everyone else, Valerius expected the guide to rise spluttering from the water, but nothing happened and he kicked Lunaris into motion as the full implications of losing the man hit him. They couldn't go forward and if they were forced back the horses would be on their knees long before they reached the causeway – if they got that far. Lunaris surged through the chest-deep water to the point where the guide had disappeared. The horse struggled to stay afloat, but Valerius's hopes rose as he saw a pale, terrified face staring up from just beneath the surface. Pale fingers scrabbled towards him and he reached down with his left hand to snatch a handful of cloth and haul the drowning man to the surface.

His success brought a cheer from the watching men, but even as he turned the horse towards the main column disaster struck. If the hunter had stayed calm it would have been the work of seconds to pull him clear. Instead, in his terror he clawed at Valerius's cloak and tried to drag himself on to Lunaris's back. Valerius was already off balance and as the hunter dragged himself to safety he hauled the Roman out of the saddle. Before Valerius had a chance to cry out the cold water closed over him and he felt the weight of his armour pulling him into the depths. He clawed at the straps, but with only the fingers of one hand it was impossible. With a thrill of fear he realized he was drowning.

Lunaris's legs kicked through the water above him and he reached out, but it was too far and what would he have done in any case? He tried desperately not to breathe, but he knew it was only a matter of time. The armour seemed to close in around his chest and he groaned with the pressure of it. Water forced its way up his nose giving him an irrational urge to sneeze. He fought panic and prayed that someone would come to his rescue, his only consolation being that saving the guide might yet save the column. And Tabitha. Maybe it would be better just to open his mouth and let the water pour in. Just as he made his decision a massive disturbance churned the water around him and his vision dimmed.

'Valerius.' The voice was soft, but urgent.

He managed to open one eye. The sun's rays framed Tabitha's concerned face and he wondered if he'd been transported to some kind of alternative Elysium. She dabbed his skull, quickly dispelling the illusion as a dart of pain made him wince. It felt as if his head had been used as a battering ram. Something moved beneath him and he realized he was lying over the backs of two horses, one of them Lunaris. Beyond Tabitha a ring of other faces stared down at him, among them Gaulan and Serpentius, but one was missing.

'The hunter . . . ?'

'They're pumping him out,' Gaulan assured him. 'He'll live, but we thought we'd lost you.'

'What happened? How . . . ?'

'Tribune Paternus's servant came to your rescue,' Tabitha explained. 'He forced his way to where you disappeared and dived in after you. We thought it was in vain, but when Serpentius joined him they were able to get you out.'

'Thank you.' Valerius turned to Paternus. 'And please pass on my thanks to your man. What happened to my head?'

'We think one of the horses must have kicked you.' Willing hands helped pull Valerius up and with difficulty he straightened in the saddle. By now the sun hung low in the western sky with the island still at least an hour away. 'Can you ride?'

'I'll be all right,' Valerius said, and immediately vomited into the disturbed water.

Darkness was falling as they urged their horses on to the low bank of earth and scrub. Not much of an island, but enough to accommodate the horses and camels and dry land, any land, was better than being in the water. They fed the animals and Gaulan set guards around the island in case the Judaeans used their skiffs to try the kind of murder raid in which the rebels specialized. Valerius sought out Paternus's servant and thanked the man, promising a more tangible reward when they reached Titus, but Gavvo only grunted and studied him with eyes as dead as one of the hunter's ducks. Valerius shook his head at the needless discourtesy and strode to where Serpentius had spread his blanket in a clump of bushes. After the Roman had changed into dry clothes a meal of stale Syrian flatbread and a handful of olives washed down by rough red wine helped revive him. When they finished he was surprised to see the Spaniard pick up his own bedding roll. Serpentius saw his look.

'I won't be far away. Shout if you need me.'

'I didn't get the chance to thank you for today.'

Serpentius shrugged. 'It was nothing. I'd probably never have got to you in time if Paternus's man hadn't reached you first. All I did was get wet and help drag you clear.'

'Thank you in any case.' There was a long pause as the two men contemplated what might have been, before Valerius spoke again. 'Gavvo appears to have had a great deal of trouble getting me to the surface. Do you think he was trying as hard as he might?'

The former gladiator looked thoughtful. 'If he was trying to kill you he disguised it well.'

Valerius let him walk a few paces.

'Serpentius?'

'Yes?'

'I remember when we were shipwrecked you told me you couldn't swim.'

Serpentius laughed. 'I must have forgotten.'

When he was gone Valerius pulled up his blanket and let the waves of exhaustion wash over him. He was too tired to even think about what would happen tomorrow. For the moment they were alive and safe. After the interminable watery ordeal of today, that was enough. He didn't know how long he'd been sleeping when the warm body in the cloak burrowed in beside him.

'This is unseemly,' he groaned.

'No,' she said. 'This is right.'

Beneath the cloak she was naked.

It was astonishing how quickly his strength returned.

XVIII

Valerius woke alone, with a sense of loss that wasn't allowed to last long.

'Come, you should see this,' Serpentius urged before he had time to don his armour.

Gaulan, Paternus and Tabitha – whose slanted blue eyes gave him a covert look that sent a shiver down his spine – were already standing by the waterline staring at the opposite shore. On the far side of the water in the soft golden light of the dawn the smoke of at least a hundred cooking fires hung in the still air like the pillars of a temple. A few dozen men and women stared back from the shoreline a hundred and fifty paces away. Beyond them hundreds more went about the business of preparing the morning meal, cutting wood and building small shelters from the branches. A man in the closest group sprang forward into the shallows and began to dance and caper, screaming what could only be abuse.

'Ah, the morning's entertainment,' Paternus sniffed. 'What does he say?'

'He's going to cut out our livers,' Tabitha translated for him. 'And feed them to his dogs.'

'Hardly original.'

'Oh, there were other things,' she laughed. 'But not the kind a lady should talk about.'

'How many do we think they are?' Valerius changed the subject.

'Not less than the thousand the scouts estimated were holding the road yesterday,' Gaulan answered. 'But there could be more in the trees. They look as if they're here to stay.'

'Wouldn't you?' Valerius studied the far bank. 'They have us where they want us. We can sit here until we're gnawing on the bones of our horses, or we can attack. If we attack it will be through water and we'll hit the shore with little or no momentum.'

'But we're archers,' the Chalcidean growled, insulted that for the second time the Roman showed no faith in his men's fighting abilities. 'We can stand off in the shallows and rake them with showers of arrows. That will soon see them off.'

'They'll have salted the shallows with traps,' Valerius countered patiently. 'See how carefully our entertainer walks as he returns to the shore. Pits with wooden spikes. And beyond them, within spear throw, they're already building barricades. All I'm saying is that we don't need to charge them like a bull at a gate.'

'So we attack them at night?'

'Just before dawn. They'll build fires along the shore at night so they can see us coming, but they'll allow them to die down as sunrise approaches. That's when we strike. When the guards are thinking about their stomachs and the rest are still dreaming.'

'But we attack?'

'Of course we attack,' Valerius grinned. 'Do you think I want to sit in the middle of this flea-ridden swamp for a day longer than necessary?'

'Can you do it?' Tabitha asked as they walked back to the main camp.

'It won't be easy,' Valerius admitted. 'But if the gods will it we can win. They are rebels and Gaulan's men and the Emesans are soldiers. If we can surprise them, our discipline will always overcome enthusiasm.'

She held his eyes for a moment and nodded. As she walked away she was immediately replaced by Paternus. 'You will allow me to join this expedition?' the tribune demanded.

Valerius reluctantly shook his head. 'This is a job for chosen men who know and trust each other's skills and courage.' He saw Paternus bridle at what he perceived as a slight to his honour and hurried on. 'I suggest you stay on the island and command the rearguard. Someone has to protect the baggage and the lady Tabitha.'

'You do not trust me to fight?'

Valerius gripped the other man's arm. 'I trust you to *lead*, Paternus.'

The scarred tribune stared at him for a long moment. Eventually he shook his arm free and walked off, leaving Valerius to wonder if he'd lost the art of command. Two years ago he would have convinced Paternus that it was in all their interests and made him feel honoured to take charge of the rearguard. When he reached his bedding, the Judaean duck hunter was waiting with Gaulan, his eyes wary, tensed like an animal ready to run for its life.

Valerius sat on his blanket and motioned to the man to take his seat opposite. 'What is his name?'

Gaulan put the question. 'He is called Simon Ben Huleh.'

'Ask Simon about the shore to the south of the island. How does it lie and what is the terrain like?'

The hunter's wide eyes darted from one man to the other. Valerius sensed the calculations going through his mind; the weighing of the scales. What was to be gained from the truth? What was the price of a lie? Gaulan drew the knife from his belt, picked up a nearby stone, studied it for grain and began to whet the blade.

Simon's eyes widened further at sight of the knife. Words began to pour from him and his hands formed patterns in the air. 'It is not the shore proper, because the lake continues for many miles, but a peninsula, shaped thus.' The Chalcidean used the knife point to draw a lopsided triangle the shape of a shark's fin, with the causeway at its base. 'On the side closest to us a strip about one hundred paces wide has been cleared over the years, because this is where the king's hunters have their camp each year when the great flocks come here to roost. They net duck and other waterfowl in their thousands and cranes by the hundred. The number of smaller birds taken is countless. This is in the month of Cheshvan, you understand, when Simon is prohibited to hunt. Despite the slaughter many more thousands escape, and—'

'With respect to Simon, I am not here to hunt,' Valerius said evenly. 'Ask him how far this shore runs to the west.'

'He has no concept of far, but a man could reach the point in a skiff in the time it takes the sun to go from here to here.' He created an arc in the sky that equated to approximately one hour.

'And what is beyond the cleared strip?'

A little later Valerius and Gaulan were joined by the Emesan cavalry prefect. Valerius felt a slight surge of irritation when Paternus followed, but knew there was

189

no changing it. Valerius was a landless exile, Paternus a ranking Roman officer who would have been perfectly within his rights to take charge of the column. Valerius sensed that something more than politeness stopped him, but he wasn't sure what. When they were gathered around the improvised map he'd drawn in the sand he outlined the situation as Simon had told it.

'I'd hoped the west of the peninsula might provide us with some kind of way out, but our guide says it's an impassable mix of forest and deep swamp. Still, that might have its advantages. Here is the forest in the centre where the Judaeans have made their shelters.' He used a twig to indicate a group of circles. 'It's possible they also spread east towards the causeway. But the key is the cleared strip, which is well guarded opposite, but runs for another mile, at least, to the west.'

'You say a night attack won't work,' Gaulan growled. 'I accept the bulk of the enemy will be half asleep just before dawn, but even if the fires are dying the guards will still be alert. The others will soon wake up if they know we're coming. How does this help us?'

'Because I don't intend them to know we're coming until we're among them.' Valerius met his unflinching gaze.

The commander of the Emesan archers snorted in disbelief. 'Are we djinns to be able to transport six hundred horses across the lake and set them down in silence among our enemies?'

'No,' Valerius admitted, 'but horses can swim.'

'The guards will slaughter the first men on the beach. You said so yourself.' It was obvious Gaulan had as many doubts as his fellow officer.

'We won't be on that beach.' Valerius struck a line through the marked defences with his twig. 'We'll use this one.' He indicated a position to the far west. 'And the reason they won't know we are there is because they'll think all the beasts of Hades are attacking them from here.' The twig flicked back to the base of the triangle.

Gaulan suddenly showed a new interest. 'How?'

'We've captured three skiffs,' Valerius reminded him. 'They ride low in the water so they'll be difficult to see in the dark. Simon,' he saw the puzzlement in their eyes, 'the duck hunter, will take one skiff west and land six men to kill any guards. I doubt there will be many because we can't escape from that side.'

'But we can attack.'

'That's right. You form up your men and wait for the signal.'

'What will the signal be?'

'Hopefully a few dozen burning huts.' Valerius smiled grimly. 'The other two skiffs will land amongst the reeds to the east. Ten men to a skiff, five on board and five hanging on to the sides, all dressed as Judaeans, or enough to look like one in the semi-dark. Twenty men can cause a great deal of chaos with surprise on their side, especially twenty men who act and sound like two or three times that number.' He turned to Gaulan. 'Charge when you see the flames, but tell your men to be vigilant for one of these.' He produced a strip of white cloth and tied it to his arm. 'Because that will be the sign of a friend.'

'And who will lead these twenty heroes who are now fighting for their lives among a thousand Zealots?'

Valerius looked up into Tabitha's appraising eyes.

It was even colder in the water than Valerius remembered. He was beginning to regret the impulse that had

191

made him insist on being one of the group hanging on to the skiff's side. His naked body had grown numb long before they approached the bank of reeds to the east of the Judaean watchfires. He flexed the fingers of his left hand and prayed it had enough feeling in it to hold a sword in a few moments' time. In front of him he could see the scarred dome of Serpentius's shaven head.

Tabitha had argued against his inclusion among the group, but Valerius knew this was where the greatest guile and, more important, the greatest resolve would be required. The only way he could ask these men to risk their lives was to lead by example. So much could go wrong. If even one guard survived long enough to raise the alarm the attack was more likely to fail than not. The defenders would swarm west with their spears and their knives and slaughter Gaulan's horsemen while they were still swimming their animals ashore. The Chalcidean had been horrified when Valerius pointed out that the only way to swim a horse so far was for the archers to float alongside them. That meant their bow strings would become wet and a wet bow string was as good as no bow string at all. So there would be no long-range killing from the shallows if they were discovered. But every archer had a sword, similar to the long *spatha* carried by Roman auxiliary cavalry. Those long blades would cause carnage and terror if they were carried against an unprepared enemy driven to panic by a determined attack on their rear. So the chance must be taken.

Paternus had wanted to bring the rearguard across from the island against the enemy flank when the main attack struck. Valerius agreed the suggestion had merit. Another surprise blow might be enough to turn a battle teetering on a knife edge into an overwhelming victory. But if the attack failed and Gaulan's men were dead and scattered it would leave the baggage train – and Tabitha – at the mercy of the Judaeans. Valerius doubted much mercy would be forthcoming. So he'd told Paternus he must hold his position. As a precaution, two of Gaulan's men would ignore the fighting and ride directly for the causeway and the road to Caesarea Philippi. If the worst happened, reinforcements would arrive by noon the following day in time to drive the victorious Judaeans away and rescue the survivors.

But that was in the future. The skiff finally reached the stand of reeds near the shore and now the packed stems were trying to tear him from the little craft. He heard the men in the water mutter muffled curses and hissed for quiet. Trying not to make a sound he used his free arm and feet to help propel him to the bank. Agonizing seconds passed until he felt one foot touch bottom and the slight crunch as the skiff hit shore. In complete silence the men on board the boats hauled the others aboard. They dried themselves off and threw on tunics and robes that had been stowed during the voyage. Serpentius helped Valerius strap on his sword and dagger and the Roman stepped ashore calling softly for the men to gather around him.

He waited till they were close enough to hear his hoarse whisper. 'I will lead. We take it slowly and make no noise until we're sure we're among them. If we're challenged, hold the guard's attention until Serpentius can deal with him. Once we see the fires we split up into fours as we agreed. One man to snatch a brand and burn the nearest hut. Kill everything that gets in your way: they will give you no mercy if the reverse is true.' After much thought, Valerius had decided that the burning huts might not be enough of a signal, hidden among the trees as they were. To make sure, he'd delegated one archer to loose a fire arrow when they had the enemy's attention. 'When you see the arrow, remember to knot the white cloth round your right shoulder, otherwise you're as likely to be killed by a friend as an enemy. Now, follow me.'

He led the way through the threatening darkness, keeping to the fringe of the forest and guided by the lights of the watchfires to his right. The clothes he wore had been taken from a dead Judaean and his nose wrinkled with the stink of another man's sweat and dried blood. He took his time, placing his feet carefully and feeling for any twigs or branches that might snap and give away his position to an alert guard.

It was unnaturally quiet. There should have been night sounds. The shriek of a hunting owl. The bark of a fox. Nothing. His ears strained for the faraway cry that would signal that Gaulan and his men had been detected, but all he could hear was the faint crackle from the fires, the soft rush of waves on the shore and the laboured, nervous breathing of the men ranged close by. Like him they would be gripping and regripping their sword hilts. Like him their hearts would be thundering in their chests fit to burst out. They were so close now they could smell the latrine stink of the scattered shit pits that were the mark of every gathering of ill-disciplined barbarians. In the darkness every shadowy bush and tree appeared as an enemy waiting to pounce, his stillness a testament to his skills.

Where were the guards? Valerius's mind screamed at him that it was a trap and to get out while they could. They must have been seen as they entered the reeds and the enemy was allowing them deeper and deeper into his territory. Serpentius was closest to him and he could sense a similar confusion in the Spaniard. With every step he expected to hear a triumphant shriek and the rush from the shadows that would herald their deaths. But it didn't come. Instead, they came level with the watchfires, still apparently unseen.

He turned to Serpentius. The former gladiator's eyes glittered in the firelight and Valerius shrugged in answer to the unspoken question in them. They'd come this far . . . Gaulan's men would be landing now, or forming up. He nodded and ran for the nearest fire, followed by four others. In the glaring light from the fires his back tensed for the strike of a spear, but suddenly he could feel the heat of the flames on his face. He picked up the unburned end of a brand out of the glowing coals and sprinted with it to the forest. Where was it? There! Just a large heap of twigs and leaves, a rebel shelter capable of holding four or five men. As his companions screamed to draw attention and hunted potential victims through the trees he thrust the brand into the twigs and waited until the material caught. In the darkness around him other shelters took light and flared up in explosions of fire and sparks. He ran through the smoke to a second shelter, leaving the others to deal with the occupants of the first. Where were the screams and the shouts of panic? Where was the opposition? He stumbled to a dazed halt as he realized it was all pointless.

The Judaeans were gone.

XIX

Valerius ordered one section of men to check the ground towards the causeway for any sign of stragglers or a surprise attack. Perhaps the rebels had been warned of Gaulan's presence and moved out to meet him, but he didn't think so. They would have left their women behind with their baggage. Here there was nothing but the detritus of an abandoned camp. He called the signaller bowman to his side and held out the glowing brand of the torch. The archer placed an arrow wound with pitch-soaked cloth against it until it lit. The moment the flame appeared the man drew back his bow and loosed so the fire arrow arced into the night before falling with a sharp hiss just off shore.

'Now loose another.' Valerius hoped that Gaulan would realize the second arrow signified a change in circumstances and would make him wary enough to rein in the headlong charge they'd planned. As the second arrow sailed skywards he called the men together and led them down to the shoreline, where the watchfires were beginning to burn down. 'Throw more wood on the fires and make sure your white cloths show clearly,' he ordered. 'No point in dying now.'

He sat on the trampled ground and stared out to where the faint outline of the island could be seen against the first hint of dawn. Tabitha would be watching the shore and wondering why she didn't hear the noise of men fighting for their lives. Would she think he was dead? He wished he had some way of sending a message to her.

The sound of muted thunder reverberating in the distance interrupted his thoughts. Not a charge, Gaulan wouldn't cut them loose until they could see their enemy, but hundreds of hooves approaching at the canter. Valerius motioned the others to stay where they were by the fires and stood up. The thunder came closer and the sound intensified until it seemed to shake the air and the very ground beneath his feet. A grey mass appeared, approaching at speed in the faint gilded light of the new dawn, rapidly transforming into individual groups of horses and men. Valerius could see the pennant of Gaulan's Chalcideans at their head. He stepped out into the open space between the shore and the trees.

If Gaulan saw the man standing in his way there was no slackening of the pace. Valerius felt as if the wall of horsemen were about to charge right over him. A blast from a trumpet finally saw the speed slacken as the leading troopers reined in their horses less than ten paces away. Gaulan stared impassively from beneath his pot helmet, his signaller and his standard-bearer curbing their excited horses by his side.

'It seems you have won this battle on your own, Gaius Valerius Verrens.'

'Alas, there was no battle,' Valerius said. 'Your fame preceded you and the rebels fled at the first hint of your coming.'

The two men grinned at each other for a long moment, before Gaulan sobered. 'Why would they leave when they had us trapped? You were wrong about the west shore. It had been well fortified. If they'd stayed they would have slaughtered us.'

'Then let us be thankful they didn't. As to the why, I think we will find out soon enough. But first let us send out pickets to guard the road while Paternus brings the baggage ashore.'

They discussed their next move while a message was sent out to the island. Gaulan surprised Valerius by suggesting they retire to Caesarea Philippi and wait until the situation became clearer. 'We can replace our supplies and get the latest news on Titus's whereabouts. Two or three days will make no difference now. Yes,' he answered the question in Valerius's eyes, 'all this has made me cautious, perhaps overly so. But these Judaeans are more numerous and cunning than I had been led to believe. We could have been wiped out.'

His view was borne out when it became light enough to count the Judaean huts. There were at least five hundred of them and signs of many more men sleeping out in the open. They'd been facing twice as many rebels as they'd estimated. Even if things had worked exactly to plan Valerius knew he'd have been fortunate if a quarter of the Emesan and Chalcidean force had survived. Despite that, he argued against any retreat. The rebels had given them a chance and they should take it, working their way south as swiftly as they could and resupplying at cities loyal to Rome.

As it turned out, the decision was made for them.

Tabitha and Claudius Paternus had just reached the shore at the head of the baggage train when one of Gaulan's scouts galloped in from the causeway. Before he could pass on his message Valerius heard a blare of trumpets that made the hair on the back of his neck stand on end. He glanced at Paternus and the scarred tribune smiled.

'A *cornu*,' he confirmed, referring to the curved trumpet used by legionary signallers.

'A legionary column marching down the road from Caesaria Philippi,' the rider blurted to Gaulan.

Valerius smiled at the Chalcidean. 'Then let us go to meet them.'

But if Gaulan's men and the Emesan archers were going to meet a column of Roman legionaries, their commanders were determined they'd be dressed like soldiers. They'd been forced to leave their protective mail behind on the island when they'd swum their horses to the gathering point for the attack. Now they had to wait until it was unpacked from the camels.

In the meantime, Valerius exchanged his blood-stained robe for a fresh tunic before riding out to meet the Roman column with Tabitha and Paternus, now resplendent in the uniform and armour of a *tribunus laticlavius*.

By the time they reached the causeway the legionary detachment's commander was already in conversation with the horsemen Gaulan had sent to guard the road. The Chalcideans looked none too happy, surrounded as they were by twenty or thirty of the legion's own cavalry. The questioner was a compact, stocky man wearing a legate's sash and gilded armour, which meant they were dealing with a full legion, or the better part of one. That surprised Valerius, but not so much as the man's identity.

One of the general's aides alerted him to the arrival of the newcomers, and he broke away with his escort from the little knot of men. He was naturally drawn to the figure in the tribune's armour, but Valerius met his eyes and saw a hint of recognition that lasted all of a heartbeat.

Paternus rapped his fist against his breastplate in salute and gave his particulars and his orders to join Titus. He introduced Tabitha as a member of the Emesan royal family, but curiously didn't mention Valerius by name, only as 'a Roman citizen travelling with our column'. Valerius bowed his head and the legate acknowledged it with a tight smile before turning back to Paternus. 'Aulus Larcius Lepidus, commanding Tenth Fretensis, and you are a welcome sight, tribune, for I am short of senior officers. It may be that I have work for you if you are willing. We both have the same destination, after all.'

Paternus said he would be delighted, though the part of his face Valerius could see didn't mirror the sentiment.

'These men,' Lepidus indicated the Chalcidean horse soldiers, 'have been telling me something of your predicament and it corresponds with our own experience. The Emperor cleared this area of rebels, but like rats they have a habit of wriggling their way back if you don't keep killing them. They were able to build up their strength during the troubles with Vitellius. The Tenth has been given the job of destroying them once and for all.' He removed his helmet and wiped sweat from his forehead before replacing it. 'We were clearing the mountains around Caesarea Philippi when we heard of a force blocking the road by the lake. You must have been a day ahead of us. We destroyed one of their bands last night and my spies told of a larger one camped in this area, though for what purpose they could not say. It was my intention to attack them at first light, but,' he gave a weary shrug, 'I see they are already gone.'

A bearded man dressed in voluminous eastern robes rode up to join the general. Tall in the saddle,

200

his aristocratic features and air of careworn nobility reminded Valerius of a man he had once seen die on a cross. Flecks of grey speckled his beard and the immaculately styled curls of his dark hair, but he couldn't have been more than forty years old. Valerius sensed Tabitha tense as penetrating brown eyes swept over them. When he glanced down her knuckles were white with the fierceness of her grip on the reins.

'My adviser on Judaean matters,' Lepidus introduced the newcomer with a hint of mockery. 'His given name is Joseph Ben Mahtityahu, but since the Emperor took the misguided decision not to cut his throat he's taken to calling himself Josephus, which is easier on us all. Josephus can smell a rebel from twenty miles, can't you, Josephus?'

'You honour me, lord legate,' the Judaean bowed low in the saddle and his tone matched the legionary commander's, 'but I fear you exaggerate my powers. There is no magic or sorcery involved. Long acquaintance with these rogues has given me an insight into their ways.'

'Long acquaintance indeed.' Lepidus's eyes fixed on the other man and Valerius noticed that there was no love there. 'We suspect Josephus was one of the instigators of the rebellion. He may even have been the man who planned the ambush that took the Twelfth's eagle, though he's understandably reluctant to claim any credit for it. Long enough certainly to become a general in their army, who commanded this entire area. Is that not so, Josephus?'

'A man of any ability will rise quickly in a rabble,' the Judaean replied with false modesty. 'And as you said yourself, my dear Lepidus, take any hundred Jews and you will find at least one general, two princes, a

201

moneylender and ninety-six priests. As for the rest? Rumour and base falsity put about by my many enemies. If there was any truth in them would the Emperor have allowed me to keep my head and raised me so high in his trust that even you accept my advice?' Lepidus's smile tightened, but before he could reply the Judaean ostentatiously sniffed the air. 'My nose tells me that this particular band of rebels are even now returning to their stronghold at Gamala.'

'Gamala?' Lepidus shot the Judaean a look of alarm. 'Vespasian razed the defences at Gamala three years ago and wiped out every rebel defending the place.'

'As you have often told me, general,' Josephus's dark eyes twinkled, 'the Jew is like the weed in a vegetable patch. Stamp him down one day and he'll reappear the next with ten of his offspring. Gamala is a natural fortress. They have restored the walls as much as they are able with their limited resources.'

The legate frowned. 'Can we take it with four cohorts?'

'Oh, I think that should be possible,' the Judaean said cheerfully. 'After all, I designed the original defences.'

Lepidus made his decision. 'Pass the word to the tribunes to water the horses and have their men fed. We march in two hours and we'll be marching fast. Have them track down any centurions who took part in the original siege of Gamala and I'll meet them in my tent in an hour.' He turned to Paternus. 'I'm afraid I'm going to have to appropriate these archers of yours, tribune. My camp prefect will give them their positions in the column, but I'll need one squadron to act as a screen out front.' Paternus frowned, but Lepidus forestalled any protest. 'Titus will thank you for it. Jerusalem will be the toughest nut he's ever had to crack. If he's going to do it his supply lines must be secure. You,' he turned sharply to face Valerius, 'mysterious traveller with no name. Come with me. I want to inspect your documents.'

In a tent by the side of the causeway, Lepidus removed his helmet and dropped into a padded chair with a sigh. An orderly brought a jar of wine. The legate filled two cups and handed one to Valerius. 'You are thinner than I remember, Valerius, and something tells me you haven't laughed for a long time. Can it really be four years?'

Valerius returned his old friend's smile. The two men had served together under Gnaeus Domitius Corbulo during his campaign against the Parthian king Vologases. Lepidus had been a tribune in the legion he now commanded. 'Four years or a lifetime, Aulus. A civil war doesn't give a man much to laugh about. You, on the other hand, seem to have prospered since Armenia?'

Lepidus stood up and started to pace the tent, as if he found stillness oppressive. Valerius had a feeling he wasn't even aware of it. 'Traianus, who then commanded the Tenth, was kind enough to commend me to General Vespasian for my diligence during the campaign. By his good offices I was awarded the quaestorship of Creta et Cyrenaica. The appointment was Nero's but the province is so insignificant that I was left to my own devices as Galba and Otho fell. When the legions hailed Vespasian I was able to repay his kindness by supporting him.' He shook his head as if he could barely believe his good fortune. 'When command of my old legion fell vacant he turned to me. Now I spend my days killing Judaeans and my nights planning to kill them.'

'I take it from the caution of your welcome that you're aware of my current status?' Valerius said warily.

'Condemned, reprieved – I congratulate you on that – and sent into the wilderness. Under normal circumstances I'd appoint you to my staff, but Titus—'

'I understand,' Valerius interrupted. 'You have to be cautious. How is he?'

'You'll find him changed. Being potential heir to the Empire weighs upon him, but not as much as the responsibility his father has placed on him in Judaea. These archers you've brought may put a smile on his face for once. When Mucianus left for Rome with the Sixth Ferrata last year he took a detachment from the Tenth and two other legions with him. Worse, he persuaded Vespasian to give him just about every auxiliary cavalry *ala* in Judaea and Syria. Titus thought he'd have them back by the time he marched on Jerusalem, but Mucianus now has his own problems on the Rhenus frontier. We need every man we can get if we're to storm those walls.' A shadow fell over the legate's handsome features. 'This is not like other wars, Valerius. You give the Germans or even the Parthians a bloody nose and they'll go back to their huts or their palaces and nurse their injuries. Only when the memory of the pain fades will they come back for more. The Judaeans are different. You destroy them in one place and they turn up in another. Josephus's tale of the vegetable patch wasn't far wrong. Kill one and another ten spring up to replace him. They're persistent. Good haters. They'll kill for a slight to their god, their religion or their family, and they don't mind dying. When Vespasian captured Josephus at Jotapata, he was the last man left alive. The rest had drawn lots and killed each other one by one. Men, women and children. They're barely human. Fanatics.'

'But not Josephus.'

Lepidus produced a bark of bitter laughter. 'Josephus is a survivor. In the early days of the rebellion his own people tried to kill him more than once . . .'

'Sicarii?'

'Or some other Zealot faction. You know of them?'

'We came across some of their work on the way here.' He explained about the encounter with Tabitha, but kept his voice emotionless as if her rescue were something he'd already put behind him.

'A rare beauty,' Lepidus grinned. 'Especially to a man who's been on a diet of fat slave girls and skinny Judaean matrons for the past year. Paternus said she was handmaiden to Queen Berenice? That doesn't surprise me. They say the lady likes to surround herself with pretty things. She's another worth a second look, by the way, but only if a man's willing to risk a posting to a dusty fort by the Dead Sea.'

'Why did Vespasian let him live?' Valerius manoeuvred the subject back to Josephus.

'Josephus may be an unprincipled turncoat who would betray his own brother, but he's a clever unprincipled turncoat. He knows the history of his own people better than any priest. When they dragged him before Vespasian, he first charmed the general, as he was then – you've seen the bastard at work – then quoted an ancient prophecy that he claimed forecast the war between Jews and Romans. And not just that. Vespasian would become Emperor of Rome. Mystical rubbish if you ask me, but Vespasian was convinced enough to keep him as a hostage and interpreter. Never underestimate Josephus's talent for survival.'

*

'You are surprised to see me.'

'I'd hoped you were dead.' Anyone watching them together by the tent Josephus shared with his servant would have seen Tabitha smiling sweetly, but her voice was filled with loathing.

'Of course.' Josephus ignored the contempt in her tone. 'I can understand that, but we must be friends, you and I.'

'I would rather befriend a cobra,' she glared. 'I'd certainly feel safer in its presence. You make my skin crawl.'

'Insult me as you will,' the Judaean said with a magnanimous wave of the hand. 'But I serve Titus Flavius Vespasian, as does your mistress. That places us on the same side of the balance – at least for now.'

'You betray your people and you take pride in it? Is there no end to your corruption?'

'I am a pragmatist.' Josephus's irritation betrayed itself for the first time. 'And in the long term my people will benefit from it. The ancients predicted that there would be a great cataclysm and a new messiah would emerge to lead the people of Israel.'

A hint of vanity in his tone made Tabitha's jaw drop. 'You think *you* are the messiah?' she demanded incredulously. 'A man who encouraged his followers to slaughter each other but didn't have the courage to do the same to himself?' He froze and she saw for the first time just how dangerous he could be. Still she couldn't stop herself baiting him. 'Oh, yes, Titus Flavius Josephus,' she spat the name out as if it were poison on her tongue, 'you were not the only one to survive Jotapata. There were others who saw through your false sacrifice. Others who knew you would not have the will to wield the knife on your own flesh, if you ever intended to. I do believe it suited you to have no witnesses after you spent most of the siege cowering in your palace. No one to stain the myth of Joseph Ben Mahtityahu, the great Judaean warrior. Well one did survive, and she reached Emesa . . .'

Her words tailed off as she realized she'd gone too far, inflamed by her hatred of this man. Josephus still had power. Within a few hours his agents would be on the way to Emesa to track down the source of these ugly truths. Tabitha had foolishly identified it as a woman survivor from Jotapata: she might as well have given them her informant's name.

A dismissive smile confirmed her suspicions. 'Lies and exaggerations from a single source? Who knows whether this . . . person was even at Jotapata? My enemies would do anything to smear my name. Anything to stop me. Of course, your dislike of me would lead you to believe her, but will others? In any case, it is of no matter. Jotapata and what happened there is in the past. Believe me, I take no pride in my surrender.' He looked her in the eyes and challenged her to disbelieve him. 'But that surrender and what I achieved in the hours following it have positioned me to deliver a greater service to my people than shedding my blood in a dusty cellar.' All around them legionaries were preparing their equipment for the march, checking straps and buckles, honing spear points and polishing swords. Josephus looked around to confirm they were all occupied and lowered his voice. 'Your mistress sent you to Chalcis and Emesa to seek out something of great value?'

Tabitha took a step back as if to escape the aura of entrapment emanating from him. Her teeth closed on her lip to ensure her silence and she wondered that it didn't bleed. Still, it wasn't enough.

'I see the answer to my next question is no. A pity. It would have saved much pain and blood if it had been in the library at Emesa.' He saw the shock on her face and smiled. 'Oh yes, I know what it is you seek, lady. How could I not when your mistress tasked me with the same mission, albeit using different methods? You are surprised? Why should that be? Surely you understand that this thing is more important than pride or anger. More important even than one man's life – or even a woman's.' Her hand went to the little dagger at her belt and now it was Josephus who took a step back, the smile widening. 'Oh, you need fear nothing from me, little Tabitha. My point is that we must be prepared to work together. I assume you have proved to your own satisfaction that this . . . treasure . . . is not in Sohaemus's library or in the keeping of Aristobulus, and I have searched every shrine and sanctuary in Galilee.' The fingers slipped away from the knife hilt and he knew he had her interest. 'So where is it and do those who keep it know the power it holds?'

She laughed at the unsubtle attempt to draw her in, but she knew that if what he said was true she had no choice but to humour him – for the moment. 'If we are to cooperate as you suggest, it might help if you were to share your thoughts with me.'

'Masada?' he suggested, naming the great mountain fortress taken from the Romans by the Sicarii three years earlier, and still occupied by them.

'If the Sicarii have it why would they send Ben Judah and his band to try to extract information from me?' Josephus's bushy eyebrows rose in surprise and this time it was Tabitha's turn to smile. 'Oh, yes, there are things even the great Josephus does not know. For a time I even believed you might have set them on me, but I see from your face I was wrong.'

'Then you are even more capable than I realized.' There was genuine admiration in his voice. 'Ben Judah is a formidable opponent by any measure. A man responsible for more deaths than the plague that robbed him of his looks. You must have required all your powers to thwart him?'

'I was fortunate,' she said curtly, sensing that the conversation was getting too familiar. This man was just as formidable as the Judaean killer, and much more dangerous, as he proved with his next words.

'Who is the one-handed Roman my good friend Lepidus is so interested in?' The way he asked it suggested the answer was of little interest to him, but Tabitha knew otherwise.

'Just a traveller who sought our protection on the way south.' She dismissed Valerius's presence as she would a servant's. 'Another dull soldier with little wit or conversation. He lost everything in the war and now seeks to restore his fortunes with Titus.'

Josephus stared at her, testing the answer this way and that, but not finding it wanting. 'Perhaps,' he nodded slowly. 'But I would not underestimate him. He may look worn out and beaten, but there is a fire burning in him that I have seen in only a few. A man like that will not be cowed by the loss of a hand or a few possessions.' She saw a shudder run through him and fought to hide her surprise. 'It was men such as he who took Jotapata.'

'You fear a one-handed man?'

'I am Joseph Ben Mahtityahu.' The grizzled head came up, lips bared in a snarl that showed Josephus, the wolf who had kept the Romans at bay in Galilee for two years. 'I fear no man. I merely counsel vigilance. I urge you, lady, to put aside your anger . . .'

They talked for a few moments more before Tabitha left. As her handmaiden took station beside her she failed to notice Serpentius sitting among a little group of legionaries outside a nearby tent.

XX

Valerius rode with Paternus at the head of the main contingent of Emesan archers. When they were clear of Simon Ben Huleh's lake the road hugged the hillside and below them the River Jordan tumbled in foaming torrents through narrow cedar-lined gorges cut in the black basalt bedrock. They were in the body of the column behind the marching legionaries, but ahead of the carts carrying the artillery: the *scorpio* catapults that fired the oversized arrows the men had good reason to call 'shield-splitters'; *onager* light catapults designed to throw a rock the size of a man's head three or four hundred paces; and the dismantled sections of the *ballistae*, the big siege artillery that could bring down stone walls. 'I wanted to thank you for not revealing my identity to the legate when you introduced me,' he said.

'It was nothing,' Paternus said brusquely. Valerius noticed he'd become more reserved since they'd joined the legionaries, as if his disability were more of a burden among his fellow Romans. The servant rode a little further back with the camels loaded with his master's possessions. Valerius could feel the dead eyes on him like a knife point pricking his back.

211

'Still,' he persisted, 'I appreciated it. Under certain circumstances it could have been embarrassing, even dangerous, for my name to be known in this company. Once more I am in your debt.'

'We were fortunate to get off the island.' The scarred tribune seemed determined to change the subject.

'Yes,' Valerius nodded. 'Fortuna favoured us. I underestimated the enemy numbers. If Lepidus hadn't happened along with the Tenth most of us would be dead.'

Paternus turned in the saddle to stare at him, as if he were reading every line and every scar on the other Roman's face. 'Sometimes a man's experiences can wear him down.' It sounded more like a portent than mere opinion. 'Inside, he feels the same, but his body is slower and his mind begins to betray him. He has doubts. He loses the ability to judge right from wrong.'

Valerius went still. What was Paternus telling him? 'Every man has doubts,' he countered warily.

'But not every man thinks he is fit to command others. From the moment we met the rebels every decision you took was wrong. You could have killed us all.' He turned his mount and rode back down the column.

As the river plunged from its gorge on to a flat plain where a second large lake shimmered on the horizon, Valerius found himself riding with Josephus, the Judaean adviser. Paternus's words troubled him more than he'd admit. Yes, the decisions he'd made had carried them into danger, but when he went over his reasoning in his mind he wouldn't have changed any one of them. He'd thought about talking it over with Gaulan, but the Chalcidean had made his feelings plain at the time. Lepidus would have understood, but Valerius still had his pride. He didn't want any man's sympathy.

Josephus tried without success to draw him out on his background and his time in Rome. When Valerius evaded the questions with shrugs and monosyllables, he steered the subject towards the Roman's travelling companions. 'An odd mix,' the Judaean mused. 'A rare beauty and perhaps the most frightening-looking man I have ever seen. Does she have the brain and the wit to match her looks, do you think?'

'I would not know.' Valerius shrugged. 'I have very little to do with her and other things to think about.'

'It would be a pity.' Josephus smiled, patently reliving some memory. 'A woman should be decorative enough to impress a man's rivals, experienced enough to make his nights satisfying and pliant enough to do his bidding. I have noticed that intelligence, if that is what one would call it in a woman, is a barrier to obedience and wit a prelude to rebellion. I prefer a woman to be a beautiful fool. And yet, she interests me. Word reaches me occasionally of her travels. Chance encounters with unusual and sometimes powerful patrons. Tales of mysterious disappearances and sudden, unexplained fatalities in her wake.' He laughed, a growl that emerged from deep in his chest. 'Why, a man could not share a bed with her without wondering if he was going to wake up dead.'

At regular intervals Josephus would ride out to meet local people in the settlements they passed, or gallop ahead to pass on information to Lepidus. While they were together Valerius continued to avoid questions about his past. Eventually, Josephus gave up and pointed to a rugged height to the south-east. 'Gamala lies on a mountain spur yonder. They have fled there because they do not think we have the strength or the will to follow. But Lepidus knows he can't leave them hovering

213

over General Titus's supply lines like a hungry vulture. He plans to slaughter them.'

'It looks a formidable place.' Valerius studied the soaring crags and sheer rock faces.

'It is.' The Judaean scratched his beard. 'Cliffs protect the town on three sides and a wall on the fourth. The only way to take Gamala is to throw down the wall. Once you have done that the fortress becomes a trap.'

'A poor reflection of the man who designed the defences, then.' Valerius deliberately tested the other man's temper.

Josephus's nostrils flared, but the flash of anger was swiftly transformed into a snort of laughter. 'You mock me, my one-handed friend, but there was a time when I could have had you hanged from the highest branch of the highest tree in all Judaea. I commanded that much power.'

'Yet now you talk of *them* and *we* and do the bidding of the invader while your people suffer.'

Still the Judaean didn't take offence. 'You do not understand me or my people. It is written that the Jews were *born* to suffer. This cataclysm was prophesied long ago, in the time of the Israelites. All those who vilify me now will be wiped away in the balefire of Rome's vengeance at Jerusalem and that is all to the good. We have a saying here. Put two Jews in a room and you will have an argument, add a third and you will have a fight. Most of our woes are a result of this capacity for dispute.' He counted the sects of Judaea on the fingers of his right hand. 'The Pharisees believe our lives are to some extent dictated by fate, but not entirely. The Sadducees say there is no such thing as fate, only the word of the law as written by Moses. So these sects are involved in an eternal argument which will never be resolved, but they are also wrought by internal divisions over the minutiae of their own opinions and philosophy. The Essenes, on the other hand, are of one mind, poor creatures. They reject pleasure as evil, regard women as mere vessels for the succession of mankind, and ensnare likely children at a pliable age and bring them up in their own image. All three find themselves at odds with the Zealots for whom the temple and the law of God are paramount and anyone who does not match their fanaticism is wanting.' He spread his hands and Valerius noticed for the first time how at odds they were with his aristocratic features. Big worker's hands; agricultural hands with thick fingers and hardened skin. 'Your Zealot believes anyone who negotiates with Rome is a traitor and must be killed. Their instruments are the Sicarii, the men of the knife. How can any nation prosper when its leaders and its thinkers would rather have their fingers around each other's throat than not?' As he talked his voice had remained calm, but a light in his eyes grew brighter with each word he uttered. Valerius had a feeling that perhaps the Zealots weren't the only fanatics in Judaea. 'God has dictated there must be a cleansing and Rome has been chosen to carry out that cleansing. When it is over Judaea will rise again and it will need leaders.'

'Of whom one will be Joseph Ben Mahtityahu?'

The Judaean turned to him and the craggy features creased in a wry smile. 'Can you think of any better qualified?'

'What if Titus negotiates a surrender and offers your enemies their lives?'

Josephus responded with another bark of laughter. 'If you believe that, you do not know these men and you do not know Titus Flavius Vespasian. The men whose word is rule in Jerusalem, John of Gischala, Eleazar Ben Simon and Simon bar Giora, would rather die than speak to a Roman. If one were to break his vow the others would kill him. And Titus has no reason to trust them. He had John trapped in Gischala, but John persuaded him not to enter the city because it was the Sabbath and used the delay to make his escape. Titus refers to him as the Snake. There will be no negotiations.'

It was mid-afternoon when they reached the entrance to a narrow valley that split the mountains to the east. Josephus showed Valerius how the only way to reach Gamala was by tortuous paths overlooked by heights that would swarm with men ready to hurl massive boulders on those below. 'I doubt the legate will waste time and men by trying to take the valley with only a few hours left till darkness. We will camp here and make the assault tomorrow.'

He was proved right when a trumpet call sounded and camels bearing the legion's eight-man tents moved forward, along with those carrying the mattocks and shovels the men would need to construct the walls of their temporary fortress. The legate's pavilion, which also acted as the legion's headquarters tent, would be the first structure erected and Valerius excused himself and rode forward to the campsite. He saw Lepidus in the distance, but he was talking to Tabitha and Gaulan, whose horsemen had operated as scouts and outriders during the march. Eventually the group broke up and Valerius dismounted and walked his horse to the legate, his heart stuttering at the look of regret Tabitha gave him in passing. There would be no secret visits in the night in this company.

'May I beg a word, sir?'

Lepidus signalled him to approach. 'Of course. If it's within my power and doesn't offend our old friend Titus, ask what you will.'

216

When Valerius made his request Lepidus shook his head. 'I'm sorry, Valerius. That is impossible.' Valerius persisted, giving his reasons for the unusual request, and eventually the legate capitulated. 'Very well,' he said reluctantly. 'It's your head after all. But I don't like it. The first cohort goes in before dawn.'

Valerius thanked him and Lepidus had his clerk write out a requisition for the equipment he'd requested. Valerius sought out the harassed armourer and handed it over, then led Lunaris to the horse lines. Serpentius appeared from between the half-erected tents of a nearby century to match stride with him. The Spaniard seemed to have recovered some of his old swagger.

'You have the look of a man who just found a dead mouse in his soup.' Serpentius gestured towards the mountains. 'You know they're planning to attack that rebel eyrie? Just be thankful that for once we don't have to put our necks on the line. They know their business, these lads.'

Valerius somehow managed to keep his face expressionless. There were some things it was better the former gladiator didn't know. 'You seem very cheerful,' he said, 'for a man with a hole in his head.'

'I've been getting to know the lady's servants a little better.' Serpentius's skull-like features split into a perplexed grin as if the memory evoked a mixture of pleasure and pain. 'Faces like angels and the bodies of Venus, but souls that drip vinegar and teeth that tear a man's flesh.'

'Then you've had your just reward for allowing your head to be ruled by that which you keep encouraging beneath your robes,' Valerius said testily. 'And why would you be doing that anyway? These aren't tavern wenches to be seduced by your boasts.'

Serpentius explained how he had seen Tabitha speaking to Josephus. 'They know each other of old, I am certain of it. Not friends to be sure,' he gave Valerius a sideways glance, 'and not lovers.' Valerius growled dangerously, but Serpentius continued. 'Their meeting had the air of conspiracy, and the Judaean looks about as trustworthy as a hungry crocodile.'

Valerius turned the matter over in his mind and came up with a dozen innocent reasons why they should meet, and one or two not so innocent. But that could wait. 'I will think on it,' he said, 'but I am sure there is a harmless explanation.'

Serpentius stared at him, but Valerius's thoughts were already elsewhere. Because tomorrow he was going to war, and there was a possibility that by the end of the day he might very well be dead.

XXI

A man must prove himself every day if he is to be the right kind of man. Paternus's words and the reproachful stares, imagined or otherwise, of the Emesans he'd led into the watery trap had cut Valerius to the bone. Until he managed to petition Titus he was still an outcast, an enemy of Rome. The only way to recover his fortunes was in the armour of a Roman soldier on the field of battle. If he was no longer capable of leading men, what would he be? Just another piece of scarred flotsam drifting from citadel to citadel in this vast eastern dust-bowl. A mercenary offering his sword to whatever petty king would pay him the price of a meal and give him a roof over his head, until the inevitable day when a blade ended his misery and his shame. An image of his father flicked into his mind; liquid, sensitive eyes belying the stern features and straight-backed rectitude of a proud but penniless patrician. What was it he had said? *You are your family's future, Valerius. Only you can restore our name. What is a family without honour or reputation?* Well, he'd restored the family's honour by his exploits in Britannia, but it had been lost once more in the festering cauldron of intrigue, backstabbing and betrayal that

219

had eventually brought Vespasian the purple. Now he must do it all again.

'Let me lead the attack on Gamala,' he had urged Lepidus. 'I will fight as a common soldier if needs be.'

But Lepidus insisted that if Valerius was going to fight it would be as a tribune. 'Acting and unpaid,' he added caustically, and only if the *primus pilus*, the centurion commanding the First cohort, agreed to take him. By good fortune, Valerius had served with Claudius Albinus on Corbulo's last Armenian campaign and the leather-faced veteran knew him by reputation.

'I'll take along another sword if the hand that holds it knows how to use it,' he spat, his narrow eyes flicking to Valerius's wooden fist. 'Even if it's the wrong hand. If you're wounded don't expect anybody to come looking for you – the foxes can have your guts for all these men care. If you get killed that's your lookout. Nobody here will mourn you. But,' his face came close enough for Valerius to smell the wine he'd drunk that morning. 'Make a mistake and one of my men dies because of it and I'll personally throw you from the top of that cliff.'

It wasn't much of a welcome, but Albinus didn't object when Valerius collected a set of plate armour from his precious stores. No question of using Sohaemus's gaudy ceremonial breastplate and helmet, but he remembered the shield was already decorated with the Tenth's symbols of the bull and the war galley. As he readied himself by the light of the oil lamp Serpentius appeared already dressed for battle, with a long sword and his little Scythian throwing axes at his belt. Of course, he'd been a fool to think he could hide the truth from the Spaniard.

'If you love me as a friend,' Valerius met the accusing stare, 'you will go back to the tent. This is something I have to do alone.'

Serpentius's teeth showed as he was about to protest this madness, but the stone-cold certainty in Valerius's eyes kept the words stillborn. With a disgusted shake of the head, he turned and walked away into the darkness.

'Close up there,' a voice hissed. 'Oh, sorry, sir. Didn't realize it was you.'

Despite the tension and the agony in his legs, Valerius smiled as the *decurio* disappeared into the silver curtain of mist that cloaked the mountain path. Ahead and to his rear the elite First cohort of the Tenth trudged silently to bring Rome's justice to Gamala. Valerius felt a sense of belonging he hadn't experienced since the deadly night fight outside Cremona, when only a man's bond with his comrades kept the fear at bay. They'd been climbing since long before dawn, their hobnailed sandals carefully wrapped in cloth to mask any noise and for better footing on the slippery black rock. It was a blessing when the darkness lifted and they found themselves still hidden from their enemies by the all-enveloping fog. The veteran legionaries hugged the cliff face as if it was a treasured friend, always wary of the long drop that fell away to their right.

They toiled upwards with shoulders hunched and eyes fixed on the ground ahead as if they were marching into a storm. Men counted their steps in their heads, trying to keep their spacing while searching for the crevice or boulder that might trip them – and betray them. Somewhere far above their enemies listened for the slightest chink of metal that would announce a Roman attack. Valerius knew the Judaeans were there, because every few moments a pebble would clatter down the rock face. He couldn't be sure whether it was accidental or deliberate, but it was certain evidence of the enemy's presence. It didn't take a military genius to work out that they would have stockpiled something much larger and more lethal than pebbles up there, ready to shower down on any legionary using the narrow path.

Valerius marched with the leading century. In the gloom behind him almost eight hundred comrades wound their way upwards, every man tensed for the sudden rush and clatter of stone that would carry him into the torrent below. The shields on their left arms might save them from smaller rocks, but a large boulder would smash the three layers of oak as if the *scutum* were a child's toy.

The man in front stopped without warning and Valerius stumbled to avoid a collision. He thanked the gods for the chance to rest his legs and drag air into his tortured lungs after the long climb; then came the niggle of fear. Why had they stopped? Had Albinus met some obstacle? Josephus had assured Lepidus the rebels couldn't block the path because they'd be exposed to archers on the far side of the gorge. Instead, they'd defend the ground where it broadened out as it reached the plateau. Valerius remembered the strained, shadowy faces in the lamplight as the Judaean described what they'd face. Gamala lay on a rocky spur overlooking the Sea of Galilee, the great freshwater lake to the west. The outcrop was in the shape of a camel's back, with a distinct hump in the centre and steep sides. Buildings covered most of the area, running right to the cliff edge.

'There is only one way to take Gamala,' Josephus insisted. 'From the north-east. The city is defended on that side by a wall, but the ground is flat enough to deploy your artillery and troops. The problem will be getting them there.'

When Vespasian besieged the city three years earlier he'd sent Titus and his Fifteenth legion far into the mountains in a hook that brought them to Gamala's rear. They'd set up camp, swept the rebels off the plateau and opened the track up for the Fifth legion to join them. With his forces in place Vespasian battered the walls to dust, allowing his troops to swarm through the streets. The campaign lasted weeks, but Lepidus didn't have weeks. He needed a quick victory so he could join Titus at Jerusalem. Jerusalem: the name was on every man's lips. The greatest prize in all Judaea. All they needed to do was storm the walls and the legionaries of the Tenth would be as rich as any man could wish to be. But first they must take Gamala.

'Once we control the plateau, we'll move the heavy artillery into place immediately,' Lepidus had told them. It would mean hauling massive baulks of timber over terrain barely fit for a mountain goat, but the men of the Tenth were hardened by years of training. 'As soon as the machines are fixed we'll start on the walls. I want them ranged before dark, so we can continue all through the night. The *onagri* and *scorpiones* to be sited and ready by daylight. Any questions?'

'Begging the legate's pardon,' Albinus's long service and experience entitled him to speak when another man would stay silent, 'but the Emperor took three weeks to make a dent in those walls, with four times as many *ballistae*. It may be asking a lot to do it in three days.'

Lepidus's eyes shifted almost imperceptibly to Josephus.

The column resumed its advance and Valerius dashed the sweat from his eyes and tried to manoeuvre the big shield into a more comfortable position. His left hand tightened on the borrowed *gladius*, testing the unfamiliar grip. Three to one was the ratio a commander wanted to achieve when he deployed his men for a siege. Three attackers for every defender. Today, the odds would be around equal, but Lepidus assured his legionaries that what the Tenth lacked in quantity they made up for in quality. The Judaeans in Gamala were the dregs of the rebel cause: old men and boys, the leavings of Vespasian's great cleansing of Galilee. It was the kind of thing every commander told his troops before an attack, but the fierce answering grins told Valerius these men believed it.

He felt the ground rising beneath his feet and again the man in front of him stopped abruptly. Seconds later a whispered watchword passed down the line from one man to the next. 'Noricum.'

One of the few auxiliary units Titus had managed to retain was a contingent of mountain troops from the high Alps. Twenty of them were assigned to the first century. Valerius heard a soft shuffling sound as two men close behind him began to climb the sheer slope to his right. Small, wiry men with a grip strong enough to crack a walnut in their clenched fists, they wore soft leather shoes so they could feel every fault in the rock. Their weapons of choice were a curved knife strapped to their chest, and the sling. Silent killers. They would be needed today.

The only evidence a dozen Judaean defenders had died on the height above was a single small stone that rattled down the slope. Before the pebble stopped rolling the man in front was on the move again and he was moving fast. Valerius picked up the pace to keep station and he could hear the soldier behind panting at his shoulder. They turned a corner in the path and it funnelled upwards, widening out until several men could run abreast. He saw four or five bodies sprawled behind a makeshift barrier of rocks thrown down by the legionaries in the van. At last the ground levelled and the century flowed out to deploy in two lines, automatically shuffling right to make way for their comrades in the next formation.

Valerius moved to the left of the line, where he could use his sword to best advantage. With the fog beginning to break up, the final century of the First cohort moved into position and the men of the Second poured from the path into the narrow gap behind. Centurions muttered at the men to be silent and curb their impatience. Albinus looked from the wispy balls of fog to the sun and back, waiting for his moment. Valerius saw him stiffen like a hunting dog on the scent. Where there'd been nothing but grey, dark shadows appeared that swiftly transformed into individual human figures.

'Sound the advance.' Albinus rapped out the command. A horn blared and the entire formation moved forward at the steady, implacable tread that had carried the legions from the heather-clad hills of Britannia to the sands of Africa. Droplets of dew twinkled amongst the yellowing grass and Valerius had a fleeting thought that he should have ordered the men to remove their foot cloths. Too late now. The last of the fog burned away and ahead of them across the long slope they finally saw Gamala. Between the walls and the advancing Roman line hundreds of men gaped incredulously at the newcomers. The rebels had been taken completely by surprise. They huddled in groups around newly lit cooking fires or squatted over latrine pits away from their rough shelters. For the sleep-dazed Judaeans it was as if the fog had spawned an army of ghosts. A few reached for their stacked spears, but most were utterly paralysed by the sight of the long lines of legionaries.

The closest shelters were less than two hundred paces away and in a heartbeat of inspiration Valerius knew what was going to happen. Albinus had seen it too.

Lepidus's orders had been to pressure the Judaean rebels and push them back into Gamala, followed by an orderly but swift siege. No one envisaged this. The mist had changed everything. Albinus was faced not with an organized defence, but by a rabble of confused and frightened men in no sort of order. It was the opportunity of a lifetime and he took it.

'Lock shields,' the *primus pilus* ordered. The command was echoed by the signaller at his side and he waited until the big painted *scuta* came together with a wooden clatter before giving his next order. 'Double march.' Again the call rang out and every man increased his pace to a steady jog.

Cries of consternation and fear came from the mass of warriors to the front. Small bands of men formed where their commanders or the bravest among them tried to create a hastily put together defence. Valerius heard the sharp crack of sling shots smacking against the wooden shields and at least once a yelp when one clattered off a helmet, but the line advanced unhindered. A group of savage faces appeared in front of him and he jerked his head to the side as a spear sliced through the ranks past his ear. A moment later the shock of a body smashing into his shield checked him for a moment before his training took over. He used his arm to angle the *scutum* and rammed the *gladius* through the gap. Oh, the joy of the *gladius*. A lethal triangular point and a decent edge. Thrust, twist and withdraw. A shriek of agony and step over the writing body. More cries as the little knots of defenders were simply overrun by a wall of legionary shields and left to be dealt with by the second and third lines.

In what seemed like moments they were among the shelters. Men simply stepped through the makeshift huts, kicking the branches aside and continuing their relentless march. Valerius looked up. The city wall, built not of solid stone but of mud bricks, was less than three hundred paces away and the space between seethed with a mass of running men. It was a rout.

Albinus wasn't satisfied to slaughter the rearmost Judaeans and let the rest escape. Now there was a fierce exultation in his voice as he gave the order. 'Sound the charge.'

A legion's greatest strengths are discipline and cohesion. In line or cohort squares it crushes the life from an enemy and pounds him into the dust by a combination of sheer power and unity, the way a grinding machine crushes grain in a flour mill. But sometimes something less subtle is required, and a legionary unleashed is an elemental force as deadly as the dart from a shield-splitter. In two paces the First cohort transformed from a disciplined double wall of shields into a pack of snarling, blood-crazed wolves hurtling down on their wounded prey. The Judaeans fought each other to reach Gamala's gate and those at the rear looked back in terror at the nemesis about to fall upon them. A few raised their shields, but most only struggled all the harder to reach sanctuary, baring their backs to an implacable, merciless enemy and sealing their doom.

The doom of their comrades, too.

A rearguard of forty or fifty brave men might have stalled the Roman attack long enough to allow the majority to escape and, perhaps, for the gates to be closed. By now it was too late. Valerius understood what the *primus pilus* had in mind and he had held back from the headlong charge, barking at the closest eight-man sections to stay with him. Mutinous growls greeted the command, but the men obeyed.

Then came the order he'd known would come. 'Valerius,' Albinus cried. 'The gate!'

'Form a column of fours in close formation.' Upwards of forty legionaries automatically locked together around him in a tight spearhead and he forced himself into the centre of the third row. 'Straight to the gate and stop for no one. The Corona Muralis and an enhanced pension for the first man into Gamala.'

A great roar went up from the legionaries in the column as they charged the cowering, cursing mass of Judaeans. Using their shield bosses to smash down any who stood in their way, they allowed the weight and momentum of the compact formation to force them through the sea of flesh. But the column's momentum would carry it only so far. When they reached the shadow of the walls it slowed, then came to a staggering halt. Now the *gladius* came into its own. The lethal triangular points darted between the outer shields to cut a way through the seething mass so the men in the column advanced across a carpet of bleeding bodies. Roaring for more effort, Valerius added his weight to the men in front and they heaved their way forward step by blood-soaked step. But the compact column was not a *testudo* with its protective carapace of shields. It was primarily an attacking weapon, and in attacks men die. A legionary in the front row took a knife in the groin and went down with a shriek of pure horror. Without conscious thought the man behind stepped forward into the gap. As Valerius hurried to fill the vacant place in the second line he stumbled and looked down into a pair of glaring, hate-filled eyes. The Judaean lay on his back, mouth gaping in a howl and a great tear in his belly, but the killing rage was on him and he was willing his heart to pump long enough to taste more Roman blood. A blade swept up in a wicked hook that would have gelded Valerius like the man before him. In the packed formation he had no room to dodge, but somehow he managed to get his foot to the knife arm. As his enemy struggled to free himself he rammed his *gladius* into the screaming mouth until he felt the point crunch on bone. No time for self-congratulation. He staggered and almost fell as the legionary behind hammered into his back with a cursed demand to get a move on.

Another man beside Valerius dropped without a sound, the victim of one of the lethal Judaean slingers. A replacement stepped unhesitatingly into his place. Valerius looked up to see the ramparts crammed with men whirling slings and hurling spears into the mass below. He hauled up his shield and attempted to protect the heads of the men in the first line. Everything was a blur. Sweat coursed from his hairline into his eyes and he had only a vague notion of what occurred around him. A great cry went up from somewhere beyond the head of the column. With a thrill of fear Valerius understood that the defenders were attempting to force the gates shut against the howling mass of bodies cramming their portals. He felt the first despair of defeat.

'The gates,' he roared desperately. 'We must reach the gates.'

His cry was taken up as more legionaries understood what was happening and joined the formation. Shouted orders from his rear told Valerius the Second cohort had joined the attack. Albinus would have them fighting their way into a position where they could best exploit Valerius's attack, or, if it failed, follow it up with one of their own.

But he would not fail. 'One more effort. Push, you bastards. We're nearly there.' He could feel the shadow of the wall now and he raised himself to his full height in an attempt to see what lay ahead. It almost cost him his life as a spear battered against his helmet, making his head ring and leaving him dazed. He would have dropped to be crushed beneath the feet of the men around him, but a hand reached out to grab his arm and hold him upright. He shook his head. What had he seen? Two oak-doored gateways, with a space of ten or twelve feet separating them. They were almost through the first pair, far enough at least to ensure there was no closing them now. But he could see the inner doors shutting inch by inch. If they managed to bar it . . . Something caught his eye above and he looked up and saw a flare of yellow that spawned a shudder of sheer terror. Fire. Of course. They weren't fools. They would be boiling oil to pour down on the attackers.

'Heave.' He heard the panic in his voice as he threw himself at the man in front. 'If they close those doors we're all dead.' Venus's withered tits, it was going to be close.

A cry of triumph split the air as the defenders managed to edge the doors closer together, but it was premature. One Judaean made a final Herculean effort to reach sanctuary but found himself wedged between them, screaming as the life was crushed out of him. It was all the incentive the attackers needed. With one final heave of their shields they smashed forward and the gates burst open.

Gamala was theirs, but could they keep it?

Beyond the gate, Valerius and his men found themselves in an open courtyard faced by a wall of nervous enemies. A moment of awed silence as if neither side could imagine what had just happened.

'Don't just stand there.' Valerius broke the spell. 'Kill the bastards.' He launched himself at the enemy in a charge filled with mindless hate and relief. One man went down under his sword and he smashed another unconscious with his shield boss before he realized that the Judaeans had fled. A flood of Roman soldiers surged past him and he knew he should follow, but he discovered he could barely move. All the energy seemed to drain from him.

A hand touched his arm. Albinus stared at him with a look of bemused admiration that didn't belong on his weathered, shrew-like face. The *primus pilus* let out a long, slow breath and closed his eyes and Valerius realized the man was almost as exhausted as he was. 'By the gods,' Albinus shook his head, 'that was a sight to behold. Now I know why they gave you the Corona Aurea.' He looked thoughtful for a moment, then his face broke into a grin. 'A pity you weren't a proper part of the legion or I might have put you up for a second.'

Valerius sheathed his gore-coated *gladius* and Albinus thrust a water skin at him. Around them detachments of battle-crazed legionaries cleared the walls and streets with relentless, demonic savagery. Valerius barely noticed them. He licked someone else's blood from his lips and drank deeply. The tepid liquid tasted of mould, but nothing had ever felt sweeter as it ran down his parched throat. 'I didn't deserve the first,' he said wearily. 'But they'll give you the Grass Crown for what you've done here.'

Albinus roared with laughter at the suggestion he might win the Empire's highest military honour. 'On the day my wrinkled balls turn square. They only give them to generals. Maybe Lepidus will award it to himself? Come,' he said, ushering Valerius towards what had once been one of the city's richer houses, 'let's see if the traitorous bastards left us any decent wine and we'll get these off.' He pointed to the blood-soaked bandages that still covered Valerius's *caligae*. 'Besides,' he reflected, 'if they'd shut those gates we'd have been well and truly fucked. Let's just be happy we've cracked this particular nut without having to bother the stone-heavers. Once we've settled with this rabble it'll be straight to the real prize.'

Jerusalem.

XXII

The rabble fought for every street and every building, but poorly equipped and without leaders they stood no chance against disciplined Roman legionaries. Valerius followed the progress of the battle through the blood-stained thoroughfares of Gamala, stepping over corpses amid the slaughterhouse stink from scattered entrails and torn viscera. He struggled to feel pity for the dead. Perhaps all the years carrying a sword had hardened him against the sight. But he knew it was more than that.

This was no Cremona, where Roman had slaughtered Roman and women and children had suffered the same fate as the men. These were enemies who had rebelled against the rule of Roman law. Not soldiers, it was true, only civilians handed a spear or a sword and told to kill. But their fate was sealed from the moment their leaders defied Rome.

Much of the place hadn't been repaired since Vespasian's attack three years earlier. Here the defenders had made their final stand within the blackened shell of a burned-out building where the charred rafters stood out like the rib bones of a sacrificed pig. Their broken and butchered bodies sprawled from the windows and hung from the roofs. What surprised him most was that so many of them were very young. The average age must have been less than twenty years and many were probably only fourteen or fifteen. It was only later he discovered exactly what Vespasian's cleansing had entailed. The fathers of these boys and young men were all dead or slaves, torn from their lives to teach Galilee a lesson it would never forget.

But they fought. And they died.

By the time he reached the camel's hump, between the two dips that had housed the bulk of Gamala's population, the Tenth had hemmed in the survivors on a series of flat-roofed buildings overlooking the west cliff. In the distance, Valerius was aware of the glittering expanse of the inland sea, but he only had eyes for the drama being acted out below. Some of the Judaeans screamed defiance and brandished swords and spears at the men who surrounded them. Most, though, gathered in small groups praying or singing. For the moment, the Romans allowed them respite, but it was only a matter of time before they finished the job and everyone knew it.

'I give you joy of victory, my friend.' Valerius looked round to find Josephus behind him staring bleakly at the spectacle. 'The next generation. The seed of Judaea's future. I would they had stayed at home.'

'They are rebels.' It was an obvious truth, but Valerius knew his voice lacked conviction. 'And you played your part in their defeat.'

'But not so much as you, it would appear. I marked you as a soldier, but how could I have known your true worth? There is not a man here who does not talk of the one-armed tribune who led the attack on the gate.' The flattery produced a snort of bitter laughter from Valerius, but Josephus ignored his scorn. 'The men who followed you would have followed no other. No other man could have achieved what you did. Mark my word, Gaius Valerius Verrens, you will have your part to play in the days to come.'

The words had a ring of prophecy that sent a shiver through Valerius, but he refused to respond to the assumption they raised. His eyes returned to the men trapped on the roofs below. 'They ran like chickens before the farmer's axe. If the rest of the campaign is like this Titus can leave the legions in their bases and his auxiliaries will do the job for him.'

He felt a hand on his shoulder and turned to find himself the focus of smouldering dark eyes. 'Do not underestimate your enemy. You surprised a band of young men barely old enough to wield a sword. It would have been different if they had stayed behind these walls. Yes,' Josephus's laugh was a hollow sham of the real thing, 'your *ballistae* would have made short work of the walls, but if they'd been given time to organize a defence of the streets you would have seen their true worth. Did you know Vespasian almost died here? It is true. You've seen how narrow the streets are. The people demolished the upper floors of their houses to provide missiles they could hurl down upon the invaders. With the lower doors and windows barricaded the Romans were crushed and broken in their hundreds. Vespasian looked for a point near here to rally them, but he became detached from the main force. He told me later that if his bodyguard hadn't formed *testudo* and dragged him out he would have been torn to pieces. He left it to Titus to take the city and before he was finished the son had to kill every man capable of bearing arms. You could not go from one house to another without stepping on bodies. This,' he surveyed the carnage around them, 'this is nothing. It will be at Jerusalem where you will see the true mettle of the Jews.'

'Tell me about Jerusalem.'

'As well defended by nature as this,' the bearded Judaean waved a hand at the ravines on every side but one, 'only greater, and the walls . . . Ah, yes,' his voice took on a ragged edge. 'I wondered. I was wrong. You will not have to wait till Jerusalem.' He turned away and walked back down the hill, leaving Valerius alone.

Below him, the men on the roofs had gathered in a crowd at the farthest edge, above the precipice. Valerius watched as they alternately bobbed their heads in prayer and looked to the heavens as if for forgiveness, or perhaps salvation. When the first threw himself off the edge and plummeted silently to the rocks below, Valerius felt his mind freeze. The act of self-sacrifice was so inconceivable it didn't seem real. As he watched, the rest followed in little groups, holding hands or clinging to each other like brothers. By the time the thousandth made the plunge it seemed almost normal. Why did he stay? Why did he not look away? Respect for the defeated? A need to see the end of it? At the time he could not have provided an answer. It was only when he saw these men's comrades defending Jerusalem's walls that he discovered the answer. He needed to know his enemy's mettle.

He walked back down the hill towards the maze of houses. Oddly, though his body ached with weariness, his mind was clear and he realized that some part of him was actually happy. Not once had he faltered. He'd known exactly what was required and never hesitated over a decision. He'd defeated fear and when he'd thought he was going to die his only thought was of eventual victory. The little worm of doubt Paternus had planted had been driven from his soul. Gaius Valerius Verrens was a wanderer no more, but a soldier who'd proved himself again on the field of battle. When he approached Titus he'd do so with pride: as the man who breached the gates at Gamala.

As he entered a narrow street that would eventually take him to the gate his thoughts turned to Tabitha. She would know by now that he'd taken part in the attack. Would she fear he was dead? And if he had been, would she have mourned him? He smiled. It didn't matter, because he *was* alive and at some point they would be together again. The smile lasted another twenty paces until he realized that dead bodies lined the street and two legionaries rifling through the robes of the corpses had stopped to study him with an odd look. He nodded and carried on his way, but he felt their eyes on his back. Of course, they thought he was mad. Why else would a man in blood-soaked armour walk down a street of the dead, in a city of the dead, smiling as if he were in a summer's meadow? For a moment images of gaping mouths spraying blood and wide terrified eyes flickered through his mind. His left hand twitched as he felt again the impact and the scraping sensation as the point of his *gladius* scored the inside of a man's skull. Perhaps he *was* mad.

His thoughts turned to Serpentius's words of half a lifetime ago at the bottom of the mountain. Tabitha and Josephus. Why shouldn't they know each other? Tabitha had said her mistress, Queen Berenice, travelled with Titus's retinue. Josephus had been Vespasian's hostage and now basked in the Emperor's patronage: of course he would have mixed with Titus and his friends. Yet why should the Judaean give the impression they'd never met when he and Valerius rode together, and why the probing about his own background?

He froze as he glimpsed someone slipping furtively through the ruins to his right. A flash of colour masked by toppled columns and collapsed roof beams, but it stirred a memory. Could it have been Josephus? The Judaean's robe was certainly similar, but he couldn't be certain. He hesitated, unsure whether to follow, but Josephus raised enough questions in his mind for curiosity to overrule caution.

Valerius climbed the steps of what must once have been a palace or one of Gamala's finest public buildings. A great oak door hung awkwardly on its hinges, the original copper sheathing stripped away, but the rivets that had held it in place still gleaming bright. Axe marks showed where someone had tried to chop it for a fire or building timber, but the ancient wood had defied them. Valerius ducked under it and into a room blackened by fire. One wall had been torn down and he could see men passing on the street outside. The place had once been covered with frescoes and painted plaster. Most was chipped away, or fallen in dusty heaps on the stone floor, but it was clear it had once been very fine. He winced as a roof tile crunched under his foot. Unlike most of the city's flat-roofed buildings, this had been tiled in the Roman fashion, but the supports were burned away and tiles lay everywhere.

Stepping carefully, he moved to a door that opened out on to a courtyard with a cistern at the centre to collect rainwater. A walkway ran round three sides and to his left was another doorway, just a black rectangle in the stone wall. Hardly daring to breathe, he moved towards it and slipped through into the gloom, taking a step to one side as he entered. A soft fluttering sound stopped his heart and he had an image of a knife spinning through the darkness to pin him through the throat. He tensed for the strike, but nothing happened apart from another soft explosion accompanied by the gentle cooing of the dove roosting in an alcove above and to his left.

Willing his heart to slow, he stood by the doorway until his eyes became accustomed to the murk, gradually becoming aware of a familiar throat-filling stench. Hundreds of scroll cases littered the floor and scattered amongst them were the contents, ancient texts now torn and crumpled into small balls of papyrus or parchment. The stink came from the human excrement that covered the floor in heaps and fouled the manuscripts. In places great smears disfigured the walls and even the scroll alcoves were dirtied. Somehow the desecration of the books had a greater effect than the slaughter he'd witnessed an hour earlier. What kind of man used a library as a latrine? The answer wasn't difficult to divine. A soldier. Like every soldier, the legionary was obsessed with his bowels. Bodily movements were the subject of intense discussion, extraordinary scrutiny and even competition. There'd been nights when he'd heard eight-man leather tents rattle to the sound of farting contests. They'd compete to see who could pass the biggest stool. He could imagine them in here, laughing as they wiped their arses on books that had sometimes taken a lifetime to write. 'Look, I've got Archimedes' screw up my bum.' The shit was old and dry – he guessed the result of Titus's depredations or perhaps a more recent Roman push into the area – but it still stank. Gamala had been abandoned for much of the time since the city's capture and destruction and the men who had occupied it recently either hadn't had the time to clean it up, or more likely were unwilling to soil their hands on Rome's leavings.

Valerius was about to take a first careful step when he heard a muffled cry from somewhere close. There were no other doors or windows in the library. He guessed whoever had owned the books used the court-yard for reading and didn't expose his treasures to the elements unless necessary. As he studied his surround-ings he noticed a break in the random pattern of shit scattering the floor. In the far corner an area had been cleared. When he looked closer he recognized some sort of trap door. A heavy cabinet stood nearby and he guessed it had covered the hidden entrance until it had been moved. He crouched over the trap and with his left hand grasped the ring bolt set into the slab and heaved it up. It rose with a slight creak and in the opening he'd created he could see a set of stairs lit by a soft glow. He raised the door to its full extent and found, to his relief, that it had been designed to stay upright without any visible support. He ducked down to look inside and was greeted by a short chamber with doors to either side.

Before he went any further he removed his sandals and placed them beside the trap. In such a confined space the sound of the hobnails on stone would be as loud as a trumpet fanfare. When he was ready he reached for his sword, then changed his mind. The stairs were steep and awkward, especially for a man with one hand, and the slightest chink of metal would give him away. He'd draw it when he needed it. He wasn't even certain he would.

One of the doors was open and he could hear the sound of a muted conversation followed by the clatter of metal, as if something had fallen. He moved slowly towards it and craned his neck to look inside.

Josephus had his back to the wall with the knife that had been knocked from his hand lying at his feet. A tall man faced him, dressed in Judaean clothing, with a cloth wound about his head to conceal his features. The tall man spoke Hebrew and held a long spear with a leaf-shaped blade to Josephus's chest, jabbing it to emphasize his words. Josephus said nothing, but Valerius could see no fear in his eyes, only calculation. Clearly he hadn't reconciled himself to what appeared to be almost certain death. The Judaean hadn't noticed Valerius yet, but that would change in a moment. He only prayed Josephus was sensible enough not to show any sign that would give him away. He stepped into the room and his fingers closed on his sword hilt. Josephus's eyes widened slightly, but otherwise his face remained impassive. Valerius pulled at the sword as he moved silently across the floor. Nothing happened. It was stuck fast in the scabbard. Fool, his mind screamed at him, to sheath it covered in blood.

No time to change that. He released the hilt and moved his left hand to his right fist. Less than three paces away the spearman heard the sharp click and whirled, lightning fast, to face the new threat. Too late. Valerius was already inside the spear point and he rammed the wooden fist into the man's unprotected stomach. All the air left him in one coughing gasp and his eyes, the only part of his face visible, widened in shock. The spear clattered to the ground and his hands clutched at his midriff. He brought the right up to his face, staring in disbelief at the blood staining his fingers. Valerius faced him, his right hand raised ready to strike again, but with a groan like a toppled tree the Judaean fell forward on to his face.

Josephus was staring at the wooden fist and the bloodied metal spike protruding from it. He took a deep breath, but otherwise the only sign of his ordeal was a slight paleness in his face. 'A neat trick,' he said seriously. 'I'm very glad you didn't experiment with it on me. Is he dead?'

Valerius heaved the body over with his foot and a pair of sightless eyes stared back at him. 'It seems so.'

Josephus moved from the wall and crouched over the dead man, careful not to touch his body. 'Please unwind the cloth from his face.'

Valerius did as he was asked. 'Do you know him?'

The Judaean stared at the bearded features. 'No.' His eyes flicked nervously to Valerius. 'Why should I know him?'

'He followed you down here.'

'A coincidence,' Josephus shrugged, returning to the wall where a shelf held several dozen scroll cases. He picked them up one at a time, discarding some, but putting others to one side.

'Why would he follow a fellow Judaean down into the depths of some palace cellar when there are several thousand Roman enemies he could have chosen from in the rest of the city?' Josephus didn't answer. 'You knew this was here?'

Josephus looked up from his books. 'Of course. Did I not tell you I designed the defences? This is the house of the High Priest. I was a guest here. I was naive then. I believed Gamala was impregnable, but I underestimated Vespasian's ability to drive his troops across twenty miles of mountains to unlock the defences from the rear. Before I left for Jotapata I left some of my writings here. I hoped they might have survived, so I came to look for them. When I turned round this brute was standing with a spear pointed at me.'

'You cried out.'

'Did I?' The Judaean's face went blank. 'I do not remember. I only had my knife, but he knocked it from my hand.' He studied the offending appendage as if it had betrayed him. 'You saved my life.' He stretched

242

out to take Valerius's hand but stopped midway as he remembered it was wooden and had a vicious-looking knife protruding from the centre knuckle.

'It was nothing. You can thank a young man called Dimitrios who runs the armoury in Emesa.' Valerius placed the point against the top of the wooden table and pushed until the blade clicked back into place. He looked from the artificial fist to the man on the floor. 'I wasn't certain it would work.'

'I'm glad it did,' Josephus said with passion. 'Mark my words, future generations will thank you for what you have done today. In these books lies the only comprehensive history of my people. Its loss would have been catastrophic.' He bundled up the scrolls he'd collected in his cloak and set off for the trap door.

Valerius stooped to go through the dead man's clothes and came up with a curved knife that looked disturbingly familiar. He slipped it into his belt and followed the Judaean, pondering on the curious mix of scholar, soldier and spy: a man who could cheerfully reconcile patriotism and collaboration; a commander who surrendered without shame and justified it by citing his people's interest, yet could look death in the face without flinching; a dissembler who lied without conscious thought and a priest who never prayed. When he reached the top of the steps Josephus surveyed the devastation and filth of the library with a look of something like sorrow on his face.

'Barbarians,' he muttered, and set off across the floor with delicate footsteps.

Valerius and Josephus emerged from Gamala's blood-soaked gateway to find Albinus making his report to the legate on the flat slope to the north of the city.

Legionaries had cleared the field of the dead and now worked to raise the banks of tonight's fort using rubble from the mud-brick walls being dismantled by their comrades. They made their way towards the little knot of officers.

'We'll leave one cohort up here to finish the job,' Lepidus said. 'They can act as the rearguard when we march tomorrow. An extra ration of wine for every man, but I want them ready to leave at dawn, Albinus.' The *primus pilus* nodded. Lepidus grinned when he saw Valerius, but his expression sobered as he saw the blood staining his tunic and armour. 'Albinus tells me I have you to thank for not having to haul my artillery all the way up here.'

'I was one of a thousand,' Valerius dismissed the compliment. 'Every soldier of the First cohort was a hero today. You are fortunate to lead such men.'

'Why, I do believe Albinus is blushing,' the legate laughed. 'Nevertheless, despite your modesty you may be sure I will say so in my report to Titus.' He looked across to where another section of wall crumbled and fell under the legionary picks and mattocks. 'I'd expected to be delayed another two or three days, which would have made the Tenth less than popular in certain circles.' He turned to Josephus. 'Were there any rebel leaders among the dead?'

'I do not believe so. They were disaffected survivors from the Emperor's Galilean campaign who have been terrorizing the communities that have accepted Rome's rule.' The Judaean's voice was a brittle mix of anger and sorrow, but Lepidus was too elated by his victory to notice.

'It is of no matter,' he said. 'Tomorrow we march south to join Titus.'

XXIII

Valerius spent the night on the plateau with the men of the Tenth. The victory celebrations had been subdued because the legionaries knew they'd be on the march at first light. As the sun crept over the eastern mountains they made their sullen, heavy-footed way down the track from Gamala with the Sea of Galilee shimmering like a great bowl of liquid fire in the distance. The sight made Valerius shiver. There was something mystical about this land, mystical and terrible, that he doubted he would ever fully understand.

The fatalism and comradeship of the Judaeans who'd leapt to their deaths and whose shattered bodies now rotted in heaps among the nearby rocks kept coming back to him. You might defeat such men. You might kill them. But you could never destroy their spirit. If one tenth of that spirit existed behind the walls of Jerusalem, many of those he had fought beside at Gamala would die there. Who knew, perhaps it would be the grave of Gaius Valerius Verrens.

But he had lived too long with death to dwell on the inevitable. It would come in its own time, and no doubt sooner rather than later, but that was in the future.

For the moment he revelled in the brotherhood of the men around him. They were the best of men and the worst. Illiterate savages who would rape and plunder and slaughter the unarmed and the helpless without compunction or conscience; who would beat an outsider to a pulp for the slightest hint of an insult. Yet they'd give their last sip of tepid water to a thirsty comrade or hold him in their arms as he took his final breath, weep over his body and pay for his gravestone. They were builders, engineers and craftsmen; artists in stone and wood and metal. Given the order, they would climb any mountain or swim any river. It was a privilege to serve with them and a privilege to lead them. All the doubt he had experienced after Paternus's warning had been swept away by the terror and exhilaration of battle. When he reached the camp below the heights he saw the scarred tribune watching his arrival along with his servant. He ignored them. Whatever threat they posed, and he was still uncertain if any existed, they couldn't touch him on the march.

Less dangerous, perhaps, but of more immediate significance, were the reproachful looks from Tabitha and Serpentius as he took his place in the column. He'd found a way to clean his armour of blood and borrowed a clean tunic before they saw him or the looks might have been worse. Part of him wanted to go to them and explain why he'd joined the attack, but he had good reasons not to. If he did face some kind of threat from Paternus, making contact might put Tabitha in danger. And then there was the mystery of her acquaintance with Josephus, which neither of them cared to acknowledge. Serpentius was more straightforward. As a former gladiator he believed that anyone who risked their life without good reason was a fool. Nothing Valerius could say would change that.

However, he wasn't surprised when the Spaniard appeared at his side an hour after the column set off along the eastern shore of the Galilean sea.

'That old bastard Albinus tells me you were a hero up there.' Serpentius kept his eyes on the road, but his voice held a grudging respect. 'Tell me there was a point.'

'There was a point.' A dozen explanations came to mind, but the Roman let them lie.

'Then we'll say no more about it.'

They rode on for a few moments before Valerius turned to his companion. 'Has the famous gladiator turned into a mother hen watching over her chick?'

Serpentius suppressed a grin. 'Watchful enough to notice that your little knife looks as if it's had some use. Curious enough to wonder why, given that the shield I packed away had more dents and cuts in it than Paternus's face.'

Valerius told him about the encounter with Josephus in the cellar of the library.

'You think this Judaean followed him there?'

'It's possible.'

The Spaniard nodded thoughtfully. 'Then there's another one who needs watching. At this rate we'll need four pairs of eyes, not two.'

'What about our other friends?'

'Nothing suspicious,' Serpentius frowned. 'Paternus is an odd one. A man with two faces, but neither of them eveals his true feelings. They keep themselves to themselves. Just sitting around their fire and watching. They remind me of some people I know.'

Valerius's interest was aroused. 'Who?'

'Us.'

That afternoon they camped outside Scythopolis, a city which had stayed loyal to Rome throughout the rebellion. The legionaries constructed their temporary fort on the flat crown of a low rise overlooking the river, the favoured location for such places. While the men worked and Lepidus rode off for talks with the city council, Valerius went to wash away the day's accumulation of dust in the waters of a nearby stream. He'd been there for only a few moments when Tabitha appeared like a wraith from the scattered bushes lining the banks. He'd stripped off his tunic and stood up to his knees in the water wearing only his *subligaculum*. His first instinct was to cover himself, but the feeling only lasted until he remembered what they had shared. She wore the dust-stained cloak she'd travelled in and her dark eyes studied his body in frank admiration.

'I had forgotten you had quite so many scars.' Her head tilted a little to one side as if that gave her a better aspect. 'Is the water cold?'

'Why don't you come in and find out?'

'Nothing would please me more.' Her laugh was like the tinkling of a tiny silver bell. 'I am carrying so much dust that if I shook myself I would cause a sandstorm. But I fear this stream will soon be very popular with our travelling companions. I only came to give you a warning.'

'Warning?' He pulled himself out of the stream and she handed him his tunic, managing it in a way that allowed her fingers to trail through the hairs on his chest. A shiver of pleasure ran through him and she must have experienced something similar because she instantly pulled her hand away as if she'd touched a glowing coal.

'When first we join Titus it must be as if we barely know each other.' She paused as Valerius slipped the tunic over his head and belted it using only his left hand.

'You are wondering why? Because it is safer for both of us. Like every court, those of Berenice and Titus are subject to undercurrents and factions. It is better that I discover who is in favour and who is not. Who is plotting and for whom. When I know everything there is to know I will go to Berenice and create some pretext for us to be together without any need for subterfuge.'

'I would like that very much.' He moved closer so he could smell the salt tang of her sweat, and something else that started a fire in his loins. The dark eyes widened and her lips twitched into a smile.

'Perhaps I will play the spy.' Tabitha's voice thickened. 'Or the concubine.'

He had an overwhelming urge to take her in his arms. Before he could act on it she put her hands on his chest to push back. But he was the stronger and he felt her body melt into his as he held her.

'No, Valerius,' she said urgently. 'Now is not the time. We will be together, but . . .'

Reluctantly, he released her. Tabitha turned away, breathing hard, as if she knew that there could only be one outcome if she stayed. When she reached the trees she looked at him over her shoulder and he saw the same desperate need he knew was in his own eyes.

'There is one other thing. Do not trust Joseph Ben Mahtityahu.'

'Why?' His voice sounded harsh in his ears. Now was the time to ask her about the discussion Serpentius had witnessed, but some inner voice urged him to keep his counsel.

'He will flatter you and you will find yourself revealing things you will later regret when they reach the ears of those with the power to hurt you.'

'Is he some kind of wizard?'

249

'No.' The smile was back in her voice. 'But, as we say in the East, he was born with a golden tongue. A man who can charm the birds from the trees as easily as the coins from your purse.'

'Then I will try to resist his charms.' Valerius returned the smile, but she was already gone.

He stooped to pick up the sheathed sword from where he'd left it on the bank, drawing it free and turning in a single movement at a rustle from the bushes.

'Didn't I tell you it's dangerous to be alone in this company?' Serpentius appeared a little further upstream.

'How long have you been there?'

'Long enough to know things are getting very complicated. Of course,' he grinned, 'I wouldn't have stayed if . . .'

Valerius felt the blood rush to his face, but he matched the Spaniard's grin. 'I'm beginning to wonder if I was wrong to free you. I liked it better when you had to do as you were told.'

For the next two days Lepidus led his legion by the glistening waters of the Jordan until they reached Jericho, where an Imperial courier galloped in to pass on an order from Titus to march immediately.

For Jerusalem.

XXIV

Jerusalem.

Valerius joined Lepidus and his staff as they spurred their way to a height east of the city where the Tenth would construct their encampment. When they reached the summit they walked their horses through a tangle of ancient olive groves.

'Venus's withered tits, have you ever seen anything like that?' The legate produced a growl of what might have been pain or admiration. 'It makes Gamala look like a morning fornicating stroll.'

The entire metropolis was laid out before them like some gigantic child's toy. Below, the ground dropped in rugged, fissured steps into a deep, rock-strewn valley, and beyond it the city sprawled across the far slope to fill the horizon. Smoke from thousands of fires formed a haze above it. Valerius could make out several huge public buildings among the claustrophobic warren of streets that populated most of the slope. His mind attempted to judge the scale of the massive walls.

'Three of them,' Lepidus confirmed what he was seeing, 'and the outer one must be at least fifty or sixty cubits, perhaps higher in places. Thick too, I'll wager.

We won't know until the engineers take a look, but I'm not sure how much damage our normal rams will do. We may need something special.' The last was almost to himself.

'I count fifteen towers on the part of the wall we can see,' Paternus ventured, 'so there can't be fewer than sixty. Not so many on the inner walls . . .'

'Plenty of wood for siege towers.' Valerius tried to inject an optimistic note. Lepidus looked at the trees around them and grunted approval.

'That's the first thing we'll do. I want the entire hilltop cleared and a defensive ditch dug by nightfall. Only post a small guard until dark; we'll need every man we've got to get the work done in time. You'll stay and help with the organization, Valerius?' Paternus gave Lepidus a look of surprise, but Valerius didn't argue. He'd planned to report directly to Titus, but the Tenth was short of tribunes and he couldn't refuse his friend. The legate's eyes narrowed. 'What do you make of the large building to the left in the walled compound? Almost a fort within a fort.'

'That is the Great Temple.' They turned to Josephus, who'd just ridden up. 'The most sacred building in all of Jerusalem, but currently in the hands of the least religious of men. It is protected to the north by the Antonia fortress and to the east by the cliff you see. Even if all Jerusalem were to fall you would still have a fight on your hands to take it. John of Gischala and his Galileans will defend it to the last, may his black heart rot. Do I have your leave to report to General Titus? I have information he might find useful.'

'Very well, Josephus.' Lepidus pointed to a large hill a mile to the north-east. 'He has his headquarters on the mountain. You can accompany the Emesan archers, but ask him if I can have them back at his pleasure. I'll feel exposed here until we get the defences set up.' The Judaean bowed and turned to leave, but Lepidus had one more question. 'What do they call this place?'

The Judaean reached up to pick a green fruit from the tree that shaded them and displayed it in the palm of his hand. 'Why, they call this hill the Mount of Olives, legate, and the valley down there is the Cedron.'

'Well, it will be the Mount of Olives no more by the time my lads have done with it.' Lepidus called for his aides. He nodded a farewell and rode across to where the Tenth's vanguard had just appeared over the brow of the hill, leaving Valerius and Paternus staring out over the valley to Jerusalem.

'Will they stand against four legions, do you think?' the scarred tribune wondered. 'Titus already has the Twelfth and Fifteenth in position, and the Fifth arrived an hour before we did.'

Valerius remembered the determined defence of Gamala and the little clusters of Judaeans throwing themselves to their deaths. *You will see the true mettle of the Jews at Jerusalem*, Josephus had predicted. 'Yes, I think they will stand.'

Paternus touched his hand to his ridged cheek in a gesture Valerius guessed was born of habit. 'Then I fear they will pay for it in pain and blood.'

'You will be reporting to Titus?' Valerius asked.

'Yes. I'll go with the Judaean.'

'Please pass on my compliments and tell him I will seek an audience when he has time to see me.'

'Of course.' The right side of Paternus's features twitched up in that curious emotionless smile. 'It appears Lepidus values your services.'

Valerius could have admitted the truth, that he'd served with the legate in Armenia, but he decided

Paternus hadn't yet earned it. 'He knows a proper soldier when he sees one,' he grinned.

The smile froze. 'Just so. I will ensure Titus receives your message.'

He disappeared off among the trees and Serpentius rode to Valerius's side. 'Lady Tabitha is leaving us.' Valerius nodded distractedly. The Spaniard looked past him to the city walls. 'So that's Jerusalem. We won't get in there as easily as we got into Rome.'

'What makes you think we'll be trying?' Valerius stared at his friend.

Serpentius produced a bark of laughter. 'If there's any shit around someone always makes sure we're the ones who're in it.'

They spent the next hour sweating in the sun with three centuries of the First cohort, helping construct the camp's fledgling defences. They began digging a proper ditch at the lower end of the site where it was most vulnerable to attack. From the slope above came the sound of axes as men cleared the dense olive groves, and the air was filled with the sweet scent of freshly hewn wood. Serpentius dug with the rest, but Valerius noticed that he kept glancing in the direction of the city.

'You think something's wrong?' He'd long ago learned to trust the Spaniard's instincts.

'I was just noticing the walls are empty, apart from a few guards.' Serpentius leaned on his mattock and stared towards Jerusalem. 'If four legions appeared on your doorstep you'd be up there with all your mates, counting their numbers and hating the bastards.'

'That's true.' Valerius followed Serpentius's gaze. 'Maybe the city council has told them to stay out of sight so we don't get a chance to gauge their strength.'

'Maybe.' The Spaniard laid down his entrenching tool and stretched for the long sword that lay within reach of his right hand. 'But I think I'll take a look— Shit!'

A hundred and fifty paces down the slope thousands of Judaean rebels suddenly exploded from a hidden gully and raced up the hill towards them armed with spears and curved swords. The attackers had climbed the rocky gorge in complete silence, the shadowy depths and their dust-coloured cloaks making them invisible to the guards above. Now they raced screaming into the open.

Valerius yelled at a trumpeter standing nearby, hypnotized by approaching death. 'Sound the alarm!'

Before they had time to react, the guards posted on the lower slopes were either slaughtered or had turned and run. Valerius saw in a single glance that unless someone made a stand the whole camp was about to be overwhelmed.

Serpentius made a movement in the direction of the attackers, but Valerius grabbed his arm. 'I need you alive with me, not a dead hero,' he said.

The Spaniard glared at him, but obeyed, automatically moving to Valerius's right side. As the strident calls of the alarm rang out across the hillside, the first instinct of the unprotected and totally surprised diggers was to reach for their weapons. Like Serpentius, all they had were swords and daggers. Their armour, shields and *pila* javelins were all neatly stacked much too far away in the centre of what would become the fort. From somewhere above Valerius heard cries of consternation and shouted orders which he hoped meant that Lepidus and his officers were already organizing a defensive position. That was all well and good, but these men would never reach them alive. There was only one chance.

'Form *orbis* on me.' He sprinted up the rising ground to a cleared area where it flattened out. Serpentius took up the cry as he matched Valerius's pace and soon hundreds of men were converging on them. Centurions hustled them into the defensive positions they'd practised a thousand times, instinctively creating the circular formation Valerius had ordered. A few dozen more arrived from the rear, led by Albinus, and Valerius saw with relief that they were all carrying shields. He ordered them forward to create a solid barrier in the front rank facing the bulk of the attackers. The veteran centurion came to his side in the centre of what was now more an extended oval than a circle, but would have to do.

'Not quite so much fun as Gamala.' Albinus spat the words through gritted teeth, plainly furious that his cohort had been surprised in the open. The last survivors clawed their way into the formation and turned to face the enemy with their swords, but behind them the slow and a few brave men who'd offered their lives to delay the attackers died under Judaean knives. Their agonized cries reached the *orbis* and a growl went up from the legionaries.

'Hold your ground, you bastards,' Albinus snarled, 'unless you want to join them.'

Valerius guessed a thousand men must be packed into the ring around him, but the Judaeans converging on the *orbis* numbered at least twice that. With no thought for their own lives the bravest immediately threw themselves against the outer ring, where Rome's finest rewarded anyone who came too close with a sword in his gullet or a mattock across his skull. More dangerous were the spearmen, who could outrange the legionary's short sword, but few were willing to hurl their weapons into the circle and leave themselves defenceless. The majority faced up to the outer rank, snarling threats and insults. Valerius allowed himself to relax a little. Although the perimeter rippled under an occasional foray he knew it was never likely to buckle unless under full-scale attack. The *orbis* was a classic defensive position where every man could support the next, but he prayed help would arrive soon. His only concern was that lack of armour and shields, and exposure to spears and slingshot pellets, guaranteed a steady stream of casualties. Apart from affecting morale, it increased the possibility that some blood-maddened section of legionaries would charge out of position and weaken the structure.

But help was close at hand.

In the centre of the crush it was difficult to see what happened. Valerius had a sense of the pressure fading, the growls of the legionaries turning to cheers and men sagging with relief as they realized they'd survived. Now it was the turn of the Judaeans to cry out in consternation and he saw the brandished swords and shields begin to waver, to draw back, and eventually to vanish as the men wielding them turned and ran. He risked a glance back up the hill and felt a surge of relief. Above the heads of his men he could see the *signum* standards of seven or eight cohorts bobbing down the hill towards the beleaguered legionaries of the First, the units they represented marching in compact squares across the rough ground.

From somewhere to Valerius's left came the shrill blast of a trumpet – not a *cornu*, which the infantry signallers used, but a *lituus*, the lighter horn carried by auxiliary cavalry – and then five hundred horsemen appeared on the crest overlooking the Judaean attackers. In an instant the retreat became a rout. The rebels sprinted over the cleared ground and half-finished ditch in an attempt to reach the sanctuary of the gully.

'What are you waiting for?' Albinus shouted. 'Finish the bastards.'

With a roar, the men of the First cohort unleashed all the pent-up anger and frustration of the last few minutes and charged down the slope. As they clawed at the fleeing Judaeans, a cohort of Thracian mounted spearmen smashed into the enemy flank, pinning the running men with seven-foot lances. The slowest were quickly overtaken and the air turned red as the legionaries struck at them with axes and mattocks or hacked at exposed backs with the *gladius*.

Valerius took no part in the butchery. He allowed the soldiers to stream past him while Serpentius remained dutifully at his side, twitching and growling like a chained hunting dog that scents blood. They watched as the last of the rebels tumbled into the gully, where their pursuers were happy to allow them to join the hundreds already streaming back into the city. Lepidus appeared at Valerius's side, his square patrician features pink with anger and frustration, but his first words expressed his relief.

'I thought we'd lost you there,' he said. 'Thank the gods we managed to salvage something from this disaster. I should have—' Something caught his eye amongst the cavalry and he groaned as a section of men broke away and trotted up the slope towards them. '*Merda*,' he hissed. 'He'll have my command for this, and maybe my head too.'

Valerius followed his gaze to where a tall figure in a gilded breastplate spurred his horse towards them at the head of his staff. Titus Flavius Vespasian drew up a few paces short of the three men. Lepidus's fist smashed into his armoured chest in salute. Valerius followed suit, reflecting that the gesture didn't have quite the same effect in a dust-stained tunic. An aide took Titus's reins and the general of the Army of the East dismounted and removed his helmet, wiping his handsome face with his neck cloth. His focus had been on Lepidus, but a narrowing of the eyes signalled recognition as he took in the wooden fist of the man at his side. Valerius could feel the hard-eyed stares of the staff officers, including Paternus, who wore a sardonic half-smile on the untouched part of his heat-scarred features.

Lepidus awaited the inevitable storm with the look of a man on the way to his execution, but Titus turned away. He studied the little clusters of dead and dying rebels and the legionaries returning up the slope carrying their casualties or supporting the wounded.

'I must apologize, general. I should have . . .' Lepidus swallowed, struggling to continue. 'A dereliction of duty, sir, for which I am willing to pay in full.'

Titus raised a hand for silence, his lips pursed thoughtfully as he continued to stare over the battlefield towards the city. Eventually he nodded to himself, and when he turned to face the legate of the Tenth his tone was surprisingly conciliatory. 'My father always says that a lesson learned seldom comes without a cost, dear Lepidus. Let us just say that you have had an insight into the true nature of our enemies. These rats are not content to stay in their holes.' His features twisted into a wry smile. 'Why, they almost had me this morning, didn't they, Tiberius?' Valerius belatedly recognized the dark eastern features of Tiberius Alexander among the aides. His expression warned that here was a man who didn't take his general's brush with danger quite so lightly. Titus ignored the stony frown and continued his story. 'We were taking a look at the north walls, near what they call the Women's Gate, and they made a sortie and surrounded us. They dragged poor Didius out of his saddle and fairly hacked him to pieces.'

'They might have done the same to you if the cavalry hadn't arrived,' Alexander growled. 'Yet you insisted on getting involved in this skirmish and risking your life again. What would your father say about that?'

Titus's hand went up to stroke his ear and Valerius almost smiled at the familiar, almost boyish gesture. 'My father would say that an officer must always put himself in the position of best advantage, no matter how much danger he places himself in. Isn't that right, Valerius?'

'With respect,' Valerius's throat seemed to be full of gravel and he coughed and spat in the dust, 'an army commander is not any officer, as I'm sure the Emperor would acknowledge.' He heard Alexander's mutter of approval turn to outrage as he continued: 'But it does the men good to know that their general is as willing to risk his life for them as they are for him.'

'Well said.' Titus laughed and clapped Valerius on the shoulder. He leaned forward and spoke quietly into the other man's ear. 'I am glad you are with us, old friend, even though your arrival is not without its complications. We will discuss it later.' He turned away with a smile. 'Now, gentlemen, let us get back to the deliberations which were so rudely interrupted by these barbarians, safe in the knowledge that dear Lepidus has learned his lesson. More guards, I think, legate; a good watch on that gate down there, and in those gullies. The Judaeans use the ground like snakes.'

He remounted, and as the party rode off towards the crest Lepidus let out a long breath. 'Lesson learned? I would rather fall on my sword than go through that

260

again.' He shook his head and turned away. 'Albinus? Where in the name of the gods is my *primus pilus*? And post some guards on that gully in case the bastards come back.'

'It's good to know he hasn't changed.' Serpentius spoke for the first time since the skirmish had begun.

But Valerius had noticed lines around his old friend's eyes and on his brow that had nothing to do with the year since they last met. 'I'm not so sure. Alexander was right. What he did today was reckless. The old Titus was always brave, but never reckless.'

The Spaniard nodded slowly as a line of men staggered past them carrying Roman dead for burial. 'I was thinking . . .'

'What?'

'We've been here less than one afternoon and we've lost a hundred men. How long do you think it will take?'

Valerius looked across to where Jerusalem's walls had filled with thousands of jeering men and women. 'How long is a lifetime?'

XXV

'Our valiant Idumaean allies have given the new arrivals something to think about,' suggested the shorter of the two men watching from the Antonia fortress as the attackers withdrew down the gully on the other side of the valley. The great fort where they stood was sited at the north-west corner of the Temple of Herod the Great, the tower so high they could clearly see the slope where the Romans had sited their camp. Zacharias had a beard of flaming red, an open, honest face pocked by the ravages of disease, and a mind capable of simultaneously juggling a hundred unsolvable problems. He was indispensable to the man by his side.

'They would have done more if John had sent his men from the Water Gate against that legion's baggage train.' Simon bar Giora knew he sounded irritated, but how could a man not be irritated when it took two days of discussion to decide on a change of guard? 'Do we know which legion it is yet?'

'The Tenth, we think, newly arrived from Jericho, but we'll know for certain when James and his Idumaeans report back. I specifically asked for any unit symbols. You can't be surprised that John wouldn't support them.

It's not six months since his men and James's were cutting each other's throats. They still would be if we weren't able to keep them apart. Thank God for the truce.'

Simon scratched his thick beard. It wasn't lice that made him tear at it until it hurt, but frustration and anger. If the Romans knew they were still killing each other they'd just sit back and watch. John of Gischala was as trustworthy as a cornered cobra. The truce with Simon's Zealots had allowed him to rest his forces until they were strong enough to take on Eleazar, whose faction still held the great temple behind them. It was only because of the truce they were able to stand here, because the Antonia was held by John's men and he would not give it up. Six months since he'd fought the newly arrived Idumaeans. Barely a month ago the slimy Galilean had used the catapults which were meant to be killing Romans to slaughter Eleazar's supporters as they prayed at the temple. Not content, he'd tried to raid the stores Simon had gathered and ended up burning most of the two-year supply he'd built up. The thought made Simon smash his fist against the parapet and his companion gave him a look of alarm. He was a giant of a man, with broad shoulders and meaty, shovel hands that had earned him the name he bore – Simon the Strong. Though usually calm and thoughtful he could be quick to anger if people or events pushed him too far.

'We must make them bleed,' Simon insisted, as much to himself as the other man. 'And be prepared to bleed in our turn.'

'Joshua believes it may have been Titus himself at the Women's Gate this morning,' his companion ventured. 'If—'

'If God had willed it he would be ours, I know. But God did not will it.' He shook his great lion's head. 'I sometimes wonder if God has abandoned his chosen people.'

'Do not say that, Simon. If anyone heard you!'

Simon gave a great bellow of laughter that started in his substantial belly and grew into his chest. 'You think he will strike me down before John or Eleazar? Come, walk with me, Zacharias. We will see what effect the Idumaean attack has had on your fellow citizens.'

They walked down the broad sandstone steps of the tower into the courtyard. No part of the city was better placed for defence, but Simon prayed it would never be needed, for if the Romans ever reached this far Jerusalem was lost. The thought made him shudder. He'd vowed the city would never be taken.

Four years earlier Simon bar Giora had halted the first Roman advance from the north. His forces attacked the legions from the rear when they least expected it and carried off their baggage train and the heavy weapons. Added to those taken from the Twelfth legion with their eagle, he hoped the *ballistae* would give the defenders something like parity in artillery.

His victory should have won him a place in the highest councils of his people, but he didn't bargain for the priests' distrust of a common farmer's son. Instead, that success, and the necessity for his followers to live off the land afterwards, caused the authorities in Jerusalem to brand him a bandit. As the Romans grew stronger it seemed certain they'd destroy Simon's force. Instead he'd fooled them by backtracking, and using the Sicarii, the shock troops of his army, to surprise and overthrow the great fortress of Masada. There he stayed, impregnable and feared, until he heard of the death of his arch-enemy Ananus, High Priest of Judaea. With Ananus out of the way he gathered support in the countryside

264

from the disaffected who were as happy to follow a peasant as a priest. Forty thousand men came to him. Forty thousand. Despite his melancholy he smiled at the memory. The immensity of it all had given him the notion of calling himself 'king'. His wife Mariam had laughed and dressed the children as little golden princes and princesses and made him understand how foolish he'd appear. Had it only been a year ago? It felt as if that had been the last time he'd been happy.

It had been the high point. In the months that followed, Rome's legions had hounded and herded Simon's forces back towards Jerusalem, and John of Gischala had become so obsessed with power he'd declared himself king and set about butchering his rivals. He was so loathed and feared that the very men who had laughed at the thought of Simon bar Giora's leading them had opened their gates to him in the hope that he would overthrow their tormentor.

Now Simon was responsible for the welfare of more than a hundred thousand people while simultaneously fighting an enemy of overwhelming strength amid a murderous three-way power struggle. Worse, this was the fourth day of the festival of Passover and the city was crammed with worshippers. He guessed several hundred thousand were camped in the city's streets: men, women and children from every corner of Judaea, and even as far as the distant Euphrates. Every one an innocent, but they were an encumbrance and he wanted them gone.

And always in the background the feral scent of Joseph Ben Mahtityahu. Bad enough that he had gone crawling on his belly to the oppressors and perhaps natural he should take such an interest in happenings in Jerusalem. But there was something else, and Simon thought he understood its nature, if not the reasoning behind it. He had acted to close off one threat. He'd hoped to hear word of the success of Shimon's mission before now, but there could be many reasons why he had not . . . He shook his head and Zacharias turned to look at him. 'It's nothing,' he said with a bleak smile. 'I was just thinking I should have stayed on the farm.'

Zacharias stopped in mid-stride and took him by the arm. 'Never say that, Simon,' he said fervently. 'I do not believe God has abandoned us. I believe he sent you to us. The people of Jerusalem know they can depend on Simon bar Giora, if no other. You are our protector and I pray that with God's help you will be our saviour.'

Simon hung his head so his friend could not see the dampness in his eyes. When he lifted it again they contained new strength. 'Come then.' He smiled. 'Let us show our people we are with them.'

In the familiar, stifling confines of the narrow streets between the fort and the lower city the tangy scents of the evening meal's preparation fought for supremacy with the all-pervading stink of the night soil containers, the dried sweat of their owners, and the ubiquitous piss pots of the dyers and leather workers. Zacharias had been born here and had known nothing else. Simon, though more used to the clean air of the mountainous south, had discovered that the very closeness of his surroundings gave an illusion of sanctuary he found comforting. As they walked, he felt people's eyes turning towards him and he could hear the murmur of voices that followed his passage. Soon the crowd following the two men was so numerous that the sound of their progress preceded them. Heads appeared from the windows ahead, wondering what the excitement was about.

'I told you you needed a bodyguard,' Zacharias muttered. 'Why couldn't you at least have brought

266

Isaac? All any one of them has to do is pull out a knife and it's finished. How do you know John's men aren't just waiting out there somewhere?'

'Why would I need a bodyguard among my own people?' Simon walked all the taller. 'You were the one who said they loved me. In any case,' his voice turned solemn, 'God is looking over my shoulder, is he not?'

Zacharias emitted a sound that reminded Simon of an exasperated camel. 'Then at least lend God your aid by keeping your eyes open for a threat. You are like a child in a sweet merchant's.'

'A man must appreciate life while he can, Zacharias. Do you know who taught me that?'

His companion shook his head and pushed his way through another group of admirers.

'Mariam.' Zacharias grimaced as Simon failed to take the hint. 'Do you know I once thought of making myself king, like that fool John? She said she would rather see me shovelling dung in the lowest farmyard than on the throne of the greatest city in Judaea. Help your people and come back to me, she said. Plant the corn and harvest it. Grind the grain and bake the bread. And she was right.' His voice turned wistful. 'But she was also wrong.' Simon met Zacharias's eyes. 'Because a man cannot turn back time, can he, Zacharias? All he can do is follow his own destiny. Will I ever return, do you think?'

Zacharias held his friend's gaze for a moment, because to turn away would be a betrayal. 'That is a question I cannot answer, Simon. It is God's will.'

The two men emerged into an open space between the second and outer walls filled with sheepskin tents. Around them sat or lay hundreds of warriors. They looked exhausted, and many tended the wounds of their

267

comrades. The bulk were flesh wounds and scrapes caused by their rushed descent of the gully during the retreat, but Simon could see some would not live the night. He searched the throng until he found the man he was looking for, a tall, fierce-looking soldier with wild, bushy hair and a dark beard.

James of Rehoboth, the Idumaean commander, looked up as they approached. 'That will do,' he told the man bandaging his injured arm. 'We would have had them,' he told Simon. 'They hadn't put out any guards and ran like rabbits when we charged from the gully. One or two of their officers made the difference. They rallied their men into a defensive circle and we couldn't break it. When their reinforcements arrived it was we who did the running.'

'A wise tactical retreat.' James's head came up and his eyes glittered with menace. He was a proud man and he would not be mocked. Fortunately, the look on Simon's face told him otherwise. 'We have to strike them when they least expect it,' the Judaean continued. 'Or fight them from behind these walls. Make them bleed for every foot of ground until they decide they have bled enough. How many did you lose?'

'Two hundred. Some of my best. You know how it is, the bravest are always at the front. Still, it was worth it if we gave the others time to ransack the baggage train. Supplies, weapons, we are short of everything.' Even as he said the words James sensed a stillness in the two men. 'They did not succeed?'

'They did not leave the city.' Zacharias couldn't meet his eyes.

James studied his arm where the blood was already seeping through the cotton bandage. 'I will kill him,' he said, the words ingrained with chilling certainty.

'You will have to take your place among a line of willing executioners.' Simon couldn't conceal the bitterness in his voice. 'How long will it take your men to recover?'

'We will be ready when you need us. We came here to fight, and to die if necessary. Some of us are true to our word.'

Simon and Zacharias made their way back through the second wall and into the city. There was no point in delay. Simon led the way along the Street of Solomon, one of the city's broadest thoroughfares. Like every open space in Jerusalem it was part filled with pens of skinny cattle and plaintively bleating goats that had been driven into the city before the Romans arrived. Tents, awnings and other makeshift shelters took up most of the rest, each of them occupied by a family of pilgrims. It was the same in the normally less populous Bezetha, the New City, between the second and third walls. They'd managed to keep the sanitary arrangements for the refugees at a tolerable level, but Simon knew it wouldn't last. With the Romans here there would be limited access to the pits at Gehenna. One more reason to get them out of the city.

He stopped in front of a tent where a woman with dark, soulful eyes suckled an infant. Two other children, a boy and a girl, blank-faced and dirty, looked on. 'Where is your husband, mother?' Simon tried to appear as kindly as one of his stature could manage. 'He should be here to keep you safe.'

She looked up and he noticed that the breast she offered the child had been sucked near dry. 'Benyamin has gone to try to buy food,' she replied. 'But there is little to spare.' Her eyelids drooped and though she tried to disguise it her voice was heavy with exhaustion and despair.

Simon nodded to Zacharias and the aide surreptitiously slipped a loaf of flat unleavened bread from the sack he carried. He split the loaf in two, then divided it again, handing the quarters to the older children before giving the intact half to the woman. With immense restraint she took a small bite before placing the grey semicircle behind her where it couldn't be seen.

'Have you come far, . . . ?'

'I am Judith,' she answered his unspoken question with lowered eyes, 'and I thank you for your kindness, though I did not ask for it. We travelled from Ephraim six days ago. It was a long journey, and hard, but by God's grace we reached Jerusalem in time to celebrate the festival in his temple.'

Simon knew of the place, a small town in the rugged hills two days to the north. A hard journey indeed. 'That was very brave,' he said. 'These are dangerous times. The Romans . . .'

'Benyamin says God will strike the Romans down as he brought down the ten plagues upon Egypt and the children of Israel will prevail.'

Her voice contained not an ounce of doubt and Simon wished he had a fraction of her faith. He allowed himself a smile that acknowledged the possibility. 'It is not unknown for armies on the march to be afflicted by such maladies. I pray daily for God's aid, but I fear sacrifice and courage will also be required.'

Judith stiffened as a shadow fell over the little shelter. 'My husband Benyamin.' There was a hint of fear in her eyes at the appearance of a heavyset man with a black beard. He wore a brown smock with a carpenter's belt at the waist. A thin boy of about thirteen stood just behind him. 'And my son Moses. I thank you again for your kindness.'

'You will be leaving soon?' Simon addressed the words to the husband.

'Not till we have completed our devotions.' Truculence hardened the man's words, as if he regarded every stranger as a threat to his world. 'Moses wants to stay and fight God's enemies, but there is the harvest to bring in.'

'I will pray for your safe return.' With a heavy heart Simon bowed his head and turned away. These people would face starvation and slaughter unless he did something about it. The animals that provided meat and milk seemed plentiful, but that was an illusion. He'd been horrified when his quartermasters had pointed out how quickly a population could consume its own weight in supplies. And that had been before the grain stores had burned. The memory stoked the fire growing inside him and he increased his pace so that Zacharias struggled to keep up. They crossed through an ancient gate in the first wall and beneath the bridge over the Tyropoeon valley. Now they were in the district known as the Lower City, in ancient times the city of David. A few minutes later Simon turned into the gateway to a substantial tower. He marched past a pair of guards, ignoring their protests and before Zacharias could stop him he disappeared up a narrow stairway, taking the stairs two by two. A group of hard-eyed men lounged near the top of the steps sharpening their swords.

'Your business?' The voice of the speaker held no welcome and Simon heard Zacharias growl as he caught up.

'You know my business very well, Aaron son of Arinus, whose father would hardly have countenanced your delaying me, since he fought at my side at Masada.' His voice softened. 'He was a good man, and I mourn him.'

271

The young man's head dropped, but only for a moment. 'He was, but still I must ask you.'

'I would talk to John of Gischala, unless he means to fight the Romans alone.'

Aaron frowned. 'Very well.' He hesitated. 'You have no weapons.'

'Do I need any?'

Aaron swivelled and looked back up the stairs behind him. When he turned back to face Simon his eyes contained a warning. 'That must be for you to decide.'

Simon bar Giora acknowledged his thanks with a brisk nod. He stepped past the reclining men and continued up the steps till he emerged into the fading light on the battlements overlooking the Cedron gorge.

Someone had set up what looked like a throne so John of Gischala could watch the afternoon's battle in comfort. Now he sat with his hands folded, his pale eyes contemplating his visitor and an amused half-smile on his thin lips. The Galilean commander had a high forehead and a long, narrow nose. He wore a fine robe of scarlet and gold and across his knees lay an iron sword, the blade polished to a gleaming finish. The two men stared at each other for what seemed an eternity before John spoke. 'You should have sent word of your coming and I would have received you in a state worthy of your rank and fame.' The smile broadened, but Simon knew it was as authentic as a hyena's laughter and in any case he hadn't come here to exchange pleasantries.

'Why did you not attack as we agreed?'

'Did we agree? I understood I was to act on my own judgement.'

'As to the timing, yes, but not whether to attack at all.'

'It was clear to me the Idumaeans must fail.' The other man gave a careless shrug that sent another wave of almost untamable anger through Simon. 'Why should I sacrifice my men to save the lives of a few desert savages?'

Simon took a step forward and the guards on either side of the throne tensed. Zacharias laid a hand on his arm, but he ignored it. 'Not to save the lives of a few desert savages – though may I remind you they are your allies and the finest warriors in the city – but to strip the Roman baggage train of supplies, to replace those you burned.'

John of Gischala's face reddened and the smile disappeared. 'A people fight all the better for being hungry.'

'A hand that wields a sword will not do so for long if its owner is starving.'

'What is done cannot be undone.' The man on the throne raised a placating hand. 'We should not bicker, you and I. As you have told me so often, we have enough enemies beyond the walls without creating more inside them. Will you break bread with me?'

Simon hesitated. For all his fine words John of Gischala had never held to a bargain in his life. To refuse another's hospitality would be ill-mannered, but he couldn't bring himself to sit down with the man. 'I must return to my family,' he lied, 'a special meal. The Romans have us surrounded now and there will be no more. They will attack soon.'

'Yes?' John's tone was guarded.

'You are prepared as we discussed?'

'Of course.' He called a large bearded warrior across. 'Tell him.'

'We defend the eastern wall. If they attack they will be forced to mass in the gorge and on the slope beyond.

We have catapults and siege engines ranged on the likely places and every tower and every inch of parapet will be filled with warriors. The rough ground at the base of the walls means they will have to build ramps if they are to get their siege engines close. We will slaughter them before they are completed.'

'Good enough,' Simon nodded. He might not be able to trust John, but this man knew his business. Something else came to him. This was an opportunity and he couldn't let pride stand in the way. 'There is one more thing. Do I have your support to ask the priests to send the Passover pilgrims home? Once the attack begins it will be difficult and dangerous for them to leave, even with Titus's authority.'

'You have it, for all the good it will do you. Phannias, that fool of a stonemason Eleazar has declared High Priest, is telling them their souls will be forfeit if they do not complete their devotions. It is only another three days.'

'Nevertheless, three days with a swarm of locusts consuming our supplies, so we must try. I will draft an appeal to Titus asking him to provide free passage. They are innocents, harmless families with children, and this is not their war. He may be a Roman, but if our foe is an honourable man he cannot refuse.'

XXVI

'No.'

Valerius and the officers gathered in Titus's command pavilion for the council of war that would decide the fate of Jerusalem struggled to hide their reactions to his unexpected decision. Sumptuous wall hangings of red, gold and purple insulated the tent for both heat and sound. The single other decoration was a bust of the Emperor looking grim and square-jawed, with more hair than Valerius remembered from their last meeting. 'There are no innocents in war. Draft a message informing the commander of Jerusalem that no one may leave the city before its formal surrender, which he is perfectly at liberty to offer.'

'I agree there are no innocents in war.' The speaker was Marcus Clemens, the new commander of the Twelfth and a long-time friend of Titus's family. Of them all he was closest enough to his commander to offer a contrary opinion. 'But surely there are practical reasons for allowing them to leave. We are told they are mostly peasant families?' Josephus, who stood at the back of the tent, nodded in agreement. 'Then they pose little danger to us outside the city. But keep them penned inside and for every family you have a protector who will fight to the death for them.'

The suggestion provoked a murmur of agreement. Titus had invited all four of his legionary commanders to gather round a map of Jerusalem. Valerius knew Clemens by sight and Lepidus of the Tenth well. The others were Titus Phrygius, a grim-faced senator who commanded the Fifteenth, and Sextus Cerealis, veteran legate of the Fifth, one of Corbulo's legions during the conquest of Armenia. Tiberius Alexander, the army's chief of staff, stood slightly apart alongside Marcus Antonius, Judaea's procurator. The only surprising absentee was Alexander's deputy, Paternus, but that could be explained by his recent arrival. Valerius had no formal role at the conference and he determined to keep his face as closed as his mouth. Nevertheless, his presence was a mark of Titus's favour and he was grateful for it.

Clemens concluded his argument. 'By refusing this offer you almost certainly double the number of men facing us and make it more difficult to fight our way through the town when the walls are breached.'

Titus nodded thoughtfully, but he was conceding the point, not the argument. 'You are right, Marcus, but this is not a military decision, it is a practical one. I believe it may save us much time and thousands of my soldiers' lives. They are short of supplies you say, Josephus?'

'Yes,' the Judaean agreed. 'They had gathered enough grain to feed the city for two years, but John of Gischala stole what he could for his own men and burned the rest. The fire happened after the last harvest and you have invested the place before the next. It couldn't have been worse timed for them. I doubt they have enough to hold out for six months.'

'Six months.' Titus's blue eyes searched the tent for any contrary opinion. 'But I do not have six months. My father will return to Rome in three and I intend to present him with Jerusalem as a gift for his homecoming. Six months' supply for a city of a hundred thousand people is a month's supply for six times that number.'

'You plan to starve them out?'

'That will be part of my strategy, yes, Lepidus. The sight of starving children will ever be a recommendation to surrender. When fathers see the flesh falling from the faces of their sons, the milk drying up in the mothers' breasts, they will be quick to make their views known.'

Valerius wondered whether Titus was again guilty of underestimating his enemy. He remembered the fatalism of the Judaeans who had leapt to their deaths at Gamala. They too had been peasants, but they'd been prepared to die rather than surrender. Would a man who'd watched his child die be any more likely to give up? But he knew his view was coloured by another consideration. He'd seen what happened when besieged cities fell. If Titus was wrong and Jerusalem had to be assaulted, all those thousands of women and children would be trapped. The screams and the scent of roasting flesh at Cremona returned to him and his stomach soured at the memory. When he looked up he found Titus staring at him.

'We are agreed then. They stay unless the tactical situation warrants otherwise. Now, to the city itself . . .'

They talked over the various possibilities, the most favourable assault points, the difficulties presented by three separate walls, the siting of artillery. The detail of any attack would be dictated by the legates, but the principle was agreed. Three legions, the Fifth, Twelfth and Fifteenth, would invest the west of the city, while the

Tenth maintained its position on the Mount of Olives to divide the attention of the defenders.

'You say this valley would provide a site capable of accommodating us, Josephus?'

'Not the valley itself, lord, the terrain is too rugged. But deploy on the plateaus to the north and south and you will have the freedom to attack the walls on either side, while ensuring the defenders must man both.'

'Very well. The final decision will be mine, but that can wait.'

'There is one more thing, general . . .' Even Clemens sounded hesitant.

'Yes?'

'The temple. It is . . .'

'Sacred to the Judaeans. I understand that.'

Clemens looked to Josephus for support, but the Judaean only shrugged. In this matter he could afford no opinion. 'If we take the city by storm, which naturally, given your earlier statements, we pray will not be necessary . . .' Titus nodded, but in a way that hinted his patience was wearing thin. 'The rules of war insist that it be destroyed; burned to the ground and every piece of plunder removed,' Clemens continued. 'Yet, as you have rightly said, it is sacred, not just to our enemies who defend the city, but to our allies. Herod, the father of the present ruler, near bankrupted his kingdom to create this wonder. His followers, some of whom will fight at our side, revere not just the structure but everything it stands for. With respect, might we not issue a special protocol guaranteeing the protection of the Great Temple and its contents? Such a gesture could erode the fighting spirit of the defenders almost as much as the tactics you have suggested.'

Titus smiled. 'A fine speech, Marcus, and a fine sentiment. It is true that, as a structure, the temple

278

has never been surpassed, and that as a fount of their religion it can never be replaced.' Valerius glanced towards Josephus and imagined he saw a mix of calculation and triumph on his face that vanished when the Judaean realized he was being observed. 'You will not be surprised that I have pondered this matter, which I agree is of great importance, and that I have taken advice from the most distinguished sources.' It seemed certain Josephus was the source Titus meant, but a titter of nervous laughter from Antonius, the youngest man present, suggested the answer might be more complex. A savage glare from Titus and a promise of violent retribution in Alexander's stare instantly silenced the procurator. 'If the building is protected it shows my father in a certain light: magnanimous in victory and tolerant of the Empire's religions, which may be no bad thing. Likewise, it is of unsurpassed beauty, which immediately makes one jealous of its welfare, much as a man might attempt to preserve his finest sculpture in a fire. Yet there is another aspect, and as a military commander it would be neglectful of me not to consider it. Look out across the valley there and what do you see?'

'A fortress,' Clemens suggested.

Titus shook his head. 'A fortress within a fortress within a fortress. Perhaps a thousand fortresses. And it is possible that we will have to expend Roman blood to take every one. I look at Jerusalem and I see a complex defensive work of a like we have never confronted before and at its heart is the most impregnable fortress of all. The temple.'

He paused to allow his words to make their mark. Each man's mind turned to the puzzle that must be unlocked and every man came to the same conclusion. Titus rose from the table and drew back the curtain covering the doorway. Framed in the opening, almost as if he had planned it, was the temple.

'One way or another we will take Jerusalem.' His voice took on a stony resolve Valerius had never heard before. 'From the information I have received, the temple will be defended to the last by these Zealot fanatics and their Sicarii allies. If that is the case, they have made their decision. It is no longer the temple, the sacred, hallowed ground of an ancient religion. It is a stronghold that is an affront and a challenge to Rome. If they choose to shed Roman blood defending it, then they and it will take the consequences. If, to save one Roman life, I must use every siege engine to batter the temple into dust I will not shrink from it; perhaps,' his eyes turned to Valerius, 'they may even choose to burn it themselves, and perish in the ashes. If that is the case I will grant them their wish. Go now and make your dispositions. We will convene again tomorrow afternoon. In the meantime, I would ask the commanders of the Fifth, Twelfth and Fifteenth to study the western defences and form alternative plans to attack.'

As the officers rose and filed from the tent Titus held a whispered conversation with Josephus. When Valerius went to follow them Vespasian's son held up a hand to signal him to stay. Eventually, Josephus nodded solemnly and walked out with a glance at Valerius that was almost conspiratorial.

When they were alone Titus sighed and rubbed his face with his hands like a weary man at the end of a long day. He turned to Valerius with a wry grin. 'Everyone has an opinion and all must be heard,' he complained. 'But it is important they know I trust them and value their experience. You too have an opinion, I suspect. You are not usually quite so backward in expressing it.'

'I am your guest, general. Guests don't offer an opinion until their host demands it.'

'Well? I saw your face when we were discussing the pilgrims. You think I am being harsh by insisting they stay and share the hardships of the rebels?'

'No.' Valerius shook his head. 'I think Clemens is correct that there are risks, but if you are right those risks are worth taking.'

'And the temple?'

'I know you well enough to know you wouldn't wantonly destroy anything of such beauty, but I was at Cremona, and in Rome when the Temple of Jupiter burned. War breeds complications. Men make mistakes. Orders are misunderstood. If the Judaeans defend the temple complex you have no option but to attack it. When you do, anything can happen.'

'Good.' Titus smiled, more friend now than general. 'I'm glad you understand. You saw the Zealots this morning and at Gamala. What do you make of them?'

Valerius met his eyes, trying to gauge the likely effect of the unpalatable truth he was about to utter. Eventually he said: 'I think you will have to wade knee-deep through blood to take Jerusalem.'

For a moment Titus looked as if he had been slapped in the face, but he recovered quickly and nodded to acknowledge the possibility. 'I will do everything in my power to avoid it, but if that is what it takes to break the rebels and deliver this city to my father, I will not shirk from it.'

In the silence that followed Valerius wondered if his friend's head was filled with the same images that haunted him, but it seemed Titus had other things on his mind.

'I had word by courier that you were on your way.' He held up a hand to forestall Valerius's question. 'It does not matter who sent it, only that they had your interests at heart. You seek a position on my staff, a command perhaps?'

Valerius kept his face emotionless and thanked his nameless benefactor for saving him the necessity of having to plead. 'I will serve wherever you think I can be of the greatest value.'

'A good answer, as always,' Titus's eyes turned knowing, 'but one you may live to regret.' He strode to the doorway and drew back the curtain. By now it was full night, but the watchfires of Jerusalem twinkled on the far side of the valley. 'Did you know that, on the day the man Christus died, the Judaeans claim it was as dark as this at noon?'

Valerius went to stand beside him. 'A cloud covers the sun,' he said. 'A soothsayer claims a miracle, the story grows with the years until it becomes truth. Before Colonia fell to Boudicca men claimed statues toppled of their own accord and the sea turned red, but I saw neither.'

'My ever practical Valerius.' Titus smiled and clapped his shoulder. 'It is reassuring to know you haven't changed. Good, that means I can be open with you. There will be no command for you in the Army of the East.' Despite himself, Valerius flinched at the blow to his hopes. Titus was astute enough to recognize his disappointment and tried to soften the impact. 'If it were my decision only, Valerius, you would have an eagle and a legion to follow it, but there are other considerations. You should know my father believes none of the nonsense uttered at your trial. In time, there will be compensations, but first he must consolidate his position. You know better than I the undercurrents and shifting loyalties in the Senate.' He waited for an acknowledgement from Valerius and the one-handed Roman nodded. 'That means my brother Domitian has an important part to play. He has laid the foundations for my father's return and he can just as easily remove them. After what happened in Rome, to give you a command in my army would be seen as an insult to Domitian. For my father's sake, and for my own reasons, I cannot afford to risk that.'

'It was asking too much.' Valerius picked up his cloak and made to leave, but Titus hurried across and took it from him.

'Let there be no misunderstanding between us, Valerius. I meant every word and dearly regret being unable to give you the command your experience and your friendship merit. Yet you said you were prepared to serve where you would be of the greatest use? Did you mean it?'

'Of course. I will serve in the ranks. Perhaps if I distinguished—'

'You have distinguished yourself enough for three lifetimes, my friend, but it would make no difference. These are political practicalities, not military ones.' Valerius stared at him in consternation. What now? 'The service I have in mind may be distasteful. It may also be dangerous. Josephus tells me you saved his life?'

Valerius blinked at the abrupt change of direction. 'It might have appeared so at the time.'

'Do not be so modest,' Titus laughed. 'I also hear you have been teaching yourself Judaean?' Now Valerius looked up sharply. The information could only have come from one source. Tabitha. An amused half-smile on Titus's lips confirmed he was perfectly aware of it.

'A little,' Valerius admitted.

'Josephus carries out certain other delicate tasks apart from being my adviser on political and religious matters in Judaea. This has made him unpopular amongst his

283

former comrades. The attempt on his life at Gamala was not the first, nor will it be the last. I want you – and Serpentius, if you wish – to act as his protectors.'

'I doubt he would want that,' Valerius protested.

'Do not underestimate yourself, Valerius. Josephus says he trusts you, and Josephus is a careful man. Of course, that may itself be a ruse, because he is also cynical and devious. Perhaps he thinks he has a use for you. But it is of no matter. What matters is that it suits Titus Flavius Vespasian for his old friend Valerius to be close to his Judaean adviser.' He let the words hang in the air so Valerius understood exactly what he meant. Protecting Josephus was only half the job. Titus decided he had to be more explicit. 'Being a student under Seneca made you as fine a reader of men as anyone I have ever come across. The work Josephus does raises certain questions; perhaps you can come up with some of the answers I would like.'

'You want me to spy on him?'

'Let us just say I would be interested in your observations. Of course, if you feel for reasons of honour . . .'

Valerius actually laughed. 'This from the man who sent me to "advise" Marcus Antonius, who wanted to kill me. In any case, you saved my life. I can still feel the chill of the executioner's sword on my neck.'

'Be certain, Valerius. It will be dangerous. I could be sending you to your death.'

Valerius took a deep breath. 'I'll do it. Nobody lives for ever, as Serpentius is so fond of reminding me.'

'How is he? He seems . . . altered.'

'The blow on the head almost killed him. Physically his skills are unchanged – he's as deadly as ever with any weapon you care to name – but sometimes his mind is elsewhere.'

Titus nodded as if the words confirmed his own observation. 'I will make sure he is looked after if anything happens to you.'

'I'd count it a favour.'

'And your new position merits a senior tribune's share of the bounty if . . . when we take Jerusalem. You could be a rich man.'

'Rich or dead.' Valerius had noticed the momentary hesitation. Did even Titus have doubts? 'One way or other it seems my days of worrying are over.'

The sentiment won a boyish grin from Vespasian's son. 'If only I could say the same. Now, you will dine with me. There is someone I would like you to meet.'

XXVII

To Valerius's surprise the meal didn't take place in camp. Escorted by a reinforced troop of a hundred legionary cavalry, they rode north until a pair of flickering torches signalled the gates of a villa or a farmstead. Trusted soldiers from Titus's old command, the Fifteenth, guarded the gateway and Valerius had no doubt more of them waited in the darkness. Whoever they were dining with was precious to the young general.

'A great deal of security.' Titus read his thoughts with a smile. 'But I have to remember that I am the Emperor's son now, and soon to be his heir. Besides, did you not chide me for exposing myself to the enemy earlier today?'

'Who lives here?'

'It is owned by a local magistrate murdered by the Sicarii, but I have commandeered it to house a friend who is visiting.' As they turned into the gateway he inspected Valerius, who wore a borrowed toga beneath his cloak, and nodded approvingly. 'You will do. The scarred tribune – Paternus, isn't it? – told me you wore a general's armour the first time he saw you.'

'A gift from Sohaemus of Emesa for a service I did him,' Valerius admitted. 'I intend to pass it on to someone more worthy of it.'

'No, you must keep it.' Titus grinned. 'Who knows, you may yet have need of it. In fact, you should have worn it tonight. Our host would have been most impressed.'

They rode up the shallow slope of a ridge in the direction of a dull glow in the ink-blue sky. Moments later the light from numerous oil lamps illuminated a building of surprising scale. They dismounted and servants took their cloaks before a chamberlain escorted them to a large room set out with cushioned couches and an ornate low table. The moment he entered Valerius had the sensation of being stripped bare under the appraisal of a pair of hypnotic eyes the colour of polished chestnut. At first glance she was no classic beauty, but a moment later he decided she was one of the most striking women he had ever seen. A half-smile as she noted his reaction said she knew it too.

Long, silken lashes framed the brown eyes and she had a narrow, aristocratic nose set above full lips that shone like Caspian rubies. Her face was a perfect oval and he guessed the wide mouth could turn sulky if – and he doubted it happened often – she didn't get her way. The dark lines of her brows arched in perfect curves across a smooth brow and her hair was styled in tight ringlets arranged in waves across her scalp. Like all her features, her ears were in precise harmony with the whole: small, delicate and hung with gold and precious gemstones that matched the necklace at her throat. She wore a dress of Roman design, but in an exotic shimmering blue that reminded him of a sunny morning off the coast of Creta, with gold braid at the neck, sleeves and hem.

She lounged comfortably on a couch arranged at the far side of the table and it took a moment before he realized she wasn't the only occupant of the room. Two other women stood behind the couch. One was Tabitha, with an amused glint in her eyes that told him she was having trouble keeping her face straight. Her presence confirmed his suspicions about the identity of the woman at the table and the reason for Titus's visit.

'Queen Berenice of Cilicia.' Titus made the introduction. 'My comrade Gaius Valerius Verrens, a valiant soldier and a holder of the Corona Aurea.'

Valerius bowed and Berenice responded with the slightest inclination of her head. Here was a woman accustomed to men's homage. When she spoke, her voice was husky, low and naturally seductive. 'Your description did not do him justice, Tabitha.'

Under the gaze of the two women Valerius felt as if his tongue had been tied in a knot. Berenice's wide eyes pinned him until Titus broke the spell.

'Valerius, I do believe you are blushing.'

The jest inspired a change in the atmosphere. Berenice struggled not to laugh and Valerius caught the mood. 'I merely reflect the glow of my lady's beauty.' He repeated his bow, catching a look in Tabitha's eyes that made him feel as if he were caught between a charge of Iceni champions on the one side and Parthian Invincibles on the other.

'Come, sit by my right side.' Berenice pointed to the couch. 'You must tell me about the first time you and Prince Titus met.'

Titus's unexpected elevation surprised Valerius, but he managed not to show it. Vespasian's son gave him a tight smile that warned this wasn't a subject for discussion. The queen gestured a servant forward and he poured wine into three of the four silver cups on the table. Of course Berenice, a ruler in her own right, would grace her lover – and Valerius had no doubt they were lovers – with a title. When he considered it, Titus, the heir to an emperor, was certainly a prince at the very least, a prince of Rome.

'If I remember it correctly I was roasting like a fish on a griddle on an Egyptian beach, with the last sip of water a distant memory . . .'

A bustle of activity from outside the room interrupted his account and a figure in military uniform appeared in the doorway. Titus looked up expectantly and frowned when he discovered the newcomer wasn't the one he expected.

'General Tiberius Alexander sends his apologies, Lord Titus, but the logistics of tomorrow's move make it impossible for him to attend.' Claudius Paternus saluted. 'He suggested you might be happy to have my company in his stead.'

The words were courteous enough, but there was a sardonic edge to the tone that made Titus's face harden as he looked up into the ravaged face. 'I am sure you have more pressing duties—'

'No,' Queen Berenice intervened with a smile. 'I am sure Tiberius would not make the suggestion without good reason. Let me see your face.' Valerius saw Paternus flinch at what could be taken as a calculated insult before he turned so that the scarred portion of his features was visible. Berenice motioned towards a position directly across the table. 'So we have two veterans with interesting stories to tell. How fitting.' She looked to Titus for affirmation and he gave an irritated nod for Paternus to take his place on the couch. 'You were telling me about your first encounter with Prince Titus, Valerius.'

Valerius glanced at Paternus, whose single eye almost smoked with suppressed fury. 'We were out of water and I doubt we would have lasted another hour,' he continued. 'If Prince Titus hadn't appeared with his auxiliaries I would not be here.'

Titus took the praise as his due. 'It was fortunate we arrived in time,' he smiled. 'But more fortunate we found your young tribune staggering across our path. If anything, he was the true hero. What was his name again?'

'Crescens.' Valerius was looking at Titus, but he sensed the man to his left stiffen and wondered why. 'Tiberius Claudius Crescens.' He'd ridden more than thirty miles across featureless desert in a near-suicidal attempt to reach help.

'Of course. A fine young soldier. What happened to him?'

'He didn't survive the campaign.' Valerius's tone signalled his reluctance to go into more detail. There was much more to Tiberius's story than the mere fact of his death, not least that Valerius had been the cause of it. Again he felt the baleful presence of the man at his left side. He turned to find Paternus's eye fixed on him, the uninjured portion of his features a stony mask. As he returned the stare his mind picked up the tiny details that had previously escaped him. By the time Paternus looked away Valerius had a feeling they'd come to some kind of understanding. So that was the way it was?

Servants brought platters of food. Simple enough fare: sliced vegetables, boiled eggs and smoked fish for the *gustus*, followed by a roast goose and a fat-tailed lamb especially slaughtered for the occasion. Honeyed grapes and delicious pomegranate seeds that popped in the mouth to release their sweet juices completed the meal. Valerius suspected Berenice would have preferred a more exotic menu, but that Titus had decreed modesty, as befitting a soldier on campaign. The wine, a fresh, pine-scented eastern variety, was plentiful. No one at the table overindulged. Again, that sense of reserve, or perhaps anticipation, as if this was but the prelude to something more important.

Throughout, Valerius was aware of a pair of eyes staring at him from the back of the room. Tabitha and her companion never moved except to provide their mistress with a personal bowl and towel to wipe her hands between courses.

At one point Titus thawed enough to make conversation with Paternus, and Valerius found himself the sole focus of the queen's brown eyes. She asked him about his journey, and Tabitha's thrill of alarm at the question conveyed itself across the room like a lightning bolt. He looked up to see a warning in her eyes and moved quickly from Antioch to Emesa, bypassing Apamea and their first meeting. Berenice listened politely until he reached the Judaean ambush by the lake and mentioned Josephus. She stiffened, and if she had been a cat Valerius had a feeling she would have hissed. The other conversation faltered.

'Thanks to the Emperor's patronage,' Berenice struggled to keep her tone civil, 'Joseph Ben Mahtityahu has set himself up as a great hero – a David to the rebel Goliath – conveniently forgetting that as a leader of the Zealots he fomented the rebellion. He encouraged his people to die then surrendered himself. But for Vespasian's good graces' – the way she said it meant

291

foolishness, and everyone at the table knew it. Titus only smiled indulgently – 'he would have ended up on a cross.'

'But you will admit he has his uses, lady,' Titus reminded her gently. 'Like you, he serves the Emperor. You are allies.'

'Berenice of Cilicia has always supported Rome.' The queen refused to be mollified. 'This is a rebellion of peasants and priests, and Ben Mahtityahu, if you need reminding, is a priest. If he serves you it is because it suits his own ends. Treachery and betrayal are his currencies. When he is not plying them against his enemies he is as like to use them to advance his position among his friends. Yes, he has his uses, but there will come a time when his usefulness is at an end. When that day comes your father would do well to complete the business he left unfinished when he captured the man. By all means use him, Titus, but please never trust him.'

Valerius listened with growing alarm to the vilification of the man he was pledged to protect. The worst of it was that he suspected Berenice was right. Nothing in his acquaintance with the Judaean signalled the contrary. In his experience, those who dealt in treachery and betrayal tended to attract it in equal measure. When the moment of judgement arrived, Valerius Verrens would be standing by Josephus's side as he faced the inevitable slings and arrows of his enemies.

Titus turned his attention to Berenice and the servants cleared the plates away. Valerius tried to catch Tabitha's eye, but she seemed to have forgotten his existence. He wondered if they could contrive a meeting alone, and was disappointed when the Emperor's son signalled that the evening was reaching an end.

'Paternus, I am sure you have much to do before morning. Inform General Alexander I will meet him at the north-west sector of the outer wall at the fourth hour.' Paternus rose from his couch and saluted. Valerius moved to go with him. 'I need you to stay, Valerius. There are things we must discuss.' Valerius bowed, but he remained standing.

'If you don't mind, lord, I will see the tribune to his horse. I have a message for Serpentius.'

Titus frowned, but nodded his approval. With a bow to Berenice the two men walked out together. When they emerged into the cool of the palace courtyard the night air was still and Paternus took a deep breath and looked to the skies. In the vast darkness above the stars twinkled like a multitude of tiny jewels.

'It is on nights like these a man truly understands that it was worth surviving, don't you think?' He turned to Valerius, the ravaged face close and his voice low. 'You must have felt diminished by your injury. A man with one hand is only part man, after all. Just as a man with half a face is. There must have been times when the point of a sword would have provided a welcome release.'

'You knew Tiberius Crescens.' It wasn't a question.

The right portion of Paternus's features creased in a bitter smile. 'So you have guessed? I am surprised it took you so long. People once said the family resemblance was remarkable. His half-brother. A little older, some would say a little wiser. Not quite so quick, but then Tiberius was truly remarkable, as I'm sure you would agree.'

'He was good.'

'But not quite good enough, because you killed him. At least, as I heard it, you were responsible for his death.'

'I would have saved him if I could.'

'Yet you didn't, Valerius.' Suddenly Paternus's words came in short, fierce bursts. 'You allowed him to die in the most brutal, vile manner imaginable. A young man, a boy almost, on a mission to dispense justice for the legitimate Emperor of Rome.'

'Nero had already lost his mind when he sent Tiberius to kill Corbulo. The general didn't deserve to die.'

'Neither did Tiberius.'

They faced each other, eyes only inches apart. For a dozen heartbeats Valerius was frozen by the memory of Tiberius Crescens' terrible end, beaten to death by his comrades after he'd failed to assassinate Corbulo. He knew Paternus's fingers were on his dagger, but he kept his arms by his side and the moment passed. A groom brought the scarred tribune his horse and handed him the reins. When they were alone again Valerius's left hand went to his belt and he drew his *pugio* before the other man could react. Paternus felt the point against his breast. His eyes widened as the one-handed Roman spun the knife so it ended with the hilt towards his accuser.

'Tiberius was my friend,' he said quietly. 'And not a day passes when I do not mourn him. If you truly think his shade will be satisfied by my death, take this and use it.'

He could see Paternus considering the possibility, but with a glance at the palace doorway the scarred soldier shook his head and pulled himself into the saddle. Before he could ride off Valerius grabbed the reins. 'Did Domitian send you to kill me?'

Paternus gave a snort of laughter. 'If he had you'd already be dead. When you were spared in Rome I knew you would run to your friend Titus. I arranged to be transferred to his staff – I still have friends in the Palatium. It was a coincidence we met in Emesa.'

Valerius wasn't sure if he believed him, but he didn't see any advantage in arguing the point. 'Why, then?'

'At first I wanted you dead, but when I discovered there were so many conflicting versions of Gaius Valerius Verrens I was intrigued. It became important to know the true value of the man who killed my brother.'

'Yet you refused my offer of the dagger.'

Paternus leaned down so his mouth was close to Valerius's ear. 'In some trials it takes time to come to a verdict. Be assured, Valerius, if you are found wanting I *will* kill you.' With a wrench he tore the reins free and spurred his horse towards the roadway where his escort waited.

Valerius was still staring down the track when he heard footsteps on the gravel.

'He hates you, I think.'

Her mere presence made him smile. 'Worse, he's not certain whether he does or not.' He turned and she was standing close; close enough for him to smell the perfumed oil on her body and close enough to touch. But not yet.

'I have to see Titus.' He shrugged. 'Then, who knows.'

'Titus has retired with my mistress,' her voice turned mock serious, 'to discuss policy, or perhaps the merits or otherwise of Josephus, or . . .' He placed a finger on her lips and she smiled. 'Come,' she said. 'The war can wait another day.'

So he did. And he was content.

XXVIII

The next morning Valerius sent a message to Serpentius to join him with Titus on the western flank of the city. He waited while Vespasian's son said his farewells to Berenice, their heads close together and hands lingering a little too long. Tabitha stood in the background, a demure handmaiden with a look of innocence that belied Valerius's memories of the previous night.

When they parted her logic had been simple. Josephus would stay close to Titus, and wherever Titus was, Berenice would be. 'Just stay alive for me, Valerius, and we will be together.'

By the time they left, dust clouds already filled the air to the west, marking the positions where Titus's legions, long on the march, were making their way to their new positions. Valerius rode at Titus's side, the toga he'd worn the previous evening covered by a nondescript cloak. The young general wore full armour, his gilded breastplate gleaming and his crested helmet glittering in the sun. Every man could see him for what he was – Valerius smiled at the memory – a prince of Rome. Aides clustered around him and couriers fluttered back and forth between the legions and their commander for all the world like bees supplying a hive.

Their route took them across a slope about a mile from the city walls on the north side of a steep valley. Titus's guards were taking no chances of another Judaean sortie of the kind that almost trapped their commander the previous day. The Tenth legion remained on the Mount of Olives, sweating as they constructed the massive siege machines that could save so many lives in the weeks to come. The Fifth and Fifteenth marched on the slope below in full battle order so their might could best be appreciated by the defenders. Each man carried his shield on his back and a pair of *pila* javelins in his right hand. Even so, squadrons of auxiliary cavalry wheeled and demonstrated on the flank of the formations, making patterns like smoke swirling in the breeze. The legions' tents, personal baggage and supplies followed them, along with the field artillery and dismantled siege cata-pults. Clemens' Twelfth Fulminata had taken a different route, for their destination was to the south-west of the city.

The slope provided Titus and his headquarters staff with a fine view of the walls. They could see the thou-sands watching warily from the parapets and the many towers that dominated this sector. Beyond the walls the roofs of scattered buildings were visible. Normally this was the least-populated section of Jerusalem, but the sea of tents erected to shelter the Passover pilgrims trapped by Titus's edict could clearly be seen.

'That will be our first objective.' Titus made his decision as they circled a group of anonymous tombs and crossed the main road leading north. 'Josephus styles it Bezetha, the New City.' He turned in the saddle towards the

Great Temple. 'Its time will come, but the New City will be the first part of Jerusalem returned to Rome's rule.'

They followed the course of the wall until they reached an area of cleared ground between two rocky spurs. Three thousand legionaries of the leading unit were already preparing a camp large enough to accommodate two legions. Men hacked ditches from the rocky soil, while others shovelled the residue into a passable bank. Engineers marked out the tent lines and the area set aside for the headquarters, the cavalry lines and the hospital. Later they'd set up the armoury and the workshops where the siege engines would be constructed.

It required an enormous effort, both in men and material, but they'd completed it a thousand times before and it came as second nature to them. Valerius didn't envy them their task, for the western flank of Jerusalem didn't have the advantages of the east. Unlike their comrades in the Tenth, these men would have to scour the countryside for sufficient timber to create three or four siege towers for each legion.

While Titus conferred with his staff, Valerius dismounted and studied his surroundings. The city wall to his front curved in an arc from the northern spur, where it followed a diagonal line down the flank of the southern. There, it joined a second, much older wall, presumably built to protect the more populated area of the city it embraced. Among the countless towers crowning the wall, one, built of white marble and the height of at least a dozen men, stood out because of its surpassing beauty.

A bulky figure dressed in eastern robes rode up the slope. 'Impressive, isn't it?' Josephus patted his horse's neck to quiet her. 'The world's greatest hope or the world's end, depending on the point of view of the man who stands here and witnesses it.'

'Just stone walls,' Valerius replied. 'And stone walls cannot stand against Rome. I'd have thought you'd have learned that by now.'

'Not stone walls.' Josephus ignored the provocation and slipped from the saddle to stand by Valerius's side. 'What you see before you is a nation, a people, a pride.'

'Are you saying Titus would be better to walk away?'

'Not at all. I have business inside those walls.'

Valerius was reminded of his promise to Titus, and Berenice's tirade against the Judaean the previous night. 'Business?' He tried unsuccessfully to keep the suspicion from his tone.

'We are not all soldiers.'

'Perhaps not,' Valerius agreed. 'But anyone who enters those walls had better be prepared to fight like one.'

'Soldiers are only interested in the here and now,' Josephus continued as if Valerius hadn't spoken. 'Some of us must consider the future.'

'So. Josephus the prophet?'

'No.' The Judaean's eyes turned bleak. 'Josephus the realist. I know what must befall my people when these walls fall. I have seen it at Gamala and Jotapata. Rome will prevail, and when Rome prevails she will impose order and discipline on those who have been unwilling to accept it in the past. That is inevitable, and I welcome it.' A frown of concentration creased his features and his gaze focused on a single area of the city. Valerius followed it to the Great Temple. 'What I would not welcome is the imposition of Rome's gods.' Valerius opened his mouth to protest, but Josephus silenced him with a wave of his hand. 'Very well, I accept that Rome does not *impose* its gods on the conquered, let us say then the *assimilation* of its gods.' He turned to Valerius and the Roman saw again the messianic zeal he'd witnessed previously. 'My people's religion is what defines them *as a people*. It *must* survive, or once again they will become a nation of slaves destined to be passed from master to master throughout the ages. But to survive it must adapt. Never again can it be allowed to divide us. Instead it must become the single factor that unites and strengthens us.'

'As I understand it,' Valerius said, 'the laws of your religion were laid down by your god a thousand years ago. Even if you challenge them, only your god has the power to alter them.'

'Not only God,' Josephus's brown eyes shone brighter still as they locked on the temple again, 'but the words of God.'

As they walked their horses back towards Titus's headquarters group, Valerius felt the Judaean's gaze on him. 'Titus tells me you are to be my watchdog. I suppose I should feel honoured that a person of such rank and lineage has accepted the task.'

'Let us not say watchdog,' Valerius responded to the baseless flattery with a dry smile. 'Perhaps companion would be more appropriate, and there will be two, though the other merits the description wolf rather than dog.'

'Very well, my *companion*.' Josephus's smile was like a piece of sea ice. 'We Judaeans have a passage in our sacred texts that speaks of *walking the valley of the shadow of death*. Many of my people believe it refers to the Valley of Hinnom yonder, whose stink fills your nostrils. It is where the unwanted dead were once left and where the abominations of the old gods were carried out. I am not so certain. I think it may be that the valley of the shadow of death is that place inside us that must be confronted when we knowingly place ourselves in peril.'

'I don't know your books,' Valerius said evenly. 'But that sounds a reasonable proposition.'

'Well, I hope you and this wolf of yours are prepared to walk in the shadow, for that is where Joseph Ben Mahtityahu intends to lead you.' As he said the words he glanced significantly back towards the city. Valerius saw his mouth drop open. 'What is that?' The question emerged as a strangled gasp.

Valerius followed his gaze and found it difficult to believe what his eyes were telling him. 'The temple is burning.'

XXIX

Simon bar Giora could have wept. First the news that Titus had refused free passage to the pilgrims. Now this.

'John has gone mad.' Zacharias's voice quivered with suppressed fury as he stared at the smoke billowing from the temple storerooms. The tangy, bitter scent of burning grain tantalized the hungry populace even as the haze hung over Jerusalem like a funeral pall. A great murmur went up from all around as they realized what was happening. 'Why would he burn supplies in a city bulging with starving people?'

'He didn't take the temple for the supplies,' Simon told him. Privately he doubted John had fired the entire contents of the grain stores. He was shrewd enough to keep enough back to feed the men under his command. 'He doesn't think we can beat the Romans simply by defending the walls. When the food starts to run out, the only way to get it will be from the enemy stores. He believes hungry men will fight harder than those with full bellies, and he may be right.'

'So the truce is over?'

'The truce is over.' Simon watched as a round object soared into the air over the temple wall and fell into the natural gorge that protected the Antonia fortress. Even now one of Simon's messengers would be running to recover it. A few minutes later the man appeared, breathing hard, in the doorway of the house Simon had taken over close to the temple walls. He displayed a battered human head by its hank of bloody hair. Simon studied the twisted grimace without any hint of recognition and nodded for it to be taken out and placed with the others. 'How many does that make?'

'Three hundred,' Zacharias confirmed. 'Including Eleazar, his deputies and Phannias.'

Three hundred men who could have helped hold the walls when the Romans came. 'He won't kill them all. Eleazar had three thousand men, John will want them fighting for him when the time comes.'

Word had come that something odd was happening in the temple shortly after the hammer blow of Titus's rejection of terms for the pilgrims. But it wasn't until the bloodied survivors started to appear that Zacharias was able to give Simon the full story.

Since the start of Passover Eleazar had made a point of opening the temple doors at noon to allow a few pilgrims to carry out their devotions in the Holy of Holies. John of Gischala discovered this and inserted a band of his warriors, their swords hidden beneath cloaks, among the waiting crowd. Once inside they'd chopped down Eleazar's guards and thrown open the gates. Hundreds more followed to join the slaughter, killing any Zealot who stood in their way.

'So ends the hero of Beit Horan.' Simon shook his head. 'A great warrior and a bigger fool. If Eleazar had joined us, Zacharias, John would have had no choice but to do likewise. What did he think he was going to achieve by holding the temple if we could not keep the Romans from the walls?'

But of course he knew what Eleazar had hoped to achieve. The fact that he had not used it as a bargaining chip meant it was still missing. Now it would be John's men who were frantically searching the temple. But the temple was a place of many secrets and soon John would have other things on his mind.

'We need to know which sections of the wall he's willing to hold.' Zacharias, as ever, appreciated the practicalities as well as Simon. 'We don't have enough men to hold it all, even with James and the Idumaeans. The main Roman force has moved camp from Mount Scopus to take up positions north and south of Gehenna. The Tenth continues to threaten us from the Mount of Olives, but the western side appears to be their favoured point of attack. The only question is where. North or south?'

'North,' Simon said decisively. 'If they attack to the south of the valley they would have to take Herod's Fort as well as the walls. We have few enough men to hold it, but it is as formidable a defensive position as Antonia.'

'Which we assume John will garrison?' Simon acknowledged Zacharias's query with a tight nod. 'Still, if they made a demonstration against the north wall to draw the bulk of our defenders . . .'

'No. It will be north.'

'Very well,' Zacharias conceded. 'We concentrate the bulk of our strength there?' Simon agreed, though his mind was already elsewhere. 'But keep enough men back to reinforce the Idumaeans, who will hold the north-east quadrant, in case the attack is a feint. John will hold the temple, and the south-east quadrant as far as the Tomb of David, which God protect . . .'

'God protect.' Simon's response was automatic. 'Arrange a meeting with John for an hour after sundown the night after next. Let him know that after we have discussed our dispositions I want a second meeting, which will include a third party.'

He saw Zacharias's eyebrows go up. This was what he had been considering since learning of John's attack on Eleazar and the taking of the temple. If it existed, it was somewhere in the temple. It could not be allowed to fall into Roman hands, where it would be destroyed or, worse, desecrated. It had to be sent from Jerusalem; even John in his egotistic madness must recognize that. But how? Who had the ability to move between Roman and Judaean lines with impunity? Which Judaean could pass a Roman guard post without being searched? And who understood the value and the importance of the thing they sought? Only one man. It was possible that this one man even knew its whereabouts. It was also possible that this one man might use it for his own purposes, but that, Simon felt, was a secondary consideration. For the sake of the children of Israel, and for Moses' legacy, it *must* survive.

He told Zacharias the identity of the third party and the normally imperturbable eyes widened. 'If John knows he is coming he will try to have him killed.'

'Undoubtedly,' Simon agreed. 'I am relying on the fact that he is resourceful enough to ensure he is not.'

'How will we contact him?'

'Are they still allowing us to feed the lepers at Gehenna?'

*

305

Work on the camp's defences continued to the staccato clatter of a thousand hammers and the rasp of several dozen saws. The craftsmen of two legions worked to piece together the frames of six enormous siege towers, each as high as the section of wall it was designated to attack. They manufactured the frames using baulks of timber a foot square and a dozen feet long, scenting the air with the aroma of newly sawn oak, juniper, cedar and olive wood. Once mighty oaks provided the main beams, while the other trunks were sawn into rough planks. These would be used to cover the frame, give the structure added strength and shield those inside. Once they were in place the entire siege tower would be clad with uncured animal skins to protect against fire.

Two of the towers were of a more complex construction than their counterparts. Josephus identified them as combined towers and battering rams. 'I saw them at work at Jotapata.' His face reflected the pain of the defeat, yet Valerius heard something close to admiration in his voice as he continued. 'Nothing could stand against them. Only the hardest woods will suffice for a ram. The arm will be created from the tallest ash tree they can find. When it is ready they will tip it with an iron head in the shape of the animal it is named for. I have seen a wall collapse with a single blow from a monstrous great ram like that.'

As the builders worked, a constant stream of horses, camels and bullocks dragged the trunks of felled trees into the camp to supply the insatiable appetite for timber. Valerius doubted there would be a stick left standing within twenty miles of the city before they were done. More timber would be needed to provide supports for the mines that would be dug to weaken the walls, still more for the earth mounds raised to support the siege towers and rams.

Josephus and his *companions* studied the preparations for an hour from a hillock close to Titus's headquarters. Watching the Judaean, Valerius thought that what was happening inside the walls was of as much interest to him as outside. When the midday sun broke from behind the clouds to illuminate the city, Valerius saw why the Great Temple was regarded as one of the wonders of the world. It shone in the sunlight like a mountain of white marble, or one of the mighty snow-capped alps of Noricum. A marvel, in a city of marvels if Josephus's boasts were to be believed. Something caught the corner of his eye on one of the higher buildings. The flash of someone cleaning a copper plate?

'I have seen enough,' Josephus said. 'If your servant will fetch the horses I would study the defences by the Valley Gate.'

Serpentius glanced at Valerius for confirmation and the Roman nodded. The route Josephus chose took them across the southern spur where they had an even more elevated view of the city. Beyond the western gate the defensive wall ran arrow-straight to the south, protected by a steep gorge, before curving eastwards. Josephus reined in and studied the gateway.

'The fortress you see is Herod's Palace.' He pointed to a massive squat building south of the gate whose flat roof provided a platform for little knots of defenders. 'Do not be deceived by the magnificence of its construction or the fact that its purpose was originally for pleasure. Even lightly defended as it is, it is impregnable. See how the three towers, Phasael, Hippicus and Mariamme, are sited to provide mutual support and interlocking fields of fire for archers and slingers. Titus considered attacking here with the Twelfth, but I advised otherwise.' The long stare he gave Valerius held the message: *You do not fully trust me, but see how I show my loyalty to your master.* 'That is why the major portion of the legion is even now marching through the hills behind us to join the Fifth and Fifteenth for the assault.'

'Have you seen enough?'

'Here, yes. But come, we will cross the valley and consider the defences from their southern aspect.'

They rode into the dip and followed the contours of the valley. A courier passed at a fast gallop, probably carrying a message to Titus from the commander of the Twelfth. A little later they were stopped by a patrol from the same legion. Josephus showed a warrant personally signed by the army commander and the patrol officer allowed them to proceed. When they reached the Twelfth's camp it became obvious why Titus had chosen to attack in the north. Clemens had sited his base on a shelf of flat land set back from the gorge separating it from the walls. His legionaries occupied small outposts along the crest. Eight-man sections stood guard, their boredom mitigated by the jeers and insults from the defenders two hundred paces away. The military presence was so obviously more about containment than threat that Valerius wondered why Josephus had brought them here. Then he noticed something curious.

A little further south a small group of civilians appeared without warning from the base of the city wall and descended into the gorge by a set of steps cut in the rock. Valerius held his breath, waiting for the moment when the legionaries reacted.

'Mars' sacred arse,' Serpentius muttered. 'Are they trying to commit suicide?'

But the expected hail of spears didn't happen. Instead, the group crossed the base of the gorge, forded a narrow stream and climbed the Roman side using a mirror image of the stairway they'd just descended.

'Let us see what is happening.' Without waiting for an answer Josephus spurred his horse down the slope towards the nearest guard post, and Valerius and Serpentius had no choice but to follow. They reached the post – a small, square defensive position behind a hastily scraped ditch and bank – just as the first civilian reached the top, gasping for breath. He was an elderly man with a long beard and Valerius saw that he carried a small cloth sack. The Roman wondered if some kind of illicit trade was being conducted between the Judaeans and the men set here to guard them. But they'd hardly do it in daylight with officers watching.

They dismounted and led their horses to where the guard commander was now in discussion with the bearded elder. The remainder of the civilians, a mixture of men and women all of a similar age, struggled up the steps to join him.

'What's going on?' Valerius demanded.

The *optio* whirled at the unexpected voice. When he saw it came from a civilian there was a moment when he was tempted to tell the owner to mind his own business. He changed his mind when he realized the tone had a soldierly authority and the man the kind of face you didn't want to mess with. If anything his feral-featured companion was even more intimidating. A man in eastern clothing stood a little apart to one side.

'General agreed to give safe passage to eight civilians at noon each day,' the soldier pointed to a wooden stockade a little further south, 'so they can feed the lepers.' He jerked a thumb at the elderly man and, followed by his companions, the Judaean stumbled wordlessly off in the direction of the enclosure. 'None of us would go anywhere near them, but he thought it wasn't right to let the poor bastards starve. They've been doing it for years and they seem harmless enough.'

Valerius watched as the elders approached the stockade and pushed their offerings through some kind of aperture in the barred gate then returned the way they'd come. As they passed the watchers one woman broke away from the group and rushed to Josephus, who frowned as she clutched at his hand, pleading in Hebrew.

'Here,' the guard snarled. 'Get away from the gentleman, or I'll take a stick to you. My apologies, sir. This has never happened before.'

Josephus stepped back with a bewildered smile. 'No, do not punish her. She was only asking for alms for the lepers, but unfortunately I have nothing to give.' He shook his head sadly and walked off towards his horse.

As they watched his retreating back, Valerius and Serpentius exchanged an intrigued glance.

It had been cleverly done and it took a practised eye to discern it, but both men had quite clearly seen the woman pass something to the Judaean traitor.

XXX

When Titus summoned Valerius to his headquarters pavilion the next day Josephus was already waiting, dressed not as a Judaean aristocrat but in the homespun robes of a common tradesman.

'Josephus has persuaded me to make one final attempt to convince the Zealots their position is hopeless.' The Emperor's son seemed uncharacteristically ill at ease. 'He believes this Simon bar Giora may be open to persuasion, given suitable incentives, and that he in turn may be able to convince Gischala. Is that correct, Josephus?'

'I believe it is worth the effort if it means the possibility of saving Jewish blood.'

'It will be dangerous, of course.' Titus turned to Valerius and his eyes were troubled, as if despite his earlier warnings he'd never thought it would come to this. 'This cannot be done in plain sight. Josephus must be able to contact Simon discreetly before they attempt to persuade John the only way to save the lives of the pilgrims is to give up the city. There is no question of marching up to the gate with a green branch and requesting entry.'

'I doubt I would live to reach it,' Josephus smiled. 'I am not much loved in Jerusalem.'

'But you still think it worth the risk?' Titus sounded as if he were trying to convince himself. Josephus nodded solemnly. 'And you, Valerius? Are you willing?'

'You tasked me with this man's protection. If he is willing to try how can I refuse?' Valerius said. 'As for Serpentius, he's a free man and can make his own choice. But yes, I will go, though I don't see how we can get inside. Unless we use the lepers' gate there's little chance of a mouse getting in or out of Jerusalem without being seen.'

'I believe there is a way.' Josephus's voice betrayed something Valerius hadn't thought to hear. Fear. 'If you are prepared to walk in the valley of the shadow of death.'

'I have walked there often,' Valerius assured him. 'And I do not hesitate to walk there again.'

'Then be ready in two hours.'

Valerius found Serpentius outside their tent playing a board game with Apion, a young legionary he'd befriended from the Fifth Macedonica. This unlikely bond was another manifestation of the change in the Spaniard, who had always tended to keep a distance between himself and other people. Valerius could only think that it was because Apion, black as a Nubian but a Roman citizen from Syria, was another outsider. When they saw Valerius, Apion marked the position of the stones and left with a sharp salute.

When Valerius explained what he knew of their mission Serpentius didn't hide his irritation at the paucity of information from Josephus. 'If he doesn't trust us let the bastard go alone,' the former gladiator spat.

'He's being careful.' Over his tunic Valerius slipped a leather jerkin of the type favoured by Titus's German auxiliaries, following it with the short chain mail vest Dimitrios had supplied in Emesa. The mail was exceptionally light, but the links were so tightly interlocked it would probably protect him as well as any plate armour. 'I thought we should be the same.' He threw the Spaniard a set of chain mail borrowed from the same source as the jerkin. 'That should fit, more or less. Apart from that all he said was that it will be cold where we're going. We should take cloaks, but make sure they're short.'

'Sounds like an invitation to a tomb robbing.'

'You may not be far wrong,' Valerius said evenly. 'But I told you, there's no reason for you to risk your neck.'

'Apart from covering your back, which is why I'm coming.'

'Good.' Valerius tried not to show his relief. 'How's your head?'

'Throbbing,' the Spaniard grinned. 'The way it does when somebody's trying to get me killed, which is most of the time.'

'Can you think of anything else?'

For answer Serpentius strapped on an odd leather chest harness Valerius had never seen before. It held the twin throwing axes he treated like his children in separate sheaths. 'It's all very well having them in your belt if you know you're going to need them,' the Spaniard said defensively. 'Sometimes a man needs to be a little faster. I had a word with that Dimitrios fellow in Emesa and he came up with this. Even with a cloak over it you can reach and throw in one movement.'

Mention of Dimitrios reminded Valerius that his own secret weapon might require attention. He poured olive oil into a wooden bowl and dipped a cloth into it. Then he pressed the button on the back of the wooden fist so the blade appeared. The button all but disappeared into a tiny depression and Valerius squeezed the cloth so a few drops of oil ran into and around it. He pushed the blade back into place and repeated the procedure with the inner button.

'Always nice to have an edge.' Serpentius nodded his approval. 'Even better if it's the whole knife.'

They met with Josephus at the appointed hour. To Valerius's surprise, instead of heading south towards the city gates they retraced their journey of a few days before until they reached the Tenth's fortified camp on the Mount of Olives. This time they were stopped and questioned several times by auxiliary cavalry, but Josephus produced his warrant and they were allowed to continue. Likewise, the warrant guaranteed them entry to the camp and an audience with Lepidus. They found the Tenth's legate squinting through reddened eyes as he pored over a sand table that replicated his area of responsibility. He looked up as they entered and his face broke into a tired smile as he recognized Valerius.

'I'm just trying to work out the best positions for the heavy artillery,' he explained. 'We have plenty of elevation, but that's not much good when you're trying to hit walls in the valley below.'

Josephus coughed to get the legate's attention and handed over a sheet of papyrus. 'I do not wish to keep you long, sir.' Lepidus darted a questioning look at Valerius as the Judaean bowed with unusual deference. 'I merely ask that your guards are informed to pass three strangers through the lines at dusk and allow them to enter the Cedron valley. Likewise to return at a time I am afraid will be unspecified, preferably without welcoming them by means of a *pilum* in the ribs.'

Lepidus still looked mystified, but the blank expressions on the faces of the three men told him he wouldn't get an answer to any of the questions their presence posed.

'Very well,' he said reluctantly. 'But you will need the watchword. Tonight it is *ballista* and the reply is *onager*. Tomorrow,' he nodded to Valerius, 'I will make it Corbulo, and the answer will be Armenia.'

Valerius smiled. 'That should be easy enough to remember.'

Lepidus drew the one-handed Roman aside. 'I hope you know what you're getting yourself into, my friend. The Judaeans haven't made any more major forays, but their patrols are as active in the valley and on the slope as ours are. You've seen for yourself how fractured this country is, all gully and cliff and scree slope. Only the locals understand how to move about quietly in the dark here.'

'That's why Josephus will be leading the way.' Valerius kept his tone light, though Lepidus had voiced exactly his own fears. 'I suspect he's lighter on his feet than he looks. And we can depend on Serpentius for quiet. I'll just be blundering along at the back.'

The legate shook his head. 'This is no joke, Valerius. This morning we found what was left of two of our wounded who'd been carried off during the raid the other day. The Zealots hadn't been gentle with them.'

'I appreciate the warning, but I have as much choice in this matter as you have about sending your men against those walls.' He would have liked to let Lepidus know that if they were successful his attack might not be necessary. The only thing stopping him was that the likelihood of survival, never mind success, was so slim it was futile to raise his friend's hopes. Instead, he said: 'I think it is time for us to go.'

Lepidus assigned a centurion to guide the three men to the Tenth's outpost line. It was held by a half cohort of the First Montanorum, Valerius's comrades from Noricum who had climbed the cliffs at Gamala. They left the camp by the southern gate and made their way carefully through the gloom, avoiding the uneven scatter of ragged stumps that was all that remained of the olive groves. Eventually, they reached a point where the ground fell away sharply. A figure seemed to rise out of the ground in front of them with a whispered '*Ballista*'? In the momentary hesitation that followed Valerius knew they were the target of a dozen *pila*, but the centurion hissed the reply and he sensed a collective sigh as the auxiliaries relaxed. They edged forward until they were in a huddle around the guard who'd challenged them. 'Anything happening?' The centurion's voice barely carried to the four men in the circle.

'The odd scrape and rustle.' Valerius heard the grin in the man's voice. 'They're out there all right, but I doubt they're looking for trouble.'

'Legate's orders. These men are to pass through into the valley.'

In the growing darkness sharp eyes studied the shadows and planes of the three faces. 'More fool them,' the auxiliary chuckled quietly. 'Those rebels can see in the dark. They have horrible long knives and they're not slow to use them. Like as not this is goodbye, comrades. But if it's Legate's orders . . . ?'

'Which it is . . .'

'The ground slopes away to the right. It's maybe a *pilum* throw before you reach a narrow path . . .'

'I know it.' Josephus spoke for the first time. His head turned to the centurion. 'Thank you, and may your gods stay with you.'

'And yours.'

Josephus rose and Valerius put a hand on his arm. 'Serpentius should lead,' he whispered. 'He's really very good at this kind of thing.'

'But he doesn't know where we're going,' the Judaean pointed out. Which was as good an argument as any, when Valerius thought about it.

As they passed through the front line the Roman heard the sentry mutter, 'Mars protect you . . . though I doubt it.'

'That's reassuring,' Serpentius muttered as he followed Josephus into the darkness.

The Judaean set a surprising pace over the rough ground and Valerius struggled to emulate it without dislodging pebbles or tripping over the ubiquitous olive stumps. It was all he could do to keep the blur of Serpentius's dust-coloured cloak in view. Fortunately, the going became easier when they reached the dusty path the sentry had identified. It cut diagonally across the steep incline and Valerius's feet told him it had once been a cobbled road. Despite the easier going, he sensed an increased alertness in Serpentius that warned against complacency. This was just the type of place the Zealots and their allies would set up an ambush in wait for a Roman patrol. He hurried to keep up, his eyes darting between the Spaniard's back and the rocks and bushes to his flank. His left hand never strayed far from his sword hilt. At the last minute he'd shortened the leather baldric holding the scabbard. Now it lay snug against his right side beneath his armpit, covered by the short-ened cloak Josephus had advised they wore.

Without warning, Serpentius stopped and dropped into a crouch. Valerius froze, his mind screaming danger as he fought to identify the threat. After a few moments a pale hand waved him forward and he breathed again, though his heart thundered against his ribs like a Parthian battle drum.

He scuttled forward to join the other two men and Josephus drew his head close, indicating an indistinct structure to Valerius's left. 'The tomb of Absalom, son of David,' he whispered, identifying the tall stone column. 'In a few moments we will pass those of the sons of Hezir and of Zechariah. This has been the burial place of my people for a hundred generations. Mark them well, for you may have to return this way without me. From here we descend into the valley and the place of greatest danger. If you lose me keep going south and stick to the valley bottom. I will find you.'

Valerius desperately wanted to ask how they were going to get into the city, but before he could put the question Josephus moved ahead with Serpentius in his wake. The Judaean seemed entirely at home in this all but invisible, fissured landscape, and confident they would reach their destination, though the gods only knew what awaited them there. On they went, down into the depths of the valley and the dangerous, boulder-strewn bed of a dried-up stream where they could feel the loom of the city walls over them. There would be guards on those walls and they would be scouting the darkness for just this kind of patrol: Roman engineers inspecting the ground to check whether it was suitable to sink a mine. Whether a siege tower would require a ramp to cross the rocky approaches or whether it could be heaved into place without. Whether the mortar that bonded the wall was solid, or whether it would crumble at the first blow from a ram. All around the perimeter men would be—

Valerius froze in position at a bright flash of light on the wall above, instantly followed by the flickering glow of flames. He looked around desperately for some cover, only to find there was none. All he could do was stay in the open and try to be part of the landscape. Fifty paces ahead a fireball arced from the ramparts and a bundle of pitch-soaked hay plummeted to explode in the stream bed, silhouetting the two men ahead. The flaming missile lit up everything around for a dozen heartbeats before subsiding into a soft flickering pyre that turned the rocky ground into a maze of shape-changing shadows. Valerius tried to still his shaking legs as he waited for the inevitable cry that would call down a hail of spears on the three intruders. Gradually, the glow subsided and they were left in darkness again. A total darkness. Where was Serpentius? He felt a moment of panic. The Spaniard must have moved off before his own night vision had recovered from the flare of light. He was alone.

'Stop standing about like a fornicating statue. We've been waiting for you.' Serpentius's hissed order came out of the darkness close to his ear. Valerius let out a long breath and followed the grey blur to where Josephus waited.

'Not far to go now,' the Judaean whispered. 'A hundred paces and then a short climb on the left.'

The left? Valerius was bemused. The left took them *away* from the city. He'd imagined a concealed doorway at the base of the wall, like the one the lepers' carers had used, though how Josephus would open it was beyond him. On the left lay nothing but boulders and dust. He clawed his way up through the dirt until he reached a part-sheltered hollow where Josephus was already on his knees poring over the ground like a soothsayer studying a chicken's entrails.

'Where is it?' Valerius could hear the Judaean whispering to himself. 'The tomb to the south. Yes. The mulberry to the north. I know it's here somewhere. The rock shaped like an eagle's beak. Or was it a dove's? They all look the same in the dark.' His hands scrabbled at the stones for so long that Valerius feared he'd gone mad.

'Is this what you're looking for?' Serpentius's whisper came from four paces away.

Josephus jumped up and hurried to him, peering at the rock in his hand. 'God be thanked.' He closed his eyes and fell to his knees.

'This is no time for prayer,' Valerius hissed, but the Judaean was oblivious. He identified the spot where Serpentius had picked up the stone and meticulously removed the rest until he'd opened up a space two paces square. Valerius knelt beside him and ran his hand over the cleared area until he found a notch in the solid rock. His face was inches away from the Judaean's and he could see the triumphant glint in Josephus's eyes.

'You seem to have a disturbing gift for finding holes in the ground that shouldn't be there.'

Josephus's teeth shone white in the shadowed features. 'The Conduit of Hezekiah.'

XXXI

It took two of them to lift the solid sandstone block that proved to cover a narrow opening cut into the rock. While Serpentius and Josephus dragged it gently to one side, Valerius dipped a tentative foot into the entrance. He was rewarded by the feel of a solid stone step beneath his sandal.

'There should be twenty-five stairs,' Josephus whispered into his ear. 'Go carefully. We cannot afford to light a torch until the cover is back over the entrance.'

Valerius nodded and groped his way downwards one step at a time. It had been dark outside, but there was something malevolent about this Stygian gloom with its clinging miasma of damp, stale air. With a lurch of the heart he felt his standing foot begin to slide from under him. He threw his hand out to steady himself, flinching at the cold touch of some slimy mucus that covered the walls. The pull of the void below threatened to swallow him as the others occupied the steps behind until he heard the soft scrape of the block being slid carefully back into position. Twenty-five stairs. It might as well have been a thousand for all he could tell. After what seemed half a lifetime his leading foot plunged into chill water. Thankfully it was only a foot deep and he splashed his way a few cautious paces across an uneven surface.

'Careful!' he warned his companions. The only answer was a soft curse and a splash as Serpentius made an uncharacteristic stumble.

The click of flint on iron was followed by the sound of someone blowing gently. Soon they saw the reluctant glow as the falling sparks were coaxed to ignite a tiny ball of dried grass laid on one of the lower stairs. Eventually a flame, and something thrust at it. The pitch-soaked torch caught with a soft whump and instantly filled the chamber with an eye-watering combination of golden light and thick black smoke.

They were in a tunnel just high enough for Valerius to stand without stooping and slightly greater than a cavalry *spatha* in width. It had been cut into the solid rock and in the sputtering torchlight he could see the tool marks where men had painstakingly chipped away at the stone with picks. Serpentius held the torch while Josephus stood on the first step arranging the skirts of his robe in a curious fashion. First he folded them back through his pale legs, then he took two wings and drew them in front of him where they could be tied into a bulky *subligaculum*-like knot.

'It is a custom of my people,' he answered their puzzled looks. 'A worker does it before he enters a muddy field, or a soldier will gird his loins in this fashion to give him more freedom of movement in battle. In this case I hope it will stop my garments from becoming wet.'

When he was satisfied he dropped into the water, which flowed from an opening beneath the stairs, and studied the chipped rock. Valerius noticed that his face had gone unnaturally pale, but his voice was steady enough. 'Hezekiah ordered this built to stop the Assyrians poisoning the city's water supply when Sennacherib brought his mighty army to besiege Jerusalem. The waters originate from the Pool of Gihon to the north.'

'You haven't been here before?'

'I have never had need,' the Judaean said. 'I knew *of* it, but I have never been *in* it.'

'But you know where it goes.' Serpentius pointed with the torch to where the tunnel disappeared into blackness.

'I am aware where we are likely to emerge, but I do not know.' Josephus's tone said it made no difference either way, because they didn't have any choice. 'Neither do I know what lies between. But this tunnel runs into the city, and as you acknowledged yourself,' he bowed to Valerius, 'not even a mouse could enter by any normal route with so many cats waiting to pounce.'

'Then let's get on with it.' Valerius spoke gruffly to hide his nervousness. The tunnel reminded him of the interior of a certain aqueduct in Rome with which he'd become much too familiar. 'I don't want to be still in here when the torch goes out.'

Josephus reached for the torch, but Serpentius brushed him aside. 'Best I go first. If anything happens to you there'll be no negotiation and no surrender.' He looked to Valerius for support and the one-handed Roman nodded.

'He's right.'

Josephus shrugged and the Spaniard squeezed between Valerius and the wall to take the lead. Valerius followed, and with the Judaean guarding the rear they splashed their way through the glittering stream, which quickly deepened until it reached mid-thigh. The ceiling of the tunnel varied in height for no good engineering reason Valerius could think of. Sometimes it soared into a black void above their heads. Sometimes it forced them to bend their knees with their noses touching the surface of the water. Likewise it occasionally narrowed so that Josephus, the broadest of them, had to turn side on to pass. It became apparent that they were on a shallow slope, taking them deeper into the earth with every step. Serpentius occasionally turned to look back at Valerius as if to make certain he was still there. The Spaniard's face was set in a rictus of such raw fury that his friend wondered if it masked fear. Certainly, the atmosphere was oppressive, as if the entire mass of the earth was weighing down upon them. Even Valerius thought he might run mad if they lost the light.

They'd just rounded a corner and Serpentius was three paces ahead when he gave a sharp cry and all but disappeared. For a moment the only thing that remained of him above water was his arm, with the torch raised aloft. Valerius instinctively stepped forward to help him and it was Josephus who reached past him to save the precious torch. The Spaniard emerged spitting water with a wild look on his face. He shook his head and a lion's mane of spray surrounded the shaven scalp.

'It's only a pace across and you should be able to edge round it.' His eyes were drawn upwards to where a shaft had been driven vertical to the tunnel, which must continue beneath him. 'By Mars's hairy scrotum,' he mouthed the oath like a prayer, 'I hope this ends soon. I'd rather face a thousand Zealots or those Sicarii than stay down here.'

'You may well get your wish,' Josephus said solemnly, backing round the edge of the underwater pit. 'But I admit I am beginning to share your sentiment.' He handed the torch to the dripping Spaniard and they resumed their progress.

They'd gone another hundred paces when the Judaean called out, 'Wait!' Serpentius turned, a sword appearing in his hand like the flick of a serpent's tongue, and Valerius stared into the darkness beyond Josephus, seeking out the threat. 'Give me the torch,' the Judaean demanded. Serpentius stretched past Valerius to hand him the flaming brand and he raised it up. This was one of the higher parts of the tunnel. In the flickering golden light they could see what appeared to be the remains of an ancient stone plaque just above head height.

Josephus reached with his free hand to remove the coating of glutinous green scum that obscured the lettering. 'Remarkable,' he breathed. 'It is in Hebrew, but of a very archaic style.' Serpentius muttered about not having time, the torch would burn out, but Josephus wouldn't be hurried. His voice shook as he recited the words as if they were a solemn prayer.

'"Behold the tunnel . . . Now this is the history of the . . . the breaking through. While each man was still wielding his axe, each towards his neighbour, and while three cubits yet remained to be cut, each heard the voice of the other calling to his neighbour . . . and on the day of the breaking through the . . . stonecutters struck, each man to meet his brother, axe against axe, and there flowed the water from the spring to the pool over a length of one thousand cubits."'

Valerius could see he was genuinely moved by his discovery, but they had to go on. 'You can return when this is over to inscribe it for your history,' he assured the other man.

But Josephus shook his head. 'I will never pass this way again unless it is on the journey to God's grace.' He swallowed and the sad smile tightened. 'I have had a horror of dark places since I was a child. Only the importance of our quest and a greater terror of being seen as a coward by two men such as you have kept my feet moving.'

'Then let us continue, and at greater speed,' Serpentius said with passion. 'I feel the same and if I am any judge the torch has only a few minutes left in it.'

Josephus acknowledged him with a weak nod and passed back the torch. With a last wistful glance at the inscription he followed in the wake of the fading glow, his feet increasing speed with every step.

Valerius counted another six hundred paces before they noticed that the pitch darkness of the tunnel turned to a leaden grey a little further ahead. He exchanged a glance with Serpentius and the Spaniard dashed the spluttering torch into the water where it died with a hiss of complaint, plunging them into total darkness. Valerius sensed Josephus freeze and took his arm before he could cry out. 'Courage. This is where you must play your part. Tell me what awaits us beyond the tunnel.'

The Judaean took a moment to compose himself. 'As I understand it, we should emerge at the Pool of Siloam, which was the main water supply in the time of David.'

'But you're not certain?'

'How can I be certain? I have never come this way before.'

'So the exit could be guarded.'

'It is possible, but I do not believe so.'

'Why?'

'Because the outflow is usually three feet underwater.'

'But that means . . .'

'It has been an unusually dry period,' Josephus agreed. 'I doubt we would have made fifty paces otherwise.'

'And if there had been a sudden storm?'

'I knew that God would be with us.'

'Can we stop discussing the weather?' Serpentius interrupted. 'We're here and we're alive, but if we don't get this done before daylight we may not be for much longer.'

He led the way slowly forward, guided by a low arch of not quite darkness fifty paces ahead. As he approached it, the tunnel widened and he whispered to Valerius to join him. After the total darkness the power of their eyes seemed intensified. Despite the gloom they could see the still waters of a large rectangular pool laid out before them, flanked by steps on every side. Beyond the steps to Valerius's left a massive wall blocked the view. He guessed it was the actual outer fortification of this part of the city, or perhaps it was an inner wall of equal strength. Titus's fortress within a fortress, within a fortress. To his right the steps were backed by a pillared portico. He imagined it filled with chattering women making the most of the opportunity to socialize while they were collecting water. But now it was empty and as far as he could tell there were no guards. Serpentius must have thought so, for he swung himself out to get a view of this northern end of the complex.

'Simple,' he said, and reached up to haul himself upwards. A moment after he'd vanished a hand appeared and Valerius allowed himself to be helped up on to a raised platform. They grinned at each other in a moment of spontaneous relief at being in the open after the long ordeal of the tunnel.

'Don't just stand there.' Josephus's urgent plea emerged from the darkness. 'Get me out of here.'

Together they pulled him clear of the tunnel and he spent a moment rearranging the skirts of his robe before studying his surroundings. 'Yes, it is exactly as I remembered it.' He led the way round the pool to the portico

327

where a gateway led to what was presumably the street. The door was closed.

Valerius pushed at it, but it held firm. When he looked closer he saw it was bolted, the bolt fixed with some kind of padlock.

Josephus pushed past him, rummaging in his bag. 'An ingenious contraption, but for any lock there must be a key.'

He fiddled with the padlock for a moment before Valerius heard a sharp snick and the rasp of the bolt sliding back.

'I thought you said you hadn't been here before?'

'No, I said I had not been through the tunnel. I hoped this was where it would emerge and God favoured me.'

Serpentius pushed at the door and peered through the opening into the street.

'Looks like we're on our own,' he whispered. 'Which way?'

They'd broken into the besieged city of Jerusalem. The question was whether they'd ever get back out again.

XXXII

'Look again.' Despite the peril of their situation the level of anxiety in Josephus's voice surprised Valerius. 'They told me we would be met.'

Serpentius opened the gate and looked up and down the broad avenue outside. 'Nothing,' the Spaniard confirmed. 'Lights in a few windows, but most are shuttered.'

'Then we wait.'

'What about patrols?' Valerius said. 'If someone comes along and checks this door . . .'

'Not in this area.' Josephus couldn't hide his irritation at the delay. 'They expect the attack in the north and John of Gischala can't spare the men for street patrols. Likewise, much of the city is full of refugees, but this is the original city of David. Like the Upper City it is reserved for the elite of the civil service and the priesthood. If, by chance, we are approached, act like mutes and allow me to do the talking. That way we may get out of here alive.'

Serpentius stayed by the gateway and Valerius took a seat on a stone bench beneath the portico and closed his eyes. Over the years, they'd spent many hours like this, biding their time in wait for the right moment or the right contact. It was nothing new to them. But Josephus paced the side of the pool muttering to himself as he counted the passing seconds and checking the position of the moon. Eventually, he could take no more.

'We don't have time.' He picked up his discarded pack. 'We must go now.'

'What about the guide?'

'He was to guarantee our safe passage. I know our destination and I can easily take us there, but . . .'

Valerius registered the mental shrug and understood immediately what it conveyed. Was the absence of the guide a result of accident, carelessness or something more sinister? But there was no point speculating. They had no choice but to continue.

Once more, Serpentius took the lead, heading north up a long paved and stepped incline between fine houses. Josephus followed, intermittently whispering directions and talking to himself as he hurried along behind. Valerius took up the rear, periodically checking his back and willing himself not to start at every shadow. His foot slipped on a patch of something wet and he winced at what it might be. It never occurred to him that it was the blood of a man lying with his throat cut in an alley a few dozen paces away. Or that he was missing four fingers of his right hand, removed by his torturers to obtain the information they needed.

The Spaniard set a fast pace up the slope, keeping to the shadows where he could and with an eye for every door and alleyway. Josephus, despite his inbred aversion to revealing unnecessary information, decided his companions needed to know their destination in case they became separated. He gave his instructions in a low whisper punctuated by gasps of exertion.

'The building we seek is a palace built by the Hasmoneans, and is close to the first wall. It is flanked by the High Priest's house and the great market, on the boundary between the two rebel factions and acceptable to both. John of Gischala, may God curse him, holds a dagger-shaped enclave that takes in most of the eastern flank of the city. It is not large, but crucially it includes the Antonia fortress and the Great Temple. Simon bar Giora holds the rest of the Upper City, the Lower and what is known as Bezetha, the New City, between the second and third walls. John has fewer men, but they are well positioned. Simon has the larger force, but even that cannot compensate for the amount of wall he must defend.'

They reached an open space and in the gloom Valerius could make out a massive, pillared structure. Serpentius hissed at them to stay where they were while he checked out the route ahead. Josephus peered at the doorway of the large building they'd reached. 'The Synagogue of the Freedmen,' he said, half to himself, 'and that must be the Hippodrome. We should turn west until we can cross through the first wall, by Herod's Theatre.'

Valerius was more interested in their interrupted conversation. 'Why do they fight each other when there are Romans to kill?'

He sensed the Judaean's shrug. 'Because John is driven mad with ambition and Simon is a good hater and a bad enemy to have.'

'Against a divided and outnumbered enemy, Titus must win, even behind these walls.'

'And so we must persuade them,' Josephus said firmly. 'The blood of thousands of innocents depends upon it.'

'All clear.' The whispered signal came out of the darkness and Valerius and Josephus moved towards the source. Serpentius was waiting for them at the corner of the next street. 'There's a building at the top of the steps that looks like the Theatre of Marcellus in Rome. Is that it?'

'Yes,' the Judaean confirmed. 'It is in the Roman style. From there we go north and the palace lies directly ahead.'

They moved stealthily through the empty streets, past grand houses that stood shoulder to shoulder with tall apartment blocks, shuttered shop fronts and closed workshops that stank of charcoal and burned metal. The first wall barred their way at the top of a steep slope, but Josephus guided them to a gate that proved to be unguarded. Hugging the curve of the theatre walls they passed safely into the Upper City. Eventually a right turn led them into an area of narrower streets. Here Serpentius became warier and despite Josephus's entreaties for speed he slowed and finally stopped. His eyes fixed on a crossroads a few dozen paces ahead.

'What's wrong?' Valerius hissed.

The Spaniard moved back to join them. 'One gleam of metal is much like another, but at a certain time and in a certain place a wise man takes heed of the message. They're ahead of us and I've had a feeling for a while we were being followed.' He shrugged and pulled his sword free. Valerius nodded and drew his own blade. Nothing to be done about it.

'We need somewhere to fight from.'

'The alley back there,' Serpentius had already made his decision, 'but we'll need to be quick.'

'But we must continue,' Josephus protested. 'The negotiations. We are so close.'

'If we keep going the only person you'll be negotiating with is your god.' Valerius hustled him back towards the cramped alleyway. 'This way at least we have a chance.' When they reached the entrance he pushed Josephus in while he and Serpentius guarded the street, each taking a different direction. 'See if you can find out where it goes,' he called over his shoulder to the Judaean. 'If there's another way out we might be able to continue.'

Josephus reappeared moments later, his face a pale blob in the darkness and his voice raw-edged with anxiety. 'It is a dead end. There's a door in the far wall, but it's barred from the inside.'

'Then we fight.' Serpentius pushed him roughly back into relative safety. 'Because they're coming.'

Led by men with torches the hunters advanced from both ends of the street, making no pretence at secrecy now they had their prey trapped. In the alley's entrance Josephus struggled to get a view of the enemy. 'Galileans,' he hissed. 'John of Gischala's men.'

The enemy had no helmets or armour, but they carried round shields and were armed with long swords or, worse, spears. Serpentius saw the danger at once.

'Move deeper inside,' he instructed his companions. 'There's only room for two men at a time and we should be able to hold them for a while.'

What he didn't say was that the logic of war dictated that men without shields and outranged by long spears would eventually be overwhelmed. Serpentius was a former gladiator and the deadliest fighter Valerius had ever known, but a gladiator's strengths lay in his speed, his skill and his manoeuvrability. Those strengths would be largely nullified by the narrow confines of the alley. The spears would flick out and their owners would advance step by step, protected by the shields. Valerius and Serpentius could parry the spear points for a while, perhaps even kill one or two of their owners. But the dead men would be replaced and those behind would push the replacements forward, forcing the defenders to retreat until their backs were literally against the wall. Eventually, their arms would tire and the spear points would seek them out.

'If you know any prayers now's the time to say them,' Serpentius hissed as two men made a tentative appearance in the entrance. The Spaniard's hand flew to his chest and his arm came forward in a single flowing movement. The man on the right cried out and threw up his arms to fall backwards with one of the little Scythian throwing axes embedded in his skull. His companion dropped to the ground and dragged the dead man away by the arm. 'That will keep them honest for a while.'

Serpentius had bought them a breathing space, but how long depended on the quality of their opponents. Valerius used the respite to study his surroundings and found no comfort in the featureless vertical walls. He could hear the sound of iron on wood as Josephus hacked at the door in a desperate but probably vain attempt to create an escape route.

It wasn't long before the Galileans tried again. This time two pairs advanced together. The two in front were protected by their shields and held their spears ready to dart forward once they came within range. Of the pair in the rear, the one on the right was ready to bring down another shield to protect his comrades from Serpentius's deadly axes. The other held a torch aloft so they could see who they were killing.

'Be ready.' Serpentius took control and Valerius was happy to let him. If they survived, and the gods only knew how, it would be because of his street-fighting instincts. 'High and low.'

'High and low.' Valerius repeated the mantra. He had only the vaguest idea what Serpentius had in mind, but he was ready when the Spaniard exploded into action. Serpentius allowed them almost to within spear-length before the second axe whipped out in a blur of bright iron aimed at the rear spearman's head. His shield came down so the axe rebounded with a solid 'thwack', but the throw had done its job. For a fleeting moment the shield blinded the two men at the back, while the two in front hesitated for a fatal heartbeat as Valerius and Serpentius attacked.

High and low. Valerius went in high. His sword swept the left hand spearman's point aside and he forced it between the two shields, feeling the resistance as it carved into someone's body. It must have been the man with the torch because, accompanied by a shriek of mortal agony, the alley was plunged into darkness. Valerius wrenched the *gladius* free as someone tried to cave in his skull with a spear shaft, hammering at the upper shield while he lashed out with his feet at his nearest opponent.

This was gutter fighting in its purest, most violent form and the art had no greater exponent than Serpentius. As Valerius made his assault, the Spaniard had executed a perfectly timed acrobat's roll that brought him in below the spears. His sword lanced point first into the unprotected groin of the right hand shield bearer. While his victim howled Serpentius ripped the shield free from his victim's nerveless fingers and rammed it into the face of his partner. The sheer speed and brutality of the assault was too much for their opponents. The survivors turned and ran, leaving two of their comrades twitching and bleeding in the filth on the alley floor. Serpentius hefted the shield and stepped forward to finish the dying men. He turned to Valerius. 'The gods forgive me,' he grinned, 'but I enjoyed that.'

Before they knew it they were laughing together in huge whooping snorts. It was madness, of course; battle madness and relief at surviving what had appeared certain death. Their laughter echoed from the walls of the alley and Josephus looked at his companions with a mix of horror and dread. What kind of men were these blood-soaked monsters?

Gradually, the laughter faded, but the grins remained. Serpentius took his position on the right, the snatched shield on his left arm, protecting Valerius when he moved in on the left. They would fight as one. Live or die as one. Brothers in arms.

Let them come.

They didn't come. Instead, the men in the alley heard the sound of charging feet, followed by a clash of swords and cries of consternation. Valerius looked back at Josephus and even in the dark he could see his own puzzlement reflected in the Judaean's eyes. He shrugged and faced the entrance, his sword at the ready.

The silence seemed to go on for ever before a commanding voice hailed them. 'Joseph Ben Mahtityahu?'

'Who is asking?' the Judaean called.

'My name is James of Rehoboth, commander of the Idumaean defenders of the free city of Jerusalem, sent by Simon bar Giora to escort you safely to the palace.'

'How do we know you can be trusted?'

'Stay, then.' James's voice was heavy with contempt. 'There are many in Jerusalem who would like to make the acquaintance of Joseph Ben Mahtityahu come the dawn.'

'No,' Josephus said hurriedly. 'We will come with you.'

'Very well.' A torch flared at the alley entrance and in its light they could see a tall man with a mane of straggly hair and fathomless dark eyes. 'Sheathe your swords. You are under Simon's truce now. John of Gischala has done his worst, but know this, Joseph Ben Mahtityahu: Do not think that because I saved your life tonight I am your friend. It will be my pleasure to take it before this is over.'

XXXIII

An avenue of torches flanked the little procession as James led the three men up the wide marble steps of the Hasmonean Palace. In the glow of the burning brands Valerius could make out a great doorway topped by two conical towers. He felt no fear in the heart of the enemy citadel, only a dull resentment at the duplicity of these treacherous rebels. Josephus had come here at Simon bar Giora's instigation. Whatever Valerius's doubts about the Judaean, he had placed his life at risk to avert the needless slaughter of his people. Yet this Simon had almost allowed him to be butchered, and Valerius and Serpentius with him.

They followed James through a maze of corridors until they reached a door clad in beaten gold, wonderfully worked into the shapes of birds, fishes and flowers. The Idumaean ushered them through into a room hung with sumptuous tapestries where the atmosphere was thick with the scent of stale sweat and antagonism.

Three chairs had been set around a large table in the centre of the room. One held a fearsome giant of a man and he jumped up to greet the newcomers. The other occupant, older and thinner, glanced up with sullen dismissal until his eyes fell on Josephus. At the sight of the Judaean his mouth twisted into a snarl of hatred and the pale eyes almost glowed with the power of his wrath. Valerius thought he might cry out, but the spasm subsided and he slumped back in his chair content, for the moment, to glare at his enemies.

The big man surprised them by ignoring Josephus and instead approached Valerius and the Spaniard. His eyes registered the dark blood staining their tunics, but his greeting barely faltered. 'I welcome you in the name of peace, my friends, though I see your passage has not been without trial. I am Simon bar Giora, and my companion is the famed John of Gischala.' He bowed his head, and Valerius's manners insisted he do likewise.

'I thank you for your greeting and hope our journey was worthwhile,' he replied with equal formality. Serpentius ignored the Judaean and glared around the room. One man stood protectively behind each of the principals' chairs while six more had their backs against the walls. What made these men different were the hands that hung poised over their swords.

Simon finally turned to Josephus, but there was little warmth in his welcome. 'Our past division means I cannot greet you with the same enthusiasm. Nevertheless, I take comfort from your safe arrival.' He glanced at John. 'Let us hope some good comes of it, God willing.'

'God willing,' Josephus echoed.

John of Gischala snorted contemptuously. 'I, for my part, can barely suffer the sight of you.' His words were warped by the strength of his hatred. 'The stink of betrayal ever hung over you. I would have killed you at Tiberias, but Jesus Ben Sapphia stayed my hand. Your death cannot come soon enough for me.'

'If you had your way tonight I would already be dead,' Josephus snapped back. 'It is only because of my companions I am alive.' With a growl he took a step towards the man in the chair, but Simon touched his arm and his anger subsided as quickly as it had risen.

'We cannot change what has been done,' the big man said. 'But we *can* promise you safe passage on your return. Please be seated. For your sake our business must be conducted swiftly.' Simon turned to Valerius. 'I apologize, but for reasons of security it is not possible for a Roman to attend these proceedings.' Valerius opened his mouth to protest, but Simon assured him Josephus would be safe. He glanced at Serpentius. 'Your savage friend speaks no Hebrew, I have your word on it?'

'He speaks no Hebrew, on my honour.'

'Then he may stay and take responsibility for your charge. He looks well capable of it, yes?'

Valerius looked into the deep-set eyes seeking the lie, but Simon met his gaze without flinching. 'You'll stay,' he told Serpentius. The Spaniard responded with a sharp inclination of the head.

'Very well. We place our trust in you to restrain your friend.' Valerius nodded at John.

'He is no friend of mine.' Simon's laugh contained no humour. 'But you may trust me in this matter. Zacharias?'

The red-bearded young man behind Simon's chair stepped forward to escort Valerius from the chamber. As they left the room, Valerius was puzzled to feel something being slipped into his left hand. Once they were alone he turned to the other man, but Zacharias gave no sign that anything unusual had occurred. 'If you will wait in the small room beyond the curtain, I must return to my commander.' He paused. 'These are difficult times. I am sorry we are at war, but a man must do what he believes is right. Do you not agree?'

As Valerius met the other man's steady gaze he could feel the tiny roll of papyrus between his fingers. 'Yes, I agree.'

Zacharias left without another word. Josephus was already seated by the time he resumed his place behind the bulky figure of Simon, but it was John of Gischala who spoke first.

'There will be no surrender,' the Galilean hissed. 'You have wasted your time.'

Josephus ignored his enemy. 'I expected none.' He addressed the words to Simon bar Giora. Despite the incomprehensible Hebrew, Serpentius picked up the tone of the exchange. He was surprised to see Josephus smile. 'I am here to discuss other matters of grave import to each of us . . . yes,' the Judaean forestalled the inevitable interruption from John, 'even to you. These matters go far beyond the enmity of three rivals, they concern the future of our people.'

Simon and John exchanged a glance and the smaller man gave an almost imperceptible nod.

'You have come for it?' Simon said quietly.

'It cannot stay in Jerusalem. If the city falls . . .'

'The city will not fall while there is one hand still capable of wielding a sword,' John snapped.

'Nevertheless . . .' Josephus gave a shrug that could have meant anything.

'Then you know its location?' Simon suggested.

'Only that it is in the temple.' Josephus looked to John for confirmation, but Gischala sank lower into his chair. 'It was brought in great secrecy to the High Priest Ananus by Jesus of Hebron.'

'A matter complicated by the unfortunate detail of Ananus's death.' John cast an accusing eye at Simon, who was not unconnected with the occurrence.

'I am told Ananus passed on the location to Eleazar before he died,' Josephus said.

'If only Eleazar were here to enlighten us.' Now Simon's tone dripped with sarcasm. 'Unfortunately someone cut off his head.'

Josephus closed his eyes. Did a people so careless with its great men truly deserve to survive?

'I have men searching for it now,' John ignored Simon's jibe, 'but the temple is of even greater extent than it appears. So many rooms: the priests' quarters, the treasury, the library, the courts, inner temples, schoolrooms, granaries and storerooms, the lepers' room, a room for sacred oil, and a room for sacred wood. Only the priests can enter the sanctuary and the Holy of Holies, but they assure me it is not there. Of course,' he said slyly, 'it would help if we knew exactly what we were looking for. Such an item can take many forms.'

'A scroll,' Josephus said after a long pause, as if his thoughts had been elsewhere. 'A substantial scroll, but a simple one without golden embellishment.'

'The library then,' Simon said triumphantly. 'Where better to hide a scroll than in a library.'

'I have had people check every volume,' John said dismissively. 'I am not a fool.'

'No? Then perhaps you can produce Eleazar.' Simon was on his feet and John rose an instant later, snarling at each other like fighting dogs across the polished table. The two sets of guards took a step forward, but Zacharias and his opposite number raised a hand to stop them. Josephus intervened to urge calm.

'You have searched the lower passages?' he asked when the adversaries had regained their seats.

'They are endless,' John complained. The other two men looked at him and he sniffed. 'I will put more men to the task. If it is here I will find it.'

'It is here,' Josephus assured him. He looked from one to the other. 'We are enemies in most things, nothing can change that, but we cannot afford to be enemies in this. When you have found it, send me a signal and whatever the conditions I will come. A truce, or another negotiation, I will create a pretext. It cannot be allowed to fall into Roman hands.' *Or certain others I could name*. The silent thought formed of its own volition.

They left by separate entrances an hour later. Valerius emerged from the waiting chamber to be met with a scowl of disappointment from Josephus. 'I have failed,' the Judaean said bitterly. 'They see the sense of surrender, and the impossibility of their position – what sane man would not – but they are fanatics. I must take the news to Titus immediately.'

James the Idumaean escorted them through the city as the first hint of dawn appeared in the eastern sky. Eventually they reached the outer wall. A narrow stairway lit by oil lamps wound down into the rock. 'My men have informed the Romans of your coming,' the bearded warrior growled. 'With good fortune you may avoid the spear point in the guts you deserve.'

Serpentius turned and took a step that brought him face to face with the big warrior. 'I've had warmer farewells.'

James met his gaze without flinching. 'I told them we should have fed you to the dogs.'

'Much easier said than done,' Serpentius replied with a dangerous smile. 'Perhaps we'll meet again to discuss it?'

343

'It would be my pleasure to kill you.'

'We're leaving.' Valerius pulled Serpentius away before the inevitable reaction. They emerged on the far side of the wall through a gate of metal bars. Someone handed Valerius a torch to guide the way down the steep slope and up the reverse face. From the stone stairs cut into the cliff he realized they were at the lepers' gate.

He waited until they reached the far side and had passed through the Roman lines, escorted by a yawning legionary, before whispering to Serpentius, 'I know it's difficult when you can't understand the words, but what impression did you get of their discussions?'

The Spaniard sent a long, searching look in the direction of Josephus's back. 'I don't know what they were talking about, but I do know one thing. Our friend there is up to no good.'

XXXIV

Titus took the failure of the mission with an equanimity that convinced Valerius he was secretly relieved. Perhaps it suited him for the Judaeans to resist at least long enough for him to prove his skill as a siege commander. To shed just enough blood to persuade his father to grant him a triumph when he eventually returned to Rome. The Emperor's son didn't enquire how they had entered the city. Spies had their ways. If the route could help shorten the siege he clearly trusted Josephus to mention it, so Valerius also kept his counsel.

'I had no great hopes for it,' Titus told them. 'These are men without the moral courage to save their people, but I thank all of you for your efforts.'

Josephus left the tent, followed by Serpentius, but Valerius hung back and Titus looked up from the map he'd been studying. He smiled. 'You look terribly weary, Valerius. You should find a bed.' He gestured to the map. 'I've been examining this city from every angle and the more I look the more difficult it becomes. What do you think of Jerusalem, now that you are one of the few in this army to have seen it from the inside?'

'Your words might have been a prophecy. A fortress within a fortress within a fortress. It was dark, but we must have passed twenty buildings capable of being fortified to keep this army at bay for a month.'

Titus nodded grimly. 'We're already running out of timber for the siege works, but I've ordered an amount kept back. I calculate that when the first assault succeeds, we will require a further three or four attacks unless the Judaeans see sense and surrender. I fear my other prophecy, that I would win this city for my father in three months, will not prove so accurate.'

'You've chosen a section of wall to assault?'

'Yes.' Titus drew him forward so he could see the map and his voice became animated. 'It must be here in the north.' He pointed to a position two miles from the legionary camps. 'The open spaces of the New City will give my legions room to fight. If we attacked the Upper City or from the Cedron valley it would be a much more difficult assault. We'd get bogged down in the narrow streets, with those buildings you mentioned a redoubt on every corner. So we will attack here, either side of the Tower of Psephinus. When we break through, the Fifth and Fifteenth will hook right and left like the pincers of a crab's claw, while the reserve cohorts from the Twelfth hold the defenders in place. With Fortuna's aid we'll kill or capture almost half of Jerusalem's garrison in a single attack.'

Valerius studied the map, drawn by Titus's engineers from a viewpoint on Mount Scopus. It was a good plan, but it depended on the cooperation of the Judaeans. If they had orders to run, Titus's claw might close on a few terrified refugees. Which raised a question.

'From the hillside we could see the tents of hundreds of thousands of pilgrims. Is it possible Clemens was correct and they will hamper your plan?'

Titus gave Valerius a sharp look. 'I see you would still advise me to allow them passage. But I need them in the city putting pressure on the Judaean commanders, not outside wondering how to stab us in the back. As to your question, I do not intend to let it happen. While the legions assault the walls I will . . . encourage . . . the civilian inhabitants of the New City to retreat through the second wall to the Upper City. See, the Fifteenth and the Fifth will attack here, and here. Meanwhile our artillery will bombard not only the walls, but the city beyond them. The Tenth will also concentrate its artillery on the tents and shelters. If they are as densely packed as we think, the arrival of a few hundred missiles and a shower of shield-splitter bolts should be enough to send them scuttling to safer positions. It must be here.' Titus sounded as if he were trying to convince himself. 'Once we've triumphed it will give us a base to draw breath for the next operation.' He pointed to the Upper City and a wall even more formidable than the one they faced.

'It is a good plan,' Valerius congratulated him. 'You seem to have thought of everything.'

Titus laughed, but he made the sign against bad luck with his fingers and didn't hide it from Valerius. 'No commander thinks of everything, as a man with your experience would know better than any. Things will go wrong. There will be setbacks, but I will take this city.' Valerius bowed, but Titus put out a hand to prevent his leaving. 'But I do not think you stayed behind to hear me talk tactics.'

Valerius shook his head. How could he have forgotten? 'When Simon barred me from the negotiations a man called Zacharias gave me this.' He handed over the tiny roll of papyrus. 'He is close to bar Giora, perhaps one of his aides.'

Titus unrolled the scroll and took an oil lamp to his campaign desk in order to study it more closely. 'Yes, it is confirmed here.' He looked up at Valerius. 'This could have been his death warrant if they'd discovered it, and yours. He asks for safe passage for his wife and child. In return he offers regular reports of bar Giora's strength and the disposition of his troops.'

'How will he provide it?'

'He talks of somewhere called the Leper Gate? His couriers will wear something red.'

Valerius explained about the leper colony and the gate in the wall and Titus scowled. 'If I'd known, I would have stopped it and had the guards whipped. Clemens should know better. You can only win a siege by being harder than the enemy. But now . . .'

'Now the situation is transformed,' Valerius completed the thought. 'The Leper Gate is like a dagger aimed at the heart of the city.'

'His wife will dress as an old woman and she'll carry the child in a basket, as if food for the lepers. He asks if we can provide some sort of distraction to allow them to separate from the others. Can it be done?'

'I don't see why not,' Valerius said. 'The question is, do you trust him?'

Titus's voice turned hard. 'Once we have his wife and child in our possession it would take a very cruel man to go back on his word.'

For a moment the tent seemed to spin and Valerius swayed on his feet. He hadn't realized quite how tired he was. Titus took his arm and steered him towards the entrance. 'Why did you not hand this to me when Josephus was here? Do you not find him trustworthy?'

'I think he is trustworthy in many things,' Valerius said, choosing his words carefully. 'But I sense he shouldn't know everything.'

Titus held his stare for just a fraction longer than necessary. 'Very well,' he said. 'You may leave us.'

Valerius blinked in the early morning light outside the pavilion. Which way to his tent? He was just beyond the circle of Titus's personal bodyguards when a slim arm hooked into his and pulled him in a different direction. 'We are in a house close by,' Tabitha whispered. Valerius staggered slightly and she stopped and looked up at him, taking in the pallor of exhaustion and the lines that had deepened overnight. 'You have had a busy night, I fear. Perhaps you'd like to go to your own bed and sleep.'

He looked into the deep blue eyes and something stirred deep inside him. 'No.' He swallowed. 'I don't think so. But I must be back by noon. Serpentius . . .'

'Can look after himself. No,' she said decisively. 'They can spare you for a day . . . at least.'

XXXV

In the aftermath of their love, Valerius was still in a dazed, bewildered no-man's-land when Tabitha's face appeared above his, her eyes reflecting his own wonder. 'It was not meant to come to this.'

'Then make the sun go backwards.' The fingers of his left hand brushed a lock of hair from her eyes. 'Otherwise you must accept it. If it was not meant to come to this, what was it meant to come to?'

'A mutual attraction.' She kissed his shoulder and his flesh muffled her voice. 'A pleasant diversion. You felt it too?' He nodded. 'At first I thought you were just another coarse military man, a typical Roman soldier, lacking manners, morals or conscience. But over time I discovered someone compassionate, fair and caring; a man I would trust with my life.'

'And with your secrets?'

A shiver ran through the slim body. 'You know?'

'I suspect. Serpentius saw you talking to Josephus in a way that made him think you knew each other. Yet Josephus made a point of seeking me out and questioning me about you as if you'd never met. Something didn't feel right.'

Valerius expected her to be angry at being spied upon, but Tabitha's only reaction was a wry smile. 'Josephus is the kind of man who can polish an ingot of copper with his fine words until you're convinced it is gold. We have never been friends, but my mistress believed he could be useful to us. In Emesa, King Sohaemus talked of a book . . .'

'I remember.'

'The Book of Enoch. Written at the very dawn of our people, before the Great Flood swept the earth clean of impurity. It foretold a new cataclysm – a second cleansing – when the Jews of Jerusalem would be destroyed by Gentiles.'

'The siege?'

'Yes. That is what we believe.'

Valerius registered the 'we', but kept his counsel. 'Josephus also mentioned a cleansing.' He told her of his mission into the city and the negotiations with Simon bar Giora and John of Gischala, and she frowned.

'Josephus knows they will not surrender, and it is not in his interest to stop what is happening here.'

'So you believe there was another reason for the meeting?'

'Joseph Ben Mahtityahu would forgo every treasure in Jerusalem to possess the Book of Enoch.' Her eyes rose to meet his. 'He must not have it.'

'Sohaemus was doubtful it existed,' Valerius pointed out. His words contained a question that demanded an answer.

'It exists,' she said firmly. 'It exists and it was sent to Jerusalem for safe keeping. The Book of Enoch lies in the Great Temple, but it is hidden and only two people alive know its exact location.'

'Josephus?'

351

'No.' She shook her head. 'But given the opportunity he is one of the few astute enough to locate it.
Only Queen Berenice of Cilicia and her faithful handmaiden Tabitha have that knowledge. You wonder
why an ancient text is so important to the future of the
Jews?' She paused, trying to find the words to explain
some complex thought process. 'The foundation of my
people's existence lies in their religion. God and his
prophets. But there can be different interpretations of
the word of God. In times past these interpretations have
led his people on two distinct paths – let us call them
the light path and the dark path. When the Jews have
taken the first of these paths it has brought them to a
place of enlightenment where art and culture prospered,
wondrous buildings were erected and peace prevailed.'

'And the dark path?'

Tabitha wrapped herself a little tighter in the blanket.
A jug of wine sat on a table by the bed and Valerius
rose to pour two cups of the sweet Judaean vintage. He
handed her one and she took a sip from it as he settled
beside her on the bed.

'The dark path led us here,' she said, meaning the
siege and the hundreds of thousands trapped within the
city. 'Those who follow the dark path twist God's words
so that power, strength and fear are the forces which
drive his people. In the past it has created a society
where the strong were encouraged to prey on the weak.
Where the weak were despised for their weakness and
poverty, but never allowed the opportunity to escape
it. In this society the sword and the spear rule. This is
where Josephus would take us. Only Berenice can lead
the Judaean people on the path of light to where God
intended. She would use the stability provided by Rome
and the power of her . . . attachment . . . to Titus to

352

create a new enlightenment. A society which values not only peace, but all the benefits peace can provide. A society not bound by the petty rules imposed by priests to maintain their power. But to achieve this, she must have the Book of Enoch.'

A cockerel welcomed the new day with a raucous cackle and Valerius rose with reluctance and pulled the cowhide stock of his artificial hand over his stump. She watched him dress as he considered the implications of her words, and the hidden suggestion at their core. 'If all you say is true, nothing can stop the destruction of this city and its inhabitants.'

'I believe so.' Uncertainty flickered in her eyes for a moment. 'If what is written is true, Titus couldn't save them even if he wished it.'

Valerius recalled the iron in Titus's voice as he'd outlined his plan of attack; the terror that would rain down upon the city's helpless refugees, the price to be paid in blood for each of the three walls and, at the last, the temple. 'If Simon and John defend the temple . . .'

This time she had no doubts. 'They see it as their sacred duty.'

'It will be utterly destroyed, and the Book of Enoch with it, unless it has been found.'

'If it is found I will know.' She didn't say how, but he knew her well enough now to believe her.

'If Berenice is to have the book someone must retrieve it for her.' He waited for a response, but Tabitha's expression didn't alter and he continued. 'It will be dangerous. They must find a way into the temple when the defenders' attention is elsewhere, but with sufficient time to escape before Titus's legions smash it to dust.' Again she didn't respond, and he sighed, bowing to the inevitable. 'Very well. I'll take Serpentius, if he's willing.

I can get us into the city, but . . .' He frowned as he realized the fundamental flaw in his hastily conceived plan.

'And I can get *us* into the temple.' She rose naked, the sinuous, pale body flowing against his, and put her finger to his lips to still the inevitable protest. 'The temple is a maze, Valerius. Only someone with intimate knowledge of that maze can find the Book of Enoch.'

He took her in his arms, torn by fear for her welfare but trapped by the truth of what she said.

'Very well,' he conceded at last. 'We will do this together. But we do it on my terms.'

XXXVI

It was all about the timing. And that depended on Titus.

Valerius knew by the sound of the big siege catapults that the attack had begun long before he reached the Fifteenth's camp. The throwing arm of each monstrous weapon measured fifteen feet and could hurl a boulder the size of a large cauldron almost half a mile. The power they generated meant they had to be pegged to the ground to stop them dashing themselves to pieces. After each throw teams of men hauled at the massive levers that helped pull the arm back against its own tension. When the sling was loaded, the engineer in charge released the arm so it flew forward to be halted by a cushion of straw-filled leather bags. The thunderous impact made a massive 'whump' and the sound echoed through the valleys to the west of Jerusalem as he approached the camp.

Titus had brought twenty of them to invest the city and, of these, fourteen hurled their missiles at the third wall close to the famed Tower of Psephinus. On the far side of the city, the Tenth legion used its catapults to add to the terror of the thousands crammed into the eastern sector of Bezetha. True to his word, Titus also arrayed his light artillery, normally kept in reserve until the walls had been weakened. The *onager* and *scorpio* catapults pitched their missiles over the walls into streets packed with refugees sheltered only by tents and make-shift lean-tos. Valerius could only imagine the effect they were having on the unprotected civilians. He'd seen a small boulder from an *onager* remove the heads of two men and eviscerate a third. A five-foot 'shield-splitter' bolt could gut one and then pin the man in the next rank so they were like chickens on a spit. It took a fatalistic courage to stand and face such anonymous, random killers. Valerius doubted the unblooded Pass-over pilgrims would stand it for long before they sought greater protection in the centre of the city.

He guided his mount past the camp towards the artil-lery line. It seemed the most likely place to find Titus, but when he reached the catapults the young general was elsewhere. He reined in Lunaris about four hundred paces from the walls.

It seemed Vespasian's son was in a hurry.

The legions were formed up just out of catapult range. It might have been a bluff to draw the defenders' atten-tion away from what was happening elsewhere on the walls, but Valerius doubted it. The Fifteenth was on the left, their ranks angled diagonally towards the Mount of Olives, their eagle proudly displayed as if challenging the enemy. To the right, the Fifth waited patiently in their cohort squares for the glory that was to come. A vexillation of two thousand men from the Twelfth would form the centre once Titus had overcome these walls. Between the legions stood their associated auxil-iary cohorts, men from Hispania and Lusitania, Syria and Thrace, Gaul and Pannonia. Thirty thousand men eager for a fight after the weeks of waiting and digging.

But first they must overcome the walls. Titus had placed his siege towers and rams in threes on either side of the Tower of Psephinus, with the ram in the centre of each trio. As Valerius watched, the legionaries who would man them formed up to haul and push the mighty towers over ground levelled by their engineers. To the front, five hundred men spat on their hands and took a grip on ropes a foot thick, while half as many added their weight behind each tower. The key was to get the enormous structure moving on its greased axles. At first the only result of their efforts was a judder through the tower and a slight tilt in the direction of the walls, where the defenders, ever more numerous, gathered to jeer at their efforts.

Titus's artillery commander had prepared for this moment. When he judged the crowds on the parapets were thick enough he called the order for the shield-splitters and the *onagri* to change their aim. Now the light artillery of three legions – the men of the Twelfth had brought their entire contingent – was brought to bear on a single section of battlements. Men turned in disbelief as the comrade next to them disappeared in a cloud of pink, before the ramparts cleared as if a single hand had plucked them clean.

'Archers!' The order elicited the blast of a *cornicen* and Valerius saw his former comrades of the Emesan column ghost forward on foot across the cleared ground. Now it became clear why Titus had chosen this as his point of attack. The Tower of Psephinus dominated an open plain beyond the walls, but to do so it had been necessary to create a parrot's beak in the defences. Of all Jerusalem's defensive positions this was the worst placed for the neighbouring towers to provide support. It allowed the Emesans to close on the wall and take their positions before the defenders could recover. Now, whenever a head appeared to brave the onslaught of the *onager* and shield-splitter missiles, it was greeted with a well-aimed volley of a dozen arrows.

With a final convulsive heave the first of the towers moved forward with a hideous squeak of wooden wheels. Soon a second followed, and a third, until all six lumbered at a hesitant snail's pace towards their goal.

The rebels had their own catapults, taken during the humiliation of the Twelfth at Beit Horan or captured when the Zealots overwhelmed the city's garrison. When the siege towers and rams came within two hundred paces the defenders launched ranging shots from within the city. Great chunks of masonry from demolished walls and buildings curved in mighty arcs to shake the ground when they landed.

Serpentius rode up to Valerius's side and produced a helmet and a leather tribune's breastplate from his pack. 'This isn't the place to be if you're not properly dressed,' the Spaniard growled. Valerius dismounted and stripped off his cloak, and allowed Serpentius to strap the breastplate into place before pulling on the helmet. The former gladiator nodded in the direction of the Judaean missiles. 'Not a good idea to be around when they arrive.'

'True,' Valerius agreed. They both had close acquaintance with the destruction that could be caused by the big catapults. 'The question is whether they can hit what they aim at. At Cremona the operators were experienced *ballistarii* who'd been working them for half a lifetime. Even then their tribune admitted they were lucky to hit anything that wasn't a mile wide.' As if to prove his point a missile fell with a crash five hundred paces to the south and nowhere near the towers, which moved inexorably towards the walls.

'They might do some damage when the cohorts go forward. Big formations make big targets,' Serpentius pointed out with the cheerful detachment of an observer who knew nobody was going to ask him to be part of one of those targets.

'But the legates will push them in fast, so they won't be targets for long. Once they get close to the walls they'll be safe enough.' He paused. 'We may have to go back into the city.'

Serpentius noted the change of tone. 'So it's our turn again, eh?'

'This isn't an order from Titus, but I have my own reasons for going.' Valerius gave the short version of Tabitha's story and the Spaniard listened with a look of sour disenchantment.

'What do we care about the future of a rabble of Jewish barbarians?' he spat.

'I care about this one.'

Serpentius turned to Valerius and his eyes were like looking into an empty grave. 'Sometimes, after I got hit over the head, I'd lose consciousness and when I went under I knew I wasn't coming back. That's how it was down there.' A nerve twitched in his cheek as he remembered the ordeal in Hezekiah's Conduit. 'What if they've blocked the exit or flooded the tunnel?'

'I don't think so. Apart from anything else I have a feeling it might be someone's way out.'

'When?'

Valerius studied the walls where the towers were creeping ever closer. 'That's up to Titus and our Judaean friends.'

'Look!' The Spaniard pointed to where four cohorts trotted in columns across the open ground to reinforce the men in the siege towers. This was clearly the moment Simon bar Giora had been waiting for. A storm of shield-splitter bolts and *ballista* missiles from hidden catapults greeted the advancing legionaries. Valerius saw men plucked out of the ranks and blood spray the air, but the compact columns ignored the casualties and were soon protected by the bulk of the towers. These had stopped just short of the wall, but the legionaries pulling the two ram towers dropped their ropes and added their weight to that of the men behind. Slowly, the two towers inched forward until the massive head of the ram could be brought against the cut stone blocks of the wall. The engineers' calculations had been perfect, for each tower topped the defences by four or five feet.

Behind the closest ram, legionaries hauled the giant ash trunk back to its full extent and then released it against the wall for the first time. The impact shook the whole tower, but strangely it was a second later before a giant clang split the air. A frozen heartbeat when it seemed the entire battlefield stood still was followed by a lusty cheer from the attackers. Another mighty clang signalled the strike of the second ram, and the rhythm was set. A rush of defenders appeared to hurl rocks from the walls down at the operators, only to be swept away by the spears of legionaries in the flanking towers. At the same time Roman artillery deluged the top of the walls with a lethal hail of missiles to deter a flanking attack.

Valerius felt his heart quicken as he imagined the nerve-shredding chaos inside the attack towers. Hundreds of fully armoured legionaries packed into the stifling gloom of the inner storeys, waiting to make their way up the ladders to the fighting platforms. To reach them they'd have to struggle through stacks of *pila* waiting to be passed upwards and past a stream of wounded being carried below to the *medicus*. Every successful strike of the ram would come at the cost of a Roman life on the fighting platform and the waiting men would be showered in the blood of those dying above. An angry murmur filled the air – the familiar background to a faraway battle – punctuated by the shrill screams of men plummeting from the battlements and the towers. His ears throbbed with the thump of *ballista*, *onager* and *scorpio* launches. Bolts and boulders flew towards Jerusalem in a constant rush and the air was split by the clang of the iron ram heads. Artillery centurions barked ceaseless commands for corrections or shouted for more ammunition.

Without warning the sound of battle changed to a higher, more urgent pitch and Valerius saw a flash of yellow on the parapet close to one of the rams.

'Bastards.' Serpentius grimaced as a streak of flame lanced out from the Judaean defences and cascaded down the animal-skin flank of the ram tower. Burning oil, carried in open buckets by pairs of men prepared to die to ensure it went where it would do most good.

'I hope by all the gods they've wet those skins properly.' A soldier's greatest fear was to be trapped in a burning siege tower with hundreds of men battling to reach the constricted trap door exits. If this one caught they would be hurling each other off ladders as the wooden structure turned into an inferno. For all the poets said, there was no such thing as a good death, but surely burning was the worst of all? Every man's eyes were drawn to the terrible drama being acted out around the pinnacle of the towers.

Every man but Serpentius.

He touched Valerius on the arm. 'See those bushes at the base of the wall just beyond the stone tower?'

Valerius strained his eyes until he could make out a patch of dusty green. 'What about them?'

'They shouldn't be there. I've been looking at these walls for days and the rebels have cleared every inch of ground around the base to give them a clear field of fire. And it's not just that. I thought I saw movement.'

Valerius looked for a senior officer to inform, but they were all occupied. In any case, what could he tell them? That Serpentius might have seen something move in a patch of bushes that some lazy work gang had ignored? But he'd known the Spaniard long enough not to ignore his instincts. He pulled himself into the saddle and Serpentius did likewise. They walked their horses forward into the killing zone, neither man quite sure why they were doing it.

'What do you think?'

'I don't know, but that stretch of wall will be out of sight of the men in those siege towers.'

Valerius increased his pace and angled his mount towards the tower closest to the danger area. 'It's probably nothing,' he didn't sound convinced, 'but we'll let them know about a possible threat and get ourselves out of there. I'd planned a quiet day.'

By now they were halfway to the siege towers, and Valerius searched the walls for anyone who might be targeting the two isolated riders with a captured *ballista*. Serpentius's face split into a knowing grin, but he kept his mouth shut.

'What?' Valerius demanded.

'I was just think—'

But Valerius would never know what the Spaniard was thinking. And his chances of a quiet day were disappearing with every hundred Judaean rebels who spilled out of those innocent bushes. He could see them making their way in a stealthy rush towards the siege towers two hundred paces away, but they were invisible to the attacking Romans.

XXXVII

'Go!' Valerius dug his heels into Lunaris's ribs and the gelding surged away in a cloud of dust as Serpentius struggled to keep up. They galloped across the stony ground roaring to alert their comrades to the unseen enemy. Valerius knew anyone who saw or heard them would probably think of them as either a pair of madmen or a threat, but they had to try. He was thankful for the helmet which identified him as a Roman. At least it lessened the likelihood of their being greeted by a volley of *pila*. His eyes darted between the Judaeans, who were all but invisible now, screened by the curve of the wall, and the attacking cohort from the Fifth.

A hundred paces to go, but it would only be moments before the Judaeans – upwards of a thousand, at least – were in position to make their final charge. 'Form line!' he screamed at the startled men in the rear of the closest cohort's ranks. 'Form line, right!'

But why should they respond to a maniac bearing down on them at the gallop when they could see no threat?

At last the siege tower loomed over Valerius. He reined in beside the vast wooden structure and threw himself from the saddle to grab the nearest man.

'Rebels,' he rasped. 'Form line, right. Where is your centurion?'

'Centurion Glico?' The legionary frowned. 'He's directing operations in the tower, sir.'

'Then forget him. Form a defensive line on the right flank, and be ready to—'

But it was already too late. The man's mouth gaped as he looked beyond Valerius's shoulder and a long ululating scream from a thousand throats announced the Judaean attack. Valerius turned to see a wall of spear-wielding men rushing towards them less than sixty paces away.

'Form line!' Valerius pushed the young legionary forward and grabbed the man next to him. 'Lock shields and prepare to receive attack.' To his right Serpentius was doing the same, pushing and pulling the legionaries into a rough line on the same axis. By now men were screaming at their comrades to join them and the inbred discipline of the legion quickly produced a rank of fifty or sixty men. It wasn't enough, but it was all they had. 'Draw swords,' he shouted to anyone, belatedly remembering that he hadn't drawn his own. He pulled the *gladius* free from its scabbard and gabbled a prayer to every god he could think of. And looked up.

As they struck.

The line was like the sand wall a child builds on a beach to hold back the incoming tide, and the attack the wave that overwhelms it. The sheer momentum of the Judaean assault carried them through the weakest points in the shields. Screaming warriors hurled themselves where the edges of *scuta* failed to touch. Spearmen instinctively sensed where a nervous hand held a sword. They poured round the flanks in their hundreds into the pocket of confusion behind, where Valerius was trying desperately to create a second rank. In moments he found himself at the centre of a maelstrom of men fighting for their lives. A gleaming spear point darted at his eyes and he twisted to allow it to slide past his right cheek, instinctively taking the step that carried him into sword range. He could smell the man's rancid breath and saw the eyes widen almost before he realized he'd rammed the point of the *gladius* forward. A twist of the wrist and the blade broke the suction of the reluctant flesh. The Judaean dropped the spear and folded at the middle with his hands scrabbling to return the slippery coils of his intestines to their natural home.

'Your right!' Serpentius's shouted warning allowed Valerius a heartbeat to parry the unseen thrust from the flank. His blade slipped down the spear shaft and a second Judaean rammed his point into the Roman's chest. If the thrust had been perfect it would have pierced the breastplate's layers of thrice-tanned bullhide, split ribs and pinned Valerius's heart. Instead, the point struck at an angle and skidded off the leather to score a groove across the flesh of his right shoulder. He screamed as a white-hot bolt of agony ripped through him and he was driven backwards and down by the weight of his enemy. As he flailed uselessly with his sword two snarling rebels jostled for the right to ram a spear into his throat. Their rivalry saved his life. A whirlwind of glistening iron appeared from nowhere and in an unreal moment one of the bearded heads parted company from its owner in a spray of scarlet. Before the second Judaean could react Serpentius smashed him backwards with a shield he'd somehow fallen heir to and kicked his spear aside to stab him in the throat.

They found themselves in a strange pocket of calm in the midst of the battle. Valerius cried out as the Spaniard hauled him to his feet by the injured arm. Serpentius flicked back Valerius's cloak to expose his bloodstained shoulder. He inspected the wound. 'It looks worse than it is, but it's just a scratch. Try to use your arm normally or it will stiffen up.'

Valerius nodded and stood on shaking legs as he studied their position. Men continued to fight for their lives all around them, but the bulk of the Judaeans had bypassed the knot of defenders at the southern siege tower to attack their real target. Dozens of rebels in the rear ranks of the Judaean assault ran in pairs and carried pots of liquid fire suspended from wooden rods.

'They're going to try to burn it from the ground up.' Despite the efforts of the ram's defenders, flames were already licking at the base of the tower where the wooden frame wasn't protected by dampened hides.

'Nothing we can do about it now,' the Spaniard said. Valerius saw he was right. Their services would make no difference to the outcome of the savage little skirmish. The legionary cohort from the northern siege tower had belatedly formed ranks and was marching to the rescue of the ram. At the same time the thunder of hooves from the direction of the Roman siege line announced the arrival of a reinforced wing of auxiliary cavalry.

The commander of the Judaean attack must have taken the sensible decision to withdraw, or his warriors made it for him. Suddenly hundreds of men in the distinctive Judaean robes were streaming past Valerius and Serpentius on their way back to the hidden portals. The only thought on their minds was to return to the safety of the city. They posed little danger, but one man came too close and Serpentius stepped out from behind the shield and clubbed him to the ground with the hilt of his sword.

Whooping auxiliaries pursued the fleeing Judaeans, mercilessly cutting down the slowest and the injured. The legionaries concentrated their efforts on dousing the flames, which had caused only superficial damage to the ram tower. Serpentius dragged his terrified prisoner to his feet and prodded him ahead with his sword point towards a little group of cavalry officers observing the aftermath of the attack. Valerius was surprised to see that Titus himself had commanded the rescue effort.

The general frowned as he recognized the two men with the prisoner, taking in the recently used swords and the blood dripping from Valerius's wooden fist. 'Even when I order you to stay safe you cannot keep out of trouble,' he smiled. 'But it seems I am in your debt once more.'

'We were out for a ride and took a wrong turning.' Valerius's face split into a weary grin. 'Serpentius has brought you a gift.' The Spaniard pushed the captive forward until he stumbled at Titus's feet. Black-bearded and stocky, he cut a ragged, miserable figure, cringing in the dust.

'Put him with the rest,' Titus ordered. 'I will see them in a moment. Ten prisoners out of so many hundreds,' he said to Valerius. 'They have a fondness for sacrifice, your Judaeans.' He gave the order for the ram to resume its work as soon as the structure had been checked. The attack would continue. 'Now, let us get this unpleasantness over.'

The ten captives sat in a huddle under the watchful eye of legionary guards. One or two appeared terrified, including Serpentius's man, but most stared defiantly at the splendidly dressed soldier who rode up to inspect them from his saddle.

'I congratulate you,' Titus called to them. 'You almost caused me a setback. Who was your leader?'

One of the prisoners stood, a tall heavyset man in a striped robe tight-wrapped at the waist in the fashion Josephus had used in the tunnel. 'Our general was John, an Idumaean commander. He lies next to the tower with an arrow in his throat. You will know him by the eye patch he wears, for he only has one – or should I say had.'

Titus nodded thoughtfully. 'You fought well, Judaean, and with courage, but now I fear you must summon more. There is a price to pay for your audacity. I cannot let the defenders who man your walls believe they can sneak out and attack our lines with impunity. To be truthful, I do not have the wood to spare, but you will be crucified in full view of the Tower of Psephinus, and your bodies left to rot, so all can witness the cost of defiance.'

One or two men groaned at the terrible end they faced, and one cried out, but their spokesman bristled defiance. 'You can crucify us by the hundred, but Jerusalem will never surrender,' he said, and spat towards Titus's horse. One of the guards moved to strike him with a club, but the general raised a hand to stop him.

'We will see how eloquent you are after a few hours hanging in the sun. Take them away.'

'No! Please, no.' The man Serpentius had struck pushed forward and dropped to his knees in front of Titus. 'I am no rebel. My name is Benyamin of Ephraim, and they made me join them. My son is dead in the fighting. I have a wife and three other children who will starve without me. Have mercy, in God's name, I beg you. I am but a simple carpenter.'

'A carpenter?' Titus studied him as if a snake or a lizard had spoken. 'All the better. You may have the privilege of fashioning your own cross.' He turned to the guards. 'Make sure he is scourged until it is perfect.'

'You may kill ten of us, Titus Flavius Vespasian,' the tall Judaean cried out, 'a thousand, or even a hundred thousand, but Judaea will rise again and Rome, the Whore of Babylon, will fall. It is written. As is your end. You may wear the purple when your dog of a father is in his grave, but not for long.'

Valerius saw his friend's eyes harden. 'My end may be written,' Titus's voice was little more than a whisper, 'but one thing is certain, you will not be there to witness it.' He nodded to the guard commander. 'When he is on the cross break his arms and legs so he knows the true meaning of punishment, and the price of insulting the Emperor.'

XXXVIII

Titus would never admit it, but the sortie by the Judaeans made him more cautious. He abandoned any thoughts of taking the wall by storm and the rams hammered at the stone blocks by day and night. One of the Roman engineers, eager to ingratiate himself with his commander, estimated the wall would fall within a week. Instead, it took thirteen days of relentless effort before the masonry began to crumble beneath the iron heads. After two more, Simon bar Giora surprised everyone by ordering his warriors to abandon their positions and retreat to more defensible positions in the inner city.

Valerius accompanied the men of the Fifteenth legion as they swarmed into Bezetha through the breaches and orchestrated the great sweep Titus hoped would denude Jerusalem of half its defenders. All they found were a few dead bodies among the shattered houses, already turning black beneath the hot sun, and the odd elder abandoned by his family. Titus decided to move his legions into Jerusalem. He ordered the third wall torn down and every house and temple in the New City demolished to create space for his camp. The rubble would supply material for new siege ramps required for the next stage of the campaign. Not even Josephus's plea could save the magnificent Tower of Psephinus from destruction.

As the work continued, Vespasian's son called a conference of his commanders. All four legates were in attendance, plus Tiberius Alexander. Valerius, his shoulder still throbbing from his wound, was invited as an observer. As they waited in the stifling atmosphere inside the heavy cloth pavilion, the generals alternately mopped their brows and plucked at the necks of their sweat-soaked tunics. Valerius had his first sight of Paternus for almost a month. The heat had turned the tribune's injured face, never the most appealing sight, a vivid shade of purple.

Between the threat of a Judaean counter-attack and his growing relationship with Tabitha, it was easy for Valerius to forget that Domitian's assassins might only be a step away. Serpentius, however, was always on the alert, and never far from Valerius's back. He reported that Paternus's dangerous-looking servant – Valerius smiled when the Spaniard referred to Gavvo, without a hint of irony, as the scarred tribune's pet killer – had gone missing. They spent the ensuing days in a high state of tension in case he was preparing some sort of attack, but nothing materialized. Valerius took the opportunity to ask politely about Gavvo's whereabouts.

'I sent him away.' Paternus stared at him with his single cold eye. 'I have a legionary more attuned to the ways of the camp than my servant. In any case,' his unscarred lips flickered into a sneering half-smile, 'anything that requires completion I am well able to carry out myself.'

'Is that a threat?'

'You may take it any way you like. My brother's death remains unavenged. I see that you, on the other

372

hand, prosper. I read our general's report on the conduct of the siege thus far and your actions took up an entire page. It seems you may yet wear your general's armour in earnest.'

'I only did my duty.'

'As must we all.' Paternus turned away as an aide ushered Titus into the command pavilion and took his cloak and helmet. The general was followed by Josephus, who met Valerius's eye with a grim smile.

A table at the centre of the room held a model of Jerusalem roughly outlined in sand and Titus walked directly to study it. 'The demolition?' he demanded.

Tiberius Alexander turned to Claudius Paternus. 'It goes well,' the disfigured tribune said. 'We have destroyed four hundred paces of wall and three towers, plus three districts of the New City. But it will take a few days before we are ready. We had to renew the ram heads.'

'And of course,' Tiberius added significantly, 'we need to know where to transport the rubble spoil.'

Titus nodded slowly, still studying the model. 'That is why we are here.' He turned to Sextus Cerealis, grizzled commander of the Fifth Macedonica. 'Legate?'

Cerealis frowned and ran a wrinkled hand over the top of his bald head. 'There has been a slight change in the situation since our last discussion. As well as holding the inner wall, the rebels have created a defensive line on the approaches to this monument . . .' He used his *pugio* to indicate an area in the west of the city close to the Valley Gate. Titus looked to Josephus for an identification.

'The tomb of John Hyrcanus, lord, son of Simon Maccabaeus.'

'Under normal circumstances,' the legate continued, 'a makeshift defensive line would make an attractive

373

point of attack. As you can see, this is different. Once we take the bank and ditch we would still be faced by the western portion of the second wall dominated by this tower. We would also, in effect, have been drawn into a salient and subject to crossfire from *ballistae* and *scorpio* artillery here and here.' He pointed to the sides forming the apex of a triangle whose point was one of the three great towers shown to Valerius by Josephus on their tour of the walls.

'What about this Antonia fortress the Judaeans make so much of?' Titus surprised Valerius by appearing to abandon his carefully laid-out strategy. 'If we take the fort and the temple our artillery would dominate the entire city and the rebels would have no option but to surrender. Can it be done, do you think, Lepidus, with your Tenth attacking the walls while the Fifth and the Fifteenth come at it simultaneously from the north?'

Lepidus's handsome face creased in a frown. 'We've done some damage to the wall with our catapults, but we haven't been able to get a ram close because of the terrain. We'll need to put in a ramp. I should also point out that the wall is at its strongest and highest where it backs on to the temple.'

'There is also the question of the approach to the tower.' Titus Phrygius, legate of the Fifteenth, nervously ventured another potential flaw in his general's plan. 'It too is protected by a hidden gorge and we would need ramps to get the rams close. It would also leave us open to flanking attacks.'

'At which we have seen the Judaeans are adept.' Titus took no offence at being proved wrong. 'Very well. We are left with the central section of the second wall. Have the engineers start work immediately on ramps here, and here. The Fifteenth will attack east of the central tower and the Fifth to the west. Marcus, I'll want four cohorts of your Twelfth again to exploit any breakthrough, and the Tenth,' Titus smiled at Lepidus, 'will once again provide covering fire with their *ballistae*. Josephus here assures me they are the pick of the army and feared by the Judaeans.'

Lepidus nodded his thanks to Josephus. 'We won't let you down.'

The officers, including Josephus, filed out, but once more Titus called Valerius back. 'How is your wound?'

Valerius assured him it was healing well.

'I'm glad,' Titus smiled. 'I may have work for you. I hope you still own this fabulous armour Paternus tells me about? Good. I want you to keep it and yourself at the ready.' Valerius left the tent shaking his head at his friend's attention to detail, but he soon had something else to consider. A messenger from Queen Berenice's court was waiting with a slip of parchment.

My mistress would talk with you. Please come soon. T, he read.

Puzzled, he told the courier he'd call on the queen when his horse was saddled. He left word with an orderly and went to look for Serpentius in the horse lines. The Spaniard's mount was missing and he pondered whether to search for him while a stable boy saddled his horse. The fine house Berenice temporarily occupied lay just beyond the hills to the north; close enough for Titus to be reached in emergency. Valerius reckoned he could be there and back by the seventh hour, unless . . . unless the entreaty was really from Tabitha?

The road was little more than a dirt track, its surface packed hard by the constant passage of Titus's timber-gathering convoys. As he rode, Valerius passed dozens of camels and oxen hauling tree trunks or stout branches harvested from land all but stripped bare of vegetation. Units of bored auxiliaries escorted the foresters, guarding against any attempt to disrupt Titus's preparations. Valerius guessed they wouldn't be worked hard in this part of Judaea. Any route so regularly traversed by the army commander with such frequency would be kept clear of any threat.

He turned off on to a side track. By the time he reached the estate the sun was past its height and he was glad he'd worn the all-enveloping cloak of light cloth provided by Ariston. At the thought of the lugubrious easterner he felt a sharp pang of conscience. Could he have done more to protect him? Reason told him not. If Serpentius hadn't been able to save him, nobody could. Still, the thought remained. He had called Ariston friend and, like too many other friends, Ariston had died.

A groom took Lunaris and the chamberlain relieved Valerius of his helmet and led him to the Queen's private chamber. Berenice sat upright on a carved wooden throne in front of a pair of doors leading to a courtyard. Tabitha stood slightly behind and to her right and Valerius felt the breath catch in his throat at the sight of her. He would have smiled, but her expression held a warning. Instead, he bowed his head in greeting and Berenice acknowledged the courtesy with a nod. The throne was the only seat in the room and he stood to attention in front of it, already half aware of the reason for his summons.

'Tabitha has told you of our dilemma?'

'Yes, lady.'

'And you are willing to undertake the task?'

Valerius glanced at Tabitha, but her face was set like a statue's. 'If you feel I can serve you.'

'Tabitha believes you capable, and I trust her judgement.' Her tone softened. 'And I suspect that it is her interests you serve, not Berenice of Cilicia.' Valerius would have protested, but a smile accompanied the words. 'I am glad you agreed, because should you succeed you will serve not only me or even the Judaean people, but Titus Flavius Vespasian and Rome. When Titus becomes Emperor – and it will happen soon, for his father plans to anoint him joint Emperor on his return to the city – he will want a Judaea at peace, a bulwark against barbarian incursion on the Empire's eastern frontier. A Judaea from which the grain flows in abundance into Rome's granaries in a bulk that will rival that of Egypt. A Judaea not riven by factional rivalries nor hidebound by traditions created by ambitious priests to protect their own interests. Only I can deliver this Judaea, but to deliver it I need control, and I can only control Judaea if I possess the Book of Enoch to act as my sword and my shield. You have seen Josephus at work?'

Valerius nodded.

'Then you know his true worth.' She paused. 'You are an interesting man, Gaius Valerius Verrens; a warrior, a diplomat, a man prepared to play the spy, not for his own gain, but to advance his Empire. When you deliver the Book of Enoch to Berenice of Cilicia, you may ask what you wish of her.' Her mouth twitched. 'Within reason, of course. At the very least, you will be a rich man who will want for nothing.'

'I would ask only one thing.' Valerius met Tabitha's eyes. They shone like glittering gemstones and not because of the light from the oil lamps. All the air seemed to be sucked from the room.

After a moment's hesitation, Berenice sighed with genuine regret. 'You would deprive me of my greatest treasure?'

'I would, lady.'

'Then so be it, and you will have my blessing.'

The interview was at an end and Valerius walked from the room. As he reached the outer door Tabitha caught him by the arm. Her cheeks were wet with tears, but she was smiling. Before he could react she kissed him hard on the mouth, and pulled him up the corridor. 'Come,' she said. 'We must make what use we can of the time we have. Soon your duties will take you away from me.'

'There will be a later,' he said solemnly.

'Yes, there will be a later.' She led him into her room and held him close, with her dark head on his shoulder. 'But for the moment we must only think of now.'

XXXIX

The track was empty as Valerius made his way back towards the camp with a head full of hopes and dreams in the dry heat of the afternoon. Find the Book of Enoch and Tabitha was his for ever. They would make a life together. Not in Rome, because Rome, with Domitian close, was too dangerous by far. Somewhere in the provinces, where Titus's friendship would protect him and Vespasian's thanks for past services would provide a position. They would not want for gold, because Berenice insisted she wouldn't allow her handmaiden to become a pauper. But first they must find the book. And the book was in Jerusalem.

It troubled him that only Tabitha could get them into the temple and knew the exact location of the book, yet there was some consolation in that they would face the danger together. They would have to use the tunnel again, and the thought gave him a shiver. What if . . .

He turned a sharp bend to find a rider facing him twenty paces ahead. The man wore a voluminous cloak in the Judaean fashion, but Valerius identified his horse as one of the big Roman cavalry mounts. His first thought was that Josephus knew of the summons from

Berenice and had come – for whatever reason – to intercept him before he got back to Titus. But why?

A clatter of hooves from his right answered the question. In the same instant the waiting rider urged his horse into motion and drew a long cavalry *spatha* from the scabbard at his waist. Valerius hauled his *gladius* clear of the cloak. Mars's arse, how could he have been so careless? One in the road to draw his attention and pin him in place, while the real threat came from the dried-out gully. He tried to turn Lunaris to meet the attack. Too late. Three of them, and they were already on him. The first rider hammered into the gelding's flank and both horses went down screaming. As he fell, Valerius threw himself aside so he wouldn't be pinned by his mount. Jagged rocks tore at his flesh as he rolled in the dust but he clung to his sword as if it were life itself. He struggled to his knees, half blinded by the hood of the cloak and lashed out at a shadow that came too close. The man laughed dismissively and kicked him in the chest so that he sprawled backwards, to be blocked by a rock wall. The hood fell back and he found himself facing a grinning, bearded auxiliary holding a long spear that darted expertly between his eyes and his throat. Valerius flicked the point away with the blade of his *gladius*, but it only came back all the faster. The other two watched from their horses in menacing silence, their faces emotionless. Half of Valerius's brain applauded the expert professionalism of the ambush and acknowledged the likely outcome, while the other half worked feverishly to find a way to stay alive.

'He's mine.' The owner of the voice was the rider who'd blocked the road. He sprang from the saddle and when he pulled back his cloak Valerius saw he was very young and that he wore the uniform of a Roman tribune. His first impression was of vivid blue eyes and handsome features set in a frown of businesslike concentration. Valerius had never seen him before in his life.

As the stranger approached, he whirled his sword in controlled, sweeping practice strokes. The razor edge whistled dangerously through the air with mesmerizing speed and Valerius's heart quailed. Here was a man as dangerous as Serpentius. As if to prove the point the tribune launched straight into the attack with powerful cuts to left and right. Valerius met the first with a flailing parry, but the heavy sword jarred his wrist as he blocked it and he struggled to deflect the next hammer blow.

The young man stepped back smiling, letting Valerius understand that the first attack was merely designed to keep him honest. 'Domitian wanted you to know why you were dying,' he said cheerfully. 'He says you are a coward and a traitor and this is the justice you deserve.' He punctuated the words with feints to the one-handed Roman's eyes and heart. Valerius ignored the provocation, using the breathing space to clutch at his jarred wrist with his right hand. He cried out at the pain as he flexed his fingers. The tribune's smile grew wider. 'Don't worry, friend, your suffering will soon be over.'

'I'm not your friend,' Valerius rasped. 'And this isn't a game.'

'Oh, but it is.' The tribune seemed surprised by his opponent's lack of appreciation. 'A killing game at which we are both adept. Unfortunately, this is the last time you will play.'

The stranger attacked with blinding speed even before he finished the sentence, but Valerius had anticipated the move. He swayed his upper body to the left, allowing the spearing thrust to the throat to slide by a hair's breadth from his neck. Only his speed saved him, because he knew he could never have parried it. His mind whirled, seeking a strategy that would keep him alive for a few minutes more. This man knew all about left-handed fighters. He would expect a counter with the *gladius*, but when it came he'd simply step to his left and saw the edge of the *spatha* across Valerius's throat. Somehow Valerius managed to bring the short sword up to push the point of the *spatha* skywards, leaving an opening for his right hand to come across in a slashing hook towards his attacker's jugular. The first spearman lunged with his point to press Valerius back and the young tribune touched his fingers to his chin, grimacing as they came away bloody. He looked down at the dagger point projecting from Valerius's right fist and shook his head at his carelessness.

'Very tricky,' he said, flicking at the artificial hand with the *spatha*. 'I should have realized you wouldn't give up without a fight. But the game is over now.' He sounded almost regretful as he called the two watching spearmen forward. 'Now you die. You wouldn't care to kneel and get it over quickly, I suppose.'

Valerius didn't bother to reply. His eyes flickered between the three spearmen and the sword point. There must have been a hidden signal. One spearman darted forward to draw Valerius's attention, but it was a feint and the shaft of another clattered into his helmet. The blow knocked it from his head and stunned him to his knees. 'Time to finish it.' Valerius looked up into the tribune's unforgiving blue eyes as the man raised the heavy sword shoulder high. He tried to raise his *gladius* to meet the blow, but all the strength had gone from his fingers.

The death sentence still hung in the air when it was punctuated by a sort of wet slap. When Valerius looked up the young assassin had sprouted a feathered shaft from the notch between chin and breastbone. He collapsed to his knees with an awful gurgling sound and clawed at his throat as he slumped forward on to his face. The closest spearman gaped in disbelief before he was punched back by a second arrow. Without another word the survivors tried to turn their horses, only to be surrounded in seconds by a swarm of auxiliary cavalry archers.

Valerius sheathed his sword and pushed himself to his feet with the aid of the abandoned spear. Lunaris stood nearby on shaking legs and the Roman walked past the still shuddering bodies to pat him on the muzzle. 'No fool like an old fool,' he confided with a sigh. 'Time they put us both out to grass.'

A shadow fell over him and he looked up into the grinning face of Gaulan, commander of the Chalcidean archers. 'You believe in living dangerously, my Roman friend. I almost didn't take the shot when I saw his tribune's armour.' He nodded to the man who rode up to his side. 'Fortunately we were accompanied by someone with more authority than I.'

'I thought you . . .' A shudder ran through Valerius at the thought of what would have happened but for the presence of Claudius Florus Paternus.

'Circumstances change.' Paternus shrugged. 'My brother's shade visited me on the night the Tenth was attacked and bade me stay my hand till I was sure. You have shown your true worth.'

'Tiberius was a good friend and a good soldier,' Valerius said. 'He did his duty to the last, as I did mine. How did you come to be here?'

'A security patrol to pave the way for Titus.' Paternus walked his horse across to where the two bodies lay bleeding in the dust and Valerius accompanied him. 'Who is he?'

'I don't know, but I'd like to find out.'

'Does anyone recognize him?' Titus Vespasian pulled back the blanket covering the dead man.

The legates of his four legions stepped forward to study the marble face. In death, Valerius's assailant seemed to have shrunk. He looked like a half-grown boy lying on the earth floor of the command tent with blood caked on his lips and the arrow still buried to the fletching in his throat.

'His name is – was – Lucius Silvanus Capito.' Phrygius winced. 'He joined the Fifteenth two weeks ago straight from Rome. An excellent young soldier with an escort of Thracian auxiliaries. I'd considered suggesting you appoint him to your staff,' he said almost apologetically.

'You will never make a politician, Phrygius.' Vespasian's son laughed to cut short the stunned silence. 'Do you have any idea who could have sent him, Valerius?'

'No.' Valerius gave Titus the answer he required rather than the truth. 'Every man makes enemies. I fear I've made more than most, but none who would want me dead.'

'Very well.' Titus called his guard. 'Take him away and have him buried.' He met the eyes of each man in the tent, leaving them in no doubt about the sincerity of his words. 'This ends here. A coincidence, a mistake or an accident. But I want it known, discreetly, that any further attempt on a fellow officer's life will not be met with mercy.'

'The Thracians?' Phrygius asked. 'Should I put them to the question? Perhaps—'

'It is finished. They are condemned by their own actions and will suffer death. But do it quietly, Phrygius. Make them disappear.'

The legate nodded.

'This is Domitian's doing?' Titus asked when he and Valerius were alone.

'It appears so.'

The young general looked up and his eyes were hard. 'His actions shame me and shame our father. This will not happen again. You will concentrate on your duties.' He returned to his papers and Valerius went to the door of the tent. 'And Valerius?'

'Yes.'

'You should look to Serpentius. He is unwell. My physician is with him.'

Valerius hurried back to his tent to find Serpentius lying on his blanket with his head back and his mouth open, snoring through his nose. The Spaniard's flesh had the pallor of a week-old corpse. Alexandros, the Egyptian *medicus* who attended Titus, stood over him watched by Apion, the black legionary.

'Is he . . .'

'I have given him a weak solution of henbane to help him sleep,' Alexandros said. 'He had a shaking fit and might have choked on his own tongue had it not been for this man.' He waved a limp hand at Apion. 'It is not uncommon among those with this type of injury.' He reached down to run his fingers gently over the depression in Serpentius's skull. 'Even if the skull isn't smashed, when a man is hit on the head with such force splinters of bone can be driven into the brain. Sometimes death is instantaneous, sometimes it is delayed, and sometimes the victim can carry on a relatively normal life, but it always has effects. Whatever the outward resemblance, your friend is not the same man he was before he received this wound.'

'Thank you. I will remember.'

'Do you want me to remain?'

'No, I will stay with him. If there is a . . . problem . . . I will send for you. Thank you for tending him.'

'You should thank the general.' The doctor's face was set in a tight smile that told Valerius he'd never have gone near a former slave if Titus hadn't ordered it.

'I also owe you my thanks,' Valerius said to Apion, who hovered by the doorway.

'He is my friend,' the Syrian said. 'And he was kind to me. It is not always easy being different. He taught me things.' Valerius nodded. He could imagine the kinds of 'things' Serpentius would teach. The open-handed blow to the nose that sent the bone up into the brain like an arrowhead; the belly punch that left you pissing blood; the pressure point between neck and shoulder that would leave a man momentarily paralysed so you could kill him at your leisure. All of them could come in useful for an outsider trying to make a place for himself among his iron-hard tentmates.

Apion left, and Valerius drew up the warped base of a cedar tree he and Serpentius used as a chair or table and sat down to watch over his friend.

XL

When Valerius woke the next day it was as if the previous one had never happened. Serpentius walked into the tent with half a wheel of fresh bread, olive oil, some dried fish and a jug of fresh water. The water came from an aqueduct that ran near the camp and originated from the famed King Solomon's Pools thirty miles to the south. Titus had ordered the supply to Jerusalem blocked to add to the privations of the defenders. Valerius supposed that if he'd known of the Conduit of Hezekiah, he would have poisoned the supply or stopped the flow. But Valerius needed the tunnel and he'd no intention of mentioning it.

'How do you feel?' he asked as they ate.

Serpentius took a moment to answer. 'A little slow in the head.' He tugged distractedly at a piece of bread. 'But otherwise no different. One minute I was with Apion watching the lads play a game of Caesar, the next I was on my bedroll with some quack feeding me a vile potion. After that, nothing till I woke this morning. What happened?'

'The *medicus* said you had a shaking fit.' Valerius studied his friend for any sign of a reaction. 'He thought

387

it might be something to do with the injury to your head. Apion probably saved your life.'

'I suppose that makes sense.' The Spaniard sucked at a hollow tooth and stared at the tent wall. 'Sometimes it feels as if the world's going on its way without me.' He bowed his head. 'I've always been in control, Valerius. Always been sure of myself, especially with a sword in my hand. Now, I have this feeling: What if? What if I'm guarding your back and it happens? You could be killed and it would be my fault. What use is a man with a sword if he's not able to use it? Maybe it would be best to get someone else to look out for you.'

Valerius clapped the Spaniard on the arm. 'Hole in the head or no, I wouldn't trust another man to be my shield in a fight. Battle turns you into a different man, Serpentius. The gods of your ancestors fight at your side. They will protect you, and you will protect me. The way it's always been.'

'I know.' The Spaniard looked up with a sheepish grin that looked out of place on his savage features. 'I'm talking like an old woman. I'm still as fast as I've always been.' He reached for the wooden practice swords they exercised with most mornings. 'Come out to the sword butts and I'll show you.'

Valerius shook his head. 'Someone gave me enough sword practice yesterday to last me a long time.' He explained about the ambush on the road from Berenice's villa and the Spaniard looked crestfallen.

'See,' he said, 'I should have been with you. Are you sure you didn't know this tribune? He must have been watching us to know where to ambush you.'

'I don't think so.' Valerius had considered the question. 'I saw plenty of escort troops guarding the timber convoys. More likely it was just chance.'

'So it wasn't old roasted face.' Serpentius said it as if he couldn't quite believe it. Paternus had been a potential threat for so long it was difficult to consider him as anything else.

'No,' Valerius said with a rueful smile, 'though if he'd had his chance earlier it's likely I'd have ended up floating down the Orontes with a knife in my back. Fortunately, he delayed long enough to appreciate my legendary charm.'

'Did they tell you we're moving? I heard it at the shit pit this morning. They've cleared enough of the town for a camp inside the old city walls. The Fifteenth are building it while the Fifth and some new recruits from the Twelfth work on the siege ramps. They've already started.'

'We should take a look,' Valerius suggested, trying to lift the Spaniard's mood.

'Better than sitting in here scratching our backsides,' Serpentius agreed.

Though Valerius had spent much of his adult life marching with the legions it still came as a surprise to discover how quickly his comrades could tear a city apart. They had an almost joyous lust for destruction. A thousand paces of wall and seven towers had disappeared since the original breakthrough. Where once had stood streets of shops, houses, workshops and temples all that remained was a field of dusty, churned-up earth. Once the buildings were demolished their rubble was turned into neat, anonymous piles. Hundreds more legionaries laboured to create the ditch and bank of a temporary fort within what had once been the New City.

'I don't understand why they didn't just make a perimeter using the walls as a base,' Serpentius said. 'It would have saved them half the work.'

'Because the walls were theirs, this is ours.' To Valerius it was blindingly obvious. 'A legionary is familiar with every foot of a marching camp. He knows what he has to build and what he has to defend and how and where to do it. He's done it so often it's become second nature. The effort of constructing the fort is worth the lives it will save if we're attacked. But it's not just that. Titus had this ground cleared to create a launch point for the next part of the siege. He wants the Judaeans to see us and fear us.'

'They see us,' Serpentius pointed to where thousands of armed Zealot warriors lined the walls, 'but I don't think they fear us.'

'They'll learn,' Valerius predicted with certainty. 'There's not a people on this earth who can stand against the legions.'

'What about that Arminius who chopped up three legions?' the Spaniard wondered mischievously.

'An ambush.' Valerius refused to rise to Serpentius's dangled bait. The Varus disaster had happened sixty years earlier, but it was still the greatest stain on Rome's military record. 'But this is no ambush.'

They walked their horses to an area where the Fifth legion had begun flattening ground and preparing ramps on the approach to the much stronger and higher inner wall.

'They won't abandon *this* position without a fight,' Valerius predicted. 'But it's still a matter of when, not if.'

Work on ramps had begun well out of range of the Judaean *ballistae* and *scorpiones*. Heaps of rubble packed between the stakes of a timber corridor gently sloped towards the second wall. Thousands of men trudged back and forth bent almost double beneath heavy baskets of earth, rubble and brush to extend the ramp another few feet. When a section reached the required elevation, teams of carpenters laid thick timber beams over the rubble to hold the weight of the huge siege towers. Once in range of the enemy, Roman light artillery pieces scoured the walls to protect the workers. In the meantime, the legionaries trotted forward with *vineae*, hide-covered shelters made of branches and wicker panels. These interlocked to form tunnels that allowed the labourers to work unmolested by spears, arrows and slingshots. Eventually the ramps would reach a height halfway up the walls and the builders would create a flat surface for the rams and siege towers.

'How long?' Serpentius asked.

Valerius studied the progress of the ramps and the height of the walls. 'Three days to finish the ramps,' he estimated, 'then another to get the towers and rams to the wall. The Judaeans will do everything they can to destroy them, but this time Titus will be ready.'

'When the walls come down do we go in with the legions?' Serpentius asked.

'Are you so interested in glory?' Valerius smiled. 'Our time will come. For now we let the men being paid for it take the risks. I want you to stay close to Titus.'

'What about you?' The Spaniard's voice contained a mix of puzzlement and concern.

Valerius grinned. 'Don't worry about me. Like all sensible generals I'll be watching from a safe distance.'

Titus summoned him at the sixth hour to receive his final instructions – 'and bring this famous armour. It's about time I saw it, but don't wear it just yet.'

Valerius arrived at the command tent with two servants carrying the weighty cloth parcels and Vespasian's son dismissed his aides. A few minutes later Lepidus joined them from the Mount of Olives.

'It was useful to be able to cut through what's left of Bezetha; it saves about two hours,' the legate smiled. 'It's good to see you again, Valerius. Staying out of trouble, I hope.'

'You hope too much,' Titus snorted. 'And you'll see plenty of him over the next few days, so let's get on with it. You have the armour?' Valerius nodded to the parcels on a couch in a corner of the tent. 'Then let's see it on, man.'

Valerius exchanged a glance with Lepidus. This was a new Titus; nervous and unusually waspish. He was reminded that the day must be fast approaching when Titus had promised his father Jerusalem and its spoils. Valerius could understand the conflicting obligations Titus was forced to juggle. It was very well for Vespasian to hand his son the throne, but unless Titus could prove he deserved it, others would surface to compete with him for the purple. Titus needed to legitimize his claim, and what better way than with a great victory? Vespasian's son didn't use up the lives of his soldiers lightly, but every life spent here might save ten later. Victory at Jerusalem and the triumph that followed would gain him the support of the legions, and not just those under his command. Military success and glory in war had long been a way of vindicating an emperor's right to the throne. Caesar had invaded Britannia to compete with the titans Pompey and Crassus. Caligula had thought to do the same, but he'd baulked at the northern sea and in the end it had cost him his throne and his life. Claudius had successfully invaded the island and reigned for thirteen unlikely years. In Valerius's eyes, Titus was better equipped than any of them to be the strong, competent and wise leader the Empire needed. How could he criticize him for having the unyielding ambition necessary to reach for the prize?

Valerius wore the fine scarlet tunic from Emesa beneath his cloak. With Lepidus's help it took only moments to don the ornate gilded breast- and backplates, followed by the greaves and the ornamental arm protectors for his wrists. The wonderful *gladius* in its elaborately decorated scabbard came next, this time slung on the baldric to fall at his left hip, as for a right-handed swordsman. Lepidus pinned the legate's cloak at the shoulder with a brooch of gold before Valerius placed the glittering helmet with its plume of stiffened horsehair and decoration of four roaring lions on his head.

Titus watched the transformation with something close to wonder. When it was complete he did a circuit of Valerius, shaking his head and chuckling. 'General? Replace the scarlet with purple and he could be the Emperor himself.' He looked Valerius in the eye. 'It should be treason to wear something like that. By the gods, it must have belonged to Nero himself. I wonder if the fat little piggy ever wore it?'

'He sent it as a gift to King Sohaemus of Emesa.' Valerius felt less than comfortable under his friend's scrutiny. 'And now . . .'

'And now,' Titus grinned, 'its bearer is a gift from the gods to Titus Flavius Vespasian. You see the resemblance, Lepidus? Perhaps a little over-prettified, but seen from afar like a pair of chickpeas from the same pod.'

'All he lacks, lord, is your natural authority. Come on, Valerius, don't be coy. Shoulders back, head up and chest out. We'll make a proper aristocrat of you yet.'

Valerius faced the two men with a wry smile. 'I'm beginning to wish I'd dumped this in the river.'

The plan, as Titus had first outlined it, was simple. Valerius, dressed in his general's uniform, would officiate at a pay parade of the Tenth on the Mount of Olives in full view of the Judaean lines. Afterwards, Lepidus would prepare his men as if for an attack, with Valerius in a conspicuous position posing as Titus. In theory, the commanding general's presence would convince John of Gischala that the main attack would fall on his positions and the preparations at the second wall were a feint. Valerius doubted it would make an appreciable difference to the outcome, but Titus would use any stratagem to achieve the victory he sought. But it seemed this wasn't certain enough.

'I have discussed it with Lepidus.' The Tenth's legate raised a surreptitious eyebrow at Valerius and 'discussed' took on a different meaning. 'Instead of putting on a display, the Tenth will make a feint attack on the Antonia fortress from the east. We'll probably have to put ramps in there at some point, so it might as well be done now. The feint will begin an hour before the genuine attack and should make the Judaeans send reserves from the inner city to the eastern wall. The cohorts I've borrowed from the Twelfth will be available to support you.'

'You don't think you'll need them for the attack on the second wall?' Valerius couldn't believe Titus would weaken his main thrust.

The general handed him a tattered piece of papyrus. 'This came from Zacharias yesterday by the Leper Gate. What do you think?'

Valerius studied the note before explaining the contents to Lepidus. 'He says the second wall is much weaker than it looks, especially in the central area. The morale of the defenders there is low, because they believe their generals have sent them there to die. They are led by a man named Judas and will run the moment the wall is breached.' He turned back to Titus. 'Break the wall and you will take the city.'

Titus nodded grimly. 'If we can get enough men through the breach before Simon bar Giora can reorganize his defence it will cause panic.' He punched his right fist into the palm of his left hand with an audible crack. 'It is an opportunity I cannot afford to ignore. When the wall is broken my legions will sweep all before them. With good fortune, we could have the entire city by nightfall.'

'Then,' Lepidus ventured cautiously, 'perhaps the assault on the Antonia will not be required.'

Titus shook his head. 'You haven't given your opinion, Valerius.'

'I think it appears a fine opportunity, but it depends on whether you fully trust Zacharias.'

'We have his wife and child,' Titus shrugged. 'Why should he betray us?'

Valerius saw that Titus's mind was made up. 'Then I would only urge you to take personal care during the assault. The streets of Jerusalem are a maze, as the streets of Gamala were.'

Titus's eyes hardened. 'You forget yourself, tribune, and you forget what kind of commander I am.'

'I apologize.' Valerius bowed his head, content he'd made his point. 'My concern is only for your welfare. Since I am to be making a display and observing, may I offer you the services of a bodyguard?'

'Serpentius?' Titus blinked. 'You would give me Serpentius?'

'Let's consider it a loan.' The one-handed Roman couldn't suppress a grin. 'He is a free man and I wouldn't like to be the person who tries to cage him again.'

Simon bar Giora sat in the grand banqueting hall of the Hasmonean Palace and cursed John of Gischala for the twentieth time that day. He hadn't slept for days, but that wasn't his greatest concern. He needed more men, especially after what he'd discovered today. Yet every time he made a request for reinforcements the Galilean pointed to the Mount of Olives and claimed the greatest threat came from the Tenth legion. Simon knew the Tenth's ferociously powerful catapults continued to cause a steady stream of casualties. A stream, but not a haemorrhage, which was what Simon faced if the second wall were to fall. Not a haemorrhage, to be honest, a massacre, unless . . . Well, he would think about that.

The plans were already in place; all he had to do was act on them. James, the Idumaean general, would command now the Romans had taken the third wall. Fine fighters, the Idumaeans; would that there were ten times as many of them. Simon had lost five hundred warriors in sorties against the Roman war machines and probably delayed them by a single day. Castor, one of his best men, had burned one of the siege towers after duping Titus into thinking he wanted to negotiate. A pity the Romans had cut him down as he tried to escape. Still, they had to keep trying.

The second wall was where the battle for Jerusalem would be won or lost, not the Antonia or the temple. Neither of them could be taken from the east, he was certain of it. The lower portion of the temple walls was a mere decorative skin upon the stone of Mount Moriah. If the Romans set their battering rams against them, all they would find at the end of a month was another wall of solid bedrock. The temple and the Antonia fortress were a single interlocking defensive system. If the temple held, Antonia would hold, and vice versa. The only way the Antonia could be overcome was if the second wall fell. Therefore the second wall must hold and John of Gischala must . . . give . . . him . . . more . . . men.

He gritted his teeth until he felt they might break. His giant hands gripped the table until it seemed the solid wood was about to disintegrate. There was a knock on the door and he took a deep breath.

'You sent for me?' Zacharias, too, looked exhausted, but then he had been on the walls for almost as long as Simon, and he had a family to worry about.

'I wanted your opinion about the state of our defences.'

'The new lines to the north of the Monument of Hyrcanus are as you would wish. Strong enough to hold, flexible enough to suck them in, but with clear avenues of escape to the Tower of Mariamme. Once they are in the salient there is no escape. We will slaughter them.'

'And in the centre?'

'We can hold them as long as the walls hold.' Zacharias sounded reluctant to give his report. 'But unless we can destroy the rams it is only a matter of time. Perhaps . . .'

'You think we should seek peace? You think we should surrender?'

'Can we win?'

'If we keep our nerve and fight and make them bleed we have a chance.' Something in the atmosphere changed and Zacharias shivered as he felt Simon's dark eyes on him. 'But we must keep our nerve.' A scrap of parchment fluttered on to the table between the two men. Zacharias's heart jumped into his throat. The dark eyes never left him as Simon continued. 'Judas and the men in the central tower have lost their nerve. What would you have me do with them?'

'Send them to the rear.' Desperation made the younger man's voice sound shrill. 'Make them dig the latrines and carry out the dead, but spare them.'

Simon sighed, and rose to his feet. He beckoned Zacharias to him and with fearful eyes his aide did as he was bade. 'I'm afraid it is too late for that. Panic and betrayal are like the miasma that overcomes an army that stays too long in one place with foul water. Only by cleansing itself will that army ever recover. Oh, Zacharias,' the words were almost a sob as he took the young man in his arms, 'what have you done?'

'I had to save them, lord.' Zacharias clung to what dignity he could. 'There has been too much death. Ruth and the child will have a life. I . . .'

Simon shook his head. 'Do you not see? You have betrayed them as you have me.'

'No,' Zacharias whispered. 'Never.'

'They can never be free. As long as a single Sicarii exists, their lives will be forfeit. Better that they had died an honourable death.'

'No.' Zacharias shook his head. 'I did what was right. What about the hundreds of thousands condemned to death by your foolish pride? All those innocents already starving on the streets of Jerusalem because Simon bar Giora does not possess the courage to utter the word surrender? Go and ask them if what I have done is so wrong.'

In the long silence that followed Zacharias felt the other man's big hands come up to stroke his cheeks, as a father would to a son. 'And what have you done, Zacharias?'

Zacharias could not bring himself to utter the words. Simon brought his cheek down to the other man's and Zacharias could feel the tears. 'Oh, Zacharias,' Simon bar Giora repeated, 'what have you done?' As he spoke the words his enormous muscles tensed and the big hands closed and twisted. Anyone listening would have heard a sharp crunch and the kind of cry a night owl makes as it pounces, followed by a long sigh.

Simon allowed the body to drop to the paved stone floor and called his guards. 'Put him with the others and do what must be done.'

Through the desperate misery of his grief he was heartened that in his betrayal the man he had called his friend might have presented him with the means to save Jerusalem.

XLI

As a courtesy of war, Titus ordered Josephus to circle the city and give the Judaean defenders one final opportunity to surrender. The offer surprised Valerius as much as any of the commander's officers. Their enemies were rebels who had defied the rule of Rome and there was an argument that the normal rules of war didn't apply.

The next day Josephus had his white horse saddled, and, dressed in his finest robes, rode from point to point shouting his exhortations. As Valerius later heard it, his call was less a plea to give up and save the thousands of innocents trapped in Jerusalem than a reminder of the terrible fate awaiting them when it fell. Since no guarantees accompanied the offer, it seemed likely to make them fight all the harder. Even his suggestion that the defenders execute his family – his mother, father and brother remained in the city – if it made them more amenable to the right decision, was more ritual than a genuine proposal.

Whatever the truth of it, the response from the Zealots and their allies came in rocks, one of which knocked him from his horse, a barrage of jeers and several anatomically impossible recommendations. There would be no surrender.

In the days before the assault a mixture of grim determination, fatalism and excitement grew in the legionary camps on the broken ground once occupied by the New City. Every man knew the day of reckoning was close. Valerius, disguised in his general's armour, rode ceaselessly across the Mount of Olives and across the ridge adjoining the Cedron valley supervising the preparations.

Lepidus had overcome his doubts about the attack. This would be no feint. 'Titus may think everything will go his way,' he told Valerius, 'but circumstances change in war. If I'm going to ask these men to die, it will be in an attack that means something. If we fail, and against these walls that's not unlikely, we fail because the Judaean defences were too strong, not because we made a half-hearted attempt.'

Two ramps had been built to take a pair of siege towers up to the walls of the Antonia fortress. To these, Lepidus added a third which would threaten the north-east corner of the temple. He hoped this would minimize the threat to the left flank of his attack on the Antonia, exposed as it was to missiles from the temple's north wall.

From his viewpoint on the Mount of Olives, Valerius could see how difficult it would be to take the fortress by direct attack. The rectangular fortification, with a massive tower at each of its four corners, stood on a rock perhaps fifty cubits high. Its south wall abutted the temple, and the city's second wall abutted the fort's north-east tower, making it impossible to outflank. To offset this, Lepidus had added his own feint: what would appear to be a direct attack on the temple itself.

A covered battering ram backed up by the four cohorts of the Twelfth legion would attack the city's East Gate. Of all Jerusalem's numerous gates this appeared to offer the most direct access, but all was not as it seemed. Zacharias had revealed that Jerusalem's finest masons had walled it up to a depth of eight feet and it was actually stronger than the wall itself.

All the preparations were carried out in full view of the Judaeans. The original purpose remained to draw men away from Titus's attack, but Lepidus still had some hopes of success.

'See how the ramps allow the siege towers to top not only the walls, but the two towers of the Antonia fortress. They are strong and the Judaeans will fight to the last, but there is space for only a limited number of defenders. If we can get enough men on to the fighting platforms and bridge the gap we could take one tower or possibly both. Once we have the towers, the fortress will follow.'

Valerius wasn't so certain, but this wasn't his fight and he wouldn't say anything to contradict Lepidus. He spent the night before the assault wide awake, more concerned for the men who would do the attacking at dawn than he'd ever been for himself. Lepidus's force consisted of five thousand of his own legionaries, plus two thousand from the Twelfth and ten cohorts of auxiliaries. The auxiliary infantry would only be used to exploit any success, but the archers would be more useful. Lepidus decided to position them in one of the few remaining areas of the New City still standing, to the north of the temple. From there, the Emesan marksmen would be able to pick off any defender who showed himself on the temple walls or the Antonia. The legate had already sent them out into the night so they'd be in position to cover the attack at first light.

In the hour before dawn, Valerius could hear the rustling of hundreds of legionaries moving into their pre-planned positions. It was accompanied by the faint chink of metal on metal, the rattle of a shield falling and the mumbled apology as one man ran into another, the hoarse, whispered curse of a centurion for one of the irredeemably clumsy fools under his command. Then, what passed for silence: the hushed, almost imperceptible hiss that might have been a light breeze passing over the leaves of a beech wood, but was actually the sound of a thousand men breathing; the shuffle of a nervous horse's hooves in the dust; the distant rumble of thunder that was the sound of his own pounding blood; and the buzz of a million bees that marked the precise moment less than a mile away when a city came awake in fear of what the new day would bring.

In truth, there was little need for silence. When the legionaries marched down the treacherous incline of the Cedron slope they'd appear as moving shadows in the first sullen, lead-grey light of the dawn. A few minutes later the rising sun would pick out the eagle, and the cohort standards of the individual units. No blasts of the trumpet to herald the advance of the Tenth. Lepidus had ordered that they march in silence until the enemy responded, the better to convey the uncompromising menace that was a legion's indelible stamp. When it rose, the sun would also light upon the glittering magnificence of the army's commander, twinkling on the ornate breastplate and the golden lions on his helmet. Valerius gentled Lunaris and tried to suppress the frustration he felt. What was he but an ornament, with no authority and no purpose other than to gull the enemy.

But he was a soldier. This was the position Titus had assigned him, and he would obey.

When he judged it was light enough for him to be seen, Lepidus raised a hand and every eye within sight turned to him. The hand dropped, and with a crunch of hobnailed sandals four of Lepidus's fourteen cohorts moved steadily down the slope, their pace set by the gradient of the uneven ground ahead.

Four hundred and eighty men to a cohort, marching in compact formations twelve men wide and forty deep. Each man took up a little more than three feet, so the cohort covered an area of fourteen paces by forty. From the hill they appeared as a shadow flowing smoothly across the earth, but Valerius knew they would be jostling, shoving, tripping and cursing as they stumbled into each other down the hillside.

A horn sounded from the city; a mighty blast as if the Judaean god had woken from his slumber and placed his own lips to the mouthpiece. The sound was accompanied by a sullen roar as the defenders of Jerusalem moved into their positions.

From the valley below came an enormous animal grunt as the men tasked with moving the three siege towers put their weights on the ropes and timbers. The rebels had attacked the towers three times over the past two days, but the big siege engines had survived and now they were less than fifty paces from their objectives. Valerius heard Lepidus muttering to himself close by, but it was impossible to tell whether it was a prayer or a curse.

A rush of disturbed air announced the arrival of the first Judaean missile, a boulder from an *onager* on the north tower of the Antonia fortress. It landed between two cohorts with an ear-splitting crack that spread a ray of jagged rock splinters. The projectile did no material damage but every man in the attacking cohorts hunched his shoulders behind his shield as if that would make him a smaller target. In seconds the air was filled with flying death and Valerius flinched as a shield-splitter bolt dissected the space between himself and Lepidus. Fortunately, the Judaean aim was usually more inaccurate. Though he saw one boulder strike carve a lane through the Third cohort in a spray of scarlet, most projectiles flew high or wide. He'd heard rumours of Roman deserters manning the Judaean catapults, but the gods be thanked none of them appeared to be on the east wall.

The four attacking cohorts reached the valley bottom and their big curved shields rose as they came within spear and slingshot range of the temple walls. Lepidus rapped out an order and his signaller blew a long blast on his *cornu* to send in the next six cohorts. Three would reinforce the assault on the Antonia fortress while the others moved against the north-east angle of the temple.

By now Valerius could see the legionaries marching across the shattered foundations of the outer wall and into the New City. Hundreds of Judaean warriors stood on the temple rampart hurling spears, rocks and darts; anything that would kill or maim an enemy.

'Now,' Lepidus whispered.

The Emesan archers rose from their hides among the abandoned buildings to sweep the rampart clear with arrows. The respite allowed the attackers to pour forward into the massive siege towers as their comrades hauled the giant structures the final few paces up the ramps to their target.

As the first legionaries reached the top of the tower it seemed Lepidus had been right and they must prevail. Moments later Valerius saw the familiar bright flare of yellow as the Judaeans hurled flaming oil to incinerate the first men who appeared on the fighting platform. A burning man plunged a hundred feet like an obscene shooting star to disappear among his comrades massed at the base of the towers.

Valerius had almost forgotten Titus was due to begin his assault on the second wall. Now he heard a subdued murmur and cries of alarm from within the city and understood it had already begun. For a moment his thoughts were with Titus and Serpentius, but his attention quickly returned closer to home.

Diagonally to his left the third siege tower had reached the point where the soaring temple wall turned towards the Antonia tower. Here, it was clear there had been some kind of miscalculation. The fighting platform of the tower should have overlooked the enemy parapet, so the attackers could fire down on to the Judaeans. Instead, the defenders had the height advantage by a few feet and they took advantage by hurling wave after wave of missiles into the men below. Valerius winced as he imagined the butchery on that blood-slick platform as the centurions propelled man after man into the slaughter when his predecessors fell.

He heard Lepidus curse and turned to him. 'At least they're dying for something,' he consoled the legate. 'They'll draw defenders away from the main attack.'

But Lepidus's attention was on the base of the tower.

The siege ramp to the temple walls had been completed during the night and should have been well guarded in the hours before dawn. But the Judaeans had either slipped through or tunnelled their way beneath the foundations. Almost wearily at first, the enormous tower the ramp supported began to tilt, picking up speed as men plunged helpless from its upper works. Too late, those at the base dived for safety in fear of being crushed. Valerius would swear he felt the ground shake as the massive siege engine crashed from the ramp on to the rocks below. Inside the shattered compartments, hundreds of men would be dead, dying, maimed and trapped, while their comrades fought their way towards the nearest escape route. But their ordeal had only begun.

On the walls above great vats of oil had been bubbling away ready to be ignited and thrown on to the attackers. Now the rebels rushed the vats to the parapet and men ignored terrible burns to manhandle them over the edge. Cascades of flame streamed down the walls with a terrible apocalyptic beauty, but the horror they caused among the wreckage was unimaginable. Liquid fire poured through great rents in the protective animal hide to incinerate the men inside and set the timbers alight. For the rest of his days Valerius would never forget the screams of men being roasted alive.

'Send a message that the second and third cohorts should join the attack on the Antonia.' Lepidus's voice shook with emotion as he gave the order. 'The others can concentrate on rescuing anything that's left alive. Have the artillery concentrate their efforts on the north wall.'

Lepidus continued the attack all morning, rotating his formations in and out of the siege towers as they tired or became depleted. He'd long since given up any idea of capturing the Antonia, but he was determined to give Titus every ounce of support. Just before the sun reached its zenith he alerted Valerius to a curious ceremony on the parapet above the smouldering ruin of the siege tower.

'What do you make of that?'

One after the other the Judaeans brought ten men to the wall and cast their bodies over the edge. Valerius winced as ropes knotted around their necks jerked tight a few feet below the parapet leaving them twitching and clawing at their throats for a few agonizing moments. Only the last appeared to be already dead before they pushed his body into the void. A square of white stood out sharply on each victim's chest, but the final man's was a stark contrast to the red stain where it appeared his captors had cut his throat.

'Deserters,' Valerius ventured. 'Or prisoners they can no longer afford to feed?' Still, the sight stirred a feeling in him he couldn't quite identify. It wasn't pity. More a sense of unease.

He cast an occasional troubled glance towards the grisly decoration hanging on the temple wall until Lepidus wearily announced that his men had done enough for now. The decision coincided with an enormous muffled roar that made the two men exchange a tired smile. Valerius reached out to clap the legate on the shoulder.

'They've done more than enough, Aulus,' he said. 'Unless I'm mistaken that is the sound of victory. Titus must have broken through.'

'Then they must fight on,' Lepidus sighed, 'because if Titus is right they'll be investing the fortress from inside the city within the hour.'

In the general euphoria it went almost unnoticed that the Judaeans had cut the hanging bodies free to plunge into the Cedron gorge. Valerius frowned when he saw the empty wall. Very gradually the significance of the timing dawned upon him.

'I need those bodies, Lepidus, and quickly.'

Lepidus rapped out an order to send a century to recover the dead men. Thirty minutes later a procession of legionaries returned carrying their lifeless burdens. One by one they set the bodies in front of the legate. 'This man's sign says he is "Judas, a traitor to his people",' a man who could read Hebrew pointed out. 'They mutilated him before they hanged him. I would guess the others will be the same.'

But Valerius only had eyes for the man whose stained chest turned out to be a flaming red beard. Zacharias's killers had cut out his tongue, and Valerius hoped it had happened after he died. A thrill of fear ran through him.

'We have to get a message to Titus. On no account is he to enter the city.'

But even as he voiced the thought, he knew it was too late.

XLII

Serpentius's hand automatically touched the hilt of his sword as he glanced across at the general. He'd seen the light in his eyes often enough to know what it meant. The light of the hunter caught up in the chase. A light that would only be extinguished by the kill.

They'd watched the rams at work from just out of *ballista* range in the ruins of the city's timber market. Titus, anonymous in a borrowed tribune's armour and helmet, fidgeted on his horse through the long afternoon. As he waited, his engineers concentrated their efforts on either side of the second wall's central tower, which had already taken a battering from the catapults.

As an additional precaution Titus had ordered the entire section of wall undermined. Protected by *vineae* and *plutei* shelters, engineers dug out the foundations and replaced them with timber props. Once the work was complete they set fire to the props and withdrew. Now, as they watched, the resulting collapse brought down the tower and a hundred paces of wall in a sullen roar of falling masonry.

Before the dust settled cohorts from the Fifth and the Fifteenth poured through the gap into the beleaguered city. If Zacharias's information was correct they should be able to punch through as far as the Antonia fortress and, in conjunction with Lepidus's Tenth, attack Jerusalem's great stronghold from three sides.

'Enough of this subterfuge.' Titus showed no emotion at his stunning success. 'Bring me my scarlet cloak so my soldiers can see I fight at their side.'

'You intend to enter the city, lord?' Cerealis and Phrygius exchanged a startled glance, but neither man was prepared to contradict his commander. Serpentius, a little apart and behind the command group, had no such misgivings.

'Begging your lordship's pardon,' he grunted, 'but street fighting's no place for cavalry. Or generals.'

Titus stared at him as an aide fixed the legate's cloak in place. 'It seems I cannot escape your master's scruples even when I send him elsewhere. When Jerusalem falls, my Spanish friend, men will say it was taken by Titus Flavius Vespasian, and none will be able to accuse me of standing back from the fray.'

'He's right, lord.' Phrygius belatedly spoke up. 'You shouldn't put your life at risk.'

But the final cohorts were already pushing their way into the city and Titus was determined to join them. 'I will send word when we reach the Antonia. Well, gentlemen,' he turned to his aides, 'what are we waiting for?'

Auxiliaries worked to widen the breach, using the rubble to flatten out the ditch, and Titus forced his way through the rear units still marching through the opening. Ahead, their comrades rampaged among the narrow streets. Jerusalem was his.

Titus's elation was almost palpable as he studied the flat-roofed buildings and sturdily built temples. In contrast, his nervous escort edged closer around their commander and Serpentius heard the centurion in charge urging his soldiers to greater vigilance. The Spaniard decided the old soldier had good reason to be wary.

The gods only knew how many of the defenders remained trapped in the houses now being checked by squads of auxiliaries who'd followed the attacking cohorts. Certainly, not many had been killed on the battlements. A few smashed bodies lay like piles of bloodied rags as a testimony to the power of the Roman artillery, but most of the dead were civilians. Every roof and every window could hide a spearman or a slinger who would die happy if his last act was to kill Titus Flavius Vespasian. Serpentius couldn't cover every threat, but he could stay close to Vespasian's son. He edged his horse into the command group.

Titus felt his presence and turned in the saddle. 'Ah, my nursemaid is still with us,' he laughed as they turned a corner into a wide market place from which narrow streets radiated in every direction.

The Spaniard drew his sword. 'You might yet have need of one.'

With every street choked with soldiers, the legionaries filled the open ground seeking an exit.

'Why aren't we moving?' Titus forced his horse through the mass of men, calling for the *praefectus castrorum* who'd led the attack on the walls.

A centurion pointed to one of the streets, and the general pushed into the narrow entrance with two of his aides, shouting to the legionaries to stand aside. Serpentius managed to stay with him, but the escort struggled to keep up, hindered by hundreds of men whose only focus was joining their comrades.

'You should wait for the escort, lord,' the Spaniard insisted.

Titus shook his head. 'I have to find out what's happening.' They heard a roar from away to their left, but it was impossible to tell whether it signalled a triumph or a setback. Titus ground his teeth in frustration. 'I must know what's happening,' he repeated. 'Where's my messenger?'

'Somewhere back there.' Serpentius pointed with his sword.

'Where is your commander?' the general called out to the soldiers they passed, but no man knew. Serpentius noticed with alarm that every door and shuttered window around them was closed. There could be only one reason. These streets hadn't yet been cleared.

'We have to get out of here, lord.' He grabbed Titus's reins and tried to turn the horse, only to be hemmed in by the crowd and baulked by the reluctance of its rider. Titus fumed at this personal outrage, but he recognized the urgency in Serpentius's voice.

'The doors,' the former gladiator shouted. 'They've blocked the street. It's an—'

A howl from the roofs finished his sentence and a hail of missiles rained down on the men packed into the streets below. A spear hurled from above pierced the neck of the tribune to Titus's right and he slumped into the saddle, sheeting his horse's neck with blood. Titus looked around in astonishment. Serpentius reacted instantly, reaching across to haul him bodily from his mount. As they fell he roared for the men around him to form *testudo*. The landing knocked the breath from him, but he picked himself up and covered Titus's body with his own.

'*Testudo*,' he repeated. '*Testudo* to protect your general. Defend General Titus.'

At last the big painted shields of a dozen men came up to form the protective carapace Rome's tacticians had evolved for just this type of situation. It would take a fortunate throw to penetrate the locked shields. Titus was shaken and bewildered but unhurt, and Serpentius helped him up to crouch beneath the shields. They had a chance. Around them some units had formed their own *testudo*. Others hammered at the doors and shuttered windows in a bid to get at the enemy, only to be cut down from the opposite side.

'General? We have to go back.' Serpentius urged the man crouching beside him in the crush of fear-tainted soldiers beneath the shields to face the unsavoury reality. 'Our only chance is to get out of this street.'

'Retreat?' Titus sounded as if the word were an insult.

'They have all the advantages—' An extra loud crash interrupted Serpentius, followed by the screaming of men who would never be the same again. 'They can sit up there and kill us a few at a time,' he continued, unperturbed, 'but it won't be long before someone decides it's a good idea to start throwing burning oil out of those windows. They didn't do this to pen us here. They did it because they think they can slaughter us. That means someone out there has a plan. If we don't want to prove him right we have to go back.'

Titus stared at him, but this time there was no argument. He nodded. 'This is your general.' His parade-ground roar pierced the clamour around them. 'Pass the order that the cohort must withdraw to the market place.' Perhaps fifty men heard the command, but they quickly passed it to those around them. The crush lessened as men took the first tentative steps backward.

There was no way of warning those in the van, who Serpentius suspected were already fighting their own losing battle. They would have to fend for themselves. Foot by painful foot they made their way back, spears and rocks rattling on the shields above.

'What the fuck's he doing in the middle of this mess?' Serpentius heard a man in an adjoining *testudo* protest. 'This is no place for a fornicating general.'

The Spaniard met Titus's eyes and Vespasian's son grinned. 'I think he's right.'

They passed a felled horse, its eyes dull and two spears buried in its side. The commander of Titus's escort lay crushed beneath it, his hands still twitching. Titus shook his head. 'I failed them.'

'No,' Serpentius hissed, 'you led them. Now you'll have a chance to avenge them.'

By the time they reached the square other units were retreating from the adjoining streets. Men carried their wounded comrades. Out of the bedlam appeared Phrygius, legate of the Fifteenth, sweat-stained and haggard. He gasped with relief as he recognized Titus.

'Thank the gods you're alive. We walked into a trap. The rebels ambushed both legions before they could reach their objectives.' He lifted a water skin to his mouth and Serpentius noticed his fingers trembling. 'We've cleared a route back to the breach. We'll get you out now and make another attempt tomorrow.'

'No.' Titus's face flushed crimson with the strength of his anger. 'We hold what we have. I want the second wall pulled down piece by piece and every building in our control demolished. We will construct our own siege wall encircling the entire city. If the Judaeans want to keep us out, so be it, we will make sure they stay in and starve. Not a loaf of bread or a jar of oil will pass.

Not a woman or child will be allowed to leave. Let it be known I will kill anyone who makes the attempt. How many prisoners?'

'Four hundred, perhaps five.' Phrygius looked perplexed.

'Then they will be the first barrier. The refugees have been escaping by the north-west route since we took the wall and our soldiers have been allowing them to pass out of pity. No more. You will crucify one prisoner for every ten paces and anyone who tries to pass will join them.'

'But—'

'Do you deny me the right?' Titus snarled.

'No, lord.'

'Then have it done,' Titus said more gently. 'They have brought this upon themselves. What they sow, so shall they reap.' He turned to Serpentius. 'You saved my life, Spaniard. This is no time to talk of rewards, but know this. If ever Valerius Verrens no longer has need of you there is an honoured place in the household of Titus Flavius Vespasian as long as he is alive to provide it.'

Serpentius bowed his head in thanks, but said no words. It was a good offer. A man could live long and well with such patronage. But he doubted he would ever take it up. He would either die in the service of Valerius or, if the gods spared him, take the long road back to Hispania and the mountains of his youth and make old bones in the earth from which he had sprung. Such was the fate of Serpentius of Avala.

XLIII

One week later

Simon bar Giora fought the despair that had been eating into him since the Romans built the siege bank that turned Jerusalem from a fortress into a prison. It was a despair shared by every one of the city's defenders and seemed to pervade the very stones around him. Before Titus's wall, ingenious people found ways to get in and out of the city; ways to pass messages and sometimes even food. Simon smuggled out refugees fifty or a hundred at a time, relying on the humanity of the individual Roman soldier towards starving women and children. Surprisingly, that reliance often proved justified, at least in part. Now the Romans had shut those ways to all.

An all too familiar stench hit him like a gust of wind as he passed a doorway in one of the big houses that lined the street. He knew what he would find if he looked inside. The Upper City was now the greater part of what remained of his holdings. These were the homes of wealthy people, but disease knew no distinctions of class or status. When he'd cut the rations for the final time the rich began dying more quickly than the poor. It seemed hunger ravaged those less accustomed to it in a shorter time than it took to weaken people who faced daily privation. That, of course, and lack of hope.

Some days earlier a delegation of priests, landowners and merchants had appeared at the Hasmonean Palace. They came to protest against his men's searching their houses for hidden food and gold, and to seek an assurance that, despite the siege, they would be treated with the respect their status deserved. Their message to Simon was that if he could not preserve their social distinctions he should hand over control of the city to John of Gischala. Or, and perhaps this was the true point of their visit, surrender it to the Romans.

Simon had stared at them for a long time, until they began to shift uncomfortably. The bones in the cheeks of a few showed they'd experienced hunger, but most still wore the fleshy look of the well fed. He thought of the thousands willingly fighting and dying to keep the Romans out of the city, the hundreds of thousands sleeping on the streets who sought only to survive, and felt nothing but contempt for these people. Simon bar Giora was a large man and his anger showed, making the men closest to him step back.

'God dictates my actions as he does yours.' He allowed fury to pervade his voice. 'It is God's will that we are here fighting for our children's future, and that of their children. We will no longer be subject to Rome, or we will die as free men. I need food so my soldiers have the strength to fight. From now on, any man who does not fight does not eat. I know you all,' he'd looked at them one by one, 'and I know you keep hidden food stores in your warehouses and your shops. I know your wives eat well while others go hungry. I know every house of yours contains a secret hoard of wealth, for you are the kind of men who would not willingly be parted from it. Well, I have a bargain for you. You have two days to bring all your food and a third part of your gold to me. If I believe any one of you has cheated me, I will have every house searched and your families put to the question. Till now I have not had the men to do this and hold the walls, but you will have noticed that my kingdom has shrunk in recent days. Now, I can give you the attention you deserve.' They stared back at him with loathing and he smiled. 'You should be thankful it is God's will there are no longer poor Jews and rich Jews in Jerusalem, only Jews fighting for survival. I have made it easier for you to reach heaven.'

John of Gischala also had a substantial hoard of food he believed Simon didn't know about. Simon needed the merchants' gold to purchase a share of it for his men. Since the attack on the Antonia fortress, John had moved into the temple complex and Simon was on his way there now. His route was complicated because the bridge connecting the temple to the palace district was sealed off. To reach the temple mount, he must go south to Herod's Theatre, then descend into the Tyropoeon valley before turning north towards the temple's main gate. On previous visits his only escort had been Zacharias, but today ten spearmen accompanied him. John of Gischala's moods were always mercurial and unpredictable, but of late he'd become ever more erratic and deadly. Of course, if John decided to kill him ten men wouldn't prevent him, but they might make him stop and think.

They turned a corner into a street of steep steps Simon found oddly familiar. This was where he'd met the woman Judith and her little family. Suddenly it became very important that they survived. The spearmen carried food to bribe any guards who decided to make life difficult. Simon decided he would give it to Judith if she still occupied the same position. His heart quickened as he recognized the little makeshift shelter, but one look confirmed his fears. A pair of bony legs protruded from the entrance, the angle of the feet a certain indication of their owner's status.

He leaned against the wall and closed his eyes. No need to look, the situation was plain enough. But he wouldn't continue without showing her this one last measure of respect. Suddenly, Judith represented all the hundreds of thousands of Passover refugees crammed into the city. He forced himself to pull back the cloth opening, careful not to touch the dead body. A single brush of the hand would require him to undergo ritual purification before entering the temple. A swarm of black flies greeted him and he closed his mouth because the stink was so thick he could almost taste it.

Judith lay on her back with a child in each twig-thin arm, but not the Judith he remembered. All dead, of course; starved, and difficult to know which died first. There'd been a baby but he saw no evidence of it. The flies had laid their eggs in dark eyes now transformed into squirming pits of maggots. A face that was mere bone overlaid by desiccated flesh. He felt the urge to vomit, but managed to curb it. What was it she had said? *The children of Israel will prevail.* Where is your faith now, lovely Judith of Ephraim? A tear ran down his cheek and his mind cried out for support. God aid me, I cannot go on without your help. Give me a sign that what I am doing is right, and not just a matter of foolish pride.

But of course there was no sign. He looked to where the gleaming roof of the temple was just visible in the afternoon sun. What if . . . No, he couldn't afford to have doubts. If he was not strong, how could he expect others to be strong? He must believe. With a last look at what had been Judith he reversed out of the shelter.

He turned to the escort commander. 'Have four men take these people and find somewhere to bury them, Isaac. We have no priest, but say what words you feel are right over them.'

'Lord, I . . .'

'Just do it.' The Judaean leader's voice held a fury that made the other man flinch. 'And when we are done with John, remove every body from the streets and the houses. It shames us that our dead lie for all to see.' He saw the doubt on Isaac's face. 'Round up every man who cannot or will not carry a sword. They too can make a contribution. I know . . .' he shook his head, suddenly death weary, 'I know we cannot bury them all. But we must do something. Is the gate to the ledge above Gehenna still open?'

'The Romans kill anyone who tries to use it.'

'Then do it at night. Do you understand?'

'I understand that.' Isaac met his gaze without flinching. 'But not why you insist on meeting John of Gischala with only six guards. Are you so fond of death?'

Simon's expression didn't change. 'What is death to Simon bar Giora, ruler of a city of the dead?'

No man could fail to be impressed by the Great Temple of Jerusalem. As he approached the Huldah Gates, Simon's eyes were dazzled by the sun's glare on the massive polished blocks of white sandstone. The beaten bronze covering the gates glowed like hot coals. Galilean warriors guarded the wide stairway, but word had been sent of his coming and they stepped aside. He passed upwards through the centremost of the triple gateways, overlooked by hundreds more of John's men watching curiously from the walls above.

The stairway opened out on to a broad court ranging the length and breadth of the complex. Massive columns supported a covered walkway. Like every Judaean, Simon knew they numbered one hundred and sixty-two. The walkway's ceiling was a wonder of carved woods – mahogany and walnut, cedar and olive – depicting figures from the Torah. In the past, men selling cattle, sheep and doves for sacrifice would have filled the precinct. Now hundreds of tents of cloth and leather covered the court, temporary shelters for John of Gischala's men. Dark patches and piles of ashes from the warriors' cooking fires stained the once-pristine paving of the Court of the Gentiles. The raw stink of fresh excrement indicated that the simple number of men had overcome both the limited latrine facilities and, more tellingly, their reluctance to defile the sanctity of this sacred precinct.

Weary eyes followed his progress through the maze of shelters, but no man attempted to impede him.

Towards the temple.

Built a hundred years earlier on the instructions of the first Herod Agrippa, the sheer scale of the building inspired awe, as its creator intended. It was constructed of the same polished sandstone as the walls and stood on a raised platform in the centre of the court. As commanded by God, it faced east across the breadth of the complex, less a temple than a giant walled fortress with a great tower at its centre.

Steps climbed to three doors in the long wall that faced him, but Simon's progress took him to the main, eastern entrance. *Ballistae* strikes from the Roman war machines on the Mount of Olives had pitted the frontage. He was thankful he'd chosen a moment when the legionaries were conserving their ammunition. Temple guards stopped him at the base of the steps and sent word inside to John of Gischala.

While they waited, Simon heard a regular sharp metallic clang and wondered what mischief his rival was up to. A few moments later a bearded officer appeared whom Simon recognized as the man who had explained John's battle plans at their last meeting.

'My commander begs your pardon, but he asks that you enter alone.' The leader of Simon's escort shook his head, but the Judaean raised a hand for patience. The soldier continued: 'Naturally, he guarantees your safety and that of your men.'

'Very well.' Simon waved aside his guard's protest. If he wanted to talk to John here it could only be on his terms. 'I place my life in his hands.'

He followed the man up the steps and into a broad, open chamber. Smoke from a brazier swirled in the soft breeze to tickle his nostrils and the air was heavy with heat and the acrid scent of metalworking. The surroundings were a sharp contrast to the industrial scene that greeted him. Sumptuous hangings in vibrant blues, reds, golds and greens covered every wall, almost giving the impression of being in the centre of an enormous garden.

This was the inner precinct known as the Court of the Women, where wives and daughters could watch the ceremonies from the galleries above. It contained four equally open secondary chambers: the Chamber of the Nazerites, reserved for a priestly sect utterly devoted to the service of God, and the Chamber of Wood, the contents normally used to burn temple offerings, but currently feeding the blaze beneath a large cauldron in the Chamber of Lepers, which was also being helped along with measured helpings from the contents of the Chamber of Oils.

John of Gischala sat upon his throne in the centre of the room watching two of his men laboriously sawing a solid gold table apart. Two others worked to free gemstones from the fastenings that fixed them in position. Despite his impatience, Simon took a moment to study this astonishing work of art being destroyed before his eyes. It must have been three paces long and one and a half broad, with legs the length of a Roman *gladius*. The top had a raised border a hand's breadth in height and formed from a single twisted rope of gold which made three continuous circuits of the surface. Cunningly worked into the inner and outer faces of the rope were layers of precious stones fixed by golden pins. More gems, fashioned into the shape of eggs, decorated the table top. Not content, the artists who created this wonder had made crowns containing ears of corn, and all kinds of fruits – pomegranates, dates, apples and grapes, all formed from jewels of the same colour as the fruits themselves – and fastened them with a band of gold to the lower part of the table. A second solid gold surface, equally elaborately decorated, served to strengthen the legs, worked in the form of lilies entwined with grapevines.

Simon winced as the teeth of the iron saw bit into the gold. It tore great rips in the soft metal and showered dust and shavings to be collected on a curtain spread below the table. Eventually the two men laid down the saw and twisted part of the upper surface free, carried it to the cauldron and placed it inside.

'It is a gaudy thing, is it not?' John of Gischala's voice brought an end to Simon's horrified inspection. The Galilean waved a hand to where another four men worked with hammer and die on circular moulds filled with gold to create coins by the hundred. 'Better to use the gemstones to bribe the Roman guards and the coins to pay my soldiers. They fight for a noble cause, but a man still needs an incentive that provides hope for the future. I hear you've been stripping the Upper City and minting your own?'

John accompanied the words with a sly leer and tossed one of the coins so Simon had to catch it. Simon looked down at the shining circle in his hand and read the crude legend circling the rim.

'What do you think?' John seemed genuinely interested in his opinion.

'Freedom of Zion? A fine sentiment.'

'We also have them in silver and bronze denominations.' John's lips twitched into that peculiar mirthless smile. 'But I so wanted a gold coin, and of course my supply is much more reliable than yours.' The knowing look in his eyes confirmed his knowledge of Simon's meeting with the priests. 'They came bleating to me to stop your ravages, but I sent them away. Bleed them dry and kill them all for all I care. A merchant without wares or a priest without a temple is just another useless mouth to feed.'

Simon was curious. 'Does it not concern you to destroy the treasures that have been in our keeping for ten generations?'

A dismissive shrug of the shoulders. 'What good is treasure if it cannot help those who hold it in their time of need? But you did not come here to talk about gold, I think.'

'I would discuss my assessment of our situation with you.'

'Very well.' John's gaze drifted towards the sweating workers. 'We will find more privacy inside.' He led the way through a curtained door between the Chamber of Wood and the Chamber of Lepers and they passed through a narrow room – 'the Court of the Israelites,' John announced, as if he were showing Simon around his home. Beyond it lay a much larger space with a massive stone altar at the rear. The altar, along with a strange-looking bronze vessel the height of a man and equipped with twelve spigots, identified the room as the Court of the Priests. Priests would use water from the laver to sanctify themselves before the ritual of the daily sacrifice. The floor on all four sides sloped away from the altar to an open conduit carrying a stream of clear water – John must have managed to maintain his own supply. Blood from a recent sacrifice still dripped down the side of the altar and ran into the conduit where it drained away in a trail of smoky pink. On one of eight marble tables to one side lay the flayed carcass of a sheep.

John saw his look. 'The priests accused me of defiling the temple and wanted to suspend their rituals, but I persuaded them that God's help may tilt the balance in our favour. An assessment, you said? I was most impressed with your little trick. You almost had them when you lured them inside the second wall. If only you had made me a part of your plans, victory might already have been ours.'

Simon stared at him. Could he really be so naive as to think a minor setback and a few hundred casualties would drive Titus away? 'We lost too many men and they did not lose enough to make a difference,' he replied. 'It won't make them give up. Has the siege dyke caused you problems on this flank?'

'They hardly need it,' John pointed out, 'when they already have the Cedron gorge. Our starving Passover pilgrims still occasionally manage to get through, but I doubt that will last. Titus has been crucifying every able-bodied man he catches whether pilgrim or not – I'm surprised he can spare the wood. You've heard the rumours?' Simon shook his head and John continued. 'Some of our escapers have been begging to be allowed back into the city.' The Galilean smiled as he saw Simon's eyes widen. 'It seems the Syrian and Egyptian guards discovered a refugee trying to smuggle gold or jewels in his stomach. Now they gut anyone they catch, man, woman and child; rip them apart to see whether they contain anything of value.'

The revelation sickened Simon. How much horror could one man take? How many of the people he'd helped to get through the Roman lines ended up butchered in the hills? 'If it's true we must work as hard to keep them in Jerusalem as the Romans.' John nodded. 'And we have to feed them.'

'But I've barely enough to feed my men,' the Galilean protested.

'I happen to know there are two storehouses filled to bursting point directly beneath us.' Simon dipped a toe in the cool water flowing past his feet and stared at the other man. 'It would be a pity if the supply to the temple dried up.' John's eyes narrowed. 'And of course, I'd pay.'

His rival took a deep breath. 'I'm sure we will find something.'

They discussed how they could work together to meet the next Roman attack, two enemies forced to combine against the greater threat. Titus's engineers had already begun to fill in the gorge to the north of the Antonia fort. 'It could be a feint,' John suggested, but Simon shook his head.

'To take the city, they need to take the temple, and to take the temple they must first take the Antonia.' They agreed Simon's men would be allowed free access across the lines to help defend the temple walls when the inevitable time came.

Simon was about to leave when his eyes fell on the steps of the Holy of Holies beyond the altar. 'You said you were certain you would find the book?'

For the first time he saw something like despair in John of Gischala's eyes. 'I need more time.'

XLIV

'My informants counted one hundred and fifteen thousand bodies carried in the past two weeks from a hidden gate to be pushed from the cliff into the valley of Gehenna. Not a dog, a cat or a rat survives in Jerusalem, but, outwith, they gorge on its leavings. I hear stories of mothers so hungry they cut up and eat their own dead children. Families sift the dung heaps and sewers for any seed of grain that may have survived another's ingestion.' Josephus paused, apparently overwhelmed by the horror evoked by his words. Valerius noticed his rugged features were pale with exhaustion and his hair seemed greyer than the last time they'd met only a few days earlier. The Judaean still wore the bandage around his forehead from the stone that had struck him. He had just returned from a final mission to negotiate Jerusalem's surrender. This time he went alone, with Titus's agreement. Despite his suspicions, Valerius felt a certain sympathy, even an affection for the man. Time after time he'd circled the walls, bearing humiliation and insult to persuade the defenders of Jerusalem to surrender, or attempting to undermine their resolve. The lion head shook as if doing so would clear it of what he'd seen and heard and he looked up. 'They say that since the siege began no less than six hundred thousand have starved to death.'

Valerius watched Titus's face for a reaction to this enormous figure and the anguish that underpinned it, but the general only nodded thoughtfully. 'But still they won't surrender?'

'Simon bar Giora would not even see me.' The lie came as easily to Josephus as reciting from the Book of Genesis. He'd used the time spent with John of Gischala to urge him to devote more men to search for the Book of Enoch, but the Galilean had argued there were only so many he could trust. 'What if one of them came across the book and somehow managed to smuggle it out to a certain person?' In the end the crazed light in the other man's eyes had persuaded Josephus to concede the point.

'Then if they will not finish it, I will.'

'Lord,' Josephus protested. 'I urge caution . . .'

Titus shook his head. 'The time for caution is past. If they will not surrender with hundreds of thousands dead and a mountain of evidence that their god has deserted them – in fact that this god now supports their enemies – they will not surrender until the final defender of Jerusalem breathes his last.'

What no other man in the tent knew, not even Tiberius Alexander, was that Titus had received a secret dispatch from his father the previous day. Titus Flavius Vespasian had arrived in Rome to discover himself the ruler of an empire with barely enough gold in its treasury to pay its soldiers for another two months. Vespasian needed Jerusalem, but even more he needed the fabled contents of the temple. And Titus was the only man who could give it to him.

'The Antonia earthworks are complete?' He put the question to Phrygius and Cerealis who would jointly command the assault. 'Everything is in place, lord,' Phrygius assured him. 'We can have the siege towers and the rams in position by first light. The engineers have undermined the walls beneath the western tower of the Antonia . . .'

'You hesitate, Phrygius?'

The two legates exchanged a glance. 'We agree it must be now. We cannot allow the Judaeans to make another successful sortie against the ramps, as they did a week ago. Every scrap of wood we have left has gone into the frame and the supports of the new ramps. Not a tree stands within a three-day march of Jerusalem, and what is left beyond is of poor quality. If we fail this time, it could be . . .'

'Months.' Titus finished the sentence for him. 'But we will not fail.' He smiled as if relieved his generals had taken the decision from him. 'I sense the hand of the gods in this, perhaps even the hand of the Judaean god. Assemble your legionaries. I will speak to them in an hour.'

Valerius saw Josephus slip out of the tent and hurried to join him. 'You seem troubled,' he said.

'All these months of . . .' Josephus shook his head wearily, but stopped abruptly as if alarmed he'd been about to say something he didn't intend. 'I mean, it saddens me to hear Titus say God has deserted the Judaeans, even these rebels who face us. John and Simon and the men who fight for them are wrong, but they are still my countrymen. Their god is my god.' The intensity in his eyes was impossible to ignore and it was directed at Valerius. 'I do not believe my god would allow so much death and destruction without allowing

431

proper recompense for the sufferers, or at least those who follow them. Something good *must* come of this, Valerius. And *someone* will feel God's guiding hand during the horrors still to come. It is my experience that God often chooses those who least expect his guidance. I believed I was that man, but perhaps he will choose another of greater resource.' Josephus placed a hand on Valerius's shoulder. 'Do not believe everything you hear about me, Gaius Valerius Verrens. And if you feel the hand of God, for the sake of the Judaean people, do not disregard it.' He walked away with the gait of an old man, leaving Valerius with a premonition of something close to dread.

The Roman's mood lightened when he returned to his tent to find Tabitha with Serpentius. She wore a dark cloak over a damson dress that surprised him by its richness, and her feet were encased in rugged sandals. It was obvious they'd been talking, but they stepped apart when he appeared through the tent flaps. Her eyes shone when she saw him and she approached to look into his face as if to fix every curve, angle and line so she would never forget it. She reached up to touch the scar on his cheek with her fingers.

Serpentius grunted something unintelligible and walked out to leave them alone.

'I think he's jealous,' Valerius smiled. 'You have bewitched him as you have me.'

Tabitha read the unspoken enquiry in his words. Her answering smile contained elements of sadness and confusion, and there was a catch in her voice. 'You, Valerius. We were talking about you. In his own fashion Serpentius loves you as much as I, but in a way no woman could ever truly understand.' She shook her head. 'How could she? You have a warriors' bond forged in the white heat of battle. You fought together, bled together, and it is only by God's grace that you did not die together. But he fears for you,' her nostrils flared and her voice turned fierce, 'and if Serpentius fears for you, I must also. He believes each man's life is a single thread and every fight and every wound cuts that thread a little shorter.' She turned away so he wouldn't see the tears that welled up in her eyes. 'I do not wish to be your death, Valerius, but I cannot turn back from the path I have chosen.'

He took her shoulders and gently swivelled her towards him. The softness of her hair brushed his face and he inhaled the fresh scent of spring jasmine. He remembered Josephus's lined face and intense, pleading eyes and the touch of a hand on his shoulder. God's hand. Fate. 'No man can escape his fate, Tabitha.' He stroked her hair with the fingers of his left hand. 'It seems our fates are entwined, but for what purpose and for how long only the gods can tell. All I know is that for us there is only the moment, and we must make what we can of it.' He led her to the blanket that was his bed and her fingers went to the brooch holding her cloak at the neck.

Much later her fingers stroked the muscular hardness of his flat belly, playing with the dark curls of the line of hair that had so intrigued her earlier. 'Titus revealed his plans to my mistress last night. How long will it take?'

'He acts like a man who has run out of time.' Valerius allowed the conference to run through his mind. 'He has tried to spare his legions the worst of it, but I think he can no longer afford to hold them back. A week, perhaps less. He must have Jerusalem, no matter what the cost.'

He felt her nod. 'We cannot delay too long before we enter the city. I must reach the temple before he destroys it.'

'He will do what he can to save it.' But even as he spoke Valerius knew he had somehow misread what she'd said.

'No, he has made his decision.' Her voice burned with emotion, and Valerius wondered if she hated his friend for making her say it. 'The reports to his father will tell a different story, but Titus Flavius Vespasian is determined there will only be one siege of Jerusalem. He will tear down this city stone by stone when he has taken it. He has said he will leave only such walls as a single legion might use as their camp, and three towers, Phasael, Hippicus and Mariamme, for their watches.'

Valerius thought of the magnificent buildings he'd seen on that first day when the Tenth set up camp on the Mount of Olives. Was it really possible Titus would destroy everything? The answer was yes. The legions had already levelled half the city during the siege. In what seemed another lifetime, Titus had called the temple a fortress within a fortress within a fortress. To leave it intact would be to present the Judaeans with a symbol of their indefatigability as a people and as a religion. A focus to which they could return and nurture the bitter taste of defeat, their hatred of Rome and their hopes for freedom. A symbol to hold and defend. Legends would spring up about the original defenders and those legends would spawn new heroes. No. The truth was that Titus couldn't afford to spare the temple, any more than the Hasmonean Palace, or any other building that reminded the Jews there was a time they called Rome equal.

'Then we leave in the morning.' He drew her to him. 'We will spend the day with Lepidus and the Tenth, discover what we can of the situation in the Cedron valley. You understand what awaits us there? Serpentius has told you?'

'I am ready.'

Rather than the direct route across the wasteland of Bezetha, Valerius, with his borrowed Judaean robes in a roll behind his saddle, took Tabitha and Serpentius in a wide arc. The reason was that he wanted to look upon Jerusalem from where he and Titus had studied it nearly six months earlier. The fighting had left more than half the city little more than a barren wasteland pockmarked by small piles of rubble. How much blood had been spilled since? How many had died?

And more blood was about to be spilled, for even as he reined in by the Caesarea road more men were already dying. The final attack on the Antonia fortress had begun.

Throughout the night the air had shaken to the diabolical heartbeat of the rams thundering relentlessly against the walls of that mighty citadel, the key to the even mightier citadel of the temple beyond. In the airless darkness beneath the Antonia's walls Roman engineers hacked at the rock and the dry earth to leave a gaping void. They worked quickly for fear of counter-mining by their Judaean counterparts, who were agile as rats in their own tunnels close by.

Titus had arranged his formations so that the Fifteenth Apollinaris faced the northern flank of the fortress and the Fifth Macedonica the west. Lepidus's Tenth would make a new assault upon the stubborn eastern towers from the Cedron. From his vantage point, Valerius could see disciplined ranks of legionaries moving into position between the big siege catapults. Cohort after cohort, their helmets and their standards glittered like individual jewels and the morning sun twinkled on their spear points. Then came the auxiliaries of the Empire's many tribes and nations, their formations a little looser, their manoeuvres visibly more laboured. Valerius suffered a sudden moment of doubt. His place was with them, not on this foolish mission to hunt down a few scraps of parchment that meant nothing to him. It occurred to him that Titus would wonder where he was and might even be justified in having him arrested for desertion. But it was only a moment, and he turned away as the thud of the first big catapult launching its missile carried across the hillside.

His eyes caught those of Serpentius and the Spaniard met his glance with a mirthless smile. The former gladiator's skeletal features seemed unnaturally pale, so the lines and the scars of old wounds stood out starkly against almost grey flesh. He had slept in the tent of his friend, the Syrian legionary Apion, and Valerius wondered if he'd had another shaking attack. But when he asked, the Spaniard only growled.

'Nothing a little action won't cure.'

When they reached the Mount of Olives Valerius found Lepidus and his staff watching the attack from a little promontory overlooking the fortress. The legate frowned when he recognized his one-handed friend. 'You again? I hope you bring a little more of Fortuna's aid than our last venture, though I doubt it. We're just fodder for their arrows and spears and to draw attention from the others. The Fifth is in the best position to make a breakthrough. What game does Titus have you playing this time?'

'No game, Lepidus,' Valerius said quietly as he drew him aside. 'But you'll remember my previous visit with the Judaean . . .'

'Ah, I thought so. You're up to no good.' Lepidus noticed Tabitha for the first time and his eyebrows rose. 'At least the company is a little easier on the eye this time. My lady,' he smiled, and bowed in the saddle.

'What I would like,' Valerius persisted, 'is the use of a tent to rest in, and a centurion to direct me towards the path we used previously. I want to have a look at it in daylight.'

'It's your neck.' He looked up at a shout of consternation. 'Jupiter's wrinkled scrotum, they've done it again. Claudius? I thought we'd stopped up all those ratholes.' Below them flame was licking at one of the siege rams where a Judaean sortie had emerged from the base of the temple's north walls. He glanced across to Valerius. 'Claudius will make sure you get what you need. I doubt I'll have time to see you before you do whatever it is you've come to do. Good luck, Valerius.' His hand reached out and touched the wooden fist.

They took what rest they could while they waited for late afternoon when Valerius intended to make his inspection of the path. Serpentius, normally catlike in his ability to sleep at any time, tossed in his blankets, and Valerius talked Tabitha through the streets he'd used when he was in the city.

'I know that long stairway,' she assured him. 'When the time comes I will be able to take us to the temple, even in the dark.'

Just before dusk, Valerius and Serpentius met a tall centurion by the camp's west gate. The sound of the battle a few hundred paces to the north was muted now as exhausted men tired of trying to slaughter each other. Valerius heard the grumble of faraway thunder and decided it must be the gods laughing at the foolishness of men.

'Good,' the centurion said, when he saw they'd changed into their Judaean clothing and grey cloaks that matched the one covering his armour. 'We'll be within range of their slingers, so we have a choice of carrying shields and asking them to use us for target practice, or being a little less conspicuous. In view of what the legate told me, I thought this was best.'

He led the way down the slope and they quickly came to the diagonal path Valerius remembered. The centurion followed it, all the time glancing at the towering walls a bowshot away. Only a few men guarded the parapets, because it seemed an unlikely place for the Romans to assault. John of Gischala needed the bulk of his Galileans to defend the Antonia. Still, someone saw them, because a lead slingshot flattened itself against a rock with a loud smack a few inches from Valerius's head. He picked it up and studied the mushroom-shaped piece of metal that would have put a hole in his head if it had been a little better aimed.

The centurion chuckled. 'They're bloody good, the slingers, but you don't have to worry about their archers. They couldn't hit a whore's left tit if they were standing on her crotch.'

They reached the pair of tombs Josephus had used as a reference point. Absalom, son of David and a pair of brothers whose names Valerius couldn't recall. Here, the Judaean had turned down into the base of the gorge, but Valerius kept to the path, his eyes always on the ground a few dozen feet below. He reached a point he recognized. A small, beehive-shaped tomb to the south and a mulberry bush to the north, with a flat platform between, and beside it a distinctively shaped rock.

'Mark that spot,' he whispered to Serpentius. 'We need to find it again in the dark.'

XLV

Serpentius led the way, sure-footed as a mountain leopard and seemingly able to see in the dark. Tabitha proved equally adept over the rough ground, and they made surprisingly good time. They only slowed when the terrain forced them to the valley bottom where the walls of Jerusalem loomed above them like a cliff to their right.

Eventually the Spaniard changed course and moved upward. Valerius heard a grunt and the soft rustle as he ran his fingers through the leaves of the mulberry bush to confirm they'd reached their destination. Valerius scrabbled in the dust until his fingers closed on the notch in the rock. He expected Serpentius to be already at his side, but the Spaniard was a hunched grey blur in the darkness. Tabitha was close enough for Valerius to see her eyes and the question in them. He shook his head.

'Serpentius?' he hissed.

The only answer was the soft mewing sound of an animal in pain.

He crept across to the Spaniard and put out his left hand to touch him, flinching as he felt the bone and sinew shaking uncontrollably beneath his fingers. He moved closer so his face was almost touching the other man's. 'Are you unwell?' he whispered. 'We can wait a few moments for it to pass.'

'I can't.' Serpentius's voice shook as much as his body and Valerius sensed he was choking back tears. His mind fought to understand what was happening. This was Serpentius, the gladiator who had won a hundred fights in the arena. Serpentius the fearless, bravest of the brave. The man who had stood beside him, unflinching, while they faced death a dozen times, and had saved his life a dozen more. 'I . . . I can't go down there again.'

Valerius put his arm round the Spaniard's shoulders and his lips against his ear. 'What is wrong, old friend?'

For a moment the only sound was that of Serpentius's harsh breathing. 'I'm not the same, Valerius.' The whisper might have been the sound of a breeze passing over the mulberry leaves. 'The man you knew is gone for ever.' Another harsh sob racked his body. 'I feel fear,' he spat the word through gritted teeth, 'and I fear death. When we last went down into that pit I understood the eternal darkness that awaits me. It has haunted me ever since. Hades awaits us down there. I cannot face it again. I am a coward.'

'No.' Tabitha echoed Valerius's urgent denial as she moved close to the Spaniard's other side.

Valerius tightened his grip on Serpentius's shoulder and turned him until he could look into the dark eyes. The depth of despair there made him want to weep, but he knew Serpentius needed his strength. He choked the words out. 'No man is less of a coward than Serpentius of Avala. This is the wound talking, not you. Every man has fears, but not every man can overcome them.'

'Not you, Valerius.'

Valerius thought back to the time he had been trapped in the pipe of a Roman aqueduct and could have laughed aloud at this folly. 'Listen, old friend, I need your help to move the stone and replace it. Give me the sack with the torches.'

'No. No,' the Spaniard insisted. 'I must come with you. A moment or two and I'll be ready.'

But Valerius remembered the previous journey through the Stygian darkness below. The thought of someone freezing or being driven mad down there unnerved him more than going into danger without his Spanish shield. 'Your place is here, Serpentius,' he said. 'Above ground with a sword in your hand.' He felt a huge sigh run through Serpentius's body and knew he'd made the right decision. 'Replace the slab when we are gone and return to Titus. He needs your sword this night more than I. With the gods' will, we will meet again at the Great Temple.'

'The Great Temple.' Serpentius repeated the words as if they were a talisman.

'Yes. The greatest danger will be when the temple falls. That is when I will call on you.'

'And I will answer.' The voice that made the solemn pledge was firmer, and Valerius hugged the Spaniard to him as he removed the bag from his shaking fingers.

'Now, help me with the slab.'

Valerius ordered Tabitha to wait on the tenth step, and when the great rock rumbled into place above his head he used the flint and iron to light the torch.

'Poor Serpentius.' Tabitha blinked as the brand flickered and burst into flame.

Valerius waited for his vision to clear, but when the ball of light finally spread he felt his guts turn to ice. They

441

had other problems to worry about than Serpentius's health. The last time he'd stood here the water had run a foot below the level of the lowest step. Now the surface shimmered six inches above the second. That meant it would be at Tabitha's thighs when they left the steps. Worse, the current flowed three times faster. He remembered the thunder he'd heard earlier. These streams would ultimately be fed from sources far in the mountains, so even if there was no rain on Jerusalem the water levels would fluctuate. Tabitha looked up at him, unaware of the calculations going through his mind. In the torchlight the water looked benign, but she didn't know what awaited them further down the tunnel. How deep would the water be, how much space between surface and ceiling? Feet certainly in the highest parts, but he remembered stretches when the stone roof had been inches above his head. Now . . . ?

'We may have to swim,' he said.

'I can swim.' She met his gaze and the dark eyes didn't flinch. 'We must have the book.'

'I think I can get us to the pool, but . . .'

She reached up to take his left hand in her right and her warmth sent a surge of belief through him. 'Do not doubt your ability or my resolution, Valerius. God is with us.'

She loosed her grip and stepped down into the swirling waters. It would be dark, he was thinking, very dark. Once the torch was wet it wouldn't light again. He tried to remember every twist and turn of the subterranean passage. Every dip and every obstacle. The place where the bottom dropped away into the sinkhole. But would they ever reach it? There was only one way to find out. He pushed past her into the mouth of the tunnel with the torch in his left hand, trailing his arm until he felt her grip the wooden fist.

At first they moved in silence, accompanied only by the rush of the water, then her voice echoed in his ears. 'I am glad we left Serpentius,' she said. 'Down here it is easy to understand his fears. When we get out of the tunnel . . .'

'We have to survive Jerusalem.'

'But first the tunnel,' she insisted with a woman's practicality. The roof was lower now, the water only three feet below it and already Valerius had to bow his head as the cut stone angled downwards. The icy cold of the water crept up his legs and the chill air seemed to permeate his bones. 'Tell me everything you know.'

He closed his eyes and let his memory tell the story. 'A hundred paces ahead the water will be up to your chin and you will think you cannot continue.' He was surprised how calm he sounded. 'The torch smokes and it will fill your nostrils and your mouth, but you must endure. Stay close. Hold my arm and try not to breathe. It will last only moments before we emerge into a section where the ceiling soars above us and the smoke will clear. There is a carved stone. Josephus said it mentioned Hezekiah, the man who ordered the construction of this conduit. After two hundred or so paces, the ceiling drops again, and the tunnel narrows, but you are slim,' he remembered the way the stones had pushed at his shoulders, 'and you will easily pass. The next trial comes soon after . . .'

'What is the next trial?' Her voice was almost in his ear.

'We will be under water.'

'For how far?'

'That depends on the depth.'

'How far?'

'Twenty feet, perhaps thirty.'

'Perhaps?' She sounded incredulous.

'Perhaps more.'

'And after?'

'Let us wait and see if there is an after.'

All too soon they reached the point where the tunnel roof dropped to meet the orange glitter of the rushing water. 'I'm going to put out the torch,' he explained. 'Stay close to me and do not fear.'

Tabitha nodded, but he heard her gasp as he used the leather bag to extinguish the flame, plunging them into a darkness so total they couldn't be sure they even existed. Valerius fumbled with the bag until he had tied the neck around the head of the torch. At least that way it had a chance of staying dry. He reached out with his left hand and felt her flinch. 'Take it, and do not let go. In this section there is room for us to swim side by side. Use your free hand on the side of the tunnel and kick with your feet. Don't rush and don't panic. If we stay calm we will easily reach the other side.'

'Valerius?' Her voice sounded very small and very young.

'Yes?'

'I love you.' He felt the warmth where her lips touched his cheek and despite everything it made him smile.

'I know. Now, fill yourself with air. I'll count to three, and on three we go under and we swim until we reach the other side. There is no going back. Do you understand?' She didn't reply, but he heard her gulping in huge nervous breaths. 'One . . . two . . .' he said a silent prayer, 'three!'

As he ducked beneath the surface the shock of the cold water threatened to force the air from his lungs, but he pushed forward and he could feel Tabitha beside him, her right hand clutching his left. He kicked with his feet and pushed at the tunnel side with his wooden fist. Despite his brave words a knife point of fear scored his brain. This was what it had been like in the pipe of the Old Anio aqueduct, with the water surging around him and no hope of escape. A little bubble of panic formed inside him, and grew until it filled his body and his mind and he thought he would go mad. Something rattled against his skull – his head had hit the tunnel ceiling – and the pain drove the panic away. He felt Tabitha's hand in his, the determination and the strength as she forced her slim body through the liquid darkness. She had no idea what lay ahead, but still she placed her trust in him. The breath seemed to harden in his chest. How long had they been under? It didn't matter, because there was no going back. Blood thundered in his ears and a great rage welled up that gave him new strength. He pushed on, keeping his head down and hammering his fist into the wall to increase his momentum. Swim and keep swimming, the pressure in his chest forcing its way into his mouth. He felt the moment her fingers loosened and she gave up. He clutched at her, but she fought him and then was gone. Bewildered, he allowed himself to float in the dark water, pushed by the current, until a hand twisted into his hair and hauled him upwards in a blinding bolt of pain. His face came clear of the water and he dragged in a long, rasping breath.

'I thought you'd decided to turn into a fish.' The soft voice was close to his ear and he could tell she was smiling. 'We could have surfaced long ago. How far until our next swimming lesson?'

Valerius pulled the torch free from the bag, but one touch of the soaking pitch-covered rag told him it would never light. 'I don't know for certain.' His voice echoed and he understood they must be in one of the areas where the roof was far above. 'All we can do is keep going until we reach the exit.' He reached out for her and drew the shivering body against his. 'Thank you,' he said.

'All I did was what you told me to.'

'I know, but thank you anyway.'

They pushed ahead through waist-deep water, successfully skirting the sinkhole that had almost swallowed Serpentius. After two or three false alarms, they reached a point where the tunnel definitely disappeared beneath the surface and Valerius judged they must be close to the entrance.

'I think this is it.'

'You think?'

'There's only one way to find out. Take my—'

He heard a splash. Silence answered his desperate cry of 'Tabitha?' 'Mars's sacred arse,' he cursed. 'The gods save me from beautiful women with minds of their own.' He dived under the surface and pushed his way forward with strong, powerful strokes. There came a moment when he sensed the tunnel widen. A few strokes later the darkness faded to be replaced with a dull red glow and he clawed his way to the surface. To his right, Tabitha was already climbing the steps of the Pool of Siloam. She had the folds of her dress in her hands and was squeezing water from them. He called out to her, but she only had eyes for the sky to their north.

It was on fire.

XLVI

As Serpentius sat in the darkness trying to control the shaking in his hands, his mind tried to come to terms with the enormity of what had just happened. The voices in the passageway faded and finally disappeared altogether and he'd never been more alone. More alone, even, than when he walked out on to the bloody sand of the arena to take another man's life in front of twenty thousand blood-hungry vultures. He felt a rush of revulsion for a people whose combined value as human beings didn't add up to the life of the single brave gladiator who knew he was about to die. How many times had he walked into danger at the side of Gaius Valerius Verrens? And all he'd ever felt was pride that Valerius chose him, a Spanish peasant, to be his friend and comrade. Even as a slave he'd known that pride, but when Valerius made him a free man it grew tenfold. And now he'd failed him.

Serpentius of Avala did not experience fear, or at least not as other men experienced it. Something inside him had always distilled the essence of fear into an elixir of power: a quickness of hand and eye and a mental dexterity that allowed him to think four moves ahead when the very best he faced could think only two. The Romans would never have taken him but for the lust for revenge that made him stand fast when he should have run. In the arena, the combination of skill and speed made him feared and respected. When others tried to make an ally of him, even a friend, he despised them for their weakness. He preferred to be hated.

Valerius had rescued him from the arena when his stubborn refusal to entertain was about to get him killed, matched against fifteen or twenty in a contest with only one end. In his turn he repaid Valerius with loyalty, and by teaching him how to turn a talent for soldiering into a talent for killing. It had been as much of a surprise to one as to the other when comradeship evolved into a type of wary friendship, and, eventually, into something beyond friendship. He looked towards the entrance slab he'd just replaced. There was still time. Valerius needed him and all he had to do was remove the stone and walk down the stairs into the darkness. But the very thought of it made him feel sick and the shakes got worse. When he willed his legs to move nothing happened.

He was a coward.

Eventually he managed to raise himself up. He retraced his steps up the slope past the tombs and exchanged watchwords with the guards at the gateway of the Tenth's camp. He found the tent with his equipment and sat with his head in his hands. Gradually, the terror faded and his mind began to clear. There was one way to erase the shame of what had happened earlier. Valerius hadn't told him everything about tonight's mission, but the Spaniard's instinct was that his friend and Tabitha were going into great danger. Valerius had said to meet him at the temple. He would do better. He would be there waiting for him.

And there was only one way to do it. He would join the attack on the Antonia.

He retrieved his horse from the lines and made his way west. Lepidus had said the Fifth was the legion with the best chance of making a breakthrough, so it was to the Fifth he rode. His route took him through the rear ranks of the Fifteenth as their siege rams continued to batter the north flank of the fortress. At a point where a few buildings survived he dismounted and continued on foot, instinctively following the sound of fighting, reading every nuance in the ebb and flow of the battle. The houses and apartments around him subdued the muffled roar, but he knew he was going in the right direction. Wounded men passed him in a stream, stumbling, staggering and crawling the opposite way.

An increase in volume confirmed his suspicion that he was approaching the Antonia. A little later he reached an area where the engineers had levelled entire streets to allow the Fifth Macedonica to deploy. Illuminated by the light of a thousand torches the Fifth's cohorts had packed into the confined space. Across their heads Serpentius could see that a combination of ram and mine had brought down the southern tower of the fort's western frontage. Marked by the burning oil the defenders had poured down it, the rubble from the collapse had provided the Romans with a new, unplanned third ramp. In a stroke of good fortune it formed a narrow valley that led to not just the upper walls of the Antonia, but to the adjoining angle of the temple portico.

Cerealis urged his men forward, the centurions screaming at them to take the wall and reminding them of the plunder that lay beyond it. To Serpentius those walls meant Valerius, and this time he would not fail his friend. He pushed his way through the soldiers, only to be blocked by the sheer mass waiting their turn to face death in the assault on the fortress.

And death was what awaited them.

John of Gischala and his Galileans were as aware of the importance of the breach as the Romans they fought. He'd placed his best men there, including James, the Idumaean general he had once called enemy. With him came the hill warriors who'd been the shock troops of Jerusalem's defence. Every Roman who ran the gauntlet of spears, darts and rocks to reach the top of the valley was driven back in a welter of blood. Serpentius saw that the only way to break the deadlock was by a concerted assault, but the centuries who made the attempt were always broken up before they reached the summit. Only the bravest would make the final climb to certain death, and many hesitated. Serpentius looked around, but he couldn't find the men he sought. What they needed were archers to sweep the walls with their arrows and cover the next assault. But Titus had always been short of archers and their lack was blunting his best chance of taking the tower and the temple.

The Spaniard forced his way through to where Cerealis stood directing the attack with his senior officers. Titus was absent, and Serpentius guessed he would be with the Fifteenth. The legate's guards stepped in front of him, but Cerealis recognized the whip-thin figure with the scarred head and welcomed him with a tight smile.

'Ah, Verrens' Spanish wolf. Where is your master? Our commander has been most concerned.'

Serpentius ignored the question. 'If you could concentrate your artillery on what's left of the tower and the angle of the temple wall, I'd be prepared to lead the next assault.'

The legate's face went blank and he struggled to contain his anger at being advised on tactics by a lowly civilian. With difficulty, he regained control of his temper. 'I fear you are too late. Oddly enough, I had already considered that.' He waved a contemptuous hand towards the breach as the familiar chopping sound of a shield-splitter being launched signalled the start of a barrage designed to sweep the defenders clear. 'The attack has already begun. I will ignore your impudence. Your suggestion is noted and your courage applauded. Now leave the professionals to get on with the battle.'

He turned away and Serpentius would have followed him but for the great roar that came from the foot of the breach. He looked round as a double century of the Third cohort launched a new attack up the rubble slope. A hundred and sixty men packed the breach, their progress impeded by the torn and blackened bodies of those who had preceded them. Above, the boulders and *ballista* bolts of a hundred catapults caused carnage among the defenders. Yet as quickly as one man fell, another replaced him and there was only the slightest diminution in the hail of missiles that hammered down on to the raised shields. The air rang with the rattle of metal on wood and the screams of dying men. Those screams took on a new pitch as a new river of fire poured down the centre of the valley scorching the legs of the attackers and incinerating the helpless wounded. The stench of roasting flesh carried on the soft breeze to the waiting cohorts and Serpentius could hear the sound of more than one legionary spilling his guts. Every man in the centre of the attacking column either fell to be devoured by the flames or fled. Only those high on the angled slopes survived to continue the attack, but even they quailed before the horror suffered by their comrades. All but one.

Serpentius recognized Apion even before he heard the Syrian's rallying call. The young legionary charged up the rubble slope gathering perhaps a dozen of his comrades as he went. A new shower of boulders, darts and arrows rained down from the defenders to meet the assault. Serpentius was certain Apion must be swept away, but the Syrian raised his *scutum* to protect himself. In the same moment a volley of shield-splitter bolts cut down the men above and the attackers clambered up the last steep section of tumbled masonry. Serpentius heard himself screaming support as Apion called to the survivors who had held back, urging them to join him. Somehow the Spaniard found himself with the front ranks of the fresh cohorts waiting to make the climb.

'Come on, you fools!' He drew his long sword and pointed to the young Syrian. 'This is your chance. Get enough men up there with him and the temple is ours.' The legionaries, frustrated by their hours of waiting, stepped forward with a growl, but their centurion snarled at them to hold their ground, looking to Cerealis for confirmation.

Taking in the situation at a glance, the legate nodded and rasped out an order to his signaller. By the time the attack call blared out, the cohort was already on the move. The rushing men swept Serpentius up in their advance and as he reached the bottom of the rubble slope he picked up an abandoned shield.

'All we want to do is kill these festering Jews,' the man beside him growled as they climbed the ramp of dusty masonry. 'They should have sent us in hours ago.' But Serpentius only had eyes for Apion. When the legionaries reached the lip of the temple wall the *ballista* crews were forced to adjust their aim. The Judaeans instantly took advantage to launch a counter-attack.

Serpentius saw the dark Syrian pushed back by two men, only to smash one aside with his *scutum* and stab the other through the body. For a moment their eyes met and Serpentius saw Apion grinning with the fierce joy of battle. A hail of missiles forced the Spaniard to raise his shield and amid the clatter of strikes he heard a cry that confirmed one had found its mark. When he looked again his heart stuttered. Apion was down, his body crumpled in the rubble. A killing rage rose inside Serpentius and he heard himself howling like the wolves of his native mountains. But Apion wasn't finished. He forced himself slowly to his feet using his shield for support. Shaking his head groggily, he turned just in time to meet another attack. Most of the men who'd made the climb were already dead, but despite the efforts of the Judaeans more legionaries were joining the little band by the moment.

'On!' Serpentius threw aside the shield and challenged the men around him. The battle madness filled him to the point where he felt his whole body was going to burst. 'Do you bastards want to live for ever? All the gold in Judaea is in that temple and it's there for any man who can lay hands on it.'

With a growl Serpentius set off up the slope. Every man there knew the gold would go to Vespasian and Titus, but they would get their share in the end. The lure of all that gleaming metal quickened their pace. They'd reached the steepest part of the slope and they pushed each other on, barely noticing the deadly hail of iron and rock. By now dozens of Roman soldiers were fighting for their lives around Apion, but they were still not strong enough to make the decisive breakthrough. The Judaeans harried the heavily armoured legionaries like packs of wild dogs. Two, three and four men surrounded each victim and hauled him to be dispatched by a knife thrust through the eye.

Serpentius and the reinforcing cohort clawed their way over the last few feet and suddenly the balance shifted. Now, apart from a few small groups wholly intent on slaughtering a downed opponent, it was the Judaeans who fought for survival. Serpentius looked around for Apion and his eye fell on a lone figure struggling under the weight of three opponents.

'Hold on!' The Spaniard forced his way through a brawling ruck of men and swung his sword at the rearmost of the Syrian's tormentors. The edge sliced into the Judaean's neck and his head parted company with his shoulders, spraying a jet of blood over his comrades. A second man turned with a great flailing slash that would have spilt Serpentius's guts if he hadn't danced back out of range. A moment later the Spaniard lunged and the man screamed as the point of the *spatha* speared his heart. The third assailant lay slumped across the Syrian's body with Apion's blade in his chest, and Serpentius rolled him aside before falling to his knees beside his friend.

Two dark eyes stared up at him, but they were the only recognizable elements of the young Syrian's face. Unable to pierce his armour the Judaeans had concentrated their efforts on their enemy's head. From the nose downwards the once-handsome features had been chopped into a gory red mess, spikes of bone and shards of teeth showing through like pearls in a grape press.

A terrible anguished groan came from Serpentius's breast as he knelt over his dead friend. Had it truly come to the point where death would be a blessed release? He shook his head. No. Not while Valerius Verrens still lived. He reached down and closed Apion's staring eyes with shaking fingers.

When he forced himself to his feet he realized the fight was almost won and his disbelieving eyes registered dawn breaking over the eastern hills. Dozens of legionaries were pouring up the rubble slope on to the roof of the cloister surrounding the temple complex, a paved walkway perhaps fifteen paces wide. From where Serpentius stood at the angle of the north and west walls, the temple sat like an enormous stone galley in the centre of an extensive outer court. Men stared up from the court fifty feet below and the first spears began to clatter among the soldiers on the roof. On both sides of the breakthrough, John of Gischala's men struggled to keep the Romans from exploiting their success. Some built barricades from bales of cloth that had appeared from some hidden storehouse. Centurions urged their men to attack before the makeshift defences could be completed as smoke began to billow up from below the walkway.

'They've set the cloister on fire,' someone screamed. 'If we don't break out of here we're dead men.'

A centurion struggled to the top of the slope at the head of a dozen men carrying a baulk of timber. Without orders they formed up at the front of four centuries preparing to attack the flimsy barricade. Serpentius watched them dash at the barrier in a compact column ten wide and thirty deep and the hastily erected structure burst open at the first attempt. With a roar of triumph the Romans surged through, tossing the bales aside and hammering at the demoralized defenders with shield and sword. The survivors screamed for mercy, but the legionaries threw them over the parapet to smash on to the paving below or cut them down where they stood. Serpentius followed in the victors' wake across the blood-soaked flagstones.

A hand caught his arm and he spun, ready to strike down his assailant. 'You?'

'I must reach the temple,' Josephus gasped. The Judaean was soot-stained and sweating after the exertion of his climb through the rubble and the bodies, but the hand that held his sword was steady enough. 'There are certain items Titus does not want to fall into the hands of his soldiers. Will you help me?'

Serpentius hesitated. Valerius had never fully trusted the man, but the temple was where Valerius would be and the Spaniard had a feeling Josephus would get him there by the most direct route.

'Very well,' he nodded. Ahead of them the legionaries had cleared the walkway as far as the opening of a stairway fifty paces ahead. When Serpentius reached it he could hear the sound of fighting below. 'Stay here until I check. Titus wouldn't thank me for getting you killed.' The Spaniard advanced warily down the first few steps until he saw that the soldiers had cleared the stair down to a pillared walkway. He gestured for Josephus to follow. By now the battle-hardened Roman cohorts must have broken through in several places because Serpentius could see the shields of three legions. Knots of men hacked at each other all over the great courtyard and the air rang with the clash of swords and the screams of the maimed and the dying. Women and children were cut down with the rest as they attempted to flee the fighting. To Serpentius's left, the entire length of the north cloister was ablaze and the torments of men trapped in the stairways pierced even the maniacal clamour around him.

'We must get to the temple,' Josephus urged. 'The entrance is on the east side.'

Serpentius searched the chaos for an obvious safe route, but could see none. 'There's only one way,' he told the Judaean. 'And that's straight through the middle.' Josephus looked at the scene unfolding in front of him with horror, but the Spaniard slapped his shoulder to get his attention. 'Stay close behind me and sing out if you see any threat.'

'But how . . .'

'Just follow me,' Serpentius snarled, 'and do what you're told if you want to live.'

They moved warily into the sea of fighting men. Serpentius led with his sword at the ready and his eyes flicking from left to right, instinctively knowing where a path would open up. His diagonal course took them towards the southern wall of the temple about twenty paces away. Josephus stayed close on his heels, almost touching the Spaniard's shoulder and starting at every clash of arms. A rebel in close combat with a legionary stepped backwards into him and turned with a raised sword at the contact. Josephus brought his blade up, but the man's face froze into a rictus of agony as the Roman slipped the point of his *gladius* beneath his armpit into his heart. As his victim dropped away the snarling killer would have turned on Josephus had Serpentius not stepped into his path and knocked his sword away.

'The watchword is Cremona and he's one of ours.' Even that wouldn't have stopped the man from slaughtering someone in Judaean clothing, but the look in Serpentius's eyes was enough to make him turn away. 'Stay with me,' the Spaniard repeated.

A man reeled across Serpentius's path with his jaw hanging off and the Spaniard dispatched him with an economic thrust that pierced his heart. A moment later he found himself facing a pair of Judaean rebels armed with spears, but after a few tentative thrusts which Serpentius parried with ease they exchanged a glance and stepped out of his path. Serpentius let them be. Josephus watched them carefully as he passed, but if they were going to die they were going to take Romans with them.

At last they reached the shadow of the temple. The great building stood on a raised platform surrounded by oversized steps. Serpentius bounded up with easy strides and turned to help Josephus. Three doorways entered the temple from this side, but all had been blocked up by the Judaean defenders. The two men were safe above the level of the fighting as long as no one else had the same idea. They made good progress along the sandstone walkway with Serpentius leading at a jog and Josephus struggling to keep up. Halfway along, a hulking legionary stepped into their path and took a swing at Serpentius with his *gladius*. The Spaniard calmly ducked beneath the blow and brought his foot up between his assailant's legs, ramming him aside to clatter down the steps.

Moments later they reached the angle of the building. Serpentius ducked down to check what awaited them round the corner. Incredibly, the first person he saw was Gaius Valerius Verrens. The Roman disappeared inside the temple with Tabitha in his wake as legionaries struggled with men who'd been guarding the doorway. Others were already removing the temple treasures.

'It's Valerius.' He half turned to grin at Josephus. 'He's got here fi—'

A bolt of white lightning exploded in the base of his spine and expanded to fill his entire being. Time didn't exist any more in a world inhabited only by pain. Serpentius tried to push himself to his feet, but something seemed to be holding him down and his sword was no help because it had dropped from his fingers.

He looked up to find Josephus standing over him with fear in his eyes and a bloody sword in his hand. As he watched the sword rise, the Spaniard's pain-ravaged face twisted into a snarl of contempt. 'Traitor.'

'Hey, you?' Two legionaries armed with spears eyed Josephus suspiciously from the base of the steps, uncertain whether he was friend or enemy. Before they could decide, the Judaean darted past Serpentius and disappeared into the doorway of the temple. Serpentius watched him go until the world closed in on him: a mother's smile, a woman's touch, the scent of an old hunting dog and a final plunge into a pit where eternal darkness reigned.

XLVII

They made their way through a miasma of death up the paved street of steps leading from the Pool of Siloam towards the temple. At first Valerius thought the bodies lying in the street must be casualties of fighting between the Judaean factions, but closer inspection indicated they'd recently died of starvation. Tabitha clutched at his arm as they passed through the crumpled honour guard, appalled at the sight of the dead women and children.

Dawn was breaking by the time they reached the hill's halfway point, but the flickering glow to the north almost outdid the rising sun. Valerius fretted that they would be too late. He had no way of gauging the progress of the attack. Titus's three legions had been fighting all night but the sullen roar in the distance, coupled with the fires, was evidence of some kind of Roman success. His suspicions were confirmed when they reached the hippodrome where the intermittent flow of refugees heading for the Lower City became a constant stream.

'They must have believed the temple was the safest place in Jerusalem,' Tabitha whispered. 'They placed their trust in God and now God has abandoned them.'

'They placed their faith in John of Gischala,' Valerius corrected her. 'And now he has failed them. John and Simon both. They should have surrendered when they had the chance.' Part of him would always wonder if that were true. Would Titus, so in need of a military triumph, have found some way to make surrender unthinkable for a man of honour or pride? 'But they're running because they are frightened and they're frightened because the Romans are coming.'

'We must reach the temple before they plunder it.' Tabitha pulled at his arm, urging him to greater speed, and they forced their way through the river of lost souls like swimmers breasting the waves pounding on a beach. Ahead the road narrowed, funnelled by the soaring walls of the hippodrome and a crumbling city wall from an earlier age. The crush became so great that the pressure lifted Tabitha's feet off the ground and Valerius feared she would be dragged away from him. Her grip on his left arm tightened and he pulled her close, growling and cursing as he shouldered his way past young and old alike. A gate appeared in the wall to their right and Tabitha pulled him towards it.

'This is the quickest way to the Huldah Gates,' she gasped. 'And the road will be easier.'

They pushed their way through against the flow. The crowd eased, but if anything the sense of terror in those they met heightened. Many ran in a blind panic, not caring who or what stood in their way, their only aim to escape what lay behind. Valerius and Tabitha could see the milky-white stone of the temple's outer walls, their magnificence made all the starker by the black smoke billowing beyond them. By now the familiar clamour of battle had replaced the sullen roar; the clash of iron upon wood vying with shouted commands, desperate cries for aid and screams of fear, defiance and death. Tabitha froze as a shrieking figure plunged from the wall away to their left. 'Keep going.' Valerius dragged her onwards up the slope to the base of a flight of broad steps leading up to two sets of gates, one double arched, the other triple.

'The triple arch is the entrance, the double the exit.' Tabitha studied the gates. In the chaos, terrified Judaean soldiers carrying wounded friends used both sets, their blood spattering the polished stones as they fled the fighting above. A guard of Galilean rebels hovered uncertainly by the gateway, unsure whether they should stop the deserters leaving or join the fighting. Tabitha glanced to one side where carved stones surrounded a pool of water and her face twisted into a grimace of uncertainty. 'I should purify myself at the *mikveh* before entering the temple.'

'There's no time,' Valerius urged. 'And you have no need. You have been purified in the Pool of Siloam, and in any case your temple is a battlefield now, defiled by the blood and flesh of the dead.'

She set her jaw and nodded determinedly. 'You are right,' she said. 'And I must be prepared to set myself beyond God's grace this day for the future of my people.'

Valerius was still puzzling over this last statement as they hurried up the steps, two narrow followed by two broad in a repeating pattern. Tabitha reached the top first. Her eyes hardened as she saw the guards stiffen. She marched straight towards the gate, throwing back her cloak so the Galileans could see the quality of the clothing beneath. Now Valerius understood her choice of fine dress.

'Why are you lurking here when your comrades are fighting to save the temple?' she demanded before the guard commander could confront her. The man's brow darkened at the suggestion of his cowardice from the beautiful woman in the dripping clothes. Her natural authority and the richness of her dress confused him at a time when his mind was already spinning with uncertainty. He and his men had been at their posts throughout the previous day and all through the night. They had orders not to leave, but the sounds of fighting echoing down the stairway from the Court of the Gentiles tested his resolve. That fighting grew ever closer with daylight, to the point where he could hear men struggling for their lives little more than a dozen paces away. A few months ago he'd been a simple farmer eking out a living outside Gadara. For all his inexperience he was a good soldier. Still, he'd been tempted, and now . . .

'I have my orders.' He eyed the hooded bodyguard lurking behind his mistress. 'The Romans . . .'

'Do you see any Romans here?' Contempt thickened her words and the guard commander sensed the spearmen behind him flinch. All around them women and children continued to flee the battle. The only civilians who'd tried to enter the temple complex in twenty-four hours were this woman and her servant. Tabitha shook her head and raised her voice. 'We expected so much of John of Gischala and his brave Galileans, but this . . . ? Did you come all this way only to stand back as your comrades spilled their blood in defence of the Great Temple?' After a moment's hesitation she made to brush past the guard commander. 'Well, if you will not fight . . .'

The commander heard the rush of feet as his men turned for the stairs, and with a last perplexed glance at Tabitha he ran to join them.

Tabitha closed her eyes and heaved a huge sigh. Valerius stepped forward and took her in his arms. 'Are you sure?' he whispered. 'You know what is happening up there.'

She stepped away and looked up into his face, appearing very small and vulnerable and young. 'I am ready,' she said. 'I have God to protect me.'

There was nothing more to say. Valerius drew his sword and led the way to the stairs. They rose to the level of the court in a series of doglegs and he signalled to Tabitha to wait while he checked the way ahead. A spear clattered close by forcing him to duck back, but whether it was aimed at him was unclear.

What he saw was like a scene from the seventh pit of Hades. Flames roared from the north cloister and black smoke filled the sky. The west was well alight, threatening to roast the hundreds of legionaries who rushed along it seeking ways to join their comrades in the court below. One glance was enough to convince him the fight could only have one victor.

This was a place of sacrifice, but Valerius doubted even the Great Temple had ever seen so much blood spilled in a single day. It covered the polished paving slabs in great dark arterial pools, ran along the cracks between like a thousand rivers, and in the form of airborne droplets had spattered every inch of the Court of the Gentiles. The stench of it filled his nostrils. For a moment he hesitated, only to find Tabitha by his side, her face a mask of determination. 'This way.' He led her towards the eastern cloister, where he reckoned they could avoid the worst of the fighting.

They hurried through the forest of marble columns unhindered apart from where a few Judaeans were being backed against the wall to be slaughtered by packs of snarling Roman soldiers. If anyone looked like contesting their passage Valerius shouted the previous night's watchword, praying no one had replaced it yet. At last they reached a point directly opposite the temple's east doorway.

'Cremona!' Valerius called, and they crossed the open space past a group of legionaries finishing off the men who'd been guarding the door. The Galileans knelt submissively to have their throats cut, and their blood mingled with that of their own previous victims. A centurion appeared in the doorway like a vision from a nightmare, gore-spattered and eyes staring. His lips curled back from his teeth in a feral snarl and he held his sword raised and at the ready. 'Cremona,' Valerius repeated. 'Special mission for General Titus.'

The centurion blinked and his eyes narrowed as they drifted from Valerius's wooden fist to Tabitha.

'Special mission, eh?' He swayed as if he were drunk. 'Well, I suppose there's more than one kind of special mission.' He gestured inside and Tabitha and Valerius stepped over the threshold into the Inner Court, moving aside as four men brushed past them struggling with a heavy golden table. The open courtyard stank of oil and Valerius could see that in one of four side rooms a great cauldron had been overturned. Its contents had spilled out to mingle with the life blood of the men who'd died trying to protect the place, whose bodies littered the floor. From an inner room came the sound of hammers and chisels, wood splintering and a curious tearing sound.

More soldiers appeared from an inner room carrying a great golden lamp holder with seven branches. A tear rolled down Tabitha's cheek as she recognized what must have been an important symbol of her religion, but her chin came up and she took his arm. 'This way,' she said. 'We are in the Court of the Women and this is as

465

close as I would normally approach the Holy of Holies. Only men may go beyond. But this temple is no longer as it was. It has already been defiled by the presence of Gentiles and the spilling of blood, and my cause is just.'

She passed through the doorway, stepping over the curtain that once covered the entrance, but now lay soaking up oil and blood. Beyond it lay a second chamber with a great bronze altar. This room too was scattered with the still bodies of the men who had attempted to defend the temple treasures. Whether by accident or design, one of them lay on his back on the altar with his head thrown back. A gaping tear in his throat still leaked blood on to the polished surface.

Tabitha barely glanced at the carnage as she strode through the room, leading the way unerringly up the steps and into the Great Temple proper. Valerius blinked as he entered a long narrow room now bare of any object apart from a dozen oil lamps. Sheets of buttery yellow gold lined every upper surface. He knew they were sheets because twenty legionaries worked frantically on ladders to tear them from the walls and throw them down to others waiting to carry them away. Something more than a curtain covered the far wall. Perhaps a foot thick, it was almost a wall in itself, but made of cloth. Holes in the ceiling close to the walls appeared to have no apparent purpose, but he guessed they might provide some form of light. Tabitha frowned, staring at a raised stone platform, and Valerius wondered if what she'd come for had already been lost to the looters.

'That is where the Ark of the Covenant should stand,' she said with a hint of satisfaction. 'Perhaps John and Simon are not the fools we believed they were. Beyond the curtain is the Most Holy Place, where the sacred ceremonies take place.'

But the Most Holy Place held no interest for her. Instead, she turned and crossed to an insignificant doorway set in a part of the walls yet to be stripped. Ignored by the legionaries, Valerius followed her to a claustrophobic stairway barely wide enough to accommodate his broad shoulders. As they climbed almost vertically through the darkness to the next level, dust rose from beneath Tabitha's feet. No one had visited this place for months, perhaps even years.

'How will we find it in the darkness?' Valerius said quietly.

'We will find it,' she assured him. The reason for her confidence became clear when she opened a trap door and they climbed into a gloomy wood-panelled attic. Yellow light from the oil lamps filtered through the slots he'd seen from below, complemented by narrow openings in the walls that provided a little natural illumination.

'These are for the priests to polish the upper walls of the Holy of Holies.' Her voice shook with emotion. 'And this,' she pointed to a series of covered niches on one wall, 'is where they keep their instruments.' She pulled back a small curtain and reached in to pull out a long pole with a cloth wrapped round one end. It surprised Valerius that such mundane implements should have individual repositories, but he guessed that, like everything in the temple, they probably possessed some kind of ritual significance.

Tabitha replaced the pole and counted the niches. When she found the one she sought she hesitated as if what it held was too overwhelming to contemplate.

Just as Valerius was about to offer his help, she reached inside. And froze. He saw her eyes widen. Was it some sort of trap? He realized he was holding his breath.

Eventually, with infinite care, she drew the mysterious object clear of its hiding place and held it in her hands, staring at it as if it were the finest jewel in all the Empire. A simple leather bag tied at the neck. She turned to Valerius with a question in her eyes. 'Yes.' His voice sounded hoarse. 'Open it. It is yours.'

Tabitha winced at a great echoing crash as the legionaries brought down another section of the golden wall. 'My mistress's.' She fumbled at the strings with awkward fingers, drawing them apart and pulling out a tattered, ancient-looking scroll attached to twin dowels of scarred, blackened wood. It was so old it looked as if it might fall apart in her hands, and she quickly returned it to the bag.

'Don't you want to check it is what you think it is?' Valerius suggested.

Tabitha shook her head. 'If it is here, this is what we seek.'

'We should go, then.'

She crept across to look down at the destruction continuing below. 'I think we should wait.' She sat back against the wall with the leather bag clasped to her body. Valerius went to her and put his arm round her shoulders. She sighed and laid her head against his chest. 'It will be over soon enough,' she said. 'Then we will be free.'

How long they sat there Valerius didn't know, but at one point he heard the sound of nailed sandals on the narrow stair. He pulled his sword as a startled legionary put his head through the trap door. 'Nothing to find up here,' Valerius assured him. 'We've searched everywhere.'

The man looked from Valerius to Tabitha and grinned. 'Share and share alike is what I say.' He raised himself on both arms only to find the point of a *gladius* pricking his throat. Above it, Valerius's eyes glowed with the promise that his next move would dictate whether it went through his gullet.

'I don't think so,' Valerius said.

'All right.' The soldier drew his head back. 'I wasn't serious. You're sure you've searched, only I've got my orders.'

'Sure.'

The helmeted head disappeared. 'Plenty more Jewish bitches where she came from.'

Tabitha shuddered and moved in close to Valerius. 'I hate soldiers.'

'I'm a soldier.'

'All but you.'

They must have slept because Valerius awoke to an unnatural quiet and he had to shake Tabitha before she'd move. 'It's time.'

She nodded and forced herself to her feet. 'I can smell smoke.'

'I think it's the cloisters.' Valerius prayed it was true, but he went down the ladder two steps at a time. When they reached ground level he held out his hand. 'Give me the book. Better if you have both hands free.' She hesitated, but only for a second, and he tied the leather bag to his belt.

When they opened the door a waft of oily smoke and the stink of burning cloth confirmed his worst fears. 'Someone has set the Court of the Women alight.'

469

'I can see flames.' Tabitha stood by the entrance. 'Check the rear chamber. There may be another way out.'

Valerius was halfway across the room when he heard a scream. He whirled with his hand on his sword, but it was already too late. Josephus had a hank of Tabitha's dark hair in his fist and the edge of his sword at her throat.

XLVIII

'I told you you would feel the hand of God, my Roman friend. The hand of God brought you here and now you will lay down your sword. Good,' Josephus said, as Valerius obeyed, his eyes never leaving the blade at Tabitha's neck. Something flickered on Tabitha's face and with the slightest shake of the head he warned her not to try anything that would risk her life. 'You understand your situation?' Josephus continued. 'Our transaction must be conducted swiftly, because I fear your comrades have accidentally fired the outer court. Now the leather bag at your waist, which I assume brought you here. Untie it, remove the object inside so I can confirm its identity, return it to the bag and place it beside the sword.' Again Valerius obeyed. The Judaean's eyes lit up as he recognized the scroll. Valerius waited for a momentary lapse in concentration, measuring his distance and his chances, but Josephus read his look and smiled. 'No, no, Valerius, I have no wish to harm the lady Tabitha, but I will have no hesitation if you force it on me. Back off from the bag and stand against the wall.' When he judged Valerius was far enough away he moved towards the scroll, his sword edge never moving a hair's breadth from the pulse in Tabitha's neck. 'My dear, you will—'

Without warning the Judaean cried out as something smacked into the centre of his back and dropped to the stone floor with a metallic clatter. The sword fell away from Tabitha's neck, but not so much that she could escape. With a groan of agony Josephus turned to stare at his attacker. Hidden from Valerius in the doorway, Serpentius of Avala lurched into the room and stood with his right hand raised, ready to throw the second of his little Scythian axes.

'I don't miss twice.' The Spaniard's voice was a rook's ragged caw. He swayed like a tree in a gale, but Josephus saw something in his eyes that told him that, even wounded, Serpentius was a deadly threat. With a last despairing glance he decided the scroll wasn't worth his life and darted towards the thick curtain at the rear of the room.

Tabitha retrieved the scroll as Valerius picked up his *gladius*. He turned to follow Josephus, but she gripped his arm. 'No, Valerius. Look to Serpentius.'

For the first time Valerius noticed the grey pallor of his friend's features. He crossed the room in three strides and caught the Spaniard in his arms as he collapsed. Serpentius let out a groan of agony and Valerius felt a warm stickiness on his hand. Laying his friend to the ground he stared at his palm with a cry of disbelief.

'I've killed enough people to know when I'm dead. That back-stabbing Judaean bastard,' the Spaniard rasped. 'Get out of here with your woman.'

Valerius tried to turn Serpentius over and inspect the wound, but the Spaniard's fingers gripped his wrist until Valerius thought they would tear the flesh. Still the Roman wouldn't give up. 'This is going to hurt.'

He took the wounded man by the shoulders and pushed him on to his side so he could see the injury. By now smoke had filled the altar chamber and flames were licking greedily at the curtained doorway of the sanctuary, sending tiny streams of sparks dancing upwards. Valerius willed himself not to panic. 'See if you can find another way out,' he called to Tabitha, trying to keep the fear from his voice.

Serpentius's tunic was heavy with blood and Valerius winced when he saw where Josephus had struck the blow. A wound low in the back like this would invariably be fatal. He found the entry point and tore the cloth apart, revealing a puncture in the flesh close to Serpentius's spine.

'I told you I was dead,' the Spaniard groaned. 'Now give me my sword. Remember?'

Valerius remembered. *A sword in my hand and a friend at my side.* The gladiator's farewell. 'We're going to get you out of here,' he insisted. Serpentius gave a grunt that might have been a laugh. Valerius had never felt such empty despair. He'd always thought of Serpentius as a big man, but now he realized that his size was an illusion created by his strength and his speed and his presence. The Spaniard felt like a bag of bones in his arms.

'Don't give up on me now.' He studied the wound again. Somehow he needed to stop the bleeding. He sawed at the hem of his robe with his sword, cutting off a long length of makeshift bandage. Taking one end he wiped the blood from Serpentius's back. It was only then he noticed the ragged edges of a second wound. A wound in Serpentius's side. It couldn't be. But when he looked again he saw the unmistakable signs of the sword's exit. His mind racing, he traced the path of the

473

wound with his fingers, ignoring the Spaniard's groans of agony. Too low! Josephus the amateur had struck too low. Maybe Serpentius had twisted when he'd struck, or he'd been forced to make the thrust from an angle. The result was a blow that had skidded off Serpentius's lower spine and under the flesh across the top of the hip bone. It must be agonizingly painful and could have nicked what Pliny called the *renes*, but it might not be a death wound. The Spaniard gasped as Valerius cut two smaller pieces of cloth from the bandage and plugged the wounds, then wrapped them in place with the rest. Ignoring his friend's suffering, he hauled Serpentius to his feet.

'You will not die, Serpentius of Avala. Do you hear me, you Spanish bastard? You will not die.'

'Leave me,' Serpentius whispered. Valerius shrank away as a gust of wind turned the curtain into a tower of flame and filled the room with a new blast of heat and smoke. 'What better end for a man like me than in the ruins of a burning city? What greater memorial than the name Jerusalem, which will be spoken down the ages?' By now the flames were licking the timbers above their heads and Valerius put an arm under Serpentius's shoulder to take his weight and hauled him bodily towards the inner chamber. 'Please, Valerius.'

'Trust me, Serpentius,' Valerius said into his friend's ear. 'Have I ever failed you?'

'There's no way out,' Tabitha's cry from the inner doorway sent a new thrill of fear through him, but his mind told him she was wrong.

'Josephus found a way out,' he insisted. 'So there must be one.'

Between them they hauled the heavy curtain aside and pulled Serpentius into an empty room half the size of the other. A dozen store cupboards had been built into the walls, but their doors hung from the hinges where the plundering legionaries had smashed them open and they'd left nothing, apart from a few pieces of furniture and vestments scattered across the floor. By now the heat was becoming intense. Smoke seeped past the curtain and they could see a glow through the gaps at the sides. Valerius looked into Tabitha's face and saw resignation.

He laid Serpentius on the marble floor. 'Look after him,' he ordered.

A padded couch with tapestry skirts stood against a bare wall and in desperation he hauled it aside. Cowering beneath was the figure of a heavily built man and Valerius's hand went to the knife at his belt. It was only when the big man raised his head that he found himself staring into the solemn dark eyes of Simon bar Giora.

The Judaean bowed his head and raised a hand as if to fend off the blade, but the blow never came. After a moment, Simon looked up into Valerius's face. 'I know you, Roman.' His voice echoed his disbelief, but his next words proved his mind was still sharp enough. 'Let me live and I can save you.'

'Kill him,' Tabitha spat. 'He more than any man is responsible for this.'

Valerius shook his head. 'I'd rather save your life than see him dead.' He looked to where the bottom of the curtain was already alight and turned back to bar Giora. 'If you can save us, why didn't you save yourself?'

The Judaean looked fearfully at the smoking curtain. Time was fast running out. 'The legionaries trapped me, then Josephus took the route that was mine. If he sees me, he will kill me. There is a tunnel that leads to the Antonia. All I ask is that you get me past the Romans there.'

'Why wouldn't I let you show us the tunnel and then kill you anyway?'

Simon bar Giora looked into his eyes. 'Because I knew the first time I saw you that you were no Josephus. Valerius Verrens is a man of his word.'

'Then show us the tunnel before we all roast.'

Bar Giora went to one of the vestment cupboards and groped into a recess above the door for a cunningly concealed lever that made the false back panel slide away to reveal an entrance.

'How did you know about this?' Valerius asked as they manhandled Serpentius through the narrow opening after Tabitha. 'It can hardly have been common currency.'

'This is but one of several.' Simon's spirits had recovered now that he had a way out. 'I was informed of their location by one of the priests in my pay. John of Gischala tortured it from Eleazar, the High Priest, before he killed him. Since I learned of John's interest I've had men waiting at the exit in the Antonia to cut him down. But you Romans took the fortress before he could use it.'

A pile of unused torches lay scattered just inside the door, cached by the priests and presumably knocked over by Josephus in his rush to escape. Choking black smoke was already filling the room behind them, but Simon delayed closing the entrance until Valerius took out flint and steel and lit one of the torches.

When the door closed behind them the silence seemed almost unearthly after the clamour of what had gone before. Valerius saw in the flickering golden light that this was no damp, crudely cut tunnel like Hezekiah's Conduit. A flight of marble stairs led down to a passage four or five paces wide, paved with stone and lined with tightly mortared blocks. He handed the torch to Tabitha and he and Simon took the mercifully now unconscious Serpentius between them.

Tabitha led the way and even struggling with their burden they made good time through the long, arrow-straight corridor. It could only have been a matter of minutes before Simon insisted they stop for a moment and lay Serpentius down.

'We are close,' he breathed. 'Someone should go ahead and check the exit is safe.'

Valerius imagined the scene as the legionaries of the Fifth and Fifteenth sacked the fortress. Carnage on every hand and not a shred of mercy to be had. 'Not you, lady.' He unsheathed his sword and handed it to Tabitha, who shifted the torch to her left hand. 'And certainly not you, Simon bar Giora. If he moves, kill him.'

Tabitha nodded and held the blade where the Judaean could see it. 'You will find a lever to the left of the doorway at shoulder height,' Simon instructed Valerius, undaunted by the lack of trust shown in him. 'It emerges into a storeroom at the rear of the headquarters building.'

With a last glance at Serpentius, Valerius moved reluctantly out of the torchlight and into the darkness. He advanced slowly, keeping to the left-hand wall, feeling his way forward, his wooden fist held in front. The fist touched something solid and he used his good hand to feel for the lever Simon had mentioned. Eventually his fingers closed round a smooth wooden shaft. Holding his breath, he pulled it firmly towards him.

He used his left thumb to arm the knife in the false hand and tensed as the door swung back soundlessly into the corridor. The opening revealed a poorly lit room of modest proportions. Everything in it appeared to be scattered across the floor in a sea of grey sludge. Sacks of flour had been slashed open so that the grainy powder mixed with olive oil and wine from the smashed *amphorae* which stuck out of the mess like jagged rocks on a mud flat. In the centre of the room a bearded man with a cut throat lay on his back staring with disinterested, long-dulled eyes at the ceiling.

Valerius picked his way through the debris to a half-open door in the far wall. It opened on to a narrow corridor, which proved empty, and in the distance he could hear the sounds of laughter and cheering. Clearly this battle had already been won.

Satisfied that he'd seen enough, he closed the door and made his way back to the passage. Within seconds of entering the darkness a chill ran through him as he sensed that something wasn't right. Something was missing. Light. The corridor was straight; the light of the torch should have been visible somewhere in the distance.

'Tabitha?'

His call went unanswered and his mind fought for an explanation. Where in Mars's name were they? He quickened his pace but couldn't hurry too much for fear Simon bar Giora might be waiting somewhere in the dark to ambush him. His senses strained to pierce the inky blackness. Somehow bar Giora must have managed to overpower Tabitha and taken the Book of Enoch. The thought that she might be lying bleeding her life out in the dark made him groan aloud.

He froze in his tracks at the faint sound of an answering whimper. Someone was there, somewhere close. He dropped to a crouch and crept silently forward, his left hand groping just above the floor and the knife point of the right extended in front. He stopped as his fingers touched something soft. Cloth . . . and beneath it flesh. Fearful of what he'd find, he ran his hands up the still warm body. Still alive. He could feel a faint heartbeat in the skinny chest. Not Tabitha, but Serpentius.

'Tabitha?' His hand reached out to the left side where she'd been sitting when he'd left them. Nothing. His situation suddenly hit home like a blow from an armourer's hammer. He couldn't move away for fear of losing Serpentius again. It meant he had to abandon her to whatever fate had overtaken her. He wanted to roar with frustration, but what could he do?

'Tabitha?' Much louder this time, his voice rising and elongating her name until it was a full blown shout that mocked him with its echo from the stone walls of the passage.

Feeling utterly defeated, he reached down to pick up Serpentius in his arms. The Spaniard let out a low moan. 'Are we dead?' he whispered.

'No, but we might as well be.'

An hour later Valerius stood in the Court of the Gentiles with Serpentius at his feet, staring up at the inferno that was the greatest building the world had ever seen. Around him several hundred legionaries ignored the bodies of a thousand slaughtered Judaeans and watched the cataclysm for which they were responsible with grins of wonder.

He'd brought Serpentius here because it was the only way to get him the medical treatment he needed to keep him alive. When he'd staggered from the tunnel he quickly found his way to a courtyard filled with the victors of the attack on the Antonia. He'd left Serpentius with the unit's temporary *medicus* and returned to

479

the passage with an escort. The only evidence of human occupancy was a red smudge on the pale golden sandstone floor that probably came from Serpentius.

The more he considered what could have happened, the more confused he became. Why had there been no screams and no sound of a struggle? He'd been less than a hundred paces away for only a few minutes. In the silence he should have heard *something*. Yes, it was possible that bar Giora, a seasoned warrior, had managed to overpower Tabitha without a sound, but was it likely? She'd been feet away from him, and she'd had Valerius's sword to protect her. And if he *had* overpowered her, why not kill her or subdue her in some other way, take the scroll and leave the body behind? Though he could barely bring himself to think it, the likeliest explanation now seemed to be that she'd gone with him willingly. But why, after all they'd been through together, would she abandon him? And, perhaps more relevant, why would she betray Berenice?

A clatter of hooves disturbed his thoughts and a cheer went up as a group of riders trotted into the court through the recently opened west gate. Among them was a familiar figure in a legate's armour, wearing the purple sash of an army commander. Titus Flavius Vespasian and his staff reined in close by Valerius and Serpentius, but the Emperor's son only had eyes for the burning temple.

'I did not want this,' he said loud enough for the closest fifty or sixty men to hear. 'I would have stopped it if I could. This has been brought upon the people of Judaea by their own god, and I take it as a sign. What he has begun I will complete. We will tear this place down wall by wall and the city with it. Perhaps, someday, there will be a new Jerusalem, but not in my time.'

The announcement was greeted with a roar of acclaim. When it died away his eyes lighted on Valerius and he smiled, only for the smile to fade as he saw the crumpled figure at his friend's feet.

'Is he . . .'

'No, but he's hurt badly. I beg you to help him.'

Titus turned in the saddle. 'Alexandros!' he roared. 'Where is that drunken surgeon of mine?'

The Egyptian doctor appeared with a servant leading a pony laden with his equipment. Titus pointed him towards Serpentius and Alexandros knelt over the Spaniard, working at the bandages as Valerius hovered close.

'Can he be saved?' Titus demanded.

Alexandros looked up. 'His injury is very grave, lord.'

The grey eyes hardened. 'I *want* him saved.' The implication was clear.

Alexandros paled and shouted a string of commands as he bent low over Serpentius, crooning to his patient in Greek as his hands fluttered across the bloodied flesh.

Titus turned back to Valerius. 'He saved my life,' he said. 'I had thought to reward him for his services. None deserves it more.'

'His life will be reward enough.'

'No.' Titus shook his head. 'If he lives he will never want again.' He turned back to the burning temple. 'There is still work to do. John of Gischala and Simon bar Giora are unaccounted for, but the taking of the fortress and the temple means Jerusalem is Rome's and the rebellion is finished. My father has his victory.'

'And you will have your triumph.'

Titus managed a wry smile. 'And you, Valerius? You did as much as any man to bring this about. What will your reward be?'

Valerius stared in the direction of the Huldah Gates and his heart lifted as he watched a diminutive figure pick her way through the carpet of dead towards them. Tabitha's expression was grave, but her eyes lit up when she recognized him. There was no sign of the leather pouch, but suddenly that didn't seem to matter any more.

'I already have my reward.'

Historical note

The siege and destruction of Jerusalem in AD 70 is one of history's greatest cataclysms. It probably cost the lives of hundreds of thousands of innocents visiting the city to celebrate the Jewish festival of Passover who had no interest in the events which brought it about. It had its roots in the Judaean rebellion – the Great Revolt – that began four years earlier when punitive taxation and Rome's heavy-handed rule under Nero finally exhausted the patience of the Jewish people.

Rebel forces had several successes in the initial stages, under the leadership of, among others, Joseph Ben Mahtityahu, and Eleazar Ben Simon, who commanded the rebels in the greatest Judaean triumph, the defeat of the Twelfth legion and the capture of its eagle, a humiliation that would have reverberated through the Empire. The Emperor Nero responded by replacing Cestius Gallus, who'd led the Twelfth's expedition, with a much tougher prospect in the shape of Flavius Vespasian. Vespasian, who would soon wear the purple himself, responded by sending his soldiers to ravage the area around the Sea of Galilee and destroy the rebel strongholds there. He was interrupted by the small matter of the Year of the Four Emperors, which made him pause while he pondered where his legions might be put to the best use in Rome's name (as it turned out, placing him on the throne).

When his soldiers made up his mind for him by hailing him Emperor, he handed over command to his son Titus, who had already distinguished himself and proved an able commander of the Fifteenth legion. With an army of four legions and tens of thousands of auxiliaries at his command, Titus forced the rebels back until they were concentrated in the city of Jerusalem. The fate of the Passover pilgrims is just one area of contention in the Jerusalem story. Roman emperors – and Titus would become one – are not known for their compassion, but starving to death hundreds of thousands of women and children appears out of character for a man whom Suetonius describes as 'kind and gracious' (though he does throw in cruel to the mix as well). The likely answer seems to be that Titus regarded the pilgrims as a weapon of war in his campaign to starve the rebels into an early surrender, and used them accordingly.

In this aim, the rebels, or at least one of their leaders, John of Gischala, went out of their way to help. The three rebel factions in Jerusalem, led by John, Eleazar and Simon bar Giora, were keener on shedding each other's blood than Roman and were at odds right until the final stages. John's men burned tons of grain Simon had stored for the siege and raided the temple and killed Eleazar and his key supporters. For narrative reasons I have truncated the events of the siege, particularly the latter part where action that took weeks is compressed into days, but most of the key scenes happened as described here, or as near as my imagination can make them. Hezekiah's Conduit exists and you can take a tour should you visit Jerusalem, but I doubt it was put to the clandestine use I have portrayed here.

Of the key figures in the book, Titus, his lover Queen Berenice and King Sohaemus of Emesa all existed and

I've tried to remain true to the historical record. The one to whom I probably owe an apology – or perhaps not – is Joseph Ben Mahtityahu, later famous as the Jewish historian Flavius Josephus. Virtually everything we know about the siege of Jerusalem and the Great Revolt is a result of his wonderfully detailed account, *The Judaean War*. But just how reliable a narrator is he? After all, this is a man who led the revolt at the start, survived the siege of Jotapata when no one else did, somehow charmed Vespasian into sparing his life when his compatriots were being butchered or sold into slavery, turned his back on his former comrades, and finally prospered under the Emperor's patronage. The one thing I think we can say with any certainty is that Josephus didn't conspire with John and Simon to save the only copy of the *Book of Enoch*, the purely fictional conspiracy at the heart of this novel.

Of course, the greatest point of contention is whether Titus deliberately meant to destroy the Great Temple, the centre of the Jewish religion and one of the architectural wonders of the age. Josephus says the burning of the temple was an accident, and that Titus did everything he could to save it. My own view is that the temple was a legitimate military objective, an enormously strong defensive position (a fortress within a fortress, as I've described it here) and one that, because of its status, would have been defended to the last. Ancient peoples had plenty of examples of what would happen if a city was taken by siege. What is beyond debate is that Titus's legions flattened the temple and the rest of Jerusalem with a brutal efficiency which cannot have been anything but premeditated.

Glossary

Ala milliaria – A reinforced auxiliary cavalry wing, normally between 700 and 1,000 strong. In Britain and the west the units would be a mix of cavalry and infantry, in the east a mix of spearmen and archers.

Ala quingenaria – Auxiliary cavalry wing normally composed of 500 auxiliary horsemen.

Aquilifer – The standard-bearer who carried the eagle of the legion.

As – A small copper coin worth approximately one fifth of a **sestertius**.

Aureus (pl. Aurei) – Valuable gold coin worth twenty-five **denarii**.

Auxiliary – Non-citizen soldiers recruited from the provinces as light infantry or for specialist tasks, e.g. cavalry, slingers, archers.

Ballista (pl. Ballistae) – Artillery for throwing heavy missiles of varying size and type. The smaller machines were called *scorpiones* or *onagers*.

Beneficiarius – A legion's record keeper or scribe.

Boars Head (alt. Wedge) – A compact arrow-head formation used by Roman infantry and cavalry to break up enemy formations.

Caligae – Sturdily constructed, reinforced leather sandals worn by Roman soldiers. Normally with iron-studded sole.

Century – Smallest tactical unit of the legion, numbering 80 men.

Cohort – Tactical fighting unit of the legion, normally contained six centuries, apart from the elite First cohort, which had five double strength centuries (800 men).

Consul – One of two annually elected chief magistrates of Rome, normally appointed by the people and ratified by the Senate.

Contubernium – Unit of eight soldiers who shared a tent or barracks.

Cornicen – Legionary signal trumpeter who used an instrument called a *cornu*.

Decimation – A brutal and seldom used Roman military punishment where one man in every ten of a unit found guilty of cowardice or mutiny was chosen for execution by his comrades.

Decurio – A junior officer in a century, or a troop commander in a cavalry unit.

Denarius (pl. Denarii) – A silver coin.

Domus – The house of a wealthy Roman, e.g. Nero's Domus Aurea (Golden House).

Duplicarius – Literally 'double pay man'. A senior legionary with a trade or an NCO.

Equestrian – Roman knightly class.

Fortuna – The goddess of luck and good fortune.

Frumentarii – Messengers who carried out secret duties for the Emperor, possibly including spying and assassination.

Gladius (pl. Gladii) – The short sword of the legionary. A lethal killing weapon at close quarters.

Governor – Citizen of senatorial rank given charge of a province. Would normally have a military background (see Proconsul).

Haruspex – Soothsayer, sometimes a priest.

Jupiter – Most powerful of the Roman gods, often referred to as **Optimus Maximus** (greatest and best).

Legate – The general in charge of a legion. A man of senatorial rank.

Legion – Unit of approximately 5,000 men, all of whom would be Roman citizens.

Lictor – Bodyguard of a Roman magistrate. There were strict limits on the numbers of lictors associated with different ranks.

Lituus – Curved trumpet used to transmit cavalry commands.

Mansio – State-operated lodging house.

Manumission – The act of freeing a slave.

Mars – The Roman god of war.

Mithras – An Eastern religion popular among Roman soldiers.

Nomentan – A superior variety of Roman wine, mentioned by Martial in his Epigrams.

Onager (pl. Onagri) – Small portable catapult designed to hurl rocks.

Orbis – Circular defensive position practised by the legions.

Phalera (pl. Phalerae) – Awards won in battle worn on a legionary's chest harness.

Pilum (pl. Pila) – Heavy spear carried by a Roman legionary.

Praefectus castrorum – Literally 'camp prefect'. Former centurion who served as a legion's third in command after the legate and senior military tribune.

Praetorian Guard – Powerful military force stationed in Rome. Accompanied the Emperor on campaign, but could be of dubious loyalty and were responsible for the overthrow of several Roman rulers.

Prefect – Auxiliary cavalry commander.

Primus Pilus – 'First File'. The senior centurion of a legion.

Principia – Legionary headquarters building.

Proconsul – Governor of a Roman province, such as Spain or Syria, and of consular rank.

Procurator – Civilian administrator subordinate to a governor.

Quaestor – Civilian administrator in charge of finance.

Scorpio (pl. Scorpiones) – Bolt-firing Roman light artillery piece.

Scutum (pl. Scuta) – The big, richly decorated curved shield carried by a legionary.

Senator – Patrician member of the Senate, the key political institution which administered the Roman empire. Had to meet strict financial and property rules and be at least thirty years of age.

Sestertius (pl. Sestertii) – Roman brass coin worth a quarter of a **denarius**.

Signifer – Standard bearer who carried the emblem of a cohort or century.

Testudo – Literally 'tortoise'. A unit of soldiers with shields interlocked for protection.

Tribune – One of six senior officers acting as aides to a legate. Often, but not always, on short commissions of six months upwards.

Tribunus laticlavius – Literally 'broad stripe tribune'. The most senior of a legion's military tribunes.

Vexillation – A detachment of a legion used as a temporary task force on independent duty.

Victimarius – Servant who delivers and attends to the victim of a sacrifice.

Victory – Roman goddess equivalent to the Greek Nike.

Vigiles – Force responsible for the day-to-day policing of Rome's streets and fire prevention and fighting.

Vineae – Hide-covered shelter used by Roman engineers when they were building siege ramps within range of enemy slings and arrows.

Acknowledgements

I'm grateful to my editor Simon Taylor and his team at Transworld for helping me make *Scourge of Rome* the book it is, and to my agent Stan, of Jenny Brown Associates in Edinburgh, for all his advice and encouragement. As always my wife Alison and my children, Kara, Nikki and Gregor, have been the rocks on which this book has been built.

Douglas Jackson's Rome series, featuring Gaius Valerius Verrens

HERO OF ROME

AD 60 – Rome's grip on Britain is weakening and the warrior queen Boudicca is ready to lead the tribes to war. In their way stand the veteran legionaries of Colonia and tribune Gaius Valerius Verrens . . .

DEFENDER OF ROME

The biggest threat to the Empire comes not from Boudicca but from within the walls of Rome itself, and Gaius Valerius Verrens has been appointed the city's 'defender'. The price of failure is high . . .

AVENGER OF ROME

The Emperor Nero's power is weakening, and Gaius Valerius Verrens is given the power of life and death over a general he worships. He must complete his mission – or risk his Emperor's wrath . . .

SWORD OF ROME

AD 68. The Emperor Nero's reign is in its death throes, and Gaius Valerius Verrens is dispatched to Rome to bring it to an end. But in its place will rise the spectre of bloody civil war . . .

ENEMY OF ROME

AD 69. In the dry heat of an August morning, as civil war grips the Empire, a soldier awaits execution. He is Gaius Valerius Verrens and he has been wrongly accused of cowardice . . .

SCOURGE OF ROME

AD 70. Gaius Valerius Verrens has been banished from Rome. To return to the city would be to face certain death and so he heads east – and into the heart of the savage Judaean uprising . . .

All available in paperback and ebook.

Don't miss the seventh Gaius Valerius Verrens adventure

SAVIOUR OF ROME

AD 72. Titus Flavius Vespasianus – Vespasian – is Emperor of Rome.

However, economic disaster threatens the city and so the Empire itself. The imperial treasure chests are all but empty, legions go unpaid, yields from the vital goldmines in Spain have fallen dramatically.

Gaius Valerius Verrens had hoped he'd left his old life behind when he received the summons from the Emperor. Vespasian wants his old friend to do him one last 'favour' – to journey to the remote, mountainous region of Asturica Augusta and investigate rumours that a bandit called 'The Ghost' is raiding the Empire's gold convoys with impunity.

What Valerius finds in this gods-forsaken land is much more complicated. The local tribes, exploited for so long, are a growing threat, but the real danger seems to come from those closer to him. Drawn into a conspiracy that, were it to succeed, could plunge the Empire into a devastating new conflict, treachery waits in the shadows. Valerius must put an end to it – but before he can, he must first establish who is a friend and who a foe . . .

Available in hardback and ebook.